About the author

Laurelle Cousins is a wool classer who lives the country life, with all its unique vibes, sounds and smells—some of which are more tolerable than others. She loves writing characters with strength and sass, her heroes and heroines always getting their happy ever after, but only after she's put them through the wringer to get there. And there's always a misbehaving animal (or two) colouring the pages of her novels.

Laurelle has been Runner-up for favourite debut author in 2022 with ARRA, for her title The Lonely Paddock and has edited a feature piece for Rural Women's Day magazine titled Childhood Memories.

Her novels available via audio version in Audible and uLibrary: Sheep Gully Road. The Lonely Paddock will be available in early 2026.

She has a sidekick kelpie named Jazz, loves wrestling sticks ten times her size. Laurelle also loves to stay in touch with her wonderful readers and would be thrilled to hear from you. You can find her at:

Website: https://www.laurellecousins.com/
Email: Laurelle@laurellecousins.com
Instagram: laurellecousins.writes
Facebook: Laurelle Cousins Writes
Pinterest: pinterest.com/laurellecousins

Other books by Laurelle Cousins

Settlers Hill Series:

Book 1: The Reluctant Farm-her

Book 2: Playing For Sheep Stations – coming soon

Book 3: The Lonely Paddock

Book 4: The Accidental Farm-her – coming soon

Forest Gully Series:

Book 1: Sheep Gully Road

Book 2: The Home Paddock – coming soon

Shearer's Arms Series:

Book 1: A Shearer's Run

Pioneer Ridge Series:

Book 1: Kelpie's Pass – coming soon

LAURELLE
COUSINS

A *Shearer's* Run

LCP

ISBN: 9781763891234
Published by LCP

Cover Design: Laurelle Cousins
Laurelle Cousins Press
Cover Images: Laurelle Cousins Photography
https://www.laurellecousins.com

For Lo-lo.

Your support throughout this whole journey has been and is:

Loyal

Unwavering

Filled with hugs, no matter the need, and there have been many!

Thank you so much. xox

Chapter One

Panicked bleating cut through the evening air as Poppy Fletcher waded knee-deep into George O'Sullivan's dam, her gumboots clinging to the stinky mud with each step. Face set, she lunged for the trapped sheep.

'Come on, you stubborn—' The words died as her boots sank deeper into the bottom of the mud like quick-setting concrete. Maybe wearing gumboots *into* the dam hadn't been her brightest idea . . .

Planting her hands on her hips, she glared at the ewe before looking up at George, who wore a smile as large as a half-moon. 'I don't think you're winning this round, young Poppy.' His weathered face crinkled with amusement from the top of the bank, his walking stick tapping against his leg. 'Better lose those boots of yours if you want to shift her.' His kelpie, Rowdy, who had only a couple of weeks ago given birth to her pups, gave a quick bark, at her or at the ewe, she wasn't sure.

She'd arrived to help George recover from his fall, and this was the thanks she got? She might love him like a grandfather, but wrestling sheep in a dam that was more mud than water—thanks to the drought—was taking things a tad too far in her opinion. But George deserved every bit of help she could give. He'd made it clear he didn't want to go into a nursing home, so this was her way of helping him stay as long as he could.

The cool breeze caused goosebumps to ripple along her damp arms as she bent to wrestle her first foot free, the squelchy mud sliding between her toes as she wobbled back and forth. She sucked in a sharp breath as she fought to regain her balance, emptying the boot ceremoniously before tossing it to the water's edge.

Narrowed eyes angled in George's direction, and she ignored the chuckle he had a cheeky habit of using when she was in a pickle, which just happened to be more often than not. 'You're lucky I didn't make you get in here,' she said, pointing a waggling finger at him despite the smile she could feel rising on her cheeks.

She released the second boot from its suction grip, tossing it to the side of the dam before she inched her way towards the ewe again.

'Baa.'

Poppy blew out a long breath, the mud clawing at her feet as her legs dragged against the dead weight of her soaked jeans. If she hadn't done her routine check of George's dams earlier that afternoon, this ewe might have been dead by morning.

She still might not make it.

'Easy, girl. I'm here to help you.' Gathering a breath, she launched herself, the ewe fighting against the suction grip of the mud to leap out of Poppy's reach.

'Watch her, Poppy,' George warned. 'She's a bit cantankerous.'

'You think?' she growled as the ewe's big, brown eyes widened and her head thrashed about.

Poppy puffed as she blinked against the splashes of water dripping down her face. She'd already had a big day, drenching George's sheep and shifting stock to newly rested paddocks. He didn't have that many sheep on the grand scale of things, but there was always enough for her to keep an eye on. The opportunity had been a godsend after . . .

Poppy looked up as the roar of a diesel engine came over the top of the hill. Twin headlights and a lightbar the length of a football field blinded her, and she squinted against the glare bouncing off the water, shying away as the ewe continued to thrash her head. The four-wheel-drive descended with a low chug, illuminating the entire dam.

'Turn down your bloody high beams!' Poppy muttered, grasping the ewe's sodden wool as the sheep fought harder. She squinted at the ute curiously. She had been in Tasmania for two weeks and George hadn't had any visitors. So why now?

The ute eased to a stop, the lights dimming, thankfully. Fighting to see through the jarring spots in her eyes, she saw a man hop out and stand beside George. His battered Akubra sat snugly on his head, casting a shadow, but she caught a flash of white teeth.

With muddied water dripping from her hair and her feet glued to the bottom of the dam, her patience snapped. The tighter she held on, the more the ewe fought, and Poppy glared at both men, not caring who the heck was with George or why he was there.

'Well?' she puffed, shaking the water from her face as she wrestled the ewe, her shoulders almost wrenched from their sockets. 'Are you planning to help or just enjoy the show?'

'All you had to do was ask.' His voice carried lazy amusement. 'Just hold on, okay?' He strolled back to his ute—actually strolled—while she stood in this rank water with an increasingly desperate sheep.

'Easy for you to say,' she called back, shaking her head as more droplets shimmied from her hair. She glanced at George with a what-the-heck glare on her face, not missing the smile he was wearing with infuriatingly bright delight. She would be having words with him later, once she was out of this pitiful predicament.

George had been her one and only Tasmanian client, visiting each year and classing his wool to help him out. With some long, hard years and low wool prices, she wanted nothing more than to see him have a good year, enough to get back on his feet. And his shearing wasn't far off from beginning again.

Poppy's jaw clenched as the stranger returned from his ute, making a deliberate loop in the rope like he was demonstrating some fancy-pants knot at a country show.

The ewe kicked out beneath the water, connecting with her shin.

'Ouch!' Her yelp escaped before she could stifle it.

'You okay there?' His cheeks lifted in a lazy smile like he had all the time in the world to spare, his eyes never leaving hers despite the ewe continuing to wrestle her head free of Poppy's grip.

'I might be if you'd hurry up and help,' she said, her teeth now chattering, the evening air seeping in deeper than her feet in the slimy mud. Drought be damned. She was going to need an hour-long shower to warm up, and free herself from this muddy stench.

He approached the edge of the dam as the glow from the ute lights highlighted the rippling water dancing about. 'Here, take this and put it around her middle.' He made to throw the rope towards her.

'You seriously want me to ask the ewe, nicely, if she wouldn't mind lifting one leg, then the other, all while I reach down below her, without her kicking me, *again*, and get that rope around her middle?'

Was he for real?

'Well, I'd rather not get wet, so yeah, that'd be good.' His damned smile, all warm and sweet, deepened, the cute dimple in his cheek unmistakable in the proximity they shared.

But his sheer audacity left her speechless—for a full three seconds. Then she smiled—the sweet smile she'd perfected especially for her four brothers when they were playing "piggy in the middle" . . . and she was the "piggy". 'Of course. How silly of me.'

Her tone must have broken through his casual confidence because his expression shifted, and with obvious reluctance, he dropped the rope, tugging off his work boots with careful precision, placing them neatly beside one another. Even his socks were folded. Poppy's eyebrows lifted in disbelief.

He slipped into the water and sidled up beside the ewe, and his arm brushed hers. She jerked away instinctively as electricity raced up her arm before staring at him, and for a moment neither of them moved.

He tilted his head back just enough for her to catch his eyes in the dim light—darker than she'd expected, studying her with compassionate intensity.

Her pulse hammered against her throat. This was exactly what she'd come to Tasmania to avoid.

'Right, let's get this done,' he said, and before she could react, he lifted the sodden ewe like she was lighter than a feather. Muscles corded along his forearms as he effortlessly held the still-struggling animal steady.

Poppy grabbed the rope, careful not to look in his direction or touch him again, threading the rope through the water and underneath the sheep. When he lowered the ewe back down, he took the rope from her, their hands brushing despite her caution.

She hiked an eyebrow before sharply looking away, perplexed by her unwanted feelings. She tried to focus on the ewe, but her distracted mind was calling her on a rebellious path she didn't want to go down. She had seen his hands, calloused from hard work, maybe fencing? The thought did funny things to her insides, and she fought to shut it down. She didn't want any romantic distractions in her life.

Ever again.

'Now push her, and I'll pull.'

Uh, what? She looked up at his expectant face, noticing the lines of concentration around his eyes. She saw it, the way he cared about the welfare of this ewe. A warmth filtered through her.

Poppy took a deep breath, mustering her strength before heaving the ewe forward as he pulled on the rope, his arms straining against the tension as though he'd done it a thousand times before. Together, they wrestled the panicking animal, puffing from the effort.

Poppy hauled herself from the water, teeth chattering as she hugged her arms around herself. She focused on emptying her boots—every last dribble—anything to avoid looking at him.

'Won't go in there with those on next time, will you?' he said, smiling lightly as he hauled the dripping ewe into the back of his ute, laying her on her side. He'd done this kind of thing before?

'Excuse me?' She straightened, boots dripping. That lopsided smile was back, along with raised eyebrows that did nothing to slow her racing heart. Who was this guy anyway? He needed a lesson in being a little less Mr Smarty-Pants and a whole lot more obliging, in her opinion.

'Just sayin'.'

She tugged on her soaked boots, fighting off her building frustration before hobbling over to George's ute. She was one-hundred percent about to be the proud owner of at least two very fat, angry blisters in her near future, but that wasn't about to have her easing her pace.

Poppy managed a tight nod as she wrenched the ute door open, pulling George's spare Driza-bone over her sodden clothes. The oil-slick fabric provided blessed warmth, but she could still feel this stranger's gaze following her as he strapped the ewe's feet together, all too aware of the broad shoulders beneath his checked work shirt.

Rick. The name popped into her mind with sudden caution. He had started with that same confident smile. She turned away, her stomach a twisted knot as memories surfaced once more.

'Thanks for the help,' she called without looking back, opening the driver's side of George's old ute.

George stepped up to the passenger door and cleared his throat, his keen gaze looking between them. 'Poppy, this is LJ.'

The way "LJ" shifted from one foot to the other caught her attention, his focus turning from her to the ewe, his hand resting on her side until she finally stopped fighting against the rope. When he looked back up and offered her a soft smile, Poppy's heart skipped an unexpected beat.

But she had to quickly remind herself why she had come to Tasmania. To forget men.

So why was this one, in nothing more than a passing moment, making that so damn difficult? She was here to forget Rick and get on with her life.

As a single woman.

Chapter Two

LJ watched George's ute taillights steadily disappear over the rise of the hill as he started his engine. He hadn't been distracted by a woman in the longest time, especially one with such depth in her gaze. After his breakup more than a year ago, any relationship other than for work was not what he needed.

No. This was a work proposal—plain and simple— brought to his attention by George. And if what he said about her ability was anything to go on, she could be the difference he was hoping for.

LJ trailed some distance behind George's ute, pulling up in front of the ramshackle house the old man called home, and shook his head slowly. How George managed to live here baffled him. It was lucky the place was still standing.

With the ewe settled in the shearing shed, he walked up

the steps to the verandah and knocked on the door, more out of courtesy—George would never have expected him to, but with Poppy in there, he felt it was right—took off his boots and went inside. In the kitchen, George stood at the cream AGA oven, stirring a pot of what looked like hearty vegetable soup. The rich, savoury aroma reminded him of home, and his heart grew heavy despite his taste buds making his mouth water. He pushed the thought aside, instead wondering if he could dare to hope for a dinner invite. It wouldn't be the first time old George had offered him a seat at his table.

But then his gaze slid to Poppy, her back to him as she stood beside the stove, trying to get warm.

George turned, his smile both generous and understanding. The loveable bugger might be getting older, but he didn't miss much.

'You stayin' for tea? Poppy here has made chicken and vegetable soup good enough to feed a shearing team, if you'd like some.' George's eyes glinted with a watery sparkle.

'Uh, yeah. That'd be great.' He gave a rueful smile, his eyes slowly lifting as Poppy cautiously looked over her shoulder at him. Her face gave nothing away, and his brow twitched in uncertainty. 'If that's okay?' He pressed his lips tight, all too aware he was close to wearing out his short welcome if he didn't tread carefully. He needed her. He couldn't afford to stuff this up.

Her silence surprised him as she turned his way and slowly blinked, offering the slightest of nods before turning back to the stove, a small shiver rifling over her body.

'The ewe is in a pen in the shearing shed, George.

Reckon she'll drip dry pretty well. Gave her a couple of biscuits of lucerne from your stash too, and some water.'

'Good job, my boy. She'll be right as rain now.' He gave a satisfied chuckle.

'Might go warm up in the shower.' Poppy offered a guarded smile before disappearing. His eyes followed her, wishing he knew what was going on in that pretty mind of hers.

He and George were discussing cattle prices when Poppy returned, her cheeks flushed with warmth and dare he say it, an ever-so-slightly improved mood given the soft, yet reluctant smile she offered, her loosely-hanging hair wet around her shoulders. Her body shook with the odd involuntary shiver, and she moved in front of the oven once more, holding her slender fingers out in front of her, her face unreadable.

LJ swallowed back his sudden rush of interest in George's wool classer. He was here strictly for business, but George had suggested it wasn't going to be an easy sell. And he'd made matters worse for himself with their earlier interaction. But with no classer, the few jobs he was clinging to were going to disappear.

Fast.

His team were depending on him—the ones that had stuck around after he had bought the shearing run. He needed to do everything he could to keep them together.

And Sam.

He had to do it for Sam.

Chapter Three

Poppy stared at the spoon in her soup, dismayed by what she'd just heard. She lifted her eyes cautiously, the struggle to keep her apprehension under control all too real.

'You . . . want me to work for you?' The words slipped out in a shallow whisper.

'I'd love it if you would. George said you were looking for work.' LJ's casual shrug contradicted the intensity of his gaze.

'Oh, he did, did he?' She shot George a pointed look as he shovelled soup like his life depended on it. She had kept her plans to herself, not willing to divulge any thoughts of her change of career to him. He'd been a long-time supporter of her classing passion.

Poppy played with her soup spoon, gathering what little

emotional control she had left. She wouldn't lie to herself. The thought of walking into another shed with a team of strangers was mildly terrifying, to say the least. Coming to Tasmania had been her chance for new horizons, a fresh start far away from the career her father had expected her to pursue.

Nursing. She had applied to the Royal Hobart Hospital to appease him, but what she'd really hoped was that helping George would give her the breathing space she needed to recover, at her own pace. She hadn't expected a classing job to fall into her lap so easily.

Her father had been relieved she had mentioned taking up nursing, especially after everything that had happened. Her mind raced with the pros and cons. Would it be so terrible? She risked a glance at LJ, heat immediately rising to her cheeks when she found him watching her. He seemed to be a trustworthy guy, even if he was above average in the annoyance department, and her chest fluttered at the memory of their fleeting touch earlier. But he also unsettled her in ways she wasn't ready to examine.

'So, you have plenty of work?' She still wasn't convinced but maybe it was worth thinking about.

'Yep, plenty for you. I prom—' He shied from her gaze, as though something was troubling him. She narrowed her eyes at him.

'Yeah, you won't have to worry.' His face shifted into a reassuring smile that he beamed her way, and she took a sobering breath. To have work immediately would be just what she needed, even if facing the thought of failure inside a shearing shed all over again threatened to send her into an instant panic. But, just maybe, George had done all right by her after all?

She used her spoon to swirl patterns in her soup, buying herself time to think and hide her flaming cheeks which were worsening by the second. If she took LJ's offer, it would be her chance to prove—to herself—that she hadn't lost her nerve. More importantly, it would show her father she could continue classing, regardless of the time it took to rebuild her confidence. All she had to do was keep quiet about it until she could ensure everything would be okay.

One week later, Poppy sat in her idling car, gripping the steering wheel as she stared at what she hoped was the Jenkins shearing shed. Sheep bleated through the motionless fog that had followed her from George's place, their desperate calls the only sound breaking the heavy silence.

Why exactly had she said yes?

Her mind drifted to the things she still had to sort out, like ringing about accommodation. George's hospitality had been godsent, but it was time to stand on her own two feet since his immediate needs had been sorted out for the time being. She hadn't bothered calling "The Lone Pony" caravan park in Longford yet, but it wouldn't be hard to secure a cabin there. The crotchety landlady had a special knack for keeping the place perpetually empty. She'd make that call at morning smoko.

Admittedly, she had come to Tassie in a rush, and George wasn't the only reason. There were people she needed to leave in her past, and helping George care for his stock and prepare for shearing was as good an excuse as any.

Her chest tightened. Those people—the ones she had trusted with her life—it had all been for nothing. She bit down on her lip, slumping back into the driver's seat. Two years of working alongside them, and she'd been completely blind to who they truly were. A lowly breath seeped from her lungs.

Squeezing her eyes shut, she drew on what little strength she still had, dreading what this new team might be like. How would she react if more snide comments and unfair jibes she didn't deserve were thrown her way? Maybe she should just pursue nursing after all. Her father's loving face haunted her thoughts, but deep down, she knew she would never be happy in a job like that. And she knew why.

Her Grandpa Isaac. He had been quite clear about that. 'There's no escaping it, my little nieta. Agriculture is in your blood. It's a done deal.'

Besides, George was right. If she was going to stay in Tasmania, she needed money, quickly. This was the job she knew she could do well, or so she had thought. All she had to do was push through her unease.

Taking one final steadying breath, Poppy reached for the door handle and stepped into the nippy air. She grabbed her paddle and work bag, then headed for the shed steps, gripping the railing tighter than necessary. She could keep her head down, stay professional, and resist any romantic inclinations her treacherous heart might threaten to develop. Then she just might be able to reclaim the career she once loved with all her heart.

Cautious hope flickered to life as she took the steps two at a time, heaving the sliding door aside. The lanolin-infused air hit her like a soothing balm, and she breathed it in deeply. There was something about a working shearing shed, knowing thousands of sheep had run through it year after year, that entranced her every time, and her tense body began to relax.

The fluorescent lights in the shed made her squint as she gathered her bearings. The chatter of voices that had filled the atmosphere a moment ago faded.

The shed fell silent.

A lone wolf whistle echoed, followed by the sound of a solid thump.

'Ow. What was that for?' came the offended voice from the far end.

'Keep your eyes to your bloody self, Whippet,' warned an unapologetic female shedhand.

Despite her nerves, the interaction brought a careful smile to Poppy's lips.

Her eyes swept the long line of empty wool bins, her heart picking up tempo. *What's in the past, stays in the past,* she murmured, lifting her chin.

A battered wool press bore the scars of countless shearings, and old cobwebs, doused in dew, hung like dreadlocks from the rafters, abandoned by their makers. Steadily, her apprehension began to lift. Grandpa Isaac had been right, she smiled, the relief palpable. This was in her blood.

But doubt clung tight as she walked to the wool press, placing her gear against the wall behind it. Not telling her father she was returning to classing, especially after what had happened with Rick . . . Was she even thinking straight? He had been so relieved to hear she was finally talking about nursing, and dare she say it, proud. Guilt settled heavily on her shoulders.

This had better not be déjà vu, she warned herself. Heavy footsteps echoed from the sliding door behind her, and she slowed. Was it LJ coming to say g'day? She ignored her flutter of anticipation.

A tall man stopped in front of her as she turned, pausing before he spoke. 'Name's Ralph. I take it you're the wool classer.' His gaze swept over her with suspicious appraisal. 'New, I see.' His voice was flat, disapproval glinting in his eyes.

The urge to grab her gear and run almost overwhelmed her. Through no fault of her own, her reputation had been destroyed by Rick's careless words and devastating actions, the icing on the cake she had been blindsided by.

And now, with this man staring at her like she was the prey he'd lined up for dinner, well, she didn't need it . . . and she didn't want it.

'Hope you know what you're doing. It's a valuable clip.' His bushy grey eyebrows drew together as he looked down his nose at her.

Poppy chose the positive approach, holding out her right hand. 'I'm Poppy Fletcher.' She summoned her best I-do-know-what-I'm-doing smile, hoping it would portray some confidence—which was dissolving at a rapid rate.

'This is . . . the Jenkins shed, isn't it? LJ's directions were so bloody sketchy, he'd be lucky to get a homing pigeon to base camp,' she said lightly, hoping for a chuckle in return. It had been near impossible to read LJ's mud map—she'd taken a chance on this shed being correct based solely on it being the only one in the area showing signs of activity, plus what looked like LJ's ute parked out the front.

'I'm Ralph Jenkins,' he said, offence creeping into his voice. 'Female wool classer . . . haven't had *one of them* before. S'pose I've got the contractor to thank for that.' His eyes shifted to the shearing board, and the entire team fell silent, watching like spectators at an accident. Her throat constricted.

What had she been thinking?

'I'm used to the men.' His unforgiving tone snatched her attention back, and she struggled to maintain her composure behind a strained smile that was rapidly fading.

Her core tensed at his sceptical stare. Maybe she should quit after this shed. Stepping away from the industry for good might help her to forget the man she thought she was going to spend the rest of her life with back in Sydney. She had spectacularly misjudged that, and now this. It was all beginning to feel like a big, fat mistake.

As if unsure what to do next, Ralph about-faced and in three long strides, stepped towards the small table opposite the wool press where the specification book waited. He grabbed last year's records—an account of all the lines of wool that had been made—studying them with his back to her.

'This is last year's speci. Dougie knew what he was doing. Damn shame he had to pull out, sickness and all.' He paused meaningfully. 'I'll be wanting him back next year.'

Had Rick's poison already spread to Tasmania? Was word out that she was incompetent? Her heart flooded with despair, alarm filling her eyes. This grower had all but written her off before she'd classed a single fleece. Or was it simply because she was a woman?

Her jaw tightened, recognising the familiar prejudice. Yup. This whole idea was absurd—she'd known it would be. Her father's words from two years ago echoed in her memory, when she'd returned from shearing at Grandpa Isaac's property, eyes bright with excitement about the wool.

'What do you want to do agriculture for, sweetheart?' he'd said to her. 'You could build a real career in something civilised and clean. I don't like the idea of my daughter breaking her back and developing muscles where they don't belong.' His eyes had almost pleaded with her.

Real career! Pfft. Poppy sighed at the memory, inadvertently glancing down at her thin arms. And there it was. She loved him deeply, but he was trapped by old stereotypes. She needed to show him how outdated they were. More and more women were entering agriculture every day, achieving incredible things.

Ralph Jenkins turned to her with a troubled frown, and a sudden urge to feel sorry for him flickered through her.

'Not sure how this will go, but I'll take what I'm given. For now.' His disappointed gaze drifted past her to the shearers.

And in a flash, the sympathy evaporated as her eyes narrowed.

He assessed her once more, a displeased grunt escaping his lips before he thrust the booklet into her hands and promptly stalked out of the shed.

Poppy fought to keep her mouth from falling open as the sliding door clanked shut behind him. She closed her eyes, pressing her fingers to her temples as a headache began building. If she couldn't perform to standard, not only would she be out of work—she'd be letting LJ down.

She would see this through, not only for this shed, but for herself.

Jimmy's voice echoed in her mind, his words settling over her like a warm embrace. 'Don't let anyone rattle you, Popps. You're brilliant at what you do. Believe in yourself a little more. They'll soon see.' Of her four siblings, Jimmy was one year older and guardian of her little secret. And she needed it to stay that way until the lies that were making her deeply uncomfortable could be set free.

Chapter Four

LJ ran a hand through his hair and turned his back on his new classer and Ralph, letting the icy air cool his emotions. Shit. Wasn't there some rule against wool classers being so distractingly attractive? Despite his best intentions, he took another glance.

Nope. The graceful way she moved, the long waves of dark hair trailing from her ponytail—Damn it, he was in trouble. He'd known it from the moment he'd laid eyes on her at George's. A skitter of nervous energy coursed through him, and he ran a hand over his face, urging himself to think straight as he stood in front of his shearing stand amongst his team, the ones he was desperate to keep in work. They had stuck by him when things were getting tough, and he couldn't thank them enough.

The purr of the shearing plants vibrated the handpieces sitting on the wooden floor of the shearing board as they sat in neutral, warming up ready for the day's work. He forced himself to focus on the familiar sounds, the comforting routine, anything but the woman efficiently organising her workspace.

'Hey LJ,' Jase said. 'What's up, man?'

Trust the young bloody shearer—he never missed a trick. LJ's smile swiftly dropped away as the truth of the shed became his all too real reality, suddenly remembering who should have been standing beside him on stand one.

His best mate.

'Nothin',' he said, giving Jase an unconvincing nod. 'Just gettin' ready to start.' He spun the handpiece in his hand, his attraction to the wool classer sharply replaced by the team's loss . . . *his* loss, so raw and so deep. It was the team's first day back after the funeral.

Sammy . . . He stole another breath. *Why'd you do it?* LJ bit down hard on his jagged emotions, working to ignore Jase's well-meaning but concerned gaze settling on him. Had it been too soon to come back to work after the accident? He'd thought he'd be okay.

Bloody promises. They were too dangerous to keep.

LJ stared down at the open chute where he'd be sending his shorn sheep, running the back of his hand along his face to remove a rogue tear before anyone noticed. There had been enough of those. The shearing run had been as much Sam's dream as it was his, and Sam would have wanted him to move forward, keeping it alive and the team in work. They were family after all, and family stuck together no matter what. He'd been grateful to have landed this job.

A sudden twang of guilt surged through him. Without Sammy beside him, even this victory felt hollow. LJ cautiously searched the faces of the rest of the team, his heartache propelling forward because he knew the truth.

His best friend's death hadn't been an accident.

He'd let it happen.

The moment the grower left the shed, murmurs and soft chuckling filled the air, sending easily spooked sheep scattering over the grating in their pens. Poppy's cheeks burned as she sucked in a tight breath. The whole team had watched her receive a serve from the cranky old farmer, and all she wanted was to disappear.

But the way she saw it, she had two choices. She could either hightail it back to the mainland for good—heaven knew it was way too small a community for her failings not to travel—or she could stay and face it like a warrior. The thought lifted her. Jimmy would say that.

Then again, country towns had a way of highlighting the good, the bad and definitely the ugly when it came to indiscretions. She knew that while their intentions might appear helpful, even genuine, the results weren't always kind.

Poppy ignored the whispers floating in the air as she studied the specification, keen to see how Dougie—the previous classer—had named the lines of wool. She glanced towards the clock at the far end of the long shearing board. She didn't have long. The shearers would start at 7.30 a.m. sharp.

She looked towards LJ, hoping he might inform her how the shed ran, but he appeared to be in conversation with the shearer to his left. So instead, she approached the workers standing around, waiting for the run to begin: shedhands, holding paddles for sweeping the wool away from the shearers' workspace. She chose the friendliest face, or so it seemed.

'Hi. I'm Poppy.' She offered a smile as her breakfast churned in her belly. The way her nerves were behaving, it was like this was her first classing job.

'Yes, we heard that earlier,' the woman said, raising her eyebrows at another woman leaning against a support pole, arms crossed and a sneer in place. Poppy switched her gaze between them, her eyes narrowing.

'So, have you worked in this shed before?' She kept her voice light.

'Ah, yeah. Duh.' The woman rolled her eyes, her head bobbing with exaggerated disbelief as she grinned at her friend.

Real nice. Poppy resisted shaking her head despite her frustration bubbling. She had met difficult shedhands before, but this one carried extra attitude that she knew would either make or break her ability to do her job properly. And she had a sneaky suspicion "break" was going to come out the winner.

With a deep breath of resolve, Poppy lifted her chin. 'Great. Would you mind showing me where you're putting the shanks and locks?' She met the woman's stare, waiting for a response.

'Find 'em yourself,' the woman sneered, looking Poppy up and down dismissively. Poppy could feel all control slipping away and sucked in yet another steadying breath, dismissing the roar of her throbbing headache. She stepped back, hoping to find someone more affable when she backed directly into a chest—of someone tall and solid and far too close for comfort.

Her heart did a double skip as she jumped forward, spinning around to face the one guy who had stopped her in her tracks only days ago. Sadness rested in his eyes despite his kind smile.

Regret settled on her. What had she been thinking coming to this job? She fumbled over her words. 'I . . . I'm sorry,' she blurted, aware her eventful arrival had the team's tongues vigorously wagging. She didn't need to add to their morning entertainment.

'All good,' LJ said, a blend of concern and amusement subtly crossing his features. 'Lucky I caught you.'

'Lucky? Excuse me?' Poppy immediately planted her hands on her hips as she stared at him. She was no damsel needing rescuing by a long shot. She could change a tyre . . . if she *had* to.

And now she found it impossible to hide her frown as her gaze zeroed in on him.

'Do you need a hand with anything in the shed?' He raised his eyebrows.

Despite herself, his suggestion only fuelled her frustration. And why did she get the feeling he was studying her like some kind of impossible puzzle?

'I'm fine, thanks.' As if she was going to ask for his help

now. He had done a dandy job of that with George's wet sheep, and she was not coming back for a second helping. She stared at him, unable to decide if he was enjoying getting a rise out of her or if he was being genuine.

'Right then, I'll leave you to it.' He nodded politely, making her feel like she was being dismissed.

Her mouth opened, ready to give him a mouthful of . . . what exactly? Now she wasn't sure. He paused, eyebrows rising in a curious arc as he looked ready to enjoy whatever was coming his way.

But annoyingly, she had nothing. And that *never* happened. She snapped her lips together and turned away. *Remember, sworn off men, forever.*

Glancing towards the clock, her eyes widened. She searched desperately for help and spotted an older man standing in the shadows, small and wiry, with a cautious expression. She pulled out a bright smile, pushing LJ to the dark depths of her mind as she approached him. If she read this other man correctly, he was hoping she'd leave him alone. But right now she had little choice.

'Hi. Would you mind telling me where everything goes in the shed? I'd appreciate your help.' She gave him an encouraging look, rolling her shoulders to shake away the numerous sets of googling eyes she could feel watching her back. He gave an apprehensive nod, his wary glance sliding to the other shedhands.

Poppy smiled, hoping to put him at ease. 'Thanks. That'd be great.'

The little man's eyes were wide as he pulled his head

back to assess her, and Poppy could have sworn he looked astonished.

'Um,' he hesitated, 'name's Little Trev. Pretty obvious, I guess.' He offered a shy smile before he shrugged, looking down at his boots.

She suppressed a small smile. The man was barely five feet tall.

No sooner had Little Trev finished showing her around than a booming voice rang out. 'Righto, boys, let's do this.'

Poppy swallowed hard as the five shearers strode into the pens, snatching their first sheep of the day and rolling them onto their backs before dragging them through the catching pen doors and onto the shearing board.

Another female shedhand brushed past, calling out towards her as she continued. 'I'm Bianca.' She gave Poppy a brief but genuine smile.

Warm puffs of air danced in front of Poppy's face as she exhaled, nodding at the woman, her nerves buzzing. Had she lost her nerve for the job after everything that had happened back home? And more importantly, was it planning on coming back anytime soon?

She watched as each man tucked a sheep's leg behind the back of their thigh, picked up their handpiece and pulled the cord.

But there was no changing one fact. Shearing had begun.

Chapter Five

Poppy was rattled. Half an hour into the run, she still couldn't find her rhythm. She'd never struggled to keep up with the rapid pace of five shearers before, but a barrage of fleeces kept launching themselves her way. If she didn't find a new gear, she'd never catch up, leaving her to be the standing joke of the shed . . . again.

And she knew exactly where the problem was stemming from.

She wiped her brow as she jogged, tightly pushing the fleece in her hands into the appropriate wool bin. It wasn't just her livelihood on the line—as the contractor, LJ had employed her for her skills. They paid him to do the organising and complete the job to a high standard. But with the grower already unhappy about having a female classer—a fact she was finding hard to ignore—LJ's reputation was also at risk.

The shed layout wasn't helping. Instead of the usual setup where she would work alongside others at the main tables, she found herself isolated at a smaller wool table behind the main sorting area. It was meant to streamline the workflow, but working alone left her feeling exposed and vulnerable.

Six shedhands worked in this shed. Two swept the board and picked up the shorn fleeces. The other four positioned themselves at the two main wool tables where the fleeces were thrown. And that's where her trouble was brewing.

Poppy frowned as another fleece landed in front of her. The two not-so-adorable shedhands she had met earlier were placing fleeces in front of her, greasy wool still attached as well as matted wool that did not fit with a fleece acceptable for sale. Each time they dropped off another fleece to her table, they snickered to each other, dumping it carelessly in front of her before swaggering away. More than once, she caught the middle finger aimed her way.

So, it was time to try out the new classer, see what she's made of was it? But she didn't have the time to redo work that should have been done correctly in the first place, especially when she had given them clear instructions before the first fleece had left the shearing board.

Poppy paused, hands deep in the warm fleece in front of her as she watched the two women work. And her concern grew. Shedhands could make or break the quality control of the wool—and her reputation as a new wool classer in Tasmania. Right now, it didn't matter whether she was staying or not. She did not need to be hauled over the coals about the contents of her wool lines for a second, humiliating time.

At the other table, Little Trev and another man worked steadily, their fleeces arriving perfectly skirted and rolled. A distinct pattern was emerging; their fleeces completed without fault.

Poppy blew a stray hair aside with a puff of air as the shearing plants wound down, quiet washing over the shed as morning smoko arrived. Chatter drifted from the tearoom, punctuated by hushed voices and muffled laughter. There were no prizes for guessing who they were talking about.

A mountain of wool glared at her from the small table. She heard her name being discussed and glanced towards the voices, her arms stilling as she stared at the overwhelming pile. Randomly, fleeces toppled to the floor around her feet.

She was the fool to think she could come back and do this. Maybe it was too soon. If she had given herself a little longer to heal, she might have been okay. Why hadn't she listened to her instincts? How long would it take for her heart to recover and her confidence to return to the job she was sure she was born to do?

Heavy footsteps stopped beside her and Poppy's heart jumped as she recognised those boots.

'What's going on here?' Ralph's voice was eerily quiet, but the tearoom chatter instantly dropped to whispers. Poppy clenched the wool in her hands and resigned herself to face him, hoping she wouldn't say something she'd regret.

But as she opened her mouth to speak, a familiar voice cut in from across the table.

'Ralph. It's her first run. How about you go have a

cuppa? Everything will be sorted when you get back.'

Poppy watched Ralph's heavy boots disappear from behind lowered lashes before turning to LJ, irritation immediately flaring.

'I could have handled him myself,' she snapped. How dare he swoop in like he was her rescuer. He wasn't as eager to rush in the other night. Although quietly, the relief was real. She'd had enough confrontation in her career, aimed at her with judgy fingers. She looked away, mortified at her reaction. Was it always going to be like this around him?

'Right, let's get this sorted then, shall we? I need a coffee after that run.'

She turned back, unable to stop a tight gasp escaping her lips as his eyes twinkled and that devastating smile settled on her.

'You don't need to help me. It's not your job. You're just a—' She caught herself. 'I mean, you need your own break.'

She cringed inwardly. Had she really almost called him "just a shearer" when he was her boss?

'No. I don't have to, but I will. You've had a rough morning, and I'd like to help.'

Poppy started classing again, but her attention wandered. The way he had stepped in—twice now—when she had felt overwhelmed . . . Was he naturally the protective type, or did he think she couldn't handle herself? She glanced his way, taking in his kind eyes and the fresh scar at the side of his head, deep and scabbed over.

Then she quickly reminded herself why she was here.

To gather back the confidence she'd lost, even if it did require a little lie . . . or three.

Chapter Six

LJ slouched on the seat in the tearoom, running a slow hand down his face. During the run, he'd found himself glancing towards the classer's table, watching the shed dynamics unfold.

And frowned.

The behaviour of his two new shedhands was unacceptable. He didn't need workplace drama on top of everything else. He scratched at his itchy week-old stubble, hoping the tension would sort itself out naturally. But what he couldn't work out was why his new classer had left what he had to assume was a secure job to come to Tasmania.

His mind drifted back to this morning's scene when he'd watched Ralph giving Poppy grief. He'd been about to intervene when she'd made that crack about his "good as gold" mud map he'd given her at George's place. A contemplative frown crossed his face. No one had ever complained about his directions before. When she'd backed into him with her dark, long locks and surprised chocolate eyes, his insides had practically groaned.

And her perfume . . . It was potent, sending shivers through him that he didn't want to acknowledge. If the boys knew, they'd string him to the rafters with baling twine. Even his ex had never affected him like that.

'Don't worry. Whatever it is, you'll work it out, my boy,' Cookie said, giving his shoulder a sympathetic squeeze as she passed him, her basket laden with all manner of goodies for smoko. Her motherly presence had been a godsend since she had joined the team with the takeover.

The aroma of her fresh sausage rolls, sandwiches, and cream jam sponge filled the tearoom, reminding him how grateful he was for his camp cook. Through the doorway, he watched Whippet reach out and pinch Bianca on the backside, earning himself yet another solid whack on the upper arm.

'Don't bloody do that here, Whippet. How many times do I have to tell you?'

'Aww, c'mon, Tweety Bird. It's too damn cute not to.' His wide grin wasn't enough to get him forgiven as she gave him a long glare.

Tweety Bird? Sheesh. LJ wanted to know how long his sister had let the shearer get away with that nickname. It would have earned him a clout on the ear.

The thought of Poppy's embarrassed smile eased his worries slightly. If things were different, he might have the mental energy to explore these feelings stirring for his new wool classer.

If only . . .

He turned his attention to a small grey mouse poking its curious nose through a gap in the skirting boards at the far corner of the tearoom, its whiskers twitching as it searched the aromas in the air.

LJ took a long sip of his stale instant coffee, cringing at the taste as he watched the brave creature tug its fat belly through the hole, pause, then scamper towards the cover of a fallen newspaper lying next to the bin. LJ absently chewed on his mouthful of sausage roll as the rodent peeked out from behind the other side of the rubbish bin, beady eyes brimming with hope. It darted out, snatching up a lonely pastry crumb before racing along the skirting boards, finding cover behind the metal ashtray tucked in the far corner.

'What's on your mind, Boss?' Bear asked, stuffing his sixth sandwich into his chubby cheeks while eyeing the biggest piece of remaining sponge. He sat back, with his legs stretched out and crossed at his ankles, chewing contentedly.

LJ stared at his shearing moccasins. 'Too much.' Work was drying up. Growers weren't ringing to book the team— they were running in the opposite direction. That's what he got for buying a shonky, rundown shearing run, wasn't it?

Last night's phone call to his father came to the forefront of his mind. Miles had answered instead.

'Get stuffed, LJ,' he said. 'No one bloody wants you around 'ere. Leave us alone.' And with that, the line went dead.

What was his brother's problem anyway? The sting of rejection cut deep, but at least Grandma Aimee's acceptance of him, and her hospitality, meant more than he could express. His mother's mother was the one person he could count on every night when he went home. He'd moved in because her house was situated centrally for the work he hoped to get, and it meant he could keep an eye on her. She wasn't frail, but he'd noticed her increasing forgetfulness, and her less-than-stable balance on uneven ground had piqued his concern.

Bear nodded with solemn understanding, and LJ felt his throat tighten. He swallowed another bitter sip of his cold coffee, rubbing at his rough whiskers he had refused to shave since the funeral.

Sam was gone. Forever.

An image of Sam's mother flew to mind—Josie, whom he had avoided at all costs during the funeral and since. His heart lurched. Keeping clear of her from now on was the only way he might be able to live with himself.

Everything pointed to a tragic work accident. But LJ knew the truth.

It was his fault.

And how long would it be before the others started to tell him so?

Any day now.

He pressed fingers to his tired eyes, hoping that might push down the pain so close to the surface it threatened to show, and his hand began to shake. He sucked in a resolving breath. He couldn't do this.

Not now.

Not ever.

What had they been thinking, buying the failing

business from Ken Cuthrow? The man was known throughout the district as a tyrant who'd worked his teams to exhaustion with long hours, no weekend breaks, and skeleton crews. Ken's antagonistic approach had driven staff away until he'd cut his losses, sold the run for next to nothing, and fled Tasmania for good.

LJ hadn't seen the writing on the wall. He and Sam had been starting an adventure they'd both hoped would last a lifetime.

It had only lasted a year.

With Sam by his side, LJ had truly believed they could turn the flailing business around. But restoring lost faith was proving harder than anticipated, farmers publicly shunning him or hanging up when he called.

And with Sam gone . . . guilt flooded him.

There seemed no point.

LJ stretched in his seat, calling on every ounce of resolve as he glanced at his remaining team. They were his family now, living in each other's pockets as they travelled together, moving from job to job. He couldn't let them down because his emotions threatened to overwhelm him.

Take Two Shearers—the name he and Sam had given their business—played in his thoughts. It had been perfect, the joint venture between two brothers by choice, ready to take on

Tasmania's shearing industry.

Now it had become take one lonely shearer who couldn't imagine life without his best mate.

Bear had refused to give up on him, standing by when week upon week, no shearing came in. Bear's wife, Cindy, had put being a stay-at-home mum on hold, starting a cleaning business in Launceston so Bear could look after the kids during the dry spells.

LJ leaned forward in his seat, his hands hiding his face, subtly smearing away the rogue tears tracing the sides of his cheeks. He drew in a sharp breath, his nose twitching as he tried to stifle any more thoughts of his painful grief.

Jase Twigg walked towards the sink—his promising young shearer who had joined the team just as Cuthrow handed the business over. He was hitting it off straight away with all the boys. Their joint friendships were so tight, they universally suffered the knife-like pain in their hearts over the loss of Sam.

'I don't know about those two new girls, LJ. Reckon they're gonna give us grief. Did you see what they were doin' to the classer?' Jase shook his head in disgust.

'Yeah, I did,' LJ said, his voice weary. 'But she's the shed boss, so I'll watch and see what she does.' He had a feeling she would sort them out, if what he'd seen from her so far was any indication. The memory of her in George's dam roused a small smile.

Besides, everyone deserved a chance, didn't they? Well, everyone except him. Second chances weren't worth the paper they were written on.

'Ya reckon? Na, man. She's soft. They're gonna eat her

up for lunch.' Jase shook his head.

'Give her time to find her feet,' LJ said. He trusted George O'Sullivan's judgement: 'She's a real good one, LJ. She won't let you down.'

He hoped so for the sake of his team, but even more so for himself.

'C'mon boys, let's get 'em,' LJ said, mustering enthusiasm he didn't feel.

The second run began at ten sharp. All five men strode into the pens with renewed energy. Bianca caught his eye, giving him her you've-got-this look that meant business. He managed a weak nod back. On the outside, he was holding up.

On the inside, he didn't know how much longer he could keep going.

He dragged his first ewe out and glanced towards Poppy, who stood leaning against a pillar, her arms crossed and a vacant expression on her face. Paul—the other shedhand— was nearby, making general conversation, laughing at his own jokes as usual. She offered distant, polite smiles and nods as he rambled.

While she didn't appear relaxed, she was getting to know the others. It was a start.

LJ enjoyed the familiar rhythm as the wool peeled away from the ewe's body in gentle arcs. He snuck a glance at his newest shearer a few stands down. Sam's death not only left an empty hole in their hearts, but also a deserted shearing stand next to him.

A timely phone call from Dave, which LJ had taken the evening after the funeral, had filled the position. LJ was grateful for small mercies, knowing Ralph Jenkins was tight with his dollars, and an empty stand would have meant hell to pay. Nope, it was better to take on a new shearer and finish the shed by the end of the week. Then, fingers crossed, he'd get the job again next year.

An hour later, halfway through the run, the boys pulled up for a five-minute break, to stretch their backs and to give Spider—the presser—time to pen up. Dave, Paul and the two female shedhands sauntered to the back pens of the shed for a smoke.

'Bloody Paul,' Bianca said, stepping up beside LJ while glaring at the man. 'The jerk is already trying to crack onto the classer with his smooth talk and smutty jokes.'

LJ glanced over his shoulder, watching Paul rest his forearms on the pen doors like he owned the place. The little shit knew smoking inside was against regulations but was obviously taking liberties. LJ twisted his body towards the group, unsure if he should wander over to the classer's table and have a word with Poppy or wait and mention it quietly at lunch time.

Strident footsteps strode down the board behind him, heading towards the pen of smokers. LJ stood taller, his elbow resting on the pen door, and Jase tapped him from behind, his brows rising.

'Right, guys,' Poppy said. 'There's a clear "No Smoking" sign at the end of the shed. Plenty of us here don't smoke, so please keep your smoking outside, starting next run.'

Paul choked on the escaping smoke as Poppy marched back down the board. Whippet and Bear smirked with approving nods, stepping into their pens and dragging out another ewe each, pulling into gear again.

'What the—' Jase's mouth slipped open.

Poppy's ponytail of waves swung in rhythm with her determined walk back to the wool table. Jase turned to LJ, who raised eyebrows in pleasant amazement, before stepping into the pen to snatch another sheep, backing out of the pen with a satisfied smile.

'Told ya she had what it takes,' Bianca said, giving him a gentle hip and shoulder as she brushed past her brother.

Hooking the sheep's front foot in behind his own, he watched Poppy stride towards the wool bins, fleece in hand. His heart skipped a beat, and for a moment, he allowed a flicker of hope to enter his mind. Could he dare to offer his love and loyalty to someone again?

But his smile immediately fell away.

No. He was better off alone.

That way, no one would get hurt.

Chapter Seven

The two smart-mouthed shedhands had made her job incredibly frustrating. So, when she smelled smoke inside the building, it was the final straw to her already smouldering mood. She'd bet money they knew the rules.

Poppy wasn't sure what repercussions would follow her confrontation over the smoking. The last thing she wanted to do was to lord it over anyone, but there came a point when things needed to be dealt with.

A staple of wool hovered between her fingers as she glanced down the board at the men bent over the ewes. Of the five shearers, LJ was the only one she'd met properly. Warmth crept up her cheeks. Despite her better judgement, she could feel herself drawn to this man who carried himself with quiet confidence, though she'd glimpsed something darker beneath his easy smile—like a sadness he was trying to mask.

Drawing her attention back to the wool, she chided herself. Men were distractions that only let her down, and the familiar prickle of hurt niggled, reminding her of Rick's broken promises and their devastating aftermath.

But her words to herself slipped away as she watched LJ work, his body moving with the sheep in a graceful dance. His arms were tanned and muscular, his biceps flexing with each new blow.

Just like Rick's used to.

She blinked away the unwelcome comparison, annoyed that LJ had her thinking thoughts she'd sworn herself off. She hadn't missed the way he and Bianca had talked closely earlier and it nagged at her despite fully knowing it shouldn't. Were they together?

But it didn't matter, she told herself firmly, refocusing her attention on the wool in her hands and pulling it firmly. It broke apart easily. She gathered up the fleece and placed it in her tender line.

The roar of the shearing plants slowed, and Poppy looked up, surprised at the time. Three fleeces remained unclassed on her table, and she allowed herself a small smile of satisfaction before her gaze hardened. The two women were back at the wool table next run, and this time she would be ready.

Poppy halted mid-step as Ralph Jenkins intercepted her walking to the tender bin with the last fleece. She decided to aim for diplomacy, offering him a confident smile. 'Your wool is lovely, Ralph. I'm enjoying—'

'By the looks of this mess, I don't think so.' His arms folded tightly over one another across his chest, his wrap-around eyebrows hanging close to his disapproving eyes.

Mess? What was he talking about? She looked at her wool lines in the large bins before turning back to him. 'I'm sorry, Ralph? Your wool is consistent so far, and in the micron range of seventeen to eighteen. It's very nice.'

'I see you've named this bin *tender*.' He stared down his nose at her.

'Yes . . .' she said slowly, trying to understand what she had done to upset him this time. It was beginning to feel like a well-worn habit.

'Have you taken a good look at how much wool you've put in there?' he said with a clipped tone. 'Near four hundred sheep have been shorn already this morning, and more than half of the wool has gone in here.' He thrust a disgruntled finger towards the bin.

Poppy's insides twisted, but she kept her voice steady, trusting her methods that had never failed her, until those wool test results from Rick's family farm. She did her best to disguise the sudden flinch she felt from her eyebrow. Tender wool always broke somewhere in the staple, the purchase price ultimately being affected because the manufacturer had increased costs to spin it into yarn for garments and other textiles. The bottom line was that the grower could get paid less for this line of wool.

'With all due respect, Ralph, I pull the staple hard. So yes, there's a lot of wool going into this line, but your strength test results should be far sounder than the expected twenty-eight or below newtons. When the buyers see this, they'll pay more for your line of wool.'

'I don't have tender wool! Dougie never—'

'Again, Ralph, no disrespect, but this is the way I class. Your sound lines,' she turned towards the other two bins situated closer to her table, 'will achieve excellent strength tests, and you should receive a premium price for them.'

Ralph Jenkins lifted his chin, studying his wool in the bins with deep thought before setting a dubious look back on her. 'We'll have to see about that, won't we?' And for the third time that day, he turned on his heels, marching his bad mood outside to bring more sheep into the shed.

Poppy exhaled slowly, her hands trembling as she put away the final fleece. She had stood her ground professionally, but Ralph's hostility was wearing her down. Back home, she'd faced similar challenges to her methods, and similar resistance too. Maybe that's all this was—resistance to new approaches, in whatever form that took? She could handle that.

She had to.

Chapter Eight

LJ shore on autopilot, making every blow look effortless as he glided around the sheep's body. He pulled out of gear and stood slowly after sending the ewe down the chute, then reached for a new cutter to change on his handpiece, his mind distracted by Poppy's determined attitude.

Bent over his own ewe, Jase glanced up sideways, with a curious look. 'You only changed that three sheep ago. The sheep aren't that dirty.'

LJ kept his focus on his handpiece. 'Lot of dust in mine.' His brows creased with intense concentration on the cutter once more. From the corner of his eye, he saw Jase shake his head in disbelief before dancing a smooth foot shuffle with the sheep to begin the long blows down her back.

Damn it. Being caught with his mind off the job was one

thing, but he was pretty sure Jase didn't know *why* he was unnecessarily changing cutters. Hopefully he'd forget about it, but a funny hunch told him he wouldn't.

He rested his handpiece back on the board and glanced towards the small wool table as he straightened. Something strange had transpired between Ralph and Poppy a moment ago, and he hoped it wasn't a repeat of this morning's confrontation.

After taking over as the contractor, restoring faith for his sparse collection of clients was paramount. Ralph was one of his pricklier farmers who had stayed with him, and for that, he was grateful. If he were honest, he'd been worried in general about the farmers' reactions to a female classer. But Poppy appeared to be managing well, and those familiar stirrings of attraction rose in his chest again.

Was she seeing anyone?

LJ shook off the random thought. With the funeral and Sam's mother fresh in his mind, he didn't need any new life complications. He was still sorting out his old one—Jacinta— who couldn't accept that their relationship had ended over a year ago.

But thoughts of Poppy offered a glimmer of hope. Her quiet strength had his attention and there was definite interest from her side. He'd seen it when he'd caught her watching him shear.

She'd blushed. He'd smiled.

He scratched his head and turned into the pen again. Enough lost time thinking about this woman—he was losing money for it. He needed to put his head down and work harder before he copped another ribbing at lunch time from the boys for his drop in tally numbers. Whippet was rounding him up, and if he wasn't careful, his unspoken 'you'll never catch me' reputation wouldn't survive.

With focus, he picked up his hand piece, pulled into gear and took the first blow.

By three o'clock, Cookie had delivered another epic afternoon smoko—cocktail franks wrapped in puff pastry, sandwiches, a fruit cake, and fruit, all served with her signature generous smile. When the boys sauntered into the tearoom, LJ hung back, fiddling with his handpiece while stealing glances towards the classer's table.

Poppy was behind again, and it added up. The cocky chicks were back on the table, clearly enjoying making her life difficult. Should he have a word with them? But after she'd handled the smoking in the shed, they'd all listened and moved outside. No, she had everything in hand.

'Those bloody women,' Bear muttered, changing his combs and cutters ready for the next run, then looking Poppy's way. 'They'd never pull that stunt if Dougie was here.' He shook his head and moved towards the tearoom, leaving LJ. He had to give it to her. Poppy was catching up faster than the first run, and he was pretty sure there wouldn't be a fleece to be seen on the wool table next time the women were back.

With the last fleece away, Poppy grabbed the nearby paddle and swept her area clean, pulling the disorderly locks into a neat pile. He watched as she bent and scooped them up in her hands, taking them to the appropriate wool pack set up in a frame by the side of the first pen. By rights, the shedhands should've been doing that job. He hid his smile of admiration. She was hardworking and patient, and his earlier doubts about her were steadily dissipating.

LJ put his handpiece down and strolled over to her wool table, the smile that had eluded him all week returning as she leaned the paddle against the wool bin and offered him a curious look.

'Hey. How's it all going?'

'I'm happy with my lines.' She nodded. 'All I need to do is sort out those delightful women who find it in their adorable hearts to make my life so difficult. But I'll figure it out.'

Oh, I know you will. LJ struggled to hide the smile rising on his lips as he recalled the way she'd "sorted them out" earlier. She was determined and the unwavering look in her eye told him she was a force to be reckoned with.

Acknowledging her with a slow nod, his eyebrows raised with interest. 'Looks to me like you're doing a good job. You look happier now.' His smile was relaxed, easy, and it felt good.

'I am happier. Just one thing though.' Her words drew his attention from the stray hair dangling softly beside her face. 'You haven't introduced me to the other shearers yet. Would you mind?'

'Sure.' LJ turned from her with a polite tilt of his head, motioning towards the tearoom door. It was only early days, but this woman who had occupied his morning thoughts was slowly easing the sharp edge off his grief, something only yesterday he'd believed would be impossible.

As she stepped in front of him, a familiar stirring rose inside his chest. He liked the way her long, slim legs were wrapped in denim jeans, and her pretty floral work shirt rolled up at the sleeves showed off her naturally tanned skin. She might have given him a drop-dead gorgeous smile, but this woman didn't come across as an easy walkover, something he found attractive.

When they entered the tearoom, LJ stepped around her.

'Right, lads. It has come to my attention that I have neglected to make some introductions.'

Poppy paid attention as LJ introduced each man in order of the stand they worked at. Jase offered her a welcoming smile, a twinkle in his eye. Whippet raised his coffee in the air as he called 'Cheers!' Dave's pale, intense eyes, the colour of iced water, sent a ripple of unease through her, while Bear stood and gave an elaborate bow that made everyone except Dave laugh.

'And you've already met Spider, presser extraordinaire.' Minding his own business, Spider munched on hot savoys she couldn't see plated at the food table.

'Thanks, guys.' She offered them a cheerful smile, their acceptance speaking louder than she'd expected.

'Hey LJ, have ya heard the latest about Sweeny's team? A bale went missin' after the shed finished last week. Reckon it's gotta be one of his blokes,' Jase said, draining his coffee.

'Some things never change, mate.' LJ shook his head with obvious disgust.

'Who's Sweeny?' Poppy said, noticing the knowing looks exchanged around the room. She got the feeling they didn't want to talk about him.

'The other contractor in the district,' LJ said finally.

Her eyes widened. Competition was expected, but there seemed to be more to this story. Then again, rumours that were started in a shearing shed—she hated that she knew this first hand—had the tendency to take off like a wildfire, regardless of whether the stories were true or not.

'The only bloody reason he's got so many jobs is 'cause the growers think they've got nowhere else to go,' Bear said, crossing his arms. 'When are they gonna wake up to themselves? He's as dodgy as they come.'

But LJ had enough work for the team, right? He'd told her as much the other night at George's. She dismissed the thought as LJ stood.

'Okay, boys. Let's go get 'em for the last run.'

'But there's two runs left,' Bear protested, and Poppy's puzzled face had him grinning with delight.

'The last run *and* the run home!'

Poppy giggled as they good-naturedly groaned at Bear for using his *old* joke on the newcomer. George's shearer—a sullen type who did his work in silence—came to mind. All Poppy heard from him was 'Good mornin' and 'See ya, tommorra'.

Regardless of her uneasy start, these guys were good to be around. This was what she wanted—a team that worked with an unspoken bond of humour and loyalty. A team that would look out for one another when the going got tough.

Not laugh her out of the shed and make her out to be the incompetent fool.

Chapter Nine

With her workday finished, Poppy grabbed her bag, popping her classer's stencil inside—her identification as a bona fide classer. Since Rick's shed, she'd made a practice of taking it with her. She was scanning her phone when LJ strolled past, heading for his ute. 'Watch out for the black ice.'

Preoccupied with a missed call from her father, she gave a token wave of thanks. She dialled his number, working to squash the apprehension rapidly building inside her chest. Others walked by and she shifted to the driver's side of her car for privacy. The sheep in the yards watched her with keen eyes, bleating at the injustice of being locked out of their green pasture.

'Hi, Dad.' She put on a cheerful voice despite the way she was feeling.

'So how was your first day?' That familiar blend of fatherly concern and pride had her body stiffening.

'It was good. Lots of patients and running around.' Her eyes darted to the gravel in front of her. She wasn't lying, only embellishing the truth a little to keep him happy. He had enough on his mind with missing Mum and dealing with work. When she'd left home, he'd been less than happy, but she had convinced him she wouldn't go back to classing. And at the time, she'd thought that too.

'There's this older gentleman called George who's been helping me settle in.' Suddenly, she wanted nothing more than to end this call, but her father continued.

'What's that ruckus in the background? Are you near a farm? I thought the hospital was in Hobart?'

The suspicion in his voice made her cringe. How could she be so stupid? He would put two and two together for sure, and then what? She'd be drowning in her own deception.

'I went for a drive after my shift and stopped near a farm. They have sheep in the yards.' She bit down hard on her lip. He knew how much she loved working with sheep. Would he let it slide, despite how obvious she now realised it sounded?

'Hmm.'

Definitely not the response she'd hoped for. Poppy glanced towards the darkening sky, a golden haze spreading across the clouds on the horizon. He had to understand she was doing this to heal from Rick's betrayal.

'You'd better ring your grandmother too. She's been trying to reach you.'

'I will soon. Bye, Dad.' Poppy hung up in a hurry before

he could probe further, stuffing her phone into her back pocket and immediately feeling guilty for being so abrupt. She wanted to talk to her grandmother, but she hated the lying already, and calling *Abuela* would only make it worse.

What had she been thinking accepting this job? Her nursing degree came to mind. When it finished, she'd tell LJ she wasn't available for more work, then return to helping George while summoning the courage to apply for nursing positions after the Royal Hobart Hospital had turned down her application—a fact she was grateful for.

LJ was sitting in his ute, his window down despite the cool air. His elbow rested on the window frame as he studied his phone.

'Thanks for everything . . . today,' she called over the top of her car, feeling the need to clarify she wasn't thanking him for the other night. Clearly she was the only one feeling awkward about their little run-in. Her feelings had run rampant then, betraying her decision to stay away from romantic relationships.

LJ glanced up, appearing surprised as if he hadn't heard her. He offered a brief smile and nod.

That's all it is, she reminded herself. He's just being friendly.

'All good. See you tommorra.' He lifted his hand in a brief wave before returning his focus to his phone.

Huh? Poppy shot him a puzzled look, hesitating as her hand gripped the door frame. Why did that sound so familiar? She frowned, brushing it aside with a dismissive shake of her head.

'Okay. I'm off then,' she called, annoyed at her own disappointment over his disinterest. A man like him could almost shake her 'anti-relationship resolve. But Rick had sealed that fate, and she wasn't going back for seconds.

Ever.

Looking to the fading daylight, she needed to reach her landlady, Mrs Potter, before dark. 'If you want to stop the squeak, you've gotta oil the wheel,' Grandpa Isaac always said.

But Poppy remembered the way the woman had dismissed her requests like they were a waste of her time last year when she had come to Tasmania to class George's wool, certain she would receive the same reaction. She groaned as she let herself sink into her driver's seat.

'I can't do nothin' 'bout your oven, luv, so don't go getting those pretty little knickers in a knot. That's me son's concern, not mine, and he ain't comin' home till the cows sing. Now get on with ya.' With that, the woman had promptly turned and walked away, muttering to herself and leaving Poppy standing in the middle of the caravan park gravel road with her groceries and no way to cook them.

Poppy didn't hold out much hope that the woman would be any more obliging this year.

Poppy's lips drew together as she blinked at the instant noodles dangling from the fork in front of her. What she wouldn't give just to sink her teeth into some of *Abuela's* delicious paella right now. She let out a lonely sigh.

Rick's smug face invaded her thoughts. Where was he right now? Probably showing off his new girlfriend—the one he'd chosen over Poppy after two years together.

I was so stupid to think . . .

She'd been so smitten with the handsome shearer from a wealthy station family, only to discover she'd been dumped because she wasn't "management material". His exact words, delivered in front of the entire team on cut-out day, when she'd questioned why the new shedhand was being promoted over more experienced workers who were far more deserving.

It was the same day she left the team, and Rick, forever . . . And the lies that were fed to enough people, she thought she might never escape the mortification and stigma for a lifetime.

Poppy played with her fork again, standing it upright in the noodles, her appetite gone as fresh humiliation hit. Where exactly was her life heading? Down the gurgler if she wasn't careful to keep her story straight, that's what. A chill ran through her, and she tugged the fleecy blanket over her shoulders, staring at her reflection in the window.

A loud *thump, thump* at her caravan door startled her from her thoughts. Her eyes widened and she looked around. Who could it be? No one knew she was here except Jimmy, and he would have called first.

'Who . . . who is it?' Her words came out shakily.

'It's Adrian Potter. You need your oven fixed?' His voice was friendly and welcoming.

'Oh, yes! Just a minute.' Her shoulders relaxed, and she left the noodles on the table for good measure. She opened the door to a short man with a neat haircut and large, bright blue eyes full of wonder. His grin was infectious and Poppy couldn't stop herself from smiling back.

'Hi. Um, you're Adrian?' Had he picked up on her puzzled expression?

'Yup, that's me.' He beamed, waiting patiently in the dark. Cold air drew itself into the caravan like it was being pulled in by a drawstring.

'Please, come in.' She held the door open.

He nodded, bent to retrieve a small bag, and stepped inside. Immediately kneeling at the oven, he opened and closed the door, fiddled with the dials, then gave her a thumbs up, his grin spreading wider. Before she could speak, he stepped outside with a torch.

She heard rattling from the front of the caravan and peered out, squinting into the darkness. Adrian's head appeared around the corner, still grinning.

'Try it now,' he said from the doorstep.

Poppy twisted one knob on the oven and lit a match.

The flame ignited.

'You did it! Thank you so much.' She hesitated, tipping her head sideways. 'What did you do?' Poppy searched his genuine, affable face.

'I turned the gas on.' His expression was pure delight, and his satisfied chuckle said it all.

'You're brilliant. I would never have thought of that. Good thing I don't have a TV. You'd need to get that working for me, too.' She chuckled lightly, marvelling. Not once had Mrs Potter mentioned anything about her son having Down Syndrome.

'That's okay.' He shrugged, then picked up his small workbag containing a spanner, a screwdriver and a torch. 'Bye.' He waved, smiling before heading back into the darkness, his torch lighting the way back to the main residence.

Poppy leaned against the door frame a moment longer, breathing in the chilled stillness of the park. A lonesome dog howled in the distance, followed by a swift "shut up".

Poppy smiled, closing the door on the darkness.

Chapter Ten

No sooner had she shut the door than her phone rang.

'What are you playing at, Popps?' Jimmy's voice was agitated. 'Dad spent the entire time at dinner ranting about wild sheep bleating in the background of your call. I reckon he's beginning to think you're working on a farm again. Oh, wait a minute. *You are!*'

'Hi to you too,' she said, worrying her brow with her fingers. 'I forgot where I was, okay? He'd rung like six times. I didn't think.'

'Well, don't do that again. You know how he gets when he's becoming suspicious.' Jimmy's tone softened slightly. 'I'm just trying to keep you covered here, but you're making it hard.'

'I know, and I appreciate it. Really.' She meant it. 'I just need a bit more time to figure things out.'

'That's fine until you forget a detail and mess up. Then I'll be the one still trying to cover for you. You do know that, don't you?'

'And you do it so well.' She closed her eyes. 'It's why you're my favourite big brother. Besides, it won't be for long. I'm planning on telling the contractor I'm finishing up after this job.'

'Hmm.' That was not the convinced voice she was wanting to hear. 'So how was your first day? How's the team you're working with?' The edge in his voice told her he was worried too, always protective of her despite her reminding him regularly that she didn't need his help.

'Well, my oven is fixed!'

'Whatcha do, kick it?'

She ignored his chuckle.

'No! That's not *always* my answer.' She laid bets he was recalling the lawn mower incident only a couple of weeks ago.

'I meant how was work?' Her brother could win a gold medal for being persistent.

'Interesting,' she finally conceded.

Jimmy was quiet for a moment. 'What's your contractor like?'

Despite herself, she felt warmth creep into her voice. 'LJ's . . . different. He seems genuine. And when the grumpy farmer gave me grief today, LJ stepped in without making me look useless.'

'Sounds like he's got your back.'

'Maybe. It's too early to tell.'

'Well, for what it's worth, I think you should give this team a chance. Give yourself a chance too.'

'I don't want to talk about it.'

'You never do. But maybe that's the problem.' Jimmy paused. 'Look, I get why you needed to get away. That bastard humiliated you in front of everyone, and it's no secret I never trusted him. But hiding out in Tasmania pretending to be a nurse isn't going to fix anything.'

'It's giving me space to regroup,' she said, hating how defensive she sounded.

'Is it? Or is it just another way to avoid dealing with what happened?'

The words burned because they felt true. She'd been so focused on running that she hadn't completely processed it. 'You don't understand. When he made those accusations about his family's best line of superfine wool, when he chose that other woman over me, when the whole team laughed . . .' Her voice caught. 'He said I wasn't good enough to class their clip, Jimmy. He made me feel worthless.'

'Hey.' His voice turned fierce. 'You are not nothing. Rick's an entitled idiot who couldn't see what he had. Don't let his stupidity define your worth.'

Tears she'd been holding back for weeks threatened to spill. 'Then why does it still hurt so much?'

'Because you loved him. And because what he did was cruel and public and intended to make you feel small.' Jimmy's protective anger warmed her even through the phone. 'But Popps, if you keep running from what you love—wool classing, working with teams—he wins. Is that what you want?'

She wiped her eyes with her sleeve. 'No. But I don't know how to go back to trusting people.'

You're brilliant at what you do, sis. Don't let Rick steal that from you.'

She felt something loosen in her chest—the first hint of hope she'd felt in months? 'What about Dad? He'll lose his mind if he finds out I'm classing again.'

'Leave Dad to me. If you decide to stay with it, I'll help you figure out how to tell him. But first, you need to decide what you actually want in your future, and not be defined by your past.'

'When did you get so wise?' she asked, managing a shaky laugh.

'Someone has to be the smart one in this family.' His teasing tone had her wanting to reach through the phone and hug him. 'Now get some sleep. And Popps? Stop hiding from yourself. You're stronger than Rick ever gave you credit for.'

After hanging up, she sat in the quiet caravan, Jimmy's words echoing in her mind. Maybe he was right. Maybe it was time to stop running and start fighting for what she wanted.

Tomorrow, she'd face those difficult shedhands head-on. And maybe, just maybe, she'd stop trying so hard to push LJ away.

For the first time in months, Poppy began to feel like her old self again.

Chapter Eleven

A cold puff of air floated in front of Poppy's tired eyes, and she curled herself into a tight ball under her doona, shivering against the cool sheet brushing her skin. What she wouldn't give for the central heating at home. This was a whole new level of cold, and the full-blown Tasmanian winter hadn't even arrived yet. Flannelette PJs and some woolly socks were at the top of her shopping list.

She jumped out of bed and tiptoed across the icy floor to the heater, flicking the switch, and all it gave back was a hollow click. Too peeved and tired after Jimmy's call last night, she'd forgotten to check if it worked. She resisted the strong urge to kick it.

Wrapped in her doona, she stared at her breath forming clouds in the frigid air. No TV, no heating, and with her limited funds, neither was happening anytime soon. She loved to read, so she added a book to her list, but decided to stay well away from anything that involved shearing sheds or romance.

A loud groan escaped as she checked the time displayed on her phone and dragged herself up to get dressed in a hurry, flicking the kettle on, holding her chilly fingers above the rising steam.

With a cup of strong black tea in front of her—like her Grandpa Isaac used to drink when he was shearing—she slid into the seat at the table with her bowl of rice bubbles, bracing against the cold vinyl. Ralph's specification sheet from last year sat beside her. She glanced over it as she munched, noting what Dougie had called the stain line. Either he hadn't seen the Code of Practice for several years or he didn't care, but she was changing it.

And she bet her bottom dollar good ol' Ralph would have something to say about it.

Poppy stepped inside the shed to friendly chatter.

'Ducks on the pond,' Bear called, and she scanned the shed, curious as to why ducks would be in the shed in the first place. They'd be cute but would need to be removed before work.

She smiled a good morning to everyone as she walked down the board.

'So, where are they?' Her curious look brought some chuckles as she glanced around, catching LJ's gaze, and butterflies erupted in her chest as he held her in a thoughtful stare. Her smile rose involuntarily before she caught herself and turned away sharply.

'Who do you mean?' Bear grinned, winking at Jase and LJ like all his Christmases had come at once.

Was this some dad joke she'd never heard before? The smirks directed her way began to make her suspicious. 'The ducks? Oh . . . hang on! She was definitely smelling a rat.

The roar of laughter confirmed it, all eyes on her. She smiled, hoping to deflect, but her face gave her away. Little Trev shuffled up beside her, his expression cautious.

'It means there's a woman in the shed,' he whispered. 'You know, usually it's a man's environment 'n all.' He glanced nervously at the others, then blinked at her wide-eyed.

'Oh!' Having only worked with younger teams, she wasn't familiar with the older terms used in days gone by. But their laughter felt good-natured, not malicious. This team, dare she think it, had the beginnings of what she hoped might be family for her.

'Well, this little duck isn't going anywhere, boys.' She rocked on her feet as the last of the remaining laughter faded, admitting she enjoyed being laughed with, rather than at.

'Glad to hear it.' LJ's voice was quiet, but Poppy turned in his direction. His slow smile and striking blue gaze hit her core, her eyes widening at the realisation that everyone was watching their exchange.

Heat flooded her cheeks as she spun towards the wool

table, letting the brisk shed air wash over her heated skin. She grabbed the wool book to check how many bales had been pressed so far, hoping no one—especially LJ—had noticed her reaction. But she knew that hope was futile. Her face had broadcast everything.

Had he just told everyone he wanted her to stay? Despite Ralph's less-than-warm welcome yesterday?

It wasn't what she wanted.

Was it?

Unable to resist another glance his way, her pleasure faded to questioning concern. His generous smile had evaporated, his handpiece hanging low in his hand as he stared at the worn floorboards like they might swallow him up.

Her brow furrowed as she leaned sideways to get a better view. His face held such sadness, she struggled to resist the urge to walk back, reach out and touch him on the arm and ask if he was okay. He pressed his thumb and finger to his eye, as if he was willing his mood away before the first run. His hand fell to his side, and he blinked hard, gathering himself with a long breath before his voice carried over the steady hum of the warming handpieces. 'Righto, boys, another day, another dollar.'

The forced cheerfulness in his smile made her chest tighten. Something was definitely wrong, and she wished she knew him well enough to ask.

The two women she thought of as troublemakers strolled in late with cocky eyebrows and chins high. They sauntered past her with smirks, heading towards where Bianca and Little Trev were doing the jobs they were supposed to be doing.

Bianca greeted them with a death stare before marching towards the wool table, stopping first to whisper something in LJ's ear. From everything Poppy had observed, Bianca was dedicated and competent, and someone you wouldn't want to cross. She threw perfect fleeces, never wasted time leaning against pen doors like some she could name, even swept the locks from under Poppy's table without being asked, and she ensured stained wool was kept separate from clean wool. She was an absolute asset, and it was pure relief for Poppy, knowing someone was keeping an eye on the quality control of the wool other than her. If only she'd had someone like that back at Rick's shed . . .

'Black wool,' Jase called, holding up the offending clump of fibre before dropping it to his side and resuming shearing. Poppy's eyes flew up from the fleece in her hands, watching the two women who continued to sweep and pick up fleeces as though nothing had happened.

No. No! Poppy left her fleece and ran to Jase. 'Did you get the black wool?' she asked the first woman, unable to hide her urgency.

'Nope.' The woman offered a snide smile and turned to her companion, who snorted with laughter.

Frustration boiled inside her. Black wool contained pigmented fibres that couldn't be dyed, and the whole clip could be ruined. Bile filled her throat, and she fought to shut down the damaging memories. She snatched up the discarded tuft and found the black wool box.

'I need this—and she held the tuft of offending wool

up—placed in here and the whole fleece taken to the spare bin behind me. Please.' The word nearly stuck in her throat, but she had to believe they might listen. Her fresh start in Tasmania depended on it.

She marked the sheep's nose with blue chalk so Ralph could draft it from the mob before taking them back to the paddock.

Back at her wool table, fleeces overflowed, matching her sagging shoulders. At the rate she was going, her chances of feeling like she wasn't going to let LJ or the grower down were diminishing at a rapid rate.

At smoko, the aroma of steaming dim sims drew her into the tearoom, and her eyes widened as she spied the cake on the table, momentarily smiling before letting it slip away at the memory it triggered.

LJ took a slice and looked at her. 'Like the look of this one, do you?' He took an enthusiastic bite. She knew her face hadn't said she did, not really, but she appreciated his attempt at trying to connect.

'It's my absolute favourite,' she said quietly. 'Mum used to make it . . . for my birthday.' She shrugged, hoping he wouldn't ask anything more. She wasn't sure if she could face a slice with the memory of her mother hovering in her mind.

'Orange and poppy seed might become my favourite

too.' His understanding smile warmed her before he moved away, leaving her watching his retreating form in dungarees disappear into the wool room. How could one guy be so distracting when she was having a weak moment? And why did she get the feeling he understood exactly how she felt?

Bianca looked up, and Poppy smiled, taking a seat beside her.

'Thanks for taking care of the fleeces while I dealt with the black wool.'

'No worries.' Bianca barely looked up.

Paul wedged himself beside Poppy, his shoulder pressing against hers. She shuffled closer to Bianca as he gave her a suggestive nudge with raised eyebrows. But before she could give him a don't-try-that-again glare, he was already attacking his first of four sandwiches cradled in his grimy hands.

She turned to Bianca. 'You're an excellent shedhand. How long have you been doing this?'

'I've been working since I left school. LJ was shearing, and I wanted to earn money, so I joined his team.'

'Are you two related?' The question slipped out before she could stop it.

Bianca grinned. 'He's my brother. Didn't he mention that?'

Relief flooded through Poppy, followed immediately by embarrassment at her obvious interest. 'No, he didn't.' A warm rush of heat crept up her neck.

'LJ's not great at introductions.' Bianca's tone held fondness. 'I won the nationals last year, and he's been National

Champion three years running. One of the best shearers in Australia.'

'That's incredible. Congratulations.' The pride in Bianca's voice, particularly for her brother, was clear.

'Thanks, but it's no big deal. I aim to do my job well, and LJ lives and breathes the work.'

Poppy offered a nod and a smile, thinking of Rick's dazzling arrogance and how it so easily drew in the girls, having them fawning over the rich farmer's son who could flex his muscles so well when he shore. At the time, she couldn't believe he'd chosen her over them. If only he hadn't—it would have saved her a whole lot of heartache.

She pushed the distasteful thoughts of him away. Even from this distance, he still felt too close.

Chapter Twelve

Another run finished, and lunchtime aromas drifted to the wool table as Poppy cleared her space of fleeces and mess. Just as she was about to head to the tearoom for roast lamb and vegetables, the familiar sound of heavy boots echoed across the floorboards.

She looked up with the friendliest smile she could muster, facing Ralph Jenkins's toad-like expression. He paused in front of her, scanning the wool bins before looking down at her over his nose—a habit she was getting used to. She drew in a slow breath.

'You still finding a lot of tender wool?' His tone held caution and, dare she think it, genuine curiosity. Where was he heading with this?

'Yes, I am.' She braced herself for another

confrontation, but instead watched in surprise as his weathered face softened slightly.

'I was thinking 'bout that last night.' His gruff voice carried less hostility, and his gaze drifted past her shoulder, as if recalling something from long ago.

'Reckon it could've been from the sudden break in the season we had over summer. We had a dumping of rain and fresh shoots of grass shot up everywhere, enough to make 'em tender, I'd say.'

She nodded slowly. Was Ralph Jenkins actually admitting he might have been wrong? 'That's possible, given where the breaks in the staple are occurring.'

He studied her for a long moment, and she caught what could have been grudging respect in his expression. 'Dougie never bothered explaining things like you do. Just called it all good wool.' He gave an abrupt nod. 'Right then. You have your lunch. I'd better bring in the next mob.' And just like that he spun on his heels, leaving Poppy with her mouth slightly gaping and a small smile creeping over it.

The rest of the day passed smoothly. Paul was keeping his distance, much to her relief, and the two women she'd mentally dubbed B1 and B2 were doing their job without too much disruption.

With a final check of her lines at day's end, Poppy

grabbed her work bag and headed for the car. She had just opened her car door when someone called out to her.

'A few of us are going to the pub for dinner. Feel like comin'?' Bianca smiled, her vivid blue eyes—so much like her brother's—waiting for her reply.

'Really? Yeah, sure. What time?'

'Six o'clock. The Night's Helmsmen. See ya there.' With that, Bianca hopped in the ute before Whippet reversed, then revved down the road.

As she listened to the loud engine fade into the distance, a flood of relief came over her and a small smile tugged at her lips. She might have left home feeling like an outcast, but right here, right now, it felt amazingly good to be included.

Home in record time, Poppy wrestled with her jammed caravan door lock with growing frustration. Her list of repairs was growing faster than the weeds rearing their seedy heads around the place. She had no time to catch Mrs Potter right now, not that the sour woman would help anyway. The lock finally released, and grabbing a change of clothes from the spare bed she'd dubbed her "bed robe", she rushed to the shower block.

Fifteen minutes later, the last of the dusk sky had faded as she pulled up beside The Lone Pony office, relieved to see Adrian out the front, watering the half-dead geraniums flanking the entrance. The darkening clouds were shedding a light misty rain, which, combined with the wind that was picking up, chilled her warm body. She tugged her jacket closer.

'Hey, Adrian. How are you?'

'I'm good.' Adrian's authentic smile was as sunny and welcoming as always. Under the verandah light, his carefully styled hair swooped across his forehead. It struck her again how this gentle, capable man could have such a gruff mother. Adrian radiated the kind of love that could only come from someone who'd received it generously—yet Mrs Potter seemed incapable of giving that. The contradiction made her think of Jimmy and how much she missed his protective warmth.

'Thanks again for fixing my oven. I'm sorry to ask for another favour, but could you look at a couple more things? My heater isn't working, and the door lock keeps jamming.'

'That's okay. That's my job.' He kept smiling as he held the bucket, slow drips seeping from the hole in the bottom and landing on his boot.

'You're a gem, Adrian. Thank you.'

The Night's Helmsman was busy for a Tuesday evening, with several patrons sitting at the bar drowning their weekly sorrows early. Poppy spotted Bianca beckoning her over to a large table where most of the team had gathered.

She'd barely taken her seat when a glass of wine appeared over her shoulder. Startled, she turned to find LJ standing behind her with a subtle smile playing at his lips.

'I figured you might like a white?' His eyebrow raised in gentle enquiry.

'You're right.' Heat crept up her neck as his blue eyes seemed to see right through her. 'How did you know?'

'Lucky guess.' He shrugged, the lines around his eyes crinkled with warmth, and she got the feeling he was reluctant to look away before he distributed the rest of the drinks, including a Coke for himself.

He doesn't drink? That wasn't what she'd expected, especially since the rest of the group had beers in front of them.

Poppy enjoyed grilled fish and salad while the group chatted easily, grateful she didn't have to do too much talking.

The team's dynamic fascinated her—Bear clouting Spider's fingers when he tried to steal chips off his plate, Bianca elbowing Whippet when he forgot to pass the salt. Their camaraderie was filled with good-natured respect, something that could only come from working closely together through good times and bad, and it left her longing.

'So what's brought you to Tassie?' Jase chewed on a piece of steak as he focused on her from the other side of the table.

The loaded question made her body clench. The real answer was too complicated and painful to share with people who were just getting to know her.

'I wanted to see more of the island.' Nervousness fizzed throughout her body. 'Having classed for George O'Sullivan the past few years, I'm ready to explore more of this part of the world.'

At least that part was true.

'I reckon you'll love it here,' Jase continued. 'I'm born and bred in these parts. Wouldn't wanna go anywhere else.' He offered a friendly smile before he dug into another slice of steak, lifting it to his mouth and chewing as he waited patiently for her to respond.

She nodded. 'I reckon I will too.' Without thinking, her eyes drifted to the far end of the table. She met LJ's gaze for a moment longer than what should have been deemed casual, acceptable, before realising it had verged on blatant staring. Heat flooded her cheeks as she forked her limp salad intently, her eyes wide. Not only had she been caught out, she was downright rattled . . . by his interest in her? She needed to keep her wayward emotions on a tight leash, not left to roam around as they pleased.

An hour later, after nursing a glass of lemon squash, she pushed back her chair. 'I think I'll catch you all in the morning.' Her smile was met with glasses raised in her direction, and she leaned towards Bianca. 'Thanks for the invitation. I really enjoyed myself.'

'No worries. Glad you could make it.' Bianca paused, studying her. 'I wasn't sure you would.'

'Oh?'

'Figured you weren't the sort to mingle. I was wrong.' Bianca shrugged, the slightest smile crossing her lips.

Poppy chuckled softly. After years of working with men, Bianca had probably seen plenty of women who did keep to themselves. Jimmy would appreciate that assessment—he'd always teased her about talking too much.

She was almost at the door when Bianca called out. 'And thanks for the shout.' She waved her beer in salute before taking a drink.

Poppy paused, taking a moment to look over the team that, after tonight, she was genuinely beginning to feel a part of. Her gaze settled on those familiar blue eyes watching her yet again. LJ raised his glass slightly, offering a subtle nod of acknowledgement that left her feeling welcomed in a way she hadn't experienced since leaving home.

Exhausted and back at the caravan, her key slid smoothly into the door lock, turning with ease. Stepping inside, she was greeted by blissful warmth from the quietly humming heater. Relief flooded through her as she kicked off her shoes.

Adrian, you're a legend.

Wrapped in her doona, she was drifting towards sleep when her phone rang. She fumbled for it with closed eyes.

'How's my little sis goin'?' Jimmy's smiling voice relaxed her.

'Hey, Jammy.'

'Wow, you are tired. The only time you call me that is when you're half-conscious.'

Poppy yawned. 'Hmm.' His voice was distant, sleep

tugging at her. 'Is everything okay? How's Grandma?'

'She's fine. I made her paella tonight with a seafood twist. Seriously good, and I do say so myself. You lucked out, Popps.'

Poppy's heart stilled. She missed being around *Abuela's* incredible cooking and her company. She missed Grandpa Isaac, too, with his gruff exterior and devoted teaching. Her family lived in Sydney's outer suburbs, so despite her qualifications, she was considered a city girl by country standards.

While her brothers played cops and robbers during school holiday visits to their grandparents' property, Poppy had trailed Grandpa Isaac like a devoted shadow, wanting to know everything about farm life. He was known for his impatience and fiery temper—warnings her brothers had heeded.

But not Poppy. She'd insisted on riding the tractor to shift hay or sit behind Grandpa on the back of the quad bike, fighting for space with Rex, his old working kelpie, whose tail constantly whacked her in her face as he stood on the back of the bike, waiting for commands.

Despite all that, what excited her most were the hours Grandpa Isaac spent teaching her in the shearing shed. She'd learned about basic wool lines, the classer's role, and how to move sheep inside the shed. In many ways, she's been like any other country girl growing up on a farm—except she'd cried every time she had to leave.

Those memories had shaped her passion for wool classing, long before Rick's betrayal had tainted it.

'That . . . sounds . . . yummy,' Poppy mumbled through another yawn and Jimmy laughed.

'Jammy, don't laugh at me. You're not nice.'

'Okay, okay. I don't think I'm going to get much sense out of you tonight, so I'll go. Sweet dreams, Popps.'

'Sweet dreams.' She ended the call with a lucky stab and drifted into dreams of sheep, wool, and a pair of stunning blue eyes.

Chapter Thirteen

LJ straightened slowly, rolling his shoulders after sending the last sheep of the run down the chute. Finally, it was the end of the week, and Bear was already reminding everyone there were two runs to go.

And the last one is the run home. LJ closed his eyes with relief.

The best news was they had final cut-out in the shed—finishing the job for Ralph Jenkins meant they wouldn't need to see him until crutching time next year. A whole nine months away.

Like worker bees inside their hive, the team picked up pace, and enthusiasm soared as the next two runs flew by and the shed wound up. LJ smiled, recalling what Poppy had called the two shedhands at tea last night: B1 and B2. Even they were showing more effort, thanks to knowing the job was finishing up.

Jase delivered the last blow on the final ewe, and the big press-up began. Spider's long arms and legs worked efficiently, cramming armfuls of wool into the press until it came close to maximum weight. He closed the bale with fasteners and removed it from the press, stencilled the appropriate bale description on the top and face, then set it aside.

The team chatted, stubbies were passed around, and everyone relaxed into final cut-out.

'Wanna beer, boss?' Bear strode up with a couple of cold stubbies in one hand.

'Nah, thanks, Bear. Can't face them anymore.' He turned his head, unwilling to let his team see the raw emotion so close to the surface—all because of Sam. He blinked several times to curb the sting.

'I get that.' Bear's face grew solemn as he handed LJ a Coke instead.

LJ took it and strolled over to where Poppy had her head down, working on the wool specification for the finished clip. He hesitated, rubbing the back of his neck before speaking. 'Uh, listen, Poppy. I should tell you—'

'Sorry, LJ, but I'm swamped right now.' She looked up apologetically, those big brown eyes making his head spin. 'I want to get this done so I don't have to come back tomorrow. Can it wait?'

'Yeah. Sure thing.' He raised his hand in apology, stepping back reluctantly. How could he explain he'd only secured a handful of sheds for the next few weeks, well short of what he had been expecting to have lined up? That growers were avoiding his calls? That he couldn't keep her on without more bookings?

She'd said she needed a regular income if she was going to stay in Tasmania. Telling her the truth meant risking losing her, even though it weighed on him that it was the right thing to do. He ran a hand through his hair. No jobs meant no need for a classer. No classer meant no future jobs.

LJ returned to his stand, gathering his combs and cutters and the rest of his gear, regretting the missed opportunity to come clean with her. But he had tried . . . hadn't he?

The sound of tyres pulling up on the gravel outside distracted him, two people stepping into the shed—a broad-shouldered man LJ didn't recognise, blocking the daylight behind him and glancing around as if searching for someone. Jase and Whippet gave a puzzled shrug.

A woman followed after him. 'Hey, Bear. Have you finished? Is LJ inside?' she asked as she breezed past Bear who was heading out to his ute.

LJ cringed at the oh so familiar voice.

Jacinta.

Bear let out a warning whistle—code that LJ's ex had found them again—as Jacinta's overly cheerful greetings filled the shed, acting like everyone was her best friend. Bianca received a hello, responding with an expressionless half-nod before turning her back.

'LJ! There you are. How are you?' Jacinta strode towards him, planting a big kiss on his lips before he could duck away from it.

LJ stepped back sharply, gripping her elbows to force some space between them. From the corner of his eye, he caught Poppy's quick glance their way before she returned to her work. A heavy sigh seeped through his lips.

'What are you doing here, Jacinta?' He struggled to hide his disbelief. How did she know where they were working?

'Were you trying to hide from me?' Jacinta waggled a playful finger under his nose. 'You can be hard to track down sometimes.'

Obviously not hard enough.

'Just working, like usual.' He continued packing his gear away, hoping his disinterest would dissuade her.

Jacinta moved towards the far end of the board and it was the break he needed. Snatching up his toolbox full of gear, he hauled it towards his ute, but not before Jase gave him a teasing wink, elbowing him as he passed by. The sound of clickety-clack footsteps immediately followed from behind.

Meanwhile, the stranger had moved towards Poppy's table. LJ watched with growing unease as the man studied her with obvious interest, like he was deciding whether to approach, Poppy clearly oblivious, absorbed in her paperwork.

'So, you've finished early? We could head to the pub and get a drink?' Jacinta sidled up beside LJ at his ute and wrapped her hands around his upper arm, squeezing it with familiarity. He looked at her with impatience. She let his arm go. 'I'd like to try the parma—'

'I don't think that's a good idea.' He quickened his pace back towards the shed, taking the steps two at a time.

That's when he saw it.

The stranger approached Poppy, and as he watched on in stunned disbelief, the man reached out and touched her shoulder. As she looked up, her face went stone white.

She knows him?

Before LJ could process what was happening, the man leaned down and kissed her—not a nice-to-see-you-again kiss, but something claiming, even possessive. Poppy immediately stood, the wool speci trembling in her hands.

And that's when LJ's stomach plummeted.

'We could all go, like old times,' Jacinta's voice continued behind him, her words distant and meaningless.

When the stranger pulled back, Poppy took an unsteady step backward, her free hand instinctively rising to her lips. Her eyes darted around the shed—panicked, trapped.

She didn't want that kiss.

Fury surged through LJ as understanding hit. This wasn't some romantic reunion.

This was something else entirely.

'No, Jacinta. It'll never be the same.' He spun around so fast she nearly crashed into him. 'Sam is gone. Nothing will fix that.' His voice trembled with emotion—grief for Sam mixing with protective anger for Poppy.

He gently but firmly moved Jacinta towards the tearoom, away from the scene unfolding near the wool table. 'Look, this won't work for me. Not now, not ever. We've been over for a long time.' He was past delivering the same message gently. She needed to accept it and leave him alone.

'I know you've had it tough lately, sweetheart.' She

touched his arm with what seemed like genuine concern. 'I'm here for you.'

'Hey, LJ. I need you to move your ute,' Whippet called, appearing at exactly the right moment.

'Sure, mate.' Relief flooded through him as he stepped away from Jacinta.

'Poppy, babe, you look fantastic. Did you miss me?'

LJ turned to see Poppy's shoulders rigid, her knuckles white as she gripped the papers. When she spoke, her voice was barely controlled.

'What are you doing here, Rick?'

The guy's laugh was casual, confident. 'Heard you were working down here. Thought I'd check out the scenery.' His eyes raked over her in a way that made LJ's jaw clench.

'You need to leave.' Poppy's voice was stronger now, but LJ could see her hands shaking.

'Come on, don't be like that. We had good times together.' Rick moved closer, and Poppy took another step back, bumping into the wool table.

That was enough.

LJ strode across the shed, his footsteps deliberate and loud. Rick turned as he approached, immediately extending his hand with calculated charm.

'G'day mate. I'm Rick. You must be the contractor. Got any work going? Always looking for good sheds.'

The elevated confidence in his voice made LJ want to grab him by the shirt and throw him out the door. He knew his sort, arrogant, smug. A lot like Miles. But instead, he ignored the offered handshake and positioned himself slightly between

Rick and Poppy.

'About right for shearers right now.' His voice was flat, final. In truth, he needed another shearer. But his gut told him he didn't want this guy in his team.

Rick's smile faltered slightly. 'Right. Well, maybe something will come up.' He turned back to Poppy, reaching out as if to touch her arm again.

'Don't.' The word came out sharper than LJ intended, and Rick's eyes snapped to his with new interest.

'Something wrong, mate?' Rick looked between them, his expression calculating. 'I see. Like that, is it?' He smiled at Poppy with cruel amusement. 'Found yourself a watchdog, have you? Hope he's trained to be nice around your boyfriend.'

Poppy flinched as if she'd been slapped, her new vulnerability something LJ hadn't quite been expecting.

'I think it's time for you to leave.' LJ stepped forward, every muscle tense, his voice level. 'Now.'

For a brief moment, Rick looked like he might push the matter further. Then he shrugged like it didn't matter at all, his infuriating smile returning.

'No worries. I'll be around, Poppy. We need to catch up.' He headed for the door, calling back over his shoulder. 'Nice meeting you all.'

The shed fell silent except for the distant sound of his car starting and driving away.

LJ turned to Poppy, her face still pale and drawn.

'You okay?' Her expression held unease, and it was a struggle for him to hold back from putting an arm around her shoulders.

She nodded without looking up, but he could see her hands still trembling as she tried to organise the paperwork.

'Poppy—'

'I need to finish this.' Her voice was barely above a whisper.

LJ wanted to say more, to ask questions, to offer comfort. But something in her posture told him she needed space to process what had just happened.

'Right. I'll . . . I'll be outside if you need anything.'

As he walked away, he caught Jacinta watching him from the tearoom doorway, her expression unreadable. The last thing he needed was her questions about what she'd just witnessed.

But all he could think about was the fear in Poppy's eyes and the commitment he'd just made to himself: that this Rick would not hurt her again. But could he really keep it? It smelt too much like a promise in his mind.

Chapter Fourteen

Poppy drove home faster than she normally would, her hands gripping the steering wheel as adrenaline coursed through her system.

Rick had found her. The memory of his unwelcome affection—was it even that—made her insides churn—the way he'd grabbed her shoulder, leaned in before she could react, claimed her lips like he still had the right. For a split second, muscle memory had responded before her mind had caught up, and she hated herself for that momentary confusion.

How dare he.

And then LJ had stepped in. The memory of his protective stance, the way he'd positioned himself between her and Rick, sent a confusing flutter through her chest. She wasn't used to anyone defending her—certainly not Rick, who'd so casually thrown her to the wolves when it suited him.

And LJ had a girlfriend? Jacinta's possessive lips on his had made that crystal clear, even if the woman's desperate pursuit seemed one-sided. What was she supposed to make of this defending she hadn't asked for? Workplace obligation? Basic decency?

Something more?

But none of it mattered anyway, she told herself firmly. Rick's appearance was a harsh reminder that she didn't need the complication of emotional entanglement with any man, regardless of how safe LJ had made her feel in the moment.

Poppy hung a right into the caravan park and couldn't help but give a sorry smile at the sight of the little white pony standing forlorn in the front paddock, and she softly smiled, despite her churning emotions. Adrian was watering the struggling geraniums again, and when she tooted, his beaming wave helped lift some of the despair.

After a hot shower that didn't quite wash away the feeling of violation, Poppy flicked on the kettle, rubbing her still quivering hands together as she waited for it to boil. Despite the afternoon sun, the air held a distinct chill she was mindful would creep in fast. She needed everything normal, routine—anything to push Rick's smug, irritating face from her mind. She took out a pen and sheet of paper to make a list of things to do.

As she was pouring her tea, a knock on the door made her jump, her heart racing before she recognised who it would be.

'Hey, Adrian. How are you?'

'I'm good.' His smile beamed up at her and some of her tension eased.

'I'm glad you popped by. I have something for you.' Turning to her small cupboard above the dining table, she pulled out a box of chocolates—originally meant to celebrate finishing the job, but Adrian deserved them more.

His face lit up with surprise. 'Are these for me?'

'Yes, to thank you for fixing . . . everything.' She waved her hand around the caravan. 'Do you like chocolate?'

'I do.' His enthusiasm was infectious, and Poppy found herself genuinely laughing since Rick's appearance.

'I have something for you, too.' He bent and picked up a small flat-screen TV, presenting it to her with pride.

'Oh wow. That's fantastic. Would you like to come in, and we can give it a try? I've made a cuppa if you'd like to join me. I'm dying for a chai tea.'

'Can I have a hot chocolate? I love hot chocolate.'

Her heart swelled.

'Do all the caravans have a TV?' Poppy asked, pouring his hot chocolate as he finished plugging it in, her smile curious.

'No, it's mine.' His eyes twinkled at her. 'You said you didn't have one.'

Her heart swelled more.

The simple generosity hit her like a physical blow. After Rick's selfishness, after feeling so alone and displaced, Adrian's kindness was almost overwhelming.

They settled around the dining table as he eagerly opened his box of chocolates. His face was priceless, and

Poppy was entranced by his childlike delight.

'Would you like one of my yummies?'

She nodded, not trusting her voice. This—this was what kindness looked like. Not Rick's manipulation or possessive claims, but genuine care without expectation.

Saturday morning's fresh air was already starting to clear some of the lingering anxiety from Rick's intrusion. The little pony stood near the front gate, steam rising from its nostrils as Poppy pulled up. Grabbing a carrot from her bag, she called the pony as she approached the fence. It glanced up, observed her with slight curiosity, then resumed its stare at the ground.

'Oh, come on, look, I've got a delicious carrot for you.' She waved it in the air, and the pony regarded her. Several blinks later, the pony's stiff legs shifted, and she loped towards the fence. With caution, she extended her nose towards Poppy, snorting nervous breaths before stretching her lips and wrapping them around the carrot.

'There you go. That was worth the effort, wasn't it?' Poppy reached out with a steady hand and stroked the pony's nose while she continued to chew.

In Launceston, she bought the practical things, like warm pyjamas, slippers and groceries. She was especially excited to find woolly socks decorated with sheep.

She had called LJ the night before to ask for the week

off to help George with his shearing. His easy agreement had been a relief, not to mention the chance to avoid Rick.

She spent the weekend baking, filling her caravan with the comforting aromas of home. And Adrian made it feel even more special with his regular drop-ins, sampling her cooking with such genuine appreciation, she found herself making extra just to see his smile.

Late Sunday afternoon, she drove towards Longford with her car filled to the brim with goodies. She wanted to load George's fridge up, put the first mob of sheep in the shed for the morning, and have tea with him.

Truth be known, George had tried his best to provide the food for both her and the shearer in the past. But when, thanks to his failing eyesight, both she and the shearer had observed their sandwiches wiggling with a few resident maggots last year, Poppy decided to take matters into her own hands. She hated to think what he ate when she wasn't around, relieved she could keep a closer eye on him now.

George was waiting on his verandah, propped by his trusty walking cane—an old stick he'd found down the paddock a few years earlier. Time had smoothed the rough edges and now it was a part of who he was. He had a grin from ear to ear, and her heart squeezed. Rowdy barked a cheerful greeting, her entire backside wagging.

George's place appeared more broken-down than a week ago, if that were possible, with fence pickets hanging at dangerous angles. Rowdy bounded to the car, giving her a welcoming bark, and Poppy bent to pat her soft ears and scruff her neck, the feel of the dog's warm fur comforting her.

'Oh, look at you!' Another set of bright eyes moved between her legs, and Poppy scooped the pup up for a cuddle, snuggling her face into its soft neck and receiving face licks for her trouble. Poppy looked on as George lowered himself onto the wooden seat, watching with obvious delight as a second pup played at his feet.

Forgetting about the food, Poppy tried to open the front gate, only to watch it collapse off its hinges entirely. She jumped back, clutching the pup protectively.

'They've grown so much, George,' she said, climbing the steps while fending off more affectionate licks.

'They're real good.' His grin turned mischievous, and she narrowed her eyes suspiciously.

'That one's for you, if you'd like her.'

Poppy froze, mid pat. 'What?'

'She's yours. One for you and one for me.' He gestured to the pup at his feet. 'The way I figure it, you'll need a handy dog now you're staying in Tassie. She's as good as any I've bred—her father's a yard trial state champion. Pretty handy in the paddock too. Reckon we've got ourselves a real nice pair.' He bent down to pat the male pup sleeping at his feet.

His words hit her. *Now you're staying.* Not visiting, not temporarily working. Staying.

The puppy gazed up at her with seal-brown eyes that seemed to see straight into her soul.

If her father found out about the dog, on top of everything else she was hiding . . . The lies were becoming a tower that could topple at any moment. But looking at this perfect little creature, thinking about Rick's violation of her safe space, and LJ's unexpected defence, not to mention Adrian's simple kindness and George's generous heart—this felt like the first decision that was purely hers in a very long time.

'Oh, George.' She pulled him into the gentlest hug his frail frame could handle. 'She's perfect.'

As she carried the food from her car with the little red and tan puppy bouncing at her heels, her mind whirled. Her father thought she was nursing. Now she had a dog to hide, a deeper commitment to this place, and Rick, who had found his way into her new world.

But watching the puppy explore her exciting surroundings with fearless curiosity, Poppy felt something shift inside her chest. Maybe it was time to stop running and start building something worth protecting.

Even if it meant the lies would have to end . . . eventually.

Even if it meant facing whatever came next with Rick.

For now, she had this moment, this place, these people who cared about her without asking for anything in return. And maybe, just maybe, that was enough to build a new life on.

Chapter Fifteen

What was wrong with him? LJ took a swing, hitting the nail dead on, securing the new weatherboard to the outside of his Grandma Aimee's house. He had no right to react when Rick had turned up, all boyfriend-like. Hell, he was acting like she meant something to him. But her eyes, wide and dare he say it, fearful, had sent off alarm bells deep inside him. He'd seen that look before, from Sam's mother, Josie.

Using his break from work—downtime he couldn't afford—he was steadily renovating the old cottage, including plans to give her a new kitchen and laundry, and new carpet for the hallway and lounge.

He liked the rhythmic hammering. It helped to quiet his mind, giving him something to focus on besides the growing list of problems threatening to destroy everything he and Sam had built. He let the hammer hang mid-swing. The team were depending on him and what was he doing? Faffing around and not securing more work for them, that's what.

He drove the nail into the wood, then bent to pick up another weatherboard, flipping it in his hands as his mind wandered to his best mate with the cheeky smile.

He and Sam had felt like they were taking on the world when they'd bought the shearing run. The partnership had offered LJ an escape from his brother's hostility, and Sam a chance to prove himself to a father who'd never shown him an ounce of respect. His younger brother had made it crystal clear that LJ wasn't welcome, though he'd never understood why.

LJ rubbed a slow hand along the next piece of wood, absently feeling for any roughness in the grain before positioning it ready to nail to the side of the house, only to let the board fall to the ground with a crash. Stepping into the shed, he squeezed his eyes tight as he pressed his thumb and index finger against them, willing the urge to weep aside.

If only he hadn't made that promise to Josie.

If only she could forgive him for his mistake, the one that had cost his best friend his life.

LJ leaned against the workbench, head in his hands. How could he have broken his promise to watch over his best mate? Sam's drinking had gotten worse over the past year, his stunts more dangerous, the memories of his father's cruelty cutting deeper. There were days LJ knew Sam had wanted the internal torment to end, and they were the days that terrified him.

LJ gasped, realising he'd stopped breathing. Josie's

words at the funeral echoed in his memory: "You promised me you'd keep him safe. You promised." Her gentle words, meshed with her tear-filled eyes, had shattered what was left of his heart.

His phone buzzed. LJ pressed weary fingers to his reddened eyes before digging into his back pocket. It was a number he didn't recognise.

'Lincoln Tanner, speaking.'

After several minutes of stilted conversation, LJ ended the call, pushing back against the shed wall, allowing his body to slowly sink down the corrugations of the wall. Each ridge hurt but he deserved it. His arms rested on bent knees as he reached the ground, his head hanging low between them.

WorkSafe were going to do an audit on his shed practices. They wanted the details of every shed he'd worked at in the last twelve months, contact information for all clients, and dates and circumstances of any incidents.

Twelve bloody months! He'd barely had time to build a rapport with his clients and couldn't be sure the audit would give a fair conclusion of his practices and relationship with them. Nor could he guarantee their loyalty to him, before or after an audit. Would Ralph Jenkins stand by him when he heard?

Would any of them?

Why'd you do it, Sammy? His chest heaved as he thumped the back of his head against the wall in rhythm to his words.

Shit, shit, shit.

Chapter Sixteen

Relief flooded Poppy as she hung up on Jimmy. She gently patted the pup, who was sound asleep on her lap. With George's shearing about to commence for the week, she would be free from Rick, *and* she wasn't the current topic of her father's interest. The less he asked about her, the less lying was required, a habit she was definitely not enjoying. Even confessing she had a kelpie would set her father off.

Her hand stilled on the pup's soft fur as her thoughts continued to race. She was resisting Jimmy's nudges to look for nursing. What she knew was how to class wool. The problem was, it held too many reminders of her "apparent inadequacies".

The mortification still burned. Showing up for work, only to be told to check Facebook, where Rick and their new shedhand flaunted their relationship for the world to see. Everyone else had known. Just not her. She'd thought she was still his girlfriend.

And then he dared to turn up, here, asking LJ for work. She had the week to work out how she was going to handle facing him, but the thought made her blood boil. Why did he have to ruin every good thing in her life?

And that kiss! Disgust shuddered through her body. She was finally seeing the side of Rick she hadn't recognised, blinded by his handsome face and farmer charm. She hated herself for being so easily lured in and manipulated. But with any luck—and she had an unsettling feeling she'd need a lot of it—he might decide to go back home since she'd given him nothing back.

Poppy stroked the pup again, determined to push Rick to the far depths of her mind as the aluminium screen door screeched and George emerged. Poppy smiled as he tottered towards her on bowed legs, his pup Sammy at his heels, followed closely by Rowdy.

Sammy spotted Poppy and charged past George, racing to leap on her lap. He woke his unusually quiet sister, planting big paws on Poppy's chest and proceeding to lick her face with gusto.

'Oh, yuck, Sammy.' Poppy cringed, swinging her head away only to meet Rowdy's equally eager tongue.

George chuckled, taking a seat at the old wooden bench on the verandah. 'So, whatcha gonna call her?'

Two arms weren't enough to fend off three excitable dogs, so Poppy quickly stood, but not before her pup squeezed in one last enthusiastic slurp.

'I've settled on Jazz. She's full of spunk and always happy.'

George nodded approvingly. 'I like it.'

Poppy stared at her pup as she stretched and yawned, her tiny tongue curling. 'Thank you again, George. This means so much to me. The closest I ever got to having a pet was a field mouse. Mum screamed when she opened the shoe box in my wardrobe and it jumped out at her.'

The old man's lips curved in amusement.

Satisfied George had eaten a hearty meal, courtesy of a spring lamb from his own flock, Poppy stood. 'Well, I'd better get going. I'll see you at six-thirty in the morning. Oh, and don't you try and move the sheep into the catching pens. Leave that to me, okay?' She gave him a knowing look, hoping he would listen to her for once. If she arrived early enough, she might beat him out of bed.

A rich glaze of sunlight cast a warm glow on the horizon as she tucked both pups into their bed next to his woodshed. 'Good night, clever girl. I'll see you tomorrow. You be good for George while I'm gone.' She gave them one last pat, then headed for home.

As she turned into the driveway of the caravan park, the little pony stood waiting with its head over the railing, blinking hopeful eyes towards her in the brightness of her headlights. Poppy's mouth twitched with a smile as she waved to Adrian, who was pulling out weeds in the fading light, before she drove on, pulling up to her van.

She grabbed a carrot and torch from inside, then jogged

back to the paddock.

'Hey, Adrian. How are you doing?' She placed her hands on her hips, slightly winded from the short run, her fitness clearly suffering since leaving netball behind.

He stood, his smile generous as always. 'Good. She likes you.' He shook his head vehemently. 'She doesn't like Mum.'

Now that doesn't surprise me.

'Does the pony like you?' A swift breeze picked up in the air, and Poppy grabbed for her hair.

'She likes apples. I toss her my apple core sometimes. Mum doesn't like me near her, says she'll bite me.'

I'd bite her, too, if I were the pony.

'Why don't you come and offer her this carrot? She's friendly.'

Adrian tucked his hands behind his back as he glanced towards the pony, then back at Poppy, blinking cautiously.

'Come on, I'm here. I'll show you how to do it without getting bitten. She's a sweet little thing.' She urged him with a nod.

Adrian giggled as the pony nibbled the carrot, its bottom lip skirting along the flat of his hand. 'It tickles.' His laugh was robust and infectious and Poppy laughed with him, her heart filling with love.

Had moving to Tasmania been for all the wrong reasons, or all the right ones after all?

'Ah, it's Poppy, my favourite granddaughter!'

Poppy shook her head as she listened to her grandfather on the phone. 'Grandpa, I'm your only granddaughter.'

'*Si*, that's why you are my favourite.'

His hearty chuckle warmed her heart. She adored this man, and she missed him.

'I have some exciting news to tell you, well, two things actually.'

'Ah, you have a job as a nurse, no? Your grandmother was talking to your father.'

Crap. Her nose wrinkled as she imagined the lies she'd need to craft, about a new patient or cranky assistant nurse unit manager who hated her. In a way, it wasn't so wrong. Not when she modelled them on B1 and B2. She gave a satisfied chuckle.

'There's a lot to tell you, but you're sworn to secrecy if I do, okay?' She struggled to hide the excitement in her voice.

'*Mamma mia*, my Poppy. What are you doing? Are you in trouble?'

I will be by the end of all this.

Poppy clenched her teeth. If she told her grandfather everything, there would be two people who knew her secret, doubling the risk of her father finding out. She didn't want him worrying about her. He hadn't been happy about her giving up her nursing degree for wool classing in the first place, thinking she had finally come to her senses. And it looked like he might have been right. But what had happened to her could happen in any job; only the shearing industry was a little more behind the times in attitude . . . on several fronts.

But she needed her grandfather's advice. He had worked in Tasmania as a young shearer before meeting the love of his life.

'I'm not in trouble. ' She decided to start with the easier admission. 'I have a working kelpie pup.'

'Ahh, now you can have a dog like you've always wanted. Is it well-bred like mine? You can be sure I will not tell your father!' The protective warmth in his voice relieved her. Her father had never allowed her to keep one of her grandfather's pups, certain it would chew his boots.

There had been no love lost between her father and her grandfather. From their first handshake, Isaac hadn't warmed to him. 'The man does not know how to laugh,' he had told his daughter. 'Why do you want a man like that?' But when she'd convinced him he was the man for her, he'd relented, wishing only for her happiness.

Her mum had always had a way of getting what she wanted through gentle persistence. It was tragic that the only thing she couldn't overcome was the breast cancer. She'd fought hard for a long time. But ultimately, she had lost out to its unrelenting grip.

'She's a gorgeous pup, Grandpa, and yes, purebred. George O'Sullivan bred and gave her to me. We start his shearing tomorrow.' It was no surprise to him that she was doing George's shearing, and she impressed herself with her subtle segue.

'Aha, and who will be your shearer?'

'Pat Tanner. Do you know him?'

'Humph. *Si,* and I do not like the man. He is nothing more than an *estafador*, a trickster who will accuse you of something you know *nada* about. Stay away from him, my Poppy.'

Poppy sat taller, a deep frown forming on her brow. Why had he responded like that? His tone warned her to drop the subject.

'I have something else to tell you and you mustn't tell anyone, not even *Abuela*, okay?' If her grandmother knew about it, she could guarantee her father would find out within hours. But she needed more time.

'Hmm, okay.' His words stretched out with caution. 'Go on, tell me my *chica.*'

'I'm not nursing.' There it was. She'd said it. There was a long pause before his heartfelt words washed over her.

'Ah, so my little *nieta* is going against her *padre's* wishes. *Si,* my *nieta* has the strength in her that I always knew. It comes from your Fernández heritage.' His voice held unmistakable pride.

If only she had that same strength when it came to returning full-time to classing. She loved it so much, but could she risk facing the humiliation she'd gone through, all over again?

'So what are you doing?'

'Classing.' She paused, relief flooding her at the thought of telling someone the truth, finally, though she braced herself for his anger about Rick's betrayal.

'Are you sure that is good for you?' The concern in his voice felt like a warm hug.

'I don't know, but a job landed in my lap and I needed the work.' She shrugged away her confusion. '*Abuelita*, have you got any books on training puppies? I'm going to need every bit of advice I can get.' Poppy was proud of her Spanish heritage and was the only one in her family to refer to her grandparents in their native names.

'*Si*, tell me your address and I'll send you one. I take it you will not be home so soon then?'

'Not for a little while. If I stay and class, I'd like to continue working with superfine wool. Do you know of any properties?' This was her favourite wool to class—silky soft, high-quality fibre that, on a beautifully structured fleece, demanded attention.

'No, my Poppy. It is such a long time since I shore down there.'

After the bust-up between another shearer and himself, long-time best mates and work partners, he left the state, determined never to return.

'There were sheds with superfine wool, but I never worked at any.'

The line went quiet, except for a dog barking in the background, probably Rex warning some sheep that had wandered away from the rest of the mob.

'I recall one property called Twin Lanes,' Grandpa Isaac said, 'but I do not know if they're still a working enterprise.'

'That's okay. I'll remember it and ask around.' She

scribbled the name on a scrap of paper.

'Oh, one more thing, *Abuelita*. Only you and Jimmy know what I'm doing here. I need you to keep it that way, for a bit longer.'

'*Comprendo*. Now, you be careful around that Mr Tanner. I cannot kick him so far, and that is as much as I trust him.'

'Sure, Grandpa, I will. Love you.' She hung up, chuckling despite feeling apprehensive about the shearer she was going to have to feed tomorrow.

Chapter Seventeen

LJ scratched at the itchy bristles he wasn't used to wearing on his face and yawned, staring at his bookwork that refused to make sense. This was the part of the job he hated—logging employee hours, then sending the details to the accountant who processed the Take Two Shearers payroll.

Take Two Shearers. The name mocked him now. Sam was gone, and LJ was failing to keep his half of the dream alive. He wearily scrubbed his face with both hands.

Once a shearer, always a shearer, LJ had mimicked his father's blows in the O'Sullivan Brothers' shed since he was three. Despite his keenness, learning the skill had been difficult because he was left-handed until his father—near to tearing his hair out in frustration—finally twigged, placing a mirror in front of him, reversing the image so he could follow the movements. Then everything had clicked into place.

LJ reclined in his chair, arms stretched out towards the dining table, thinking about his Pa Pat who had taken his shearing to the next level. When his father, Stan, had stepped away from shearing to run the farm full-time, Pa Pat taught LJ the stockman ways, including moving mobs into the sheds efficiently and penning up cunning old sheep. LJ had lived and breathed lanolin-infused air, perched on the pen railings as he waited for his chance to pen up more sheep, desperate to impress his grandfather.

At fifteen, he spent every school holiday break in the shed with a handpiece in his hand, crutching mobs of sheep before the shearers shore them. Then, starting with fifteen sheep a run, building up to twenty-five, he hit his stride when shearing thirty-three, which was pure elation in his books. These days, shearing fifty a run—or more, depending on the breed and condition of the sheep—was normal.

But the numbers weren't what mattered. The simple act of shearing had made him who he was. Now, with Sam's blood on his hands, he wasn't sure who he was any more. He was a contractor on paper, but that counted for zip if he couldn't get work for the team.

The uncomfortable image of Poppy's face when Rick had kissed her flashed through his mind—that trapped, violated look she'd worn. At least she was safely at George's this week, away from that bastard. But what happened when she came back? How could he be there for her when he might not have a business for much longer?

Besides all that, why did he care so much about what

happened to her? It wasn't like they had known each other long—at least not long enough for him to be experiencing these confusing feelings. But still, they were there, refusing to leave him alone. His heart quickened.

LJ rubbed his eyes, trying to regain focus. The books weren't going to get themselves done on their own.

Grandma Aimee tottered into the dining room, clasping a cup of coffee and a plate with a piece of warm raspberry jam slice fresh from the oven. The aroma brought back childhood memories and he smiled up at her.

'Eddie, I've made you your favourite.' As she turned around to look for her deceased husband, her legs wobbled from under her.

'I've got you.' LJ sprang up, supporting her elbow and waist as she squeezed her eyes shut, overcome with dizziness.

'Thank you, my dear. I don't know what came over me.' She brushed a hand over her forehead before patting his hand, her smile as surprised as his frown. It was the third time this week she had lost her balance for no apparent reason.

Increasingly, LJ felt the responsibility to keep an eye on his grandmother and at least with no work, he could be here when she needed him. His chest immediately tightened with worry. But if he did by some miraculous circumstance secure work for the team, what would happen when he wasn't there to catch her?

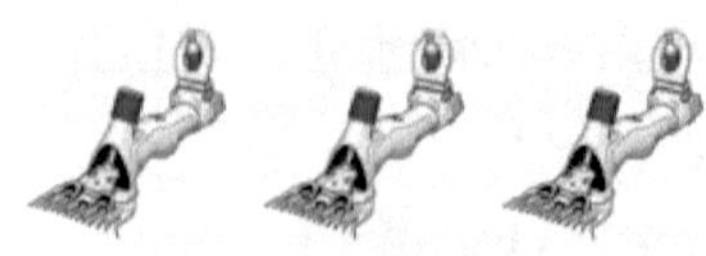

Frigid air gushed in through the ute's vents as LJ drove to his parents' house for tea. He cranked the heater to full blast. His fingers clenched the steering wheel as the shearing shed came into view. Miles was standing in the yards, moving sheep into the shed.

'Crutching time.' The words slipped from LJ's lips as he watched his brother disappear inside the shed. They were crutching them ready for shearing. The thought of missing the milestones of the farm hung low and heavy.

When Ken Cuthrow had conducted the shearing contracts in the Longford district, Stan and Pa Pat had refused the cutthroat tycoon access to their property. 'The man can't be trusted. Don't have anything to do with him,' they'd always said. Small country towns were deceivingly big when it came to negative reviews, and Ken's reputation had spread to much of northern Tasmania, so much so that growers didn't want any of the team near their sheep. Care needed to be taken, particularly when shearing soft-skinned superfine merinos, and Cuthrow had blown his reputation with too many cut sheep, not to mention hamstrings, causing losses the growers weren't prepared to keep suffering.

So, when LJ mentioned buying Cuthrow's failing shearing run, Stan was dead against it.

'I don't care how cheap it's going for, son. It'll only buy you trouble. No one will want to employ your team, regardless of how well you shear.

'But they know me—our family,' LJ had argued, holding out his hand as though it was the key to convincing his father. 'That's gotta count for something.' LJ believed in people's loyalty and their trust in family connections.

'It won't make a difference, son. Cuthrow's carved too much mistrust into this state. People's memories are long.'

Pa Pat was the only one to side with LJ, recognising the potential in his level-headed grandson. Unbeknownst to Stan, Pat had even offered money towards the business purchase. It galled him to give hard-earned dollars to a man of ill repute, but if it would propel his grandson into a promising career, he'd do what it took.

So LJ went against his father's advice, but banked on his family to employ his team for crutching and shearing. That way, he reasoned, he would never lose touch with the farm or his family.

He'd been so wrong.

He pulled up at the homestead, recalling his latest phone call with Miles. 'That's too bloody expensive, LJ. You tryin' to live like a prince or somethin'?' Miles had hung up on him— again. Now his team sat idle while his family employed Sweeny's crew, the same dodgy contractor who'd had a bale "mysteriously" go missing last week. The betrayal cut deeper than any business rejection from strangers.

'LJ!' His mother came out of the house, embracing him on the verandah with a hug before stepping back to look up at her boy, holding him at elbow length. She took his face in her hands and his wry smile filled them.

'I've missed you. Promise you won't stay away so long next time.'

Promise? Ha! The word hit him like a physical blow.

There was no chance he was making promises again in his lifetime. He only broke them, along with hearts and lives, his own included.

'Is that lamb I smell?' He forced a smile, desperate to change the subject. Nothing beat his mother's slow-cooked, home-grown meat, even if the thought of eating made him feel sick.

The front door slammed shut. LJ glowered as he followed his brother's disgruntled footsteps until they disappeared down the hallway.

'Guess he saw my ute,' he said quietly as his mother tugged the roasting tray from the oven. The smell of roast potatoes filled the air, but all he felt was the familiar knot of tension in the back of his neck.

Chapter Eighteen

Poppy was run off her feet. Although Pat Tanner was almost seventy, he peeled wool from George's sheep with enough speed to keep her chasing her tail. *Must be the cake that's pepped him up*, she thought wryly.

Crisp air in the shed was tempered by the sun streaking through broken weatherboards in George's well-worn shed. Poppy soaked in its warm glow against the cold, clinging tightly.

George took great pride in his product, and his wool always excited her. Superfine, fifteen to seventeen micron, dreamy soft to touch, bright white with a lustrous appearance and all the "look at me" vibes any top-notch fleece deserved. She was setting aside the best fleeces, planning to show them to George at lunch with her suggestion that he might like to enter one into the Bendigo Sheep and Wool Show competition next July, where the annual event raised funds from the donated fleeces for a nominated charity.

By lunch time, Pat had shorn fifty sheep. He stood, stretching his crooked back from too many years of being hunched over sheep, and something about the gesture piqued her curiosity. It was familiar somehow. The way he scratched his neck, the particular twist of his shoulders, was uncannily familiar. Was it someone from her old team? But who?

Shrugging off the notion, she grabbed the fleece in front of her and placed it in the wool bin before the three headed over to George's house where the drifting aroma of lasagne wafted from the warmth of the AGA oven, making her belly grumble.

'George tells me you're a permanent resident now, givin' classin' a real go.' Pat shovelled a large forkful of lasagne into his mouth, leaning forward, his elbow on the table. He chewed loudly while waiting for her to answer.

What exactly did she say to that? That her love for the work had all but died the day Rick had shattered her heart? That her confidence might never recover? With Rick turning up unexpectedly, she wasn't holding onto much hope that she might be able to forget what happened anytime soon.

'I've got a grandson who's a contractor. Already has a new classer, though. Pity. I coulda told him about you.'

Poppy looked up, surprised, then shrugged off his comment, too absorbed in her own thoughts. 'I'm classing . . . for now. But you never know what's around the corner.' She offered a careful smile, feeling George's concerned gaze on her.

'Not so much work up north, then?' Pat's inquiring glance felt pointed as he shovelled another forkful into his mouth.

A rueful smile crossed her face. 'I like it here, and George is my favourite client.' She beamed at the old man, giving him a teasing nudge. She had told him she wouldn't be charging him again this year. LJ had plenty of work for her, so it didn't matter.

But Rick . . . Why did he have to continue to ruin everything?

That evening, Poppy sat on her chair outside her caravan, wrapped in her doona and Ugg boots, the clear night bringing a light breeze that made her body wriggle with a shiver. She was in the mood for a thorough sulk.

She absently contemplated the idea of nursing. Would it be that bad? But what if her father expected her to return home and carry on working there? Soon she'd return to LJ's team. And what if LJ had changed his mind, and Rick was working for him after all? She'd have to face him while working alongside the people she'd begun to care about, pretending his presence didn't make her skin crawl.

The sound of heavy footsteps crunched against the gravel in the darkness, making her shrink down inside her warm capsule. The sound moved closer. Louder.

'Hey there, Poppy. What are you doing out here? It's freezing.' Adrian's cheerful voice drifted towards her, and she willed her thundering heart to slow down.

'Hi, Adrian,' she breathed, relieved. 'What are *you* doing out here in the dark? You almost made my heart seize.'

'Sorry.' His light giggle told her he wasn't sorry at all, and despite her mood, she found herself smiling.

Adrian searched the stars in the dense sky as he stood beside her, his back to the caravan. 'I felt like a walk.'

The image of Mrs Potter danced in her mind. She didn't blame him one bit. She'd want to get away from that cranky woman, too.

'It's too cold out here. Come on. How about I make us a hot chocolate.'

'Oh, yum.'

With the heater pumping, they sipped on their drinks. Having discovered Adrian's sweet tooth, she'd popped three fat marshmallows into both of their mugs to soften and ooze. His eyes lit up watching them float in the hot liquid, and when he took a sip, a marshmallow moustache stuck to his top lip.

'Do you like living here, Adrian?' Poppy wrapped her hands around the mug, mesmerised by the rising steam.

'Sometimes. I like it when I see you.' The blush creeping up his cheeks . . . his lowered eyes, made her heart squeeze with affection.

'Thank you for being my friend. I don't have many here yet. It gets lonely.' She'd sent Jimmy some money to buy a plane ticket—the only sure way she knew would make him come—and couldn't wait for him to visit.

'Will you leave?' A deep frown creased Adrian's brow, his big blue eyes searching her with concern.

The question hit harder than expected. With Rick threatening to weasel his way back into her professional world, and her web of lies growing more complex daily, staying felt both necessary and impossible.

'I'm not going anywhere.' She reached out to squeeze his forearm reassuringly. 'Especially if I can find some superfine wool to class.' She wouldn't say no to a clip like that if given the opportunity. LJ had to have some sheds lined up that grew wool like that.

Adrian sat taller in his seat, his eyes suddenly wide and excited. 'I know a farmer.' He almost bounced in his seat. 'You can class his nice wool!' The innocent desperation in his tone tugged at her heart.

Was there actually a chance Adrian might know a superfine woolgrower? The property that *Abuelo* had mentioned surfaced in her mind. What were the chances of Twin Lanes being the one Adrian was referring to? Next to zero, she sighed. But there had to be properties that LJ had connections with. So regardless of whatever Rick was up to, staying with LJ was a must. She would just have to get on with her job and ignore the jerk. And eventually, he might get the hint and shift back to New South Wales, where he belonged.

'Thank you, Adrian. That'd be great.' If only he were able to make that happen. But deep down, she doubted he understood what her job actually entailed.

Chapter Nineteen

'Your wool is all done. And just in the nick of time. That sky doesn't look friendly.'

'You're right,' George said, glancing at the black clouds approaching before giving Poppy a nod. 'They've been talking up this front and I reckon it could be savage.'

'What about we have a hot date at the pub to celebrate, like last year?' She gave him a cheeky wink. They'd be able to have a meal and be home before things got too nasty with the weather.

George's whiskers crinkled around his approving smile. 'Ah, Poppy, you're the daughter I never had, aren't you?' He shuffled towards the shed door.

She tried to smile, but deep down, all this really meant was she was about to go back to LJ's team, which would have been a good thing if she knew Rick wouldn't pull his "Surprise, I'm here. Come and greet me with illustrious bows", impromptu arrival again.

Chimney smoke filled the crisp night air at The Night's Helmsmen as Poppy darted around to the passenger door to help George out of the car.

Grateful to get away from the spits of rain, they entered the warmth of the lounge, a buzz of voices and laughter filling the atmosphere. With George on her arm, she scanned the room for an empty table, eager to sit. Her feet were full-blown aching after penning up, shifting sheep into and out of the yards, and classing, and she was ravenous for a meal she didn't have to cook herself.

'Looks like we have the best seats in the house,' George beamed, sidling up to the fire near their table and rubbing his hands together.

'I'll just grab us a drink,' she smiled. 'Roast lamb, like usual?'

'With extra gravy, please.'

Returning to their table, she placed the glasses down and began to pull her chair out when she noticed a couple seated near the far window. Her gaze narrowed. Who was with LJ?

'Is everything alright, my dear?' George leaned forward in his seat, puzzlement filling his gaze as he reached for his glass.

'Um, yes. Don't mind me.' Poppy shrugged off George's curiosity with a dismissive wave of her hand, attempting to focus on the menu, but instead found herself sneaking glances over George's shoulder more often than she cared to confess. Whoever he was with was a similar age to George. If they were to join tables . . . they could do a double date. The thought sent her heart into a double beat.

With their orders taken, Poppy snuck yet another peek. *Damn it.* He'd seen her too? Sudden heat raced up her neck and she began to peel off her jacket. And damn those intense eyes holding hers like he was attempting to send some telepathic message.

She recognised defeat deep within his eyes, like something had robbed every ounce of joy from him.

She looked away, grateful her meal had arrived despite her appetite having run for the hills thanks to the gorgeous contractor sitting not so far away, the one she'd struggled to shake from her thoughts all week. She nibbled at her chicken parmigiana, pleased to see George's appetite had improved over the week since feeding him up. He might not have put any real weight on, but his hollowed cheeks were definitely looking a little fuller.

Finally immersed in a relaxed conversation about the wool market and the possible upcoming prices for George's wool, she looked up in surprise when two strong legs approached their table. His leather dress shoes looked worn in and comfortable, his hands deep inside his pockets.

She willed herself to look up.

'Hey, Poppy.' Her genuine smile eased his apprehension. 'Hi, George.' He offered his hand in greeting. 'Did you get all your wool baled up?'

'Young Poppy here, did.' George beamed with admiration. 'She's a keeper, this one. You should get her on your team.' George gave LJ a knowing wink, chuckling.

'You're right, George,' but at his words, his confidence flailed thanks to the reality of his situation. The last thing he wanted was to lose her from the team. But what other choice did he have? The strain of a tension headache began to pulse in his temples.

And Rick. The chauvinistic moron had left his mark on LJ's mind. He'd sorted him out once, but letting her go from the team . . . Where did that leave her if he found her again? But the reality of his situation pressed hard in his mind. With a heavy heart, he knew what he had to do.

Whisps of hair hung softly around her face, soft highlights of red shimmying through her dark locks in a pinned up bun, and LJ's heart squeezed a little tighter, knowing the enormity of this moment. His work was running out faster than he could say 'sheepo'. Farmers were continuing to choose the other local contractor, prepared to turn a blind eye to the drinking in the shed that began at first smoko. It pained him. Especially knowing his team could do a far more reliable job. But that didn't change the facts.

Had he and Sam been that naïve, believing they could be a successful, trusted contracting team that provided reliability alongside a great rapport with all their clients? Had he been so desperate to see a future for them both that he had totally missed what was happening in his present? That Sam was no longer here, and it was futile to think he could make the contracting run work without him.

A barbed lump formed in his throat.

He *and* Sam. Not him, on his own. He scrubbed a hand over his face at the thought of letting his team down.

He glanced over his shoulder at Grandma Aimee, who waved his way with a sweet smile. He turned back to see Poppy looking at her, then at him.

'You're . . . not here with Jacinta?' Curiosity laced her expression, and he was almost grateful it deferred him from facing the inevitable.

'No. Why would I be?'

'Oh, I thought she was your—'

'She's not my girlfriend.' His tone came out sharper than he'd intended, the enormity of what he had to tell her weighing heavily.

Was she surprised? Relieved? His heart buoyed a little, before deep regret swamped him again. He had to tell her, he urged himself. It probably meant losing her, for his work and dare he think it, for him, for good. Just another round of promises he'd failed to deliver on. Cuthrow's curse had won. This contracting run was doomed before it had a chance to begin.

Her light, affable smile reached inside his chest, tugging his heart with a familiar pull despite his melancholy. She was pinning her hopes and dreams on him, and he was about to blow them up.

He searched her steadfast gaze, running a sweaty hand

over his mouth as he summoned the courage.

'Listen, Poppy, I need to let you know, I don't have a lot of work left for the team, and I'm . . .' He turned away, unable to keep those deep brown eyes in the centre of his focus. Why did he have to say it out loud, especially to her? He turned back, his heart almost breaking from the sincerity in her eyes. 'I'm going to have to let you go.'

There, he'd done it. He let the last of his long breath slip from his lips in a deflated sigh. He wasn't just letting her down. He was letting himself down, too.

And letting Sam down.

He had effectively blown his chance to show the farmers he was pulling together a reliable team they could count on. Shame gnawed at his conscience.

And he'd lost any chance of something with Poppy, whatever that could have been. Was it so wrong to believe he deserved something good in his life?

But letting go of one employee meant he could keep the rest of the team working for another week, maybe two. He had his classing ticket and, in a roundabout way, knew what he was doing. She had to understand that, right?

Chapter Twenty

Nursing, here I bloody well come.

Poppy looked to the lights on the ceiling of the pub, unsure what she was angriest at: her failed chance to kick-start her career again, or the fact LJ had all but lied to her. The idea that her future might not be her own choice chilled over her skin.

'So . . . you've known all along you didn't have any more work for us? And yet you told me, no wait, you *promised* me I'd have as much work as I liked?' She wanted to be understanding and empathetic towards him. The way he looked so forlorn and broken stirred places in her heart she'd wanted to keep shut down forever. But the enormity of what he'd done, pulling her options from under her feet . . . she was definitely allowed to feel ripped off.

Her voice remained calm despite her shock. She'd tried to leave Rick's broken promises behind, and here she was, faced with more?

She stared at him in disbelief. 'What am I meant to do? You gave me your word.' But the desperation in his pleading expression begged her to understand. Only, she wasn't ready to. The wool industry was what she knew and loved. She needed his work to stay in Tasmania. But what about Rick? With him here, she still wasn't free. Perhaps she should go home? Only, if she did, she'd be facing her father and his expectations, which she didn't want. She fought against the sting of threatening tears.

'Did you know you were running out of work . . . before you asked me?'

At least LJ had the decency to look sheepish now, and in that moment, she didn't need to hear his answer. It was all there in the way his Adam's apple bobbed sharply as he tried to swallow.

'Okay,' she said, staring at her plate as she tried to dredge some semblance of a smile for him despite her confidence hitting the floor. Her well-thought-out choices were being stripped from her one by one, and she didn't have many left she believed she could count on.

'Well, I guess I'll be looking for another job then.' Maybe George would take her in again because she definitely wouldn't be able to afford to stay at The Lone Pony for too much longer.

Adrian . . . Her heart ached at the thought of leaving him in the hands of his heartless mother, and at not being able to come home after a long day, and see his brighter-than-life smile. Already he was becoming like a little brother to her, and she would miss him. Deeply.

Did LJ care about any of this? Perhaps he did? She looked up at him again, his eyes full of compassion, regret, and sorrow. Then again, maybe it was mostly about whatever he was going through, as though some deep sadness filled him endlessly and he might never be able to shake it.

Nestled neatly on top of her worry was her ever-growing attraction to him. She had to admit she was quietly relieved to discover he didn't have a girlfriend after all, but she was still gutted that he was letting her go. Damn men and their way of catching her in a weak moment. Poppy was well and truly past falling for someone who broke their word.

'I . . . um, think that's my call to leave,' he said. 'I'm really sorry, Poppy. Good to see you, George.' He turned away, his every step slow and heavy.

Thank goodness she had locked her heart up tight. It was the only way to protect it. But as she watched him slump into his seat, her heart stirred, her mind a tangle of thoughts and questions.

What if there was a good man hidden in there?

No. Right now, it wasn't smart to ask that.

Poppy picked up her fork, forcing the next piece of chicken down her clenched throat. Had she been too hard on him? But he deserved it. Didn't he? Thanks to him, she now didn't have a job, had Rick on her heels, and was about to lose the only family she had, in accommodation she could no longer afford. He had lied to her, just like Rick had. She chose to ignore the little red flag flying smartly in her direction, reminding her she had some lies of her own. She had promised Adrian, and more so herself, that she would find a way to stay here, and that's exactly what she was going to do.

LJ propped his head on his fist, despondently tossing the carbonara with his fork. Poppy's comeback was direct, and he'd deserved every word. He had seen so clearly the confusion, disappointment, and above all, vulnerability morphing on her face. Why hadn't he been up front with her, told her the truth from the start?

Because telling Poppy was like admitting defeat and he wasn't ready for that, not for himself and definitely not for Sam. He was holding out, desperate enough to believe farmers would support him, trusting he was worth taking a chance on. So much for hoping they might realise relying on him was smarter than trusting his competitor's contracting team.

But more than that, he was desperate to believe his team knew he wouldn't give up on them. They depended on him keeping this show on the road. It had to be the right thing letting her go. Wasn't it? Despite himself, remorse and regret pounded in his ears, knowing he'd let her believe he wouldn't let her down. Guilt tapped hard and fast on his shoulder, for Josie, Sam—the whole team. He didn't deserve their loyalty, and he most definitely didn't deserve their trust.

And now Poppy. He didn't want to lose her. She was his hope for a future with Take Two Shearers. And dare he think it, she might be the hope he needed for him. His heart stirred as he thought of her sitting within reach, yet so far away, and a big part of him wanted to turn around, go back to her table, and tell her it was all a big mistake and that he'd have work for her when she'd finished George's shearing.

That word she'd used. Promise. He hadn't seen that one coming, and it stung. Without realising it, he had done it again, unable to keep the very thing he'd sworn he would. He felt like a dog. He'd been no better than her ex, according to Bianca. Rick had not only dumped her publicly, he'd announced to the world she couldn't do her job, all the while Poppy thought she was going to marry the guy. What would possess someone to do that to someone as loyal, steadfast, and strong as her?

Class act, Tanner! You've really got the touch.

LJ set his fork down, leaned his elbows on the table, and put his face in his hands. What was he meant to do? He'd failed Sam, ended his team's hopes, and his small chance at connecting with Poppy on a deeper level had just been flushed down the gurgler.

He was hanging on by the thinnest of threads, with one last property lined up for next week, just waiting on confirmation. Balancing the fine line between telling the team they no longer had work, all while waiting until the eleventh hour—just in case some did come in—was getting harder by the second to pull off.

Would he ever stop failing the people he cared about?

A flash of lightning lit up the sky, stirring unwanted memories as he drove them home, of the night Sam had died. LJ glanced to the passenger seat, Grandma Aimee blissfully asleep despite the rain pelting against the ute.

He squeezed the steering wheel a little tighter, fighting against the sadness trying desperately to strangle him. That night was a blur to his mind's eye, every part of it. Except when he'd rushed to his best mate's limp body . . .

And he couldn't do a thing to change it.

'Ah, shit.' The words left his mouth in a sigh. WorkSafe. He ran a slow hand over his face, staring into the rain glistening in the brightness of his headlights. Audited. If he hadn't been sitting down already, the word might have knocked him flat to the ground. And if they began asking his team about the night—his conduct—would they back him? Defend him? Especially when he knew he wasn't worth defending? Why would they do something like that when he was on the verge of letting them all go?

Poppy's shocked face after he'd all but fired her filled his heart with deep remorse. Where else was she going to get some classing if it wasn't with him? *Sweeny.* The name hung on his lips like a bitter aftertaste. But she was smarter than that. She'd heard what they'd said about the man. No. He was confident she wouldn't do it.

But the phone call he'd heard at the end of her first day

with the team continued to play in his mind. He frowned. Something didn't make sense. He'd tried to tune out to her conversation, her calls no different to his. Private.

But still, he'd heard.

It was clear she'd been speaking to her father, but why had she made excuses about being near the sound of bleating sheep? And working with an old man? The only old man he figured she knew was sitting with her in the pub.

Chapter Twenty-One

'Thank goodness for you, Jazzy pup.' Poppy lay on her side, scratching behind the ears of the pup who was lounging on the bed beside her like a literal real-life princess, a gentle snuffle of pleasure escaping from her whiskery mouth. A regular tink, tink sounded from the saucepan collecting water as it dripped from the hole in her roof.

After dropping George home last night and making sure his door was locked, she had braved the storm to collect Jazz and take her home for the night. She wasn't sure if animals were allowed at the caravan park, but if she was quiet, Mrs Potter would be none the wiser. The caravan had shuddered in the gale-force winds, keeping her awake. Or was it because she no longer had a job? Jazz hadn't helped, whining at the door at least twice, "wet dog" eau de cologne filling her caravan for the rest of the night.

Humph. Poppy's hand paused on the pup's head, and Jazz's curious hazel eyes innocently opened, shining in her direction. Had LJ actually sacked her? Her face crumpled, dejection settling in. All she'd wanted was a fresh start and to regain some of her lost confidence. But she was good at what she did. Had he been that unimpressed with her work? Had he heard what had happened back at home? Had Rick told him? Any wonder LJ was cutting ties with her. She was a liability he didn't need.

Humiliation clawed its way inside her, reminding her of what Rick had announced, boldly and unashamedly, firstly to the team, and then to the world. Black wool. In his family's clip. What she didn't understand was how that had happened. Had she missed something? Not heard a call from the shearers?

But there was no point wallowing in self-pity, even if doing so did make her feel a little better. What she needed was to work out her plan B so she could remain in Tasmania, stay well away from Rick, and learn to live with the shame and guilt that came with such a devastating mistake.

Poppy clambered over the pup, and Jazz watched on with sleepy eyes while she got dressed. 'Come on, let's go for a walk. Then I'll get us some breakfast.'

With Jazz on a lead, Poppy snuggled into her down coat and Ugg boots, and swung the door open, the wind blustering her hair as Mrs Potter came tramping past in her flower-topped flip flops, lairy purple cardigan, and hair rollers. The woman slowed, looking in her direction. Poppy tugged the lead behind her back, using her boots to block Jazz from peeking out.

'Good morning, Mrs Potter,' she said, hating the way her voice suddenly squeaked with tightness. She put on her brightest how-are-you smile, hoping the woman wouldn't see through the guilt dripping from it.

Mrs Potter's narrowed eyes scrutinised her up and down. Poppy froze. The wind continued to whip at the tattered awning, masking Jazz's soft whine.

'You think it's a good morning, do ya? You're a strange one then,' the woman scoffed. 'Couldn't get a wink of sleep 'cause of this bloody wind.' She waved an angry arm in the air. 'Knocked down trees, some of 'em landin' on me caravans. Flattened one roof completely.'

Mrs Potter took a step forward, pointing a sharpened finger at Poppy. She sucked in a gasp.

'You're darned lucky it wasn't yours!' Her face carried a downcast snarl as she turned to look at the damage.

'Is anyone hurt?' Poppy stretched forward, peering in the direction Mrs Potter was looking, recalling hearing a loud crunch during the night.

'Nope, thank goodness. That would've been a lawsuit for sure.' She gave Poppy a glaring warning. 'And don't you go getting any fancy ideas, young miss. I don't want no trouble 'round 'ere.'

Poppy's eyes widened. Did the woman see anything good in anyone? Her heart ached for Adrian. She ducked back as the woman pointed a gnarly finger her way once more, eying her suspiciously before finally heading off.

Poppy was reaching a hand behind her to give Jazz a quick pat when a bellowing holler erupted.

'Adrian!'

Poppy snatched the pup up in her arms, shut the door, and headed towards the bushland behind the park, but Jazz pulled against the lead, whining and planting her front paws stubbornly in the dirt.

'You're going to get us both in trouble,' Poppy hissed, scooping up the squirming puppy. 'I'm already in enough!' Rounding the tree line, she was heading back to her caravan when the rumble of an all-too-familiar ute had her pulse quickening, LJ's ute pulling up not far from her caravan.

Jazz squirmed in her arms as Poppy stared, transfixed despite herself. Why is he here? And why did he have to look so damn good after firing her? Her heart betrayed her mounting anger, skipping a beat as his long legs in perfectly fitted jeans stepped from the vehicle.

'Hey. What are you doing here?'

What am I doing here? Her head tilted in disbelief. What was *he* doing here? That was the more pressing question, all smiley and chirpy. He truly was unbelievable, and she worked her disgruntled frown into a fine art form while Jazz proceeded to nip at her chin.

LJ strolled towards her, all calm and casual, his smile as gorgeous as ever, infuriating her all the more. Jazz stilled in her arms, panting lightly as she watched him approach.

'Is this where you're staying?' He swung around, trying to size up which caravan she had made home.

She shook her head, wishing she could deny where she was living and ignore his frustratingly alluring appeal.

'Yeah.' She put the pup down. Jazz eyed him

quizzically before pouncing on her front paws with a come-play-with-me bark.

'What are you doing here?' She had to know, unable to resist making a show of lacing her arms over her chest. Was he here to offer her the job back? She'd be more than happy to say no thanks purely on the principle of the matter, regardless of her common sense screaming for her to take it back. Immediately.

'Wet sheep thanks to the storm. Won't be shearing for a couple of days I reckon. Mrs Potter rang, asking if I could remove a fallen tree.' His smile lifted. 'Nice looking pup. What's her name?'

Nope. No job back. And just one minute. Did he *know* her landlady? She tapped the ground with her foot. 'Jazz.' If he had to know. The pup sat as he spoke, and Poppy looked down in amazement. 'Clever girl,' she said quietly.

'I like it.'

He liked the name Jazz? The thought did funny things inside her. What else did he like? She might consider taking her job back after all—after she'd watched him squirm.

A breathtaking smile rose on his lips, and Poppy sensed warmth rising up her neck. But she refused to be swept away by his dazzling smile and his maddening patience that threatened to make her do something she might regret. Thanks to his lie, he'd proven he was like every other man she knew. Untrustworthy. Except for Jimmy, of course. So why did she have this unrelenting urge to step closer and hope he might kiss her?

'What do you think you're doin' with that mutt in my

caravan park? Pets are *not* allowed.'

Poppy winced as Mrs Potter approached from behind LJ. Before Poppy could speak, LJ stepped forward. 'It's my pup, Mrs Potter. Poppy's just taking her for a toilet stop.'

'Oh, well,' the woman chuffed, 'that's alright then, if she's yours, LJ.' Mrs Potter pressed a hand to her chest, turning an equally bright shade of pink as Poppy had, dismissing her annoyance to the wind.

What was happening? The man who'd fired her spectacularly last night . . . was now defending her? And her cantankerous landlady had a crush on him?

'Hey, Adrian, good to see you again.'

Poppy's eyes widened. *So we're old buddies now, are we?* Her fingers dug into her forearm through her jacket, hard enough to leave a bruise.

'You too, LJ.' Adrian stepped up and shook his hand, giving a polite nod and smiling like an adoring younger brother. Poppy's heart melted.

But irritation continued to needle her. Did the man know every damn person in Tasmania? Did he break promises with them, too? Her blood simmered dangerously close to boiling point.

Mrs Potter's pleasant tone turned from LJ, morphing into the snarl Poppy was more familiar with. 'And what do you think you're going to do with that . . . mutt?' Her chin jutted forward. Could it be . . . the woman was actually onto her?

Jazz gave a sharp bark from between Poppy's legs, and she worked to smother a satisfied smirk. *Clever girl. Remind me to teach you how to go for the throat.*

'I'm leaving now, so you can calm your farm.' Poppy couldn't hide her sarcasm as she scooped the pup into her arms and marched towards her car.

'Thanks for minding her for me. I'll see you at George's place.'

Poppy spun around like someone had told her she had to run from a bomb. 'Why?'

LJ's half-smile tugged at the corner of his mouth, and despite everything, her heart stuttered. Her attraction overrode her anger for one dangerous moment. He needed to stop looking at her like that. She turned away before the urge to smile back could betray her.

From behind, Mrs Potter's voice sharply morphed from the whip lashing she'd dished out to her, to irritatingly sweet, dripping honey.

'And what did you call the little pup, LJ?'

'Jazz.' LJ grinned at Poppy.

She wanted to scream; to punch something, anything. First, he lied to her. Then he proceeded to save face for her? And claim her pup in the process? The man had a massive screw loose.

Poppy drove with no real destination in mind. The wind from last night had calmed considerably, but the occasional bluster still managed to take her by surprise, rocking her car. The winding roads were slippery with stray branches strewn everywhere.

She thrummed frustrated fingers on the steering wheel, her thoughts shifting to Jimmy, and her heart ached. He was working for a large construction company in Sydney, building high-end custom homes. While it was hard for him to take time off, he had managed to secure a week in October to visit her, and she could hardly wait. She pulled off to the side of the road, skidding, tugging her phone from her bag.

'Hey, little sis. How's the sheep wrestling going?'

'I've lost my job. I've got a pup I can't afford to keep. I have a mini water tank rapidly filling on the floor of my caravan, thanks to a raging storm last night, and I don't know what to do about finding more work.' The words tumbled out in a defeated rush, a lonely tear hot on their heels.

'Oh wow, way to go, sis. Can you look for another contractor? Sounds like the one you have isn't reliable.'

'You have *no* idea.' She pressed her face into her hands, fighting back more tears. She'd have to Google contractors in the area. The shearers had been talking about one, but from what they had said, the team sounded a lot like the crew she'd fled—cocky upstarts who thought they were better than anyone else.

'Hey, you'd better be ready. Dad's gonna give you a ring tonight. Stay away from any noisy animals, okay?' The humour in his voice was unmistakable.

'Hardy ha ha.' She lifted the corner of her mouth in annoyance, wishing he could see it. 'Do you think he'd like to hear shearing plants going too?' She loved Jimmy, and his intentions were good, but sometimes he drove her crazy.

Poppy sat forward in her seat, remembering the last words her mother had said to her before she had passed in her arms. *'Always strive for your dreams, Poppy. Don't let anyone sway you otherwise.'*

Thanks, Mum.

A fresh tear trickled down her cheek. If her mother's illness had taught her anything, it was that life was short and you should love what you do. She hoped she could draw on some of the strength her Mum had, to find a way to make that happen.

'I reckon there's more to it,' Jimmy said, interrupting her thoughts. 'Last night he was talking about hospitals not offering enough help for sick patients.'

He went quiet for a moment. 'He does care, you know.'

Chapter Twenty-Two

Poppy shivered in front of the shower block mirror as she tugged her damp hair into a poor excuse for a ponytail. She paused, studying her reflection as a thought surfaced—one she'd barely had time to consider. What had happened to LJ's forehead? The scar was scabbed and still a little angry—only recently closed over—as if he had suffered a nasty blow. Did it have anything to do with the remorseful expression he wore when he thought no one was watching?

But no, she chided herself, his image teasing her heart like a carrot on a stick. She needed to distance herself from him if she was going to stay. Perhaps the other contractor hadn't heard what she'd done. She could only hope.

A smiling face met her at her caravan door.

'Hey, Adrian. I'd kill for a morning coffee. Feel like a

hot chocolate?'

'You're funny, Poppy.'

She smiled at his wide grin. 'Come on, then.' She beckoned him inside.

The sun offered warmth against the wintry atmosphere as it streamed through the open door. She poured the drinks and gave Adrian two deck chairs to set up under her awning.

Wrapping cool fingers around the steaming mug, she took a long sip, closing her eyes in bliss. Tasmania was teaching her many things, and slowing down was one of them, even if she hadn't felt like she had a choice. She liked the feeling.

'I brought something for you.' Adrian's smile was infectious, his eyes dancing as he waited for her response. He set his mug down and stood, glancing both ways cautiously before stepping behind her caravan and returning with an animal crate.

Poppy eyed it with puzzled amusement.

Adrian lowered the crate, his face turning serious. 'It's for Jazz,' he whispered, as though it was a secret of the utmost priority. 'Then Mum can't tell you off.' His big eyes searched hers with delighted excitement.

'Oh, Adrian, I love your thinking!' She offered her hand up for a high-five, and he slapped it enthusiastically.

'But how did you know she was mine?' Her voice remained guarded as she glanced around like the trees had ears.

He giggled, covering his mouth. 'I saw you sneak her from your car. I saw her tail under your coat.' His chuckling grew, his shoulders shaking. 'It was waggling fast.'

Poppy leaned back, struck by the wonderful friendship she'd found in Adrian. For someone with his challenges, he didn't miss much. If only his mother would take the time to see it.

'It's a great idea.' She paused, considering her new friend while taking a thoughtful breath. 'Would you like to come out to the farm with me today? You could see Jazz and her brother. George would love to meet you.'

'I would. I would.' His eager grin danced across his cheeks as he bounced in his seat.

'Great. Finish your cuppa, and we can head off. Better let your mum know too. Then we can go.'

Adrian took a rushed final gulp, hurrying to his feet and calling for his mother as he jogged away. He turned back to her, urgency in his voice. 'I'm going now, Poppy. Wait for me.'

His infectious enthusiasm made her want to leap for joy. Almost.

She might manage it if she got some kind of work for the coming week.

And, if LJ's gorgeous smile would stop haunting her thoughts.

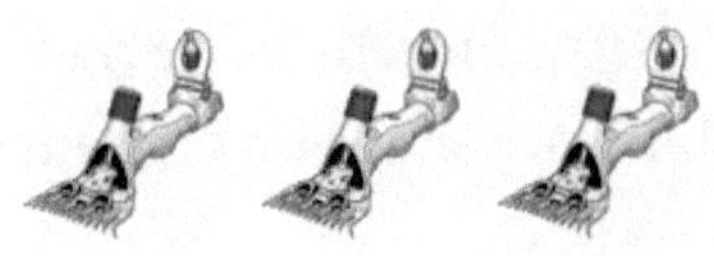

'No, Tom. I understand. Just, please consider us next time. I guarantee we'll do a great job for you. My team is reliable and—'

LJ pulled his mobile away from his ear to check if he had lost reception mid-conversation.

Disconnected. He'd been hung up on.

Again.

His lips pressed tight. Tom and Bob Brown were farming brothers who needed a shearing team this week. Jase had heard from the local produce store owner only yesterday. Sure, they'd been having squally weather, but since the storm, nothing that warranted stalling shearing. Was this the latest excuse growers were using to cancel on him? He paced the concrete path beside Grandma Aimee's shed.

This isn't right. They've known me since I was a kid. How hard can it be to trust me?

But a dark voice spoke louder, and he gave a defeated nod.

Because you bought a failing business from a dishonest man, and they'll never believe otherwise. He stopped at the shed door frame, leaning against it as he blew out a frustrated breath.

LJ turned his gaze towards the house, his attention on Grandma Aimee as she absently stared out the kitchen window, her face tranquil. They were waiting on the test results to confirm the doctor's suspicion that she had suffered a TIA—a mini-stroke. It explained her loss of balance and intermittent short-term memory issues.

Pushing off the door frame, he moved to the workbench where he was constructing a wooden planter box, the first of two—a gift for her birthday in a couple of weeks. He was going to plant a pink daisy bush in each, to sit on either side of the front door, standing out against the grey painted weatherboards.

Early in the afternoon, his mobile stopped him mid-swing. He ran his hand over the smooth wood as he put the phone to his ear without checking the caller ID.

'LJ. It's Stephen Matthews. How are you?' The man's deep voice reverberated down the line.

'G'day, Stevo. Can't complain.'

That was the polite thing to say, right?

He stared at his feet, surprised the owner of Oxley Falls Station might be calling. 'Wish I had a bit more work for the team, but I'm keeping busy.' Upbeat and onwards, that's the ticket. He picked up the new tin of pearl white paint, spinning it in his hand. With one final sanding, he would have the planter boxes ready for a lick of colour.

LJ heard a pen tapping in the background, suggesting Stevo was thinking before he spoke. 'Well,' Stephen paused, 'I was thinking I might be able to help change that.'

Heavy thumps pounded inside LJ's chest, and his hand stilled on the wood. The Matthews were also shearing this week. His rival contractor, Ryan Sweeny, had their job tightly secured. LJ hadn't bothered calling him, certain his chances were zero.

'Are you available this coming week? I have three thousand wethers needing shearing. Sale prices are good, and you can consider this a trial run if you like. If I'm happy with the job your team does, I'll give you the spring shearing too.'

Had he heard right? LJ stood taller, his mind racing with the logistics of having a team ready to start tomorrow for a six-stand shed. Stevo had rung at the right time. It was no surprise to him that the other job he had been waiting on had fallen through. Sweeny had an uncanny knack for stealing work from under his nose.

What about Poppy? Could he ask her back after letting her go not twenty-four hours earlier? Would she consider it? He didn't like his chances after her reaction at Mrs Potter's.

And Rick. He needed another shearer if he was to take this job. He wasn't sure he could handle watching Rick kiss her again. She might decide to take him back after all, his brow furrowing at the thought.

He stared out the shed window, surprised by how much the idea of seeing her again excited him. Why was his love life never straightforward?

Regardless, the simple truth was—he needed her.

'Listen, I've known you a long time. What do you say?' Stephen said, interjecting LJ's racing thoughts. If he didn't take this opportunity, he might never get another.

'Sure, Stevo. Give me a couple of hours to round everyone up and I'll ring you back to confirm.'

'Excellent. Just what I wanted to hear. I knew I could count on you.'

LJ quickly interrupted Stephen as he was about to hang up. 'Oh, and Stevo, thanks. We won't let you down.'

The call ended with LJ's heart racing and brain whirring as he stared unseeing at the shed floor. He had work for the team, but it would be a rush to make it happen. He set up a group text and wrote a concise message, asking them to reply within the hour.

Then came the final task—calling his classer. He needed this job. They all did, especially with the chance to secure permanent work. The Matthews family were big players in the sheep farming industry, running a large superfine stud with a sound reputation. This job could be the start of a turnaround for his team. He could feel it.

He pressed call and waited. Did she want her job back? The answer was a definite maybe.

Chapter Twenty-Three

LJ's fingers flexed in anticipation. The team were ready to go, and some had already left for the property under an hour's drive away. He had also managed to get hold of a local shearer he knew of but hadn't used before to make up the six-stand shed. With Rick in the mix, he had the shearers he needed. What he hated was the feeling he'd let Poppy down by having to include him in the team.

The sound of a small car engine slowed out the front of Grandma Aimee's house and LJ squinted as headlights reflected on the windowpane in the evening darkness. He covered his eyes with his hand to ease the glare from the glass and grinned. Poppy had come.

He let the curtain fall back into place, kissed his grandmother goodbye on the cheek, and exited through the front door. She had remained alert and focused all day, and his mother was dropping by in the morning to check on her. If necessary, she could stay the three days he was going to be working.

The tally of sheep they had to shear couldn't have been better. It was a short amount of time to be away, and it would give Poppy a chance to see if a camp-out was something she wanted to do with the team.

LJ's diesel engine roared to life and he backed down the driveway, cranking up the heater before giving Poppy a brief wave and pulling onto the road. Excitement, anticipation, and a good dose of hope stirred inside his chest as he headed off, unable to fully express the relief he felt over it.

He had been so close to strolling over to her car before they'd left—knowing she would put down her window—for nothing other than to lean in a little closer and smell her perfume, or tell her he was grateful she was coming to the shed with him. And damned lucky. She wasn't exactly welcoming him with open arms right now.

Darkness shrouded his ute, leaving him too much time to think about the woman travelling behind. Jacinta had consistently haunted his every move since their breakup. Would he ever be free? His fingers were crossed that she wouldn't find him this time. But even if she didn't, he didn't stand a chance with Poppy. Forget Rick being there. Could he wholeheartedly trust himself not to break her heart and risk ruining her life?

In the beam of his lightbar, the glint of red and white reflectors on the post with an old milk can for a letterbox came into view. He flashed his hazard lights to let Poppy know they were close.

LJ drove on autopilot along the two-kilometre-long driveway, slowing as the car reverberated over the cattle grate before he slowed in front of the huts, where he was greeted by Little Trev waving frantically.

'Thank goodness you're 'ere, boss! There ain't no hot water. I can't start work tommorra' if I haven't had me shower! It ain't right for a man to start work dirty 'n all.'

'Hang on, Little Trev.' LJ swivelled around and reached to the back seat of his dual cab, snatching a torch.

Poppy hopped out of her car and strolled over, smiling and speaking before he could continue. 'It could be the gas not turned on at the bottle.' Her eyes danced with a dash of determination and a hint of unforgiveness if he read her right, which he totally deserved. Reinstating her after firing her, well, he was damned lucky she had said yes. He caught B1 eyeing him with a suggestive glint in her eye from the steps of the large dormitory used for their accommodation.

Ignoring her, he smiled at Poppy, impressed by her suggestion. The more he got to know about her, the more he liked. She had shown herself to be practical, engaging, and a leader through and through. He tugged himself away from her enticing eyes that had a habit of penetrating his senses. Whenever they were on him, he was sure she was peering inside his soul, digging deeper than he wanted her to see.

'Uh, did anyone check that?' he said, more to himself than anything as he stepped from the ute, avoiding Poppy's gaze so he had some chance of concentrating on the matter at hand.

'Nah, boss. I was the only one wantin' me shower.' Little Trev's face frowned with anxious turmoil, and LJ took pity on him, putting a firm hand on his shoulder.

'She'll be right, Little Trev. I'll go turn it on now. Then you'll have hot water in an hour or so.' He glanced at Poppy with a thank-you nod. Her raised eyebrows told him not to push it.

'But me bedtime . . . it'll be too late.' Little Trev was almost jigging on the spot now.

LJ faced him, a patient smile on his lips. 'What if we ask Cookie to boil the kettle? Would you be okay to have a quick wash instead?'

'I,' he searched the grass at his feet, 'I guess it'll 'av' to be.'

'Good then. Let's go see Cookie.'

Poppy found it hard not to smile; from the way Little Trev had danced foot to foot, or from the look of guilt LJ wore, she wasn't sure. But seeing his admission pleased her more than she wanted to admit.

Rick leaned against his ute, watching on as she talked with Little Trev and LJ. The way he crossed his arms smacked more of arrogance than patience, and despite her attempts to ignore him and move away as fast as possible, he intercepted, his attempt at a charming smile doing little to convince her she was wrong about her decision to forget him altogether.

'It's good to see you here, Poppy.'

'What do you want, Rick?' She raised a single eyebrow, willing him to say whatever he needed to, and then go.

He took a step closer, offering genuine surprise when she took a step back. 'You, Poppy.'

'You only want *what* suits you, *when* it suits you, Rick. I'm not interested.' She made to move away.

'You can't tell me you didn't want that kiss,' he called out.

She stopped, looking over her shoulder. She would put an end to this now, for good. 'On the contrary, Rick, yes, I can. And don't ever pull a stunt like that on me again.'

Was he serious? He had no right to second chances or stealing kisses she didn't want to give, and after this shed, she wasn't sticking around to let him think so.

Turning away, she ignored his disingenuous pleas to listen, focusing on the entrance of what looked like a large school camp dormitory. A single globe lit up two concrete steps that led into a long corridor. As she approached, B1 and B2 blew puffs of cigarette smoke, and Poppy fought the urge to swipe her hands through the air as they eyed her up and down in disapproval.

Inside, the smell of dust filled the air down the long hallway, several rooms feeding off it, with floorboards harbouring beer and coffee spills gathered from more than fifty years of after-work drink-ups and cut-outs.

Nearing the end of the long hallway, she turned right at

the T-junction and peered inside the large room filled with people. Floating dust particles danced about in the room.

The atmosphere was contagious, and Poppy caught the all too familiar fever for the start of a new shed rushing inside her. Almost everyone was crammed in there, including Rick. Her heart immediately sank. He had some nerve, expecting her to fall at his feet at the idea of taking him back. Turns out he didn't know her at all, despite them being together for two years. She wasn't about to let him ruin this job for her. She had work, and it was with superfine wool.

But a deep, unsettling feeling clawed at her. Would she make the same mistake again? She was in a shed with Rick, like the last time it happened. If he even smelled her fear, her anxiety that was resurfacing like nobody's business, he'd latch onto it like a bloodhound, tearing her reputation to shreds again. And if that happened, most certainly she would have to consider giving up wool classing for good. There were only so many chances you got before you had to accept your failings, cut your losses, and move on to other pastures . . . like working in a hospital.

Her stomach stabbed her with nausea. Just this job. She could do it. Then she would try the other contractor, she reminded herself. Rick would look a right fool if he followed her a second time in the same town. And he didn't like looking like the fool.

Bianca caught her eye and offered a smile, inviting her to come in. 'Have you found your room yet?' she said over the racket of the TV and enthusiastic chatter.

'No, not yet.'

'You're not in with us. You have a separate room in the small hut. You would have driven past it on your way in.'

Bianca leapt up and her foot clipped Paul's leg as she walked past.

'Hey, watch it, bit—'

Bianca whirled around, stepping towards him with a look that could scare the savviest slimebag. One look from her and he shut up, quickly turning his attention to the TV as he shrugged his shoulders, attempting the "it's cool" act.

'Come on, I'll show you.' Bianca's business-like smile put Poppy at ease.

It took three hip and shoulders from Bianca before the classer's hut door scraped against the concrete floor and opened. Straight ahead was a porcelain vanity basin attached to the wall, a tiny mirror hanging above it. Poppy walked in, fingering the dust on the sink before peering around the corner to the left. There stood a cast-iron bath with a large rosette shower head, the kind that beckoned her to take a long, hot soak.

Bianca turned to her right and, with another shove, she nudged the next door open against the aged floorboards, dust swirling around the corded light hanging from the centre of the small room.

There was a fireplace with wood stacked against the wall, and a two-person couch. Her bedroom adorned an aged antique dresser pitted with borer holes, and a single bed artfully dotted with old mouse droppings.

'So, make yourself at home. Do you need any help?' Bianca's expression offered little care or concern, but Poppy knew she was loyal to a fault.

'Thanks, but I'll be right.' It was ten-thirty p.m., and she needed to do the basics like make her bed and set up her clothes for the morning. As Bianca left, she gave a drawn-out yawn, shutting the door to her hut.

With her mattress dusted down and sprayed with a good once-over of Pine-o-clean, and her bed made, she was ready to hit the sack.

But sleep evaded her.

2.30 a.m.

2.45 a.m.

3.05 a.m.

3.55 a.m.

Poppy's arms thumped the mattress beside her body, and she let out an exasperated groan. The old bed gave a grinding squeak every time she turned, and an unknown thud under the floorboards at irregular intervals had her wondering who her guests were. The full moon shone through her window, casting shadows over her room as her mind churned. Was this grower going to make her life as tiresome as Ralph Jenkins? Was she good enough to do the job?

And then there was Rick. He'd looked at her with expectant hope in his eyes, but she knew that was just an act. What he liked was the thrill of the chase, until something new and shiny came along. She wasn't about to be fooled a second time. Would she ever be free of him? She turned on her side with a huff.

Dull morning light finally filtered through the window, and Poppy forced one exhausted eye open, squeezing it shut again in defiance. But with a sudden jolt once she'd registered the time on her phone, she sat up and rushed to get dressed.

Tugging the doors of her hut open, she was slapped by the sharp, frigid air, and she ducked back inside for her woolly lumber jacket. It was one of Jimmy's. She snuggled into it, the soft scents of his deodorant and aftershave calming her apprehension and tiredness.

In the dawn light, the buildings were set apart like a game of Monopoly with everything laid out for a small community to thrive. It reminded Poppy of what a small gold rush town might have started out like. The shed out the back stored a supply of firewood, and a steady *thud, thud* suggested someone was already using the splitter to cut more for the evening fire. Along the fence line was a meat house where two fresh carcasses were hung, and she found herself thinking about tea with anticipation. Cookie had fresh lamb on the menu.

Voices came from a building parallel to the main sleeping quarters, and the tantalising aroma of bacon made her mouth water. A covered open-ended walkway led to the kitchen entrance. At the opposite end, layers of picturesque fog hung suspended over grassy undulations, large native gums dotting the landscape, reminding her of a fairy-tale wonderland.

Swinging the door open, a steamy warmth hit her as she stepped inside the kitchen.

'Morning, Cookie.' Poppy strode over to the pass, helping herself to a plate.

'Good morning, Poppy.' She was a short woman with a delightful double chin and an ever-present tea towel that hung over her shoulder. She twisted her head towards Poppy, her hands continuing to scrub the plates in the hot water. 'How did you sleep?'

'Not good. I hope you've got something full of sugar planned for afternoon smoko. I'm gonna need it.' She gave Cookie a pleading gaze.

'How about orange poppy seed cake? I know how much you love it.' Cookie raised her eyebrows encouragingly before turning her attention back to the sink.

With her toasty eggs and bacon sitting snug in her belly, Poppy was sipping on her steaming cup of tea when LJ strolled in, not noticing her. She stilled as he strode towards Cookie at the stove, grinning as he leaned over the woman's shoulder to pinch a piece of bacon from her frypan. Tilting his head, he gave the cook a teasing smile before popping the bacon into his mouth, and Poppy's heart fluttered. The man was the right slice of perfect, even if she did—on an all too regular basis—want to wring his neck, and her heart rate quickened as she was momentarily drawn in by his playfulness.

'Oh, get on with ya,' Cookie laughed, flipping the tea towel from her shoulder and giving him a good-natured flick on the leg as he jumped out of reach. Just watching the interaction made her want to step nearer and share the moment. But deep down, she knew it was a moment she couldn't have.

With her shoulders set, Poppy stood, took her plate and rounded the corner, strolling towards the sink. 'Good morning, *boss,*' she said with a touch of sarcasm, eying him from over her shoulder and holding his gaze. Then and there, it suited her to rub the title in. Was this going to be her last job if he decided to sack her again? He was damned lucky she had said yes. Mind you, she hadn't wanted to—out of principle, pure and simple— but she also didn't have much choice.

'G'day, *classer*. How are you today? Sleep well?'

His smile warmed her from the inside, and once again, she chanced a glance at his lips, knowing just how perfect they would feel on hers. Her cheeks warmed at Cookie's discerning eyes as she slid her plate and cutlery into the soapy suds.

'Fine and dandy, thank you very much.' Her sleep? She didn't need him worrying over whether she could do her job so omitted answering that, sensing a telltale grin forming on Cookie's lips, but she refused to look her way. So instead, she lifted her chin and spun around to face LJ. 'I was wondering if you could tell me a bit about the shed. Did the grower leave a speci for me to look at?' Could he hear her heart thundering as loud as it was in her ears, his body moving closer as he stepped forward?

'Sure. I'll go clean up and meet you at your hut in five.' He stepped towards the door, leaving her wanting for more . . . of his time, his smile, his gaze? He called back to Cookie, his eyes dancing with cheekiness. 'Thanks for the bacon.' His gaze slipped to Poppy, his mouth lifting in that delightfully annoying half-smile that made her insides shimmer every time, before he shut the door behind him.

Cookie's ample bust bobbed up and down as she chuckled, her head swivelling from side to side. 'He's a bit adorable, that boy.' Her eyes settled on Poppy once more, and she got the distinct feeling the lovable woman was up to something.

Chapter Twenty-four

Poppy paused at the doorway as she listened to the hum of the shed. Hundreds of feet shuffled in the pens with nervous energy as the team readied paddles and bats in position for the day ahead.

She swallowed, stealing her resolve as she saw Rick fiddling with his handpiece, deep in thought, and her eyes narrowed. She would get this job done and be out of here. She had a life to live, not a history to dwell on.

LJ left his stand and introduced her to the property owner, Stephen Matthews. 'We work hard to produce a reliable product that buyers will be eager to purchase. And prices are on the rise right now, so I'm keen to see how the job comes up.'

No pressure, she thought, her insides erring on the side

of icky and mushy rather than calm and unfazed like she needed them to be.

In other words, he'd be watching how she did. Stephen's manner was politely self-assured, and she knew how much was riding on this, both for her and for LJ. But questions buzzed in her mind. If she did a good job, would LJ offer her permanent work? Did she want that? Last night, she hadn't thought so.

And a bigger question than any of those was, could she continue with the team if Rick stayed? Resentment stirred in her. He had no right following her every move. It was downright intrusive, and creepy, and she wasn't fooled. He may have needed work, but she knew his main objective, to win her back or take her down like a sinking ship.

By afternoon smoko, Stephen had reduced his visits to the classing table, leaving Poppy unsure if that was a good sign, or . . . No. She refused to go down the negative path. She trusted that she knew her job, despite Rick's ongoing presence fighting to wear her down, break the little confidence she'd salvaged back, and downright frazzle her. Placing the fleece in the appropriate bin, she stepped back to check her lines, happy with how they were looking.

Weariness from concentrating, lack of sleep, or working overtime to avoid Rick, had Poppy pressing weary fingers to her eyes before she took a slice of the orange poppy seed cake Cookie had promised. She was licking the icing from her fingers and contemplating a second slice when B1's voice rang out.

'So, what's the story with Sam? He get sick of ya

company or somethink?' Her voice carried in the tearoom, and everyone stopped, their faces suddenly stricken.

'What the . . .' Bear said, as LJ stood swiftly, eyes wide with disbelief, raising a calming palm towards Bear. Jase sprang up beside LJ, and the two men formed an instant wall, protective and impenetrable.

'I don't know what you've heard, but you'll hear it from me only once,' LJ said, leaning forward towards the woman. 'Sam is no longer with us and we're all the worse off for it.'

Poppy choked on a cake crumb, smothering her cough as she tipped forward in her seat, the delicious orange flavour now lost. Who *was* Sam? No one had mentioned the name before. She glanced around the tearoom, all eyes alert, concerned, and instantly defensive. She watched LJ, his expression clouded with what looked like guttural grief, the mention of Sam's name elevating a heightened level of caution and unified silence.

'You're nothing but a pack of soft pansies. Grow some balls,' Rick said, his heartless chuckle impressing only himself and the two women.

'Touchy, aren't we?' B1 smirked, clearly enjoying the reaction she'd provoked. 'Must've been some story.'

'The only story here is you keeping your smart mouth shut,' Jase said, stepping into her space. 'We don't need your shit-stirring in the shed.'

'You're here to work, nothing else.' LJ's words were level, final.

'Right then, let's get back to it.' Whippet clapped his hands sharply, breaking the tension as his lanky legs strode back to his stand.

Bianca saw the confusion on Poppy's face. 'Hey, come with me.' She beckoned Poppy to follow, and a sense of dread enveloped her. Whatever she was about to learn, Poppy had the uncanny sense she'd need to brace herself for it.

Chapter Twenty-five

Sam was LJ's best mate, and he had just died? Poppy reeled at the news Bianca had told her. She might not have known Sam, but it made so much more sense why the team had reacted so strongly. And rightly so. Rick had always had trouble keeping his mouth shut, especially when his opinions weren't wanted. What had she ever seen in him, and why was it only now that she was seeing what an honest-to-goodness douche-bag he was? And dealing with a loss of someone so young . . . that had to be like dealing with a death in the family for LJ—for the team.

The rest of the week carried on in a disquieting symmetry that had Poppy snatching regular glances at LJ with heartfelt sadness and concern. She'd tried the occasional smile at first, but he'd become insular in his focus, disconnecting from the team, and from her, which affected her more than she was expecting. Clearly, what B1 had announced in front of the whole shed had cut deeply. And she understood it. Rick had made it all too clear her classing skills were less than adequate for what he required for his family-run farm, and it also happened to coincide with his deepening interest in a shedhand called Tiffany who had been elevated from "averagely skilled" status—which the whole shed witnessed—to the shedhand who was able to call the shots when it came to orders and changeover positions.

Three days in, and the shed wound up with little pomp or ceremony—no drinking fest like that of her previous team. Rick left the moment he'd sent his last sheep down the chute—with his bad mood—a stubbie in his hand, not a moment too soon for her. He hadn't even chased her down to say good-bye—a little confusing to say the least—but what she did know was that she could suddenly breathe easier with him gone. The only thing left to do was her detailed speci. After that, it was a nervous waiting game until her test results came back.

A week later, Poppy was sunning herself like a lizard on her deck chair. Little Jazz lay on a rug next to her, breathing out a relaxed sigh. With the laptop resting on her knees, Poppy scanned the collection of emails she'd chosen to ignore over effective time-wasting and puppy play she liked to call bonding.

Casually scrolling through the emails with her usual disinterest, her fingers slowed, her eyes wide with apprehension and deep-seated curiosity. She clicked on the message from the local stock and wool agent. Oxley Falls test results were in, and if they were good, her job with this grower would be secure, her reputation improved within Tasmania, and the big job in September just might be confirmed.

Her heart raced, and her fingers shook as she pressed on the link. While that all mattered, it wasn't as important as her finding out if the wool she'd classed was, in fact, free from anything that shouldn't belong in it.

Chapter Twenty-Six

LJ swung by his parents' place to grab the pies his mother had asked him to pick up, and while he was looking forward to one, there were more pressing matters on his mind.

Hopping from his ute, he strode towards the shearing shed, his emotions in a scramble as he walked into the shed. Stan was at the wool table, methodically washing his combs and cutters with hot soapy water, laying them out on an old towel to dry.

'G'day, Dad.' LJ glided past him, feeling the undeniable tug of home. People said all shearing sheds were the same: same basic look, similar layout, same smells. But for him, being in his family shed was so much more than that. It was his core, like his soul was somehow attached to it. He slowed as he neared the shearing stands, running his hand down the pull cord rope, stopping at the knot at the end. This shed held so many important memories for him, from the first time he shore forty-two sheep, to the time he and Sam brought in a mob of wethers and shore them the day before shearing started, just to get themselves warmed up and job ready. A low smile surfaced on his face as he ran attentive eyes over the catching pens, the realisation that he may never shear in his family's shed again, haunting and real. The memory of Miles's voice pounded in his ears like a jackhammer following their most recent phone call. 'Now that I'm running the place, your services are no longer required.' LJ's face pinched at the surprising aggression the words had stabbed him with.

It had been painful for LJ to step away. Not that he minded shifting into their grandmother's cottage. But letting Miles step up and take on the farm hadn't sat well with him, but assuming it was what Stan had wanted, he'd decided pursuing the contracting run was what was meant to be. What Stan didn't realise was that LJ wanted to run the contracting run from home, working the farm as a family enterprise when shearing was quiet.

A dangle of thick cobwebs floated in the subtle draft of the shed, and LJ crossed his arms as he leaned his shoulder against a post of the sheep pen, letting himself be hypnotised by it.

Heavy feet thumped up the steps to the shed, shaking LJ back to reality.

'Dad, have you seen—' Miles stopped, and LJ swivelled around, straightening to full height, and the two brothers eyed one another suspiciously.

The shed fell quiet.

'Stan?' Mum hollered from the house. 'Can you come help me? I'm trying to move the kitchen dresser and it won't budge.' The back door thudded shut behind her. Stan nodded in acknowledgment, and LJ couldn't read in his expression if he was happy to remove himself from the immediate tension in the shed, or if he had no clue what was really going on.

LJ's eyes followed his father out the door before they slid to his brother, the pause strained and uncomfortable.

'Why weren't you at Sam's funeral, Miles?' It was a question that had been burning in LJ's mind.

Miles's right eyelid gave the slightest flinch. 'I had a previous appointment in Launceston that I couldn't break.'

LJ waited for an apology.

There was none.

'He was a brother to you, too. So, when you die, it'll be okay if I have something more pressing to do instead of turning up to your funeral?' His voice was even, calm, everything he wasn't feeling. Was his brother for real?

'Sam was *your* brother! More than I ever was,' Miles snapped back, his finger poking the air towards LJ. 'Neither of you wanted me around. I got left in this godforsaken place while both of you gallivanted around the bloody countryside like carefree cowboys.' He swung his arm in the air. 'You didn't care about the farm. Face it, Lincoln, you left me with the shit job and let me do it by myself.'

What? That was the last thing the farm was. He'd wanted it all his life, until Miles had made it clear he didn't want him around.

'Did you want to come shearing with us? You could have—'

But that wasn't what he really wanted to know right now. LJ took a step closer, keeping his voice level despite the quiver he could feel rising in his throat.

'What was so important, Miles? If it had been you who had died, Sam would've been there in a heartbeat.'

'Bullshit. You two only cared about what you both wanted. And it's none of your bloody business where I was.' Miles spun around and stormed out of the shed, leaving LJ more confused than he already was.

He walked back to his ute, his mind whirring. His brother was pushing him off the farm for reasons he had no clue about, and he was hiding something. So why did he get the feeling that finding out what it was might be worse than not knowing?

Chapter Twenty-Seven

Since living with Grandma Aimee, not a day went by that LJ didn't wonder why Miles had such a hatred for him. He squeezed the steering wheel a little tighter, hoping some reasoning might miraculously come to mind. If he knew, he might be able to do something about it.

LJ's ropeable mood began to settle as Pa Pat's weathered cottage came into view. The old man had always been his anchor, and right now, LJ needed every skerrick of grounding he could get. His grandfather was tinkering in the machinery shed, cursing as his screwdriver slipped from his hand and clattered onto his boot.

'Cor, that blasted screw. It's too bloody small for these old eyes.' Pa Pat glanced up. 'And about bloody time you visited your Pa. Come here. I need those young eyes of yours to put this darned screw back in me glasses. If I can find the confounded thing.'

Frustrated puffs and grumbles followed, and LJ grinned, walking towards the workbench. 'And how many times has that screwdriver dropped to the ground this time?'

'Only three, but that's none of your concern.' Pa Pat's glare held familiar warmth as he bent down to search the floor. 'Confounded screw dropped off in me cereal this mornin'. Had to fish it out with a bloody sieve!'

'You mean you didn't swallow it this time?'

'Now don't you get smart with me, young fella.' Pa Pat's gnarled finger waggled in LJ's face. 'That was an accident, and you know it.' He continued to poke the air at his grandson, but the mischievous glint in his eye was unmistakable.

LJ took the screwdriver from his grandfather, tightening the arm. He held the glasses to his face, wobbling them up and down like Groucho Marx.

'Oh, get on with ya.' Pa Pat snatched them from LJ's fingers, placing them on his face and giving LJ one last measured glare, for good measure.

'Hey, Pa, do you recall a shearer by the name of Isaac?'

'I most certainly do.' The change in his grandfather's expression caught LJ off guard.

'Thievin' bastard of a man.' Pa Pat took a step towards him. 'He accused me of double-clickin' me counter. Swore black and blue to the grower I'd been stealing numbers for me own gain. Haven't seen hide nor hair of him since, and I never want to!'

LJ's stomach knotted. On the fly during one of the smokos, Poppy had casually mentioned a shearer named Tanner that her grandfather had shorn with in Tasmania. It had been awkward at the time to tell her the man was his own grandfather. She hadn't elaborated, dismissing the subject thankfully. It was the last thing he needed to add to his list of many things she was angry at him about.

They headed inside the quaint cottage, situated on the outskirts of Launceston, for a drink. LJ poured their coffee and opened the cake tin from his mother, releasing the warming scent of cocoa and mint. Pa Pat's eyes lit up as he swooped on the largest slice of chocolate cake with peppermint crisp on top.

'Damn good cook that mother of yours.' Cake crumbs tumbled from his mouth as he spoke. 'So, how's the team goin'?'

LJ watched cake crumbs fall, resisting the urge to brush his own chin. 'Going okay. Got a couple of . . . questionable workers.' How much did he tell his grandfather, who had helped fund a business that was about to go under? LJ would never be able to repay him his share if it did. Guilt dug deep. The last thing he wanted to do was let Pa Pat down. He ran a hand through his hair haphazardly.

'Ah, it's always gonna happen in this industry, son. Fire the troublemakers and you've got nobody left to hire.' Pa Pat chuckled knowingly before sipping his coffee.

Truth was, LJ wanted better for his contracting name. Without reliable workers, he'd lose both his decent employees and his scarce clients.

Whatever Poppy had done, she had the magic touch and LJ couldn't have been more relieved or grateful. Since the test results had come back from Oxley Falls, LJ was receiving more calls enquiring about his team's availability, making him exceedingly thankful to Stevo for spreading the word. Could he hope that growers were beginning to think about taking a chance on him? He had to hope so.

A steady smile lifted his mouth as he pulled up at The Lone Pony caravan park. All he had to do now was ask his classer back.

Permanently.

He knocked on her caravan door, his heart racing. What if she refused? He might lose her from his team, but worse than that, he might lose any chance with her personally.

The door swung open, making the breath trapped in his lungs hitch. Standing there, sexy as all heck in faded trackies, a worn windcheater and decidedly raised eyebrows that studied him with measured curiosity, was his classer—or at least he had to hope beyond all hope she would be, if she would do the one little thing he needed her to, no biggie, just . . . forgive him.

Where was he meant to start? And why was this suddenly so hard? He'd planned to ask straight out, but her expression—like she was ready to feed him to the lions—made him hesitate.

'What was that?' she asked with mock innocence. 'You

. . . want me back?' She moved down to the bottom step of her caravan, crossing her arms, her smug eyebrows arching impossibly high. And right there and then, he wanted to step in, take her in his arms and kiss that smugness away, but if he did, she'd likely tell him to take his job and throw it in the sheep dip.

Instead, cheeks burning beneath his whiskers, he nodded sheepishly. 'Yeah. I do.' He stared at the ground before giving in to the desperate need to drink her in. The mistrust in her eyes made him ache, but as her expression softened, his insides turned to liquid.

He risked a step closer.

'I want you to know . . . I've missed you.' And he meant it. Totally. Completely. Before any second thoughts could anchor his racing heart, he stepped in, cupping her face and watching her searching eyes before he drew closer to her lips, nearer, nearer, watching them lift with the faintest of smiles. He found her mouth, kissing her tenderly, their lips moving against one another in perfect rhythm.

And it wasn't just him kissing her.

She was kissing him back.

Poppy stretched her arms above her head at the end of another exhausting but satisfying run, making her way to the tea room for smoko. Word was spreading in all the good ways about their contracting run, and she had her job back. She might have made him work for it, his hesitant, and dare she think it, shy smile more alluring than she wanted to admit when he'd rocked up to the shed this morning. Her mind buzzed with giddy excitement, and now, watching him leave the shed to take a phone call filled her with a sudden, unexpected loss.

Unable to help herself, she slipped towards the door, where LJ's voice carried in what sounded like a serious phone conversation. She peered around the door, admiring his shoulder muscles flexing against his singlet, the winter sun giving his skin a sun-kissed glow. When he caught her eye and smiled, ending his call to stride towards her with what she felt certain was downright enthusiasm, his gaze held an intensity that made her heart skip. His eyes lingered on her lips with a smile as he approached, standing close enough that nervous energy danced in her stomach.

Chest fluttering, she watched a small smile crease the corners of his mouth until Rick strolled past, shattering the moment, his satisfied smirk saying it all. Frustration clenched her fists. Why did he ruin every good thing she had going? She tried to refocus on LJ, searching for why she wanted to talk to him. She'd make up something if she had to.

'Can I ask you something?' She side-eyed Rick, who remained watching on, wishing she could yell at him to disappear—for good.

'Sure.' He sounded pleased she'd stopped him, and suddenly her confidence wanted to slip away.

'Um.' She squirmed, hoping he could hear the sensitivity she intended. 'What happened to . . . Sam?' At the mention of his name, Rick turned and left, the relief so deep, she wanted to cheer.

But her eyes widened as LJ's face instantly crumpled, his gaze dropping to the floor as his endearing smile vanished. She reached for his arm but he stepped back, with a gentle shake of his head, and the rejection hit her like a physical blow. After the longing she'd seen in his eyes a minute ago, this wasn't what she'd expected. Had she crossed some invisible line she hadn't known existed?

'It's not something you need to worry about.' He stubbed his shearing moccasin on the ridge in the floorboard, gave her a pained grimace, then walked away.

Poppy felt stripped bare, like a puppy abandoned in a cardboard box, watching its owner disappear.

What had just happened? Bianca came over, offering an apologetic smile.

'Sam died at a camp-out,' she whispered, then fell silent for a moment. 'His death is being investigated.'

'What do you mean?' Poppy stared at Bianca, realising she might have just destroyed any chance she had with LJ. She'd clearly stuck her nose in where it wasn't welcome, leaving her feeling foolish and isolated.

Poppy followed Bianca back into the tearoom in silence, mechanically grabbing a sausage roll before finding a quiet seat in the corner. She stared at the food in her hand, her appetite gone as LJ addressed the team.

'We've got some bad news and some good news.' He leaned over the table to grab a couple of triangle toasties and a piece of apple slice before finding an empty seat.

He glanced around the room, and Poppy was acutely aware he was avoiding eye contact with her. She bit her lip.

'We've lucked out on the job at Powranna Station, but Stevo from Oxley Falls officially booked us for his main shearing.'

'Oh, yeah!' Bear gave Jase a high-five, and even the "bananas" smiles appeared genuine. The women had almost given up on making Poppy's life miserable, moving onto their new focus, Jase, who B1 had taken a liking to.

Relief flooded through her as LJ finally looked her way, giving her a you've-got-the-job nod. If she couldn't hope for more, at least she had that, and she managed a smile back.

LJ's phone rang again, and the tearoom fell silent once more, all eyes fixed on him.

'G'day, Ron. Yeah, sure, we can fit you in.' He glanced around the team, his gaze lingering on her. Was he checking to see if she'd changed her mind about staying?

'When do you want to start?' His eyes focused intently on her.

Poppy leaned back, nibbling her sausage roll and not daring to make eye contact. Right now, everything about him was self-assured, confident and calm, nothing like the pain she'd just witnessed. He treated the farmers with genuine respect, even when they dismissed him. She found it both attractive and endearing.

Only she couldn't have it for herself.

But why had he recoiled from her when she'd asked about Sam? There was nothing to be ashamed of. Was there?

Why was everyone so secretive about how this shearer

had died?

Chapter Twenty-Eight

Sunlight glinted through the windscreen, and LJ reached for the visor, tugging it down to shield his eyes. Smile lines caressed the skin behind his sunnies. 'Yes!' he said exuberantly, punching the steering wheel with the palm of his hand and bopping to the music on the radio. Things were on the up. With Ron's sheep to shear, they'd get his shed finished fast enough to start a new shed, should one come their way. And with the calls he'd received today, his team had work for the next few weeks. It was a big shift from five weeks earlier when it had looked like he wouldn't be able to hold his team together. Bear's family came to mind, and LJ dared to hope he might be able to offer financial security to all his employees at long last.

'Ah, Sammy, our plans are working out. Buying the run

from Colin *was* worth it after all.' Instantly, all air whooshed from his lips as his smile fell away. 'We were a team, and a bloody good one.' Could've been the best in Tassie. LJ's lips began to tremble.

'If you hadn't gone on another drinking binge. If you hadn't—'

LJ pressed a hand to his mouth, cutting off the memory. Not only did it hurt too much, but thick guilt also gripped him when he admitted that if he'd been the true friend he claimed to be, he would have made sure it *didn't* happen.

'Promises. They're all bullshit,' LJ blurted out, his hand roughly rubbing the back of his neck, his good mood stolen. He bit down on his bottom lip, happy to feel the burn. Sam had suffered pain his whole life—his father beating both him and his mother on a whim when in a drunken rage.

He drove on, one hand atop the steering wheel and his head propped against his fist on the window ledge. They'd been planning on entering the State Championships again. LJ's lips lifted in a regretful smile. While he'd won more often, he'd known the day was coming when Sam would round him up. His numbers were increasing, his precision the best LJ had seen. Everything had been pointing to a year of success for Sam.

But there were moments when Sam was plagued with self-doubt and worthlessness. Not a day went by that LJ didn't evaluate his best mate's mood, watching for the tell-tale signs, wishing he could turn back time, change what had happened. Both concerns for the success of the business, and the small fire in Cookie's kitchen when they had been away on a job—

the thought made him sick—had distracted LJ that terrible night. Despite his desperate efforts, he hadn't been able to remember those final moment's he was about to have with Sam, or exactly how much grog he'd had to drink.

Fighting the dampness in his eyes, LJ blinked against the glare from the sun as he fought for the umpteenth time to remember the final circumstances of that day. But like every other damn time, he couldn't dredge the details to the forefront of his mind, thanks to the sheet of iron that had been ripped from the shearing shed roof during the wild storm, knocking him out cold.

The muscles in his forearm tensed as he recalled hearing Bianca's panicked scream moments before, calling Sam's name—so uncharacteristic of her. But it was only when she burst through the door to the kitchen, screaming and pointing for him to get over to the windmill at the woolshed, that he paid attention.

And then it was too late.

Chapter Twenty-Nine

Jazz and Sammy leapt down the paddock, jumping boulders and playfully sniping at one another. Poppy sank her hands deep into her jacket pockets as her gumboots squelched through the slippery mud. With her beanie tugged tight around her ears and thick scarf wrapped around her face, she was dressed for the Antarctic.

Wishful thoughts of LJ played in her mind, and Jacinta, who had miraculously found them again at Ron's shed. Did the woman have spies on the inside? But that wasn't possible given the way everyone responded to her arrival each time. And what was Poppy meant to do with the fact that Jacinta wouldn't leave LJ alone? He didn't appreciate her there. His face said it all every time. But what if there was some unfinished business between them?

His damned kiss had complicated everything, that's what. Now he was definitely avoiding her—she was sure of it—by eye contact, and definitely by not talking to her, unless was absolutely necessary. Didn't he want her in his team anymore?

Reaching the house gate, she shoved it open with her hip, and all three ran for shelter under George's verandah as a savage outburst of hail lashed the ground.

Inside, George huddled close to the AGA stove, feeding another piece of wood into its hungry mouth when Poppy and the pups burst into the kitchen. The pups ran to Rowdy, who offered a low growl when they tried to snatch a drink. She had weaned them three weeks ago, but it didn't stop them from trying. On the kitchen table sat a mixing bowl, steady droplets pooling inside it from the roof.

Poppy stared in dismay. While the house managed to hold tight during the dry times—be it ice cold from lack of insulation in the walls—the wet created another issue she was unable to do something about herself. And it added to her worry about George coping on his own in the future if things changed. She was falling in love with Tasmania, despite Rick hanging around like the proverbial bad smell. Spider had heard he wasn't working, having been given his marching orders by LJ now he was no longer required. He'd eventually get bored and head home to his pampered life and princess shedhand, or at least she could hope.

Pushing her dreary thoughts aside, she gave a determined smile and tugged the cake container from the corner of the bench, grabbing a cutting board as the kettle whistled. With her back to George, she decorated it with candles, then turned around. His peppery whiskers moved as his lips rose, revealing four missing teeth.

Poppy placed the board on the rickety table, and all three dogs trotted over, noses high in the air.

'What's all this then?' George's delighted smile lit up his face.

'It's a special day and I wanted to surprise you.'

'Well, you definitely did that, my dear.'

Much to her relief, it took George six blows to put the candles out on the carrot cake that Poppy had generously laced with cream cheese frosting. She didn't want to think about how long they might have been waiting for a slice if she'd put all eighty-three on.

Poppy cut a slice each as George looked up at her. 'So, how's the job going? Is LJ a good boss?'

Hesitating, she studied his face for a moment before handing him a plate. She brewed the tea in George's pot, pouring them each a hot cuppa. A jug of milk sat to the right, just the way George liked it.

'He is.' She stalled. 'There's talk of a couple more weeks of work left, but . . .' A frown crossed her brow, and she stared at her slice of cake like it was only meant to be admired, not eaten. Was his work drying up again? It was an all-too-frequent pattern that continued to directly affect her. But more than that, it was the loneliness she sensed rising in her chest at the thought of not seeing him every working day that had her missing him like she'd already left. Would his contracting run end, forever? She wished he would let her help.

'I'm thinking I might look around for another contractor, you know, see if I can find more work.'

George offered a thoughtful gaze as he munched on his mouthful. He swallowed. 'I know I'm a silly old fool, but I'd be inclined to stick with what you have. The boy is a good lad, respected 'round these parts. You'd do well to give him a go.' His watery eyes held hers, and she checked herself, unsure if his look suggested something worth paying closer attention to. Regardless of her growing feelings for the man with a sexy smile who turned her insides to mush every time she thought of him, that couldn't compete with her need to find a way to continue staying in Tasmania.

Poppy lowered herself onto the kitchen chair, and Jazz lifted her front paws onto her thigh, as if sensing her melancholy mood. Her happy eyes begged Poppy to spare a small morsel, or more.

She stroked the pup's head, her mind awash with confusion. If she stayed with LJ, who knew when his work would run out, and would he even bother telling her? The thought needled her with a sharp stab. She'd had enough of being dumped by boyfriends and bosses. But if she joined another contractor with an established clientele—far more than what LJ appeared to have—her scope would undoubtedly broaden.

So, there really was no choice.

Chapter Thirty

LJ's concerns were growing faster than the weeds in Grandma Aimee's garden. After the initial flurry of inquiries resulting in a handful of bookings, there hadn't been any more phone calls or emails regarding future work. And with this week and next left on the books, letting his team down weighed heavily on LJ's mind. He scrubbed his face with his hands. Why did it have to be so bloody hard?

He finished shearing the belly of his next sheep, grabbed it and tossed it to the board. He moved onto the first back leg, his thoughts far from the job. The text he'd received earlier had him squeezing his handpiece tight.

'It's real nice you handed over your family's clip to us for crutching. Pretty sure we've got the main shearing too.'

Ryan. Bloody. Sweeny. The thieving bastard.

LJ could picture the smug grin on Miles's face right now. Didn't loyalty count for anything, the same loyalty his father had drummed into them? But Miles's opinions no longer meant anything anymore—not since he realised his brother couldn't stand Sam.

'We're all in this game to help each other, and word is your work's running out. Can I have Bianca, and that new classer of yours?'

Did Sweeny actually think he'd be pleased as punch to hand them over to a tool like him? Like hell he would.

A strange unease filled LJ's mind, and he frowned, glancing towards Poppy, who was busy doing her work to her own beat. He lay his sheep on its side, commencing long blows as his handpiece ploughed through the wool, glad to feel the strain on his back and arms. It helped to keep him distracted from the wandering thoughts—which he had no real control over—when it came to his classer.

Bianca wasn't a worry. His sister was loyal to the core. But Poppy . . . she liked being in the team, he was sure of it. But would she stay if she got the chance of more work?

But the truth was, he didn't deserve any relationship. Not with WorkSafe looming. It wasn't fair for him to be dragging her down in his personal life.

LJ sent the ewe down the chute and stood, looking nowhere in particular. Jase did the same, straightening his back as he glanced LJ's way.

LJ took a step forward, their toes less than an inch apart. He needed to vent. 'Bloody Sweeny's started poaching again. Wants Bianca and Poppy.' He stared out the small window above his stand, watching clouds drift across the sun. Helping other contractors with crew from time to time was fine—professional courtesy. But Sweeny ran his own agenda, and it was never about lending a mate a hand. It was about playing for keeps.

'For what job?'

'Dad's.'

'What! Why didn't your dad take us on? What's changed?'

LJ shook his head, the muscles in his jaw flexing against his clenched teeth.

'Miles. That's what. Told Dad we cost too much.' Miles was calling all the shots for the farm, and his father couldn't see through it.

'Don't bloody give them to him, LJ. The bastard can find his own workers. He'll only use and abuse them, then spit 'em out.'

But it wasn't Sweeny that was on his mind. It was Miles. He knew his brother was up to something, and it smelled of more than straight-out sabotage. LJ just had to figure out what.

Poppy hung up the phone, her ear buzzing after being quizzed by her father. She'd managed to fob him off, feeding him a line about a patient cutting his palm on a handpiece. And it was true—she managed to convince herself. Whippet had been showing off to Spider, claiming he could shear five sheep in under ten minutes. On the fourth sheep, he looked up, yelling out to Spider to be ready to shout the bar Friday night as his handpiece travelled towards his left hand holding the back leg in position.

In the same moment, an almighty 'frickin' hell' hollered through the shed as blood gushed over the sheep and onto the board. Poppy grabbed the first aid box, cleaned, disinfected and bandaged the wound, but Whippet had refused medical attention. So she kept a close eye on him, making him sit while she changed the bandages at each break despite his leg bouncing nervously.

It had taken constant badgering—something she loathed doing—and Bianca's pointed silent treatment before he'd finally listened.

'You don't have to go to the doctor, Whippet. As long as you don't mind it going septic.' She paused. 'And of course, any chance of catching LJ's numbers disappears if it gets amputated.' She'd walked away with the first aid kit and a satisfied smile at his stricken face.

Who said you couldn't scare a shearer?

With one man down, the job was behind by half a day. Once they were done, LJ's sheds were winding up. And there was no word from him of any more until Oxley Falls in September. Her mind raced. She needed to find more work. If LJ couldn't do that for her, then she'd find it on her own, making sure she was back for Oxley Falls. The thought of leaving him—and the team—left her feeling hollow. But LJ wasn't in the game of making any promises, a fact he'd already proven. She had to show as many growers as possible that she was available. As word travelled, she'd establish a reputation as a classer in this state. Then all she needed was for Rick to leave, and the courage to tell her father the truth.

Saturday morning was frosty and crisp underfoot as Poppy stepped from her caravan, rubbing her gloved hands in front of her face and blowing warm puffs of air into them. The late winter sun was rising in the cloudless sky, and she studied the gumtree forest a hundred or so metres away. Each tree glowed with fresh, white frost, glimmering as it caught the warm rays. This was her first heavy Tasmanian frost, and its beauty was breathtaking.

She had promised Adrian she would take him to George's today, and hopped in her car, cranking the heater up as the engine purred to life. Adrian scooted down the steps at the sound as she headed back inside her caravan.

'Wait for me, Poppy.'

She laughed, stepping out with a bucket of steaming hot water. She was lifting it towards her front windscreen when he yelled out, his panicked hands waving in the air.

'No, no, Poppy. Stop.' He jogged as fast as he could towards her.

She studied the thick layer of ice on her windscreen which encased the wipers, lowering her bucket as he stopped in front of her, breathless.

'Why not? We won't see where we're going if I don't.'

'Do it with cold water,' he puffed. 'Hot water . . . breaks the glass.' He rocked on the spot, watching her anxiously.

'Oh?' Poppy twisted her lips. She paused a little longer before dumping the water on the icy ground, steam rushing into the frigid air. Returning with a bucket of cold water, she drizzled it over the glass under Adrian's close eye. He smiled as they watched the ice steadily melt away, assisted by the gentle heat from inside her car.

'You saved me, Adrian.' She loved how he was filling her loneliness when Jimmy was so far away. He was fast becoming another brother to her, and she hoped she'd get the opportunity to take him home to meet her family someday. Only, that would require another lie . . . or ten before it could happen.

'I saw you, Poppy.' Adrian gave a shy giggle, and when Poppy glanced at him in the passenger seat, his cheeks were a ripe shade of cherry red.

'Saw me where?' She frowned.

'At your caravan. With LJ.' His giggle came again, this time a little louder, his hand over his mouth.

She turned to watch him a little longer this time, a look of confusion on her face until— 'Ohh.' Had he really seen LJ . . . *kissing* her? A sharp rush of heat flushed her cheeks, and she fixed her gaze on the road. There was no denying it, but the disappointment that came with the memory robbed all exhilaration of the moment from her mind.

'Yes, LJ came to say hi.'

'He kissed you.' Adrian giggled behind his hand, his eyes darting to her and away again, as though he might get in trouble.

'Yes. Yes, he did.' Was there nothing this guy missed?

The roads to George's were slippery with black ice. But Poppy was learning fast. This was normal for a full-blown Tasmanian winter, and she drove with caution, barely hitting the speed limit. Along with the drive, Adrian's cheerfulness was infectious, and Poppy flashed him a grin as she slowed at George's driveway.

'Here we are.' She waggled her eyebrows, and he jiggled in his seat. If only his mother could see how much pleasure it gave her son to be taken on an outing. Poppy offered him a high-five in the air.

But Mrs Potter wore the shame of a disabled son like a well-loved jumper. She'd been dealt a raw hand in life, becoming more bitter and spiteful as Adrian aged. Deep down, Poppy was sure Adrian knew his mother resented him, but to his absolute credit, he never let on. He went on camps for Down Syndrome kids and was one of their key leaders. His love for life knew no boundaries.

All three dogs bounded to the car as they pulled up. Adrian's hearty giggle delighted Poppy, though she gave the obligatory stern warning about jumping on visitors. They spun away from Adrian, jumping on her instead.

The highlight of Adrian's day was a bareback ride on Belle. George's twenty-nine-year-old Clydesdale. She'd once pulled the plough for George before he and his brother renounced the old ways, buying a tractor. Belle plodded beside

Poppy as Adrian yelled 'yee--haw' and 'come on, horsey', giggling when she broke out in a gentle loping trot.

But when they pulled up at The Lone Pony, Poppy's heart sank. While a warming residue from the happiness of the day glowed on both their faces, Mrs Potter's expression killed it instantly. Adrian's enthusiasm didn't falter, recounting his adventures to her rigid back as she turned towards the house.

Back in her caravan, Poppy lay on her bed and stared at her phone. The day had been great, but it had also reinforced how much she wanted to stay. That meant researching what her options were when LJ's work dried up, and Google was going to help.

Chapter Thirty-One

Day one for the final shed LJ had organised for the team was done, their last week-long camp-out, and maybe the last one for team Take Two Shearers, forever. He stared at the open fire in his shearer's hut, the distant sound of chatter and the TV audible from the communal lounge some twenty metres away. His transfixed gaze watched the flames twirling around the sticks he'd collected earlier, as the comforting smell of smouldering smoke rose inside the room.

The Shermers were new to the farming community and extremely green when it came to running a sheep property. LJ recalled his conversation with Max.

'I've got a real good kelpie that the last owners left behind when they moved out. Nice little thing. Um, should she be rushing the sheep and biting them? Kath doesn't like it 'cause the sheep might get hurt.'

LJ had smothered a rueful smile at the phone. 'How about I swing by before we start and give you a hand?'

It was obvious why the previous owners had left the dog behind, and LJ had kept the over-zealous—some might say out of control—dog on a lead as they got the sheep into the yards.

'You know, you were the only one to accept my job, LJ. The other contractor said he was too busy.'

LJ swallowed hard. The comment had caused both suspicion and concern for him. These were good people giving rural life a real go—keen to learn. He wasn't surprised that Sweeny had snubbed them. Newcomers like ex-townies were notoriously prickly when it came to practical animal management. But Max was genuine, ready to get dirty and embrace the farming way, and LJ knew his team would have the job next year, if they could manage to get their sheep in again, that is.

Now, as he contemplated both his future and that of the team, dejection crept in. He'd worked hard to push aside—for the most part—the circumstances surrounding Sam's death. And he thought he was managing to do so pretty well. But more often, Sam was becoming a hauntingly real presence in his memory.

It was always Sam who stayed upbeat when LJ had worried about where their next dollar would come from. His practical jokes and antics always brought a smile to everyone around him and empowered LJ to see the positive over the negative.

'Don't worry, LJ. The next phone call's only one bleat

away. The McKenzies will ring. Just you watch,' Sam had said, offering a cheeky wink, which, at the time, had settled LJ's apprehension.

He shuffled in his seat as he ran his hand along the bristles on his face, pausing as his thoughts collided. Sam had told him that not a week before he had died.

And the McKenzies hadn't rung.

He blew out a languished puff of air, resting his hands on his outstretched legs crossed at the ankles. Out of habit, he listened for any unusual noise or commotion from the huts—a sign there could be trouble of some kind—as the skittering flames continued to do their tango.

A loud knock at his door startled him, and he reluctantly eased himself up from the chair. Was it Poppy? His heart gave a little flutter of hopefulness before he squashed it back down.

Then again, was something wrong? The last thing he needed was someone doing something stupid, or dare he think it, another death on his already bloodied hands.

'Come in.'

His door burst open, and blonde flowing locks and a beaming smile greeted him. A heavy groan slipped from his throat as he slumped back into his seat, wishing the flames could make him disappear.

Or her.

'Hello, Jacinta.' His voice was hollow as he hid his face behind his hand. He was so over her uncanny ability to find him. Hadn't he made it clear enough last time that he wasn't getting back with her? What was it going to take?

'Hello, my darling.' She paused and glanced around his

room. His dirty clothes were scattered across the floor, and his bed lay unmade. A pile of wood and sticks lay dumped in the corner of the room next to the fire, a box of matches and a packet of firelighters sitting on top of a thin layer of dust on the ledge above the fireplace.

'Look at you. You're a mess. Good thing I—'

'Why are you here, Jacinta?' He turned with an accusatory glare. 'Because if it's not important, you need to leave.' He glared back at the fire.

Would she get the message *this* time? He wanted her to go, to let him suffer the loss of his friend for the rest of his life. It's what he deserved, and he knew it. His reddened eyes began to sting and he tried to convince himself it was from the heat of the fire.

'What do you want, Jacinta?' He breathed the tired words out.

'Well,' she chimed, 'I have some news.'

'You could've rung.' He reached for the bridge of his nose, knowing full well that if she had, he wouldn't have answered.

'I thought you'd like to hear it in person.' She took an important deep breath. 'I was in the café this morning, you know, our favourite one . . . and I saw a man in a suit and tie, jacket and pants . . . you know, the lot.' She ran a hand down her torso. 'Smart looking.'

LJ closed his eyes, the thud of a headache forming.

'And he asked if I knew you.'

LJ's hand fell, hanging mid-air as his eyes swivelled towards her. It irked him to see her glean the fact that she had his full attention.

'The logo on his shirt said WorkSafe.'

Oh, shit.

Chapter Thirty-Two

Poppy froze the moment she stepped out of her hut. Jacinta was in the process of throwing LJ's door open with theatrical gusto, and her heart plummeted. With her mini speech written and rehearsed, she'd been about to tell LJ that she would seek alternative work due to his sheds winding up. She'd wanted to plead her case, promising to be back in September, in time for Oxley Falls. But deep down, she hoped he would object, perhaps say he'd received a call from another shed, or tell her he didn't want her to leave. She wanted to stay with the team, but more than that, she wanted to stay with him.

Just as she was ready to tell him, the girlfriend, or ex—she had no idea what Jacinta was other than a source of gushy smiles and oozy affection—had turned up. No doubt he was pleased to see her. The thud of her rejected heart pounded against her ribs. Was she ever going to learn?

Bianca had insisted Jacinta was in LJ's past, but the regularity with which the woman turned up at all their jobs, including camp-outs, left Poppy unconvinced.

Poppy shook her head and closed the door, pressing her back to it, desperately searching her room for answers. But the only thing that rang true in her ears was the flowery laughter from Jacinta.

Moving to her bed, she snatched up her phone, put on some music, and opened Google again. He'd sacked her once. Now it was her turn to repay the favour.

She found LJ's direct competitor and dialled the number. '*El mandigo* cannot be choosers,' she whispered to herself—words Grandpa Isaac often recited to her—and she tapped the green phone on the screen, waiting for the call to connect.

LJ had managed to move Jacinta on using the lame excuse that he was exhausted. And it was true. Sam's death, concerns about leaving Grandma Aimee at home—alone, letting his team down, Miles, and worries about WorkSafe were mounting rapidly. Plus, there were his fluctuating emotions for his wool classer, which didn't help. He found himself searching for opportunities to meet with her again, to hold her in the warmest of embraces, savouring her perfume and the feel of her body close to his.

He'd caught her watching him as he turned into the pens, but her expression had confused him. Where she'd smiled or blushed in the past, there was now a look in her eyes that held his with determination and, if he were brave enough to admit it, a decided strength. His brows had snapped together as she broke their contact, continuing with her work like he meant nothing to her other than that he was her boss. What he wouldn't give to know what was going on in that gorgeous mind.

His past relationship with Jacinta had always felt forced and contrived. But with Poppy? His senses were on high alert at every damn turn. His heart cartwheeled when she locked eyes with him; when he noticed the thick dark wisps of hair that escaped her ponytail and fell on either side of her face. He knew he was in trouble the moment he'd forced his hands deep inside his pockets to resist the urge to brush them from her face.

LJ placed one last piece of wood on the fire before putting the wire screen across it for the night. He lay in bed, hands behind his head, as he tried to sort through his complicated life, but one thing continued to resurface.

Poppy Fletcher.

He needed to do something about this woman who hovered in his background thoughts every workday and in his dreams at night. After this job, and with the next week, or more, without work—he thought sadly—he'd ask her out for tea, or even a picnic lunch. Anything. He needed to know if what he was feeling ran parallel with her thoughts, or was so far off, vertical could never meet horizontal.

Chapter Thirty-Three

Poppy set off, her first day with her new team completed. As with LJ's team, it had been a little awkward at first, but thankfully, they were focused on the job rather than giving her grief.

She'd met Sophie, a pregnant shedhand who she'd taken an instant liking to. The girl was a hard worker, regardless of how close she was to her due date. And Ryan Sweeny, he appeared likeable enough, introducing her to his team and the grower who was keen to see what she could do with his fine micron clip.

But deep down she missed her old team, with Bear's terrible dad jokes and Spider's gangly limbs perfect for grabbing armfuls of wool to feed into the wool press. She even missed the "bananas", who'd mellowed lately. Would she find another team that genuinely welcomed her? Or would she regret abandoning team LJ?

Her pulse quickened as she thought of LJ, and she blinked hard to clear his image. The brutal truth was simple: any team without LJ wasn't a team she wanted to be in. Her chest deflated with regret at the no-win circumstance he'd put her in.

Poppy turned into The Lone Pony gateway, and Adrian greeted her with his brilliant smile as he scratched between the pony's ears. Seeing him was like glimpsing Jimmy, and after her gloomy drive home, she needed a brother figure to hang with right now. She pulled up, leaning over to open the passenger door.

'Hey, Adrian. Do you feel like fish and chips for tea?' *If the dragon will let you out.*

'Yep. I do.' His enthusiastic nod made her smile.

'I'll get cleaned up and then we'll go. I'll toot when I'm ready, okay?'

'Yup!' He clapped his hands.

Watching him from her rear-view mirror, Poppy realised that life without Adrian in Tasmania would be almost unbearable. His friendship was unshakable, and that meant everything. Without him and George, who would she have? A thread of loneliness gnawed at her wavering confidence. They were the only family she had right now.

Adrian cradled the hot fish and chips, his fingers dancing over the paper in rhythm with the radio. His questioning eyes caught hers.

'Why were you sad today, Poppy?'

She studied the road ahead. 'I've started work with a new team, and I'm not sure they're the best fit for me. And I'm pretty sure my phone is dead. It went for a swim in a puddle this morning.'

'That's not good.'

'No.' But she needed to stick with this team. Her thumb tapped on the steering wheel, her mind a long way from the road in front.

'What's wrong with LJ? I thought you liked him.'

She ignored the question, but her traitorous thoughts drifted to the way LJ's t-shirt hugged him close, his smile breaking down layer after layer of her protective walls. Her heart jittered out of rhythm. If she was honest with herself—which she wasn't—she missed LJ already. Had it only been a couple of days?

'Did he upset you?'

The guy never quit! She took a calming breath.

'No, he didn't. He hasn't got any more work for me.'

'I know a shed.' Adrian's voice held hope like it could be bottled. But she refused to hold onto any false hopes.

'Thank you for trying to help, but this is just something I need to do on my own.' She immediately regretted her dismissive tone. But how could Adrian possibly know farmers, let alone those growing superfine wool?

His unconvinced expression caught her eye, and she attempted a grateful smile.

A shaft of sunlight streamed through Grandma Aimee's lounge room window, causing particles of dust motes to linger and dance. LJ stared through it with a blank stare. He was furious.

And hurt.

He'd put his heart on the line last Monday, asking if she wanted to go out for lunch—they both had no work after all. But it was Friday, and silence was his only answer. He despised feeling like some lovesick teenager, checking his phone hourly.

He hadn't picked her as the ghosting type. She'd answered his calls and texts for work every time. A twinge of guilt hit him as he realised it was much better than how he'd treated her those few weeks ago, and he stiffened. What a hypocrite, Tanner.

By Wednesday, curiosity had driven him to The Lone Pony, where he'd found Adrian mowing around her caravan. After some gentle probing, he'd learned the devastating truth: she was working for Ryan Sweeny. Betrayal burned through him as he raked frustrated fingers through his hair. Sweeny was his competitor, known for dodgy dealings, cheating farmers, and outright theft. Poppy knew his team's opinion of Sweeny, yet she'd chosen him?

LJ paced the room, stopping in front of the window

again. *And would it have hurt her to let me know she was ditching us?*

But the deep-down truth gnawed at him: avoiding promises meant no one got disappointed. Or killed.

Ever again.

He collapsed onto the couch with a thud.

But why did Poppy's departure wound him so deeply? He told himself it was genuine concern for her welfare, frustration at losing his only classer—a damn good one.

Nothing more.

But his leg jigged as his mind raced. Dave had made the same choice, and LJ was relieved to see the douchebag go— birds of a feather and all that.

LJ pressed a hand to his neck, muscles tense. He had to warn Poppy about Sweeny's reputation, without seeming desperate—though desperation was exactly what he felt. Her reputation was at stake. As shed boss, she'd be held responsible for any missing items. He couldn't let that happen.

But what could he do?

LJ reined in his emotions as a cheerful voice called from Grandma Aimee's gateway, which was laced with a fragrant jasmine vine that cascaded to the ground.

'Hellooo? Are you there, honey? Can you give your mother a hand?'

'Sure, Mum.' LJ stood, offering a reluctant wave to her from the lounge window. He cleared the croak from his voice. 'Hang on.'

Friday morning was here again, and with it, a guarantee of warm home-cooked meals, slices, and as always, a delicious cake. That had to be enough to improve his listless mood.

He swung the front door open, and the gentle breeze carried with it the appetising aroma of cinnamon and banana. 'Something smells good.'

Strolling along the path towards his mother's car, their eyes met, and her smile dropped away. LJ ignored her concern as he gave her a peck on the cheek.

Jen stepped back. 'I know that look.' Her knowing gaze measured him, her head tilting. 'What's wrong, honey? Bad day?' She rubbed his arm with motherly tenderness.

'You could say that.' He shrugged, his voice distant, offering her a reluctant half-smile as he watched a car pass by.

'I'm sorry, honey. We all miss him.'

He nodded, his sad eyes on hers. Jen's tears welled on cue, and he fought against their magnetic pull. He'd shed enough tears for Sam already. They had to run out sometime.

Jen took a shaky breath. 'I saw Josie a couple of days ago. She's doing okay.' She gave a sad smile. 'As well as she can do, given . . . everything.' She paused meaningfully.

'She asked if you could call by and see her. Said she needed to talk to you.' Her gaze urged him to agree.

He turned towards the kerb as his heart jackhammered. *I can't. She wants to tell me she'll never forgive me for what— for what I didn't do . . . for Sam.* LJ was like a son to her, but didn't anyone have a clue what *he* was carrying, trying to live with? Did they think he was blind to his own failures?

LJ swept up the basket of goodies at his mother's feet before reaching into the back seat for the box of meals, hooking them under his free arm. But before he could step away, Jen placed a gentle hand on his back, his resilience glass-thin.

She smiled sadly and touched his cheek with fingers cold from the morning chill. A memory rushed back. It was the same touch she'd given him when he'd fallen over and hurt his knee, or his hand as a kid.

'It'll get easier, honey, I promise. Just not yet. And remember, it's okay to never forget. That's what makes your heart stronger.' She sniffed back her sorrow.

But how could it get easier? He felt broken, shattered, and completely destroyed. He'd tried not to remember. The pain of asking for forgiveness was unbearable. And the longer he chose to forget, the less love he'd be able to offer anyone. Especially Poppy.

The contracting run was finished. All that remained was deciding when to tell everyone.

Chapter Thirty-four

Friday afternoon finally arrived, and Poppy couldn't escape the shed fast enough, desperate for the weekend to regroup and decide whether she could continue with this team. She'd already overheard a couple of the shearers discussing how "handy" some of the farmer's drench, which was sitting inside the door of the shearing shed, might be for their own mobs, but she couldn't tell if they were only joking.

'See ya, Soph. Have a great weekend.' Her pregnant friend shuffled out, one hand on her belly as she took careful steps out of the shed. Sophie was due any day now, and Poppy wasn't sure how much longer she could keep going. But Sophie needed to keep working to support herself and her baby.

'Ah, Poppy,' the farmer said, approaching her with a smile. 'Hoped I'd catch you. Wanted to tell you that you're doing a real good job with the wool. I'm more than happy.'

'That's great to hear.' Those words were almost enough to live off. But it was only when she saw the test results that she would know how she'd done. A ripple of unease floated in her mind.

'I'd like you back again for our next shearing, if you want the job. Is this your usual team?'

Poppy caught the slight hesitation in his tone, suddenly unsure how to answer him. Part of her wanted to say yes, because she needed the work. Her love of classing was steadily recovering every day. Another part wanted to scream that she'd never work for Ryan Sweeny again.

If only LJ could have secured more work.

'It is, for now. My other contractor ran out of work for me.' The familiar ache hit her chest thinking of them all, especially LJ.

He nodded thoughtfully. 'Hmm, hmmm.'

Dread flooded through her. She hadn't heard that familiar murmur in ages. Dad! Had he been trying to contact her? With her phone drowning in rice, she hadn't thought to call home. And Jimmy. Her shoulders slumped. She was in so much trouble.

'Interesting. Haven't taken to this team if I'm honest. Too rough with the sheep and too many cuts. Who do you usually work for?'

'I've been working for Take Two Shearers.' Her voice stilled, the thought of Sam missing from that title saddening her despite never meeting him. How was LJ coping, and, was he missing her?

'Okay. I'll keep your phone number on hand, and when I need you back, I'll give him a ring.' He smiled obligingly. 'See you Monday morning.' He left the shed, and Poppy, reeling. Could her classing actually bring in work for LJ? That would be an interesting turn of events.

Poppy found a pay phone outside a petrol station and dialled Jimmy's number.

'Thank God. Where the hell have you been? I was about to book a ticket and start a search and rescue party. Do you have *any* idea the stress you've caused me? Dad is beside himself and reckons you're hiding something. Funny that! I've held him off, but I don't know for how much longer. Not answering his calls wasn't your smartest move, little sis. And don't go rolling your eyes like that!'

How did he know? She sucked in a controlled breath. 'Firstly, you should already have a ticket if you got your act into gear and bought one with the *money* I put in your account. And secondly, my phone went for a swim. It still hasn't come up for air. It's currently swimming in a bowl of rice.' She cringed. 'Pretty sure I've killed it.'

'Okay. That explains your phone, but why didn't you think of ringing some other way? It's been *five* days. I started thinking you'd found yourself a new favourite brother.'

Poppy chuckled. 'I have,' she teased. 'Remember

Adrian? He's a pretty good replacement for you. Better, actually. He doesn't have a smart mouth like you, and farts way less.'

'He sounds like no fun at all.'

'Ah, but he likes hot chocolate and my puppy. Anyone who likes those is a winner in my book.' She giggled. Jimmy loved dogs and had said Jazz looked cute in the photos she'd sent him. 'Nah, you're irreplaceable.' She smiled into the phone, knowing he'd get a complex if he thought Adrian was actually replacing him.

'Listen, do me a favour and ring Grandma. She's having kittens, and Dad's wound up tighter than a tractor spring. Count yourself lucky he's tied up with work and can't drag you back to Sydney right now. This job is going to set him up with enough super that he won't run out before he hits the dirt.'

'Jimmy! Don't talk about Dad like that.' Love and guilt suddenly twisted in her chest—for leaving, for lying to him.

'Just ring him! Then he'll get off my back. And Popps, pull that little stunt again and I'll remove you from my Christmas list.'

'Aww, you love me that much? Aren't you the sweetest?' The thought of not receiving his gifts was a clever threat on his behalf, and she knew her mockery was pushing her luck. And although it was on the tip of her tongue to tell him about her rough week, now wasn't the time. His protective instincts would have him hovering over, around, beside, and under her every move. She had to manage this on her own.

'Poppy, you're gonna have to come clean real soon, I swear.'

'I will, I will,' she growled. 'I need to time it right, that's all. I'm with another team now. Give me a few more weeks, enough to prove to the growers they can trust me with their clips, and then I'll tell him. I promise.'

'You'd better, because being your favourite big brother is wearing thin.'

There was a smile in his voice, but she knew he was right. The longer she stalled, the worse it would be, especially if Dad found out from someone else. Distance had its advantages . . . and its disadvantages. She hoped her time wouldn't run out before his parental instincts for his only daughter did. At least she didn't have to suffer Rick anymore, or him reminding her she'd failed his family's wool clip worth thousands of dollars.

'And little sis. Do me a favour and buy yourself another phone.'

Chapter Thirty-five

The pub was unusually quiet for a Friday night despite the speakers pumping out familiar country tunes. Jase nursed a cold beer while LJ sipped his usual Coke at the rickety barstools in The Night's Helmsmen. Bianca and Whippet chatted at a table behind them.

LJ rubbed his forehead, staring at his boots. He didn't have work for the coming week, and he was exhausted from trying to find a solution. The sticky carpet clung to his boots like chewing gum, and he shifted his feet to the steel bar running along the length of the bench.

'Wanna know something?' Jase broke the silence between them.

'Hmm?' LJ raised his eyebrows. It had been a brutal day he couldn't shake. Why hadn't Poppy returned his calls or texted? It worried him, and for more reasons than the simple feeling he'd been stood up.

'I'm gonna miss Poppy.'

LJ's spine stiffened as he studied his friend. Did Jase have feelings for Poppy? He hadn't picked up on it before now. She was gorgeous, with her striking Spanish looks and smile that took him to destinations he'd never imagined visiting. And no matter how often he tried to push thoughts of her aside, he failed miserably. But Jase? They'd be perfect together. The thought sat like lead in his gut.

LJ took another sip of his cold Coke, swallowing hard. 'Yeah, me too.'

'What possessed her to leave us? Did she tell you she was going? Damn stupid of her if you ask me.'

'She didn't say a word I found out when I saw Adrian Potter.' He stared at the bubbles running up the side of his glass. He wouldn't mention the real reason for seeing Adrian, that he'd stressed over not hearing back from Poppy after putting himself on the line. 'Guess she wanted to chase the work.' But LJ had picked her to be smarter. And from what he'd heard on the shearers' vine, Rick was apparently working on his own, so it couldn't be because of him.

Jase changed the topic, chuckling as he recalled Bear doing his Mr Bean impersonation on the way into the pen to grab another sheep last week, but his voice faded in LJ's mind. Instead, he was visualising Poppy working, determined to prove herself as though her life depended on it. But she didn't need to, so good at her job. Exceptional even. But he hadn't taken the opportunity to tell her. He hadn't taken the time to tell her a lot of things.

And if Jase was romantically interested in Poppy, how could he stand in his way? But could he let someone else sweep away the only girl who'd consumed his thoughts ever since she'd arrived? Confusion tormented him. His mind said mates didn't compete—not in his team, not after everything they'd endured. But could he let her go without a fight?

The front door of the pub swung open, a sharp breeze rushing in with a rowdy crowd. LJ's eyes were glazed and distant, his thumb and forefinger circling the top of his glass as the condensation drizzled down the sides.

Jase lifted his elbows from the bar, half-turning. 'LJ.' His tone sharpened. 'LJ, you'd better sit up.' Jase nudged him.

LJ roused himself enough to focus, but he didn't have the energy to care. His face cast shadows of sadness, despondency and self-loathing. Jase's eyes widened with empathy for his friend before he looked back at the crowd making their way towards the bar.

'Well, well, well. Look who we have here, boys and gals. Why, it's our charming competitor. Got any more sexy classers for us to try out?' Sweeny tugged a stool alongside LJ and ordered himself a beer. LJ's stare remained fixed on his glass, fingers tightening their grip. Sweeny glanced at the bar mirror reflecting assorted wines and spirits. Above hung the head of a huge stag shot by a local over fifty years ago.

'So, Bianca,' Sweeny called out, his eyes remaining glued on LJ, 'you coming to work for me too? Your dear big brother can't manage enough work for you, but I've got plenty.'

LJ side-eyed Bianca, noticing Whippet's firm hand restraining her leg under the table—preventing her from springing up to tear Sweeny's throat out.

Sweeny cocked his head towards the barman. 'I take it that's a no. Bianca mustn't want work.' His eyebrows flicked smugly. 'Don't say I didn't offer.'

LJ swallowed his rising anger as Sweeny winked appreciatively, snatched up his beer and shoved his stool aside.

Arresting vigilance pumped its way through LJ's blood, and he felt something shift inside him. As far as he was concerned, Poppy remained his employee until he heard official word otherwise. The longer he didn't hear, the more time he had. All he had to do was convince her his team was the one to stick with.

But with no work in the foreseeable future, he had little to persuade her with.

While Sweeny's team had accepted her, she continually reminded herself why she was doing this, questioning her wisdom when she suspected—more and more—that equipment was going missing. Only, she couldn't prove it.

She'd managed a brief hello to Dave on Monday morning, realising he too had chased work when LJ couldn't provide more.

Sadness washed over her as she watched Sophie

struggle with her bulging belly as she tried to pick up the fleece. The poor girl was due in a week.

At smoko, Poppy took a chair outside to sit in the warming sun as she mulled over her savoury scone and stared into the distance. What was LJ doing right now? She smiled, remembering his endearing grin when he'd glanced up mid-sheep to watch her. But what good did it do her to be thinking about him? What exactly were they anyway? Friends? She could hardly hope for more. If she knew what was good for her, she'd stop her errant thoughts. Only problem was, she didn't want to.

'Mind if I sit with you?' Poppy turned, pleasantly startled, then jumped up to grab another chair for Sophie.

'You're doing so well.' Poppy smiled, eying her as she sat awkwardly. 'How are you feeling?' She couldn't imagine working in Sophie's condition.

'I'm okay, only the occasional twinges here and there.' Sophie paused, staring at her sandwich. 'I'll go for as long as I can. The hospital isn't too far from this shed.'

Did she actually believe she was going to go into labour at work?

'Can I ask, are you . . . on your own?' Poppy hadn't heard Sophie mention a significant other in the short time they'd worked together.

'Yeah.' Sophie's voice faded. 'He left when he found out I was pregnant.'

'Well, he doesn't know what he's missing out on.' Poppy was appalled. Of all the low acts, especially when Sophie was so loyal and dedicated.

'Sweeny doesn't want me to finish up because he'll be short a shedhand. And I can't afford to stop. At least not until this little one arrives.' She placed a protective hand on her swollen belly. 'I have to keep paying rent.' She offered a sad half-smile, weariness overwhelming her features.

Poppy gave a slow nod. Didn't she know it.

The week rolled by with Poppy keeping to herself, watching out for Sophie and her expanding baby bump. She remained upbeat and excited for her, but Poppy knew the enormity of what lay ahead—a seventeen-year-old approaching adulthood and motherhood simultaneously in a crazy rush. Daunting didn't begin to cover it. Poppy could hardly imagine the apprehension Sophie had to be feeling.

By the time she'd packed up and reached her car, everyone had left. She enjoyed her drive home each night, the stretching shadows of oranges and pinks of the setting sun over the hills easing her mind. This was the time in the day she truly breathed, knowing her aching shoulders could relax rather than being tense with apprehension. She wound down her window a little to let the cooling breeze ease the heat trapped inside the car from the day's sun.

The country roads in these parts were only wide enough for single cars. She pulled out, sitting below the speed limit. Twin lambs in the paddock to her left caught her attention as they galloped over a hill, racing one another, their panicked mother bleating for them to return. Poppy smiled. Even for a sheep, being a parent brought constant stress from concern for your kids.

Mum, I miss you.

The familiar pang of guilt wove its tentacles into her core—thoughts of her grandmother's cooking, Jimmy's voice, and Grandpa Isaac's parting words. 'Now you be careful around that Mr Tanner. I cannot kick him so far, and that is as much as I trust him.' They filled her mind so deeply, she failed to notice the blinding driving lights of a four-wheel drive ute eating up the asphalt behind her.

Honk! Honk!

Poppy jumped from her reverie, glaring at the rear-vision mirror and squinting at the massive bull bar bearing down on her tail. Where had that come from? And what was she meant to do? Speed up and keep the driver happy. Slow down and let them pass?

Or pull over? She eased her foot off the accelerator, flicking on her blinker. Immediately, her brow furrowed. 'What on earth?' This ute was pulling in behind her. Poppy swallowed hard, her heart racing. She kept her engine running.

The ute door shut with a thud, crunching footsteps walking on the stony edge of the road towards her. Was it Sweeny? Why hadn't he just rung her to pass on a message about next week? She squinted against the blinding reflection of lights in her side mirror, making out the casual, yet purposeful walk of a man. He paused at her window and tapped on it, his smile set.

'Rick?' Poppy wound down her window. What the heck was he doing here? She'd hoped he might have realised what a ridiculous move he'd made and gone back to the mainland.

'Hey, Poppy. You're looking good.' His words were a token gesture, ones she knew she couldn't trust. He was all charm, his big smile as confident as ever. But she was well past its magnetic pull. He was wasting her time.

'What are you doing here, Rick?' The last thing she was going to tell him was that he'd scared her half to death. He didn't need any incentives to rattle her.

'Apparently, I just missed you at the shed. The farmer said you headed this way.'

'What do you want?' She didn't hide the building frustration in her tone.

'I've come looking for work.' He nodded, blinking at her like it should have been music to her ears.

'You don't need me for that. You can get it on your own.' He was seriously getting on her nerves. 'Go home, Rick.' *Back where you belong.*

'Thought I'd try Sweeny.' He shrugged, like that was his only logical choice.

'He gave you a job. Figured if it was good enough for you, it's good enough for me too.'

That smile. Again.

He was torturing her, with his persistence to stay all too close to her, and his sheer determination to make it sound so reasonable, especially when she had the infuriating hunch it wasn't because he was looking for work at all.

'What about LJ? Thought you wanted to work with

him.'

'I'd rather work with Sweeny.' The glint in his eye sent a ripple of unease throughout her body, and she fought to not let it show as he watched her closely. If she even let on she was uncomfortable, he'd likely turn on her like a hungry shark. She'd seen the occasional signs not long before she'd left—an angry flick of his hair, him holding her a little firmer than necessary—so she had to make it look like it didn't matter to her, whatever he did.

'Please yourself, Rick. Just don't expect me to be over the moon about it.' And with any luck, Sweeny wouldn't be able to take him on.

She pulled back onto the road without a wave, leaving his headlights and his sceptical eyes in her dust.

Chapter Thirty-Six

LJ checked his phone for what felt like the umpteenth time, then tossed it onto the passenger seat with disgust. If Sweeny was so busy that he couldn't accept any more work, how come the growers weren't contacting him instead? He'd heard one local had employed a contracting team from as far away as Hobart, rather than use either of them. Was he destined to chase false hopes forever?

Everything he heard from growers and wool reps confirmed clients were growing increasingly disgruntled with shonky shearing contractors and unreliable teams. He'd spent the last week dropping flyers and business cards into every agricultural business and stockfeed store within two hundred kilometres. If this idea didn't pay off, then he'd wasted a whole lot of time and fuel he couldn't afford.

The early-morning sun hung low in the sky, mixing with overnight dew to create a blinding glare as he drove to Bear's place. He absently rubbed at his eyes before tugging his sunglasses from the top of his head.

These back roads stirred childhood memories of touring sheds with Pa Pat, penning up for the shearers, and standing at an empty shearing stand, mimicking his grandfather's every blow. He'd practised using his favourite plush toy "Sheepie", dragging him from the pen, then pretending to shear.

A nostalgic smile crossed his face as the ute devoured the white lines. This was why he'd wanted to become a shearer—the romance of working long, hard days in the freezing cold and stifling heat. It made his heart quicken every time he thought about it. And it was the badge of genuine pride he wore when someone asked him what he did for a living.

And yet, it was so much more than that. It was in his blood.

But Miles was another story.

LJ's finger tapped the steering wheel to the soft beat of music on the radio. He despised Miles's smug confidence. Even as kids, his brother had mastered a cunning knack of avoiding regular farming chores, disappearing while LJ willingly stepped up in his absence.

Then Sam had moved in.

Sam and Josie had lived with the Tanners until Josie had saved enough money to get a place of their own. That had taken several years, thanks to her drunken ex booting them out with nothing but the clothes she'd managed to snatch from the washing line as she ran, and Sam's tatty toy sheep which never left his arms.

LJ gave a small smile, recalling Sam's anger when Miles duped them, promising lollies from the school canteen if they did his chores. But Sam was a boy full of mischief, with an inclination to teach someone a lesson when he'd been shortchanged. Life was a game to him, good or bad, and LJ knew Sam had learned many life lessons earlier than his peers.

Easing his foot off the accelerator, LJ dropped down the gears, pushing aside thoughts of his irritable brother. There were better things to do than dwell on his irritating brother, like visiting a mate for a coffee, and dare he hope it, a bit of advice. He turned into Bear and Cindy's driveway. He needed to get some kind of reassurance that his team not only continued believing in him but were still his friends.

'I don't understand. Why aren't they giving us a call?' Frustrated fingers rubbed his at his forehead as Bear stared at the table, mug in hand.

'I dunno, mate.' He gave a consoling smile.

Bear's five-year-old son bounded into the kitchen. 'Dad, can I have a new bike for my birthday, pweeese?' The boy's big brown eyes didn't have to be looking at LJ for him to be hit in the gut by the pleading gaze.

'When?' he said, the word coming out as a whisper.

'Not sure, but I can feel it. Cindy and I know you're doing everything you can, and I'm not going anywhere, okay?' This time his gaze held firm on LJ, and he felt guilty for nodding, just to appease his mate. He was starting to believe the turnaround Sam had steadfastly believed in wouldn't happen at all.

Bear had hope in him, but did he have even a speck of it for himself? If he didn't get the confidence of more growers soon, the drastic decisions he'd been holding off, would happen.

He had to show his father that buying the contracting run would pay off.

LJ pulled up in front of Grandma Aimee's cottage, only to be greeted by his mother's ashen face. He stepped from the ute and walked to the front gate, meeting her embrace, which told him everything.

'She has mild hypothermia. Oh, LJ, it could've been so much worse. Thank goodness last night was milder than normal.'

The overnight temperature had reached a minimum of eleven rather than the more regular four degrees or below for this time of year. Grandma Aimee had gone for an evening stroll last night, looking for her Eddie.

Regret dug deep as remorse tugged hard in his heart. 'I'm so sorry, Mum.'

'She keeps asking for you. The doctor wants to discuss her living arrangements. They're concerned about her wandering off again.'

LJ's hands clenched into fists. Another failure. Another person he'd let down. How many more promises would he break before this was over?

Chapter Thirty-Seven

Did she feel bad for speaking to Rick like that? Maybe a little. Did she regret it?

Not one bit.

Poppy balanced on the edge of her bed with Jazz at her feet, staring at the cold cup of tea resting in her lap. The young dog watched expectantly, her tail swishing on the floor as Poppy tossed her the crust from her toast.

The morning news came on the TV, but the words fell on deaf ears. Sweeny had given Rick work, what was it, from the goodness of his heart? She wouldn't be surprised if Rick had blackmailed the guy. She'd done her best to ignore him, and for the most part, he seemed to be getting along well enough with the team, leaving her alone. But there was the occasional steady glance in her direction that left her distinctly on edge. Since he'd come to Tasmania, he was more . . . intense, focused. When it came to his work, that approach was great, even if his father and brother had constantly badgered him to slow down and cut less. But when her skin crawled and she looked up to see his cool eyes on her, she wanted to run from the shed.

Flopping backwards, she watched a daddy-long-legs do a side-step to snatch a gnat caught in its web. Could things get any worse? She was beginning to believe they could.

Standing, Poppy tipped the remainder of her tea down the sink, wishing she could flush Rick out of her thoughts in the same way. 'C'mon, Jazzy pup. Let's get to work.' The dog sprang to her feet, and Poppy longed for some of that enthusiasm in her own step. She grabbed her work gear, shutting her caravan door a little harder than necessary.

Poppy kept one eye on Sophie, who had told her she was experiencing niggles every day now, Braxton Hicks contractions preparing her for the real thing. She paused, the staple of wool hovering between her fingers as she watched Sophie rubbing her belly with a suspiciously pained expression.

It was ten minutes before afternoon smoko when a frightening scream hollered from the board.

'Oh, no.' Poppy dumped the fleece in her hands, and

Jazz—tied to a post nearby—sat up tall as Poppy raced down the board, alarmed shearers pausing mid-blow to stare at the shedhand. Sophie was bent over, one hand supporting her massive belly, the other gripping the post.

Poppy caught Sophie from behind in the nick of time, supporting her under her arms as another sharp contraction gripped. Her heart hammered. Was this really happening? Now?

Rick pulled out of gear, returned his half-shorn sheep to the pen and approached, unexpected disquiet on his face.

'Um, do you . . . need anything?' His eyes held hers before Sophie buckled over her belly again.

She'd comfortably settled into her approach of full-blown ignoring him since yesterday, when he turned up to start working for Sweeny. But right now, she couldn't have been happier he'd asked.

'Ring for an ambulance. And find the farmer's wife. Ask for some towels and hot water. And a pair of scissors.'

'Shit, Poppy. What do you want scissors for?' Rick's face paled, his customary self-assured demeanour suddenly vaporised.

'Just get them, Rick!' Poppy smelled the apprehension in the shed, the men's body odour suddenly stronger than the usual sweat they worked up from a day's physical work. But as Sophie squeezed her hand with such intensity that Poppy thought one of her bones might break, she turned her attention back to her patient.

Sophie clambered to stand again, pacing the length of the board with Poppy right by her side. The shed fell silent, the shearers finishing the run in an unspoken agreement for an early smoko. What Poppy wouldn't do to blink them all away, but instead, she trained her eyes on Rick as he re-entered the shed. 'Are they on their way?'

'Who?' A long pause followed as Rick glanced towards the others, his cocky assertiveness barely discernible. He looked back at her. 'I got the wife. And the scissors.'

She sucked in an impatient breath. Despite her complete distrust of him, she needed to know, deep down, that he might recognise the enormity of the situation and set his perpetual conceit aside for the duration of what she was very sure was about to happen. 'You need to call 000 *now,* Rick. Put your food down and *ring.* I'm not a midwife and don't like the idea of becoming one, especially in a filthy shearing shed.'

Pain gripped Poppy's hand once more, and she turned back to Sophie, who was whimpering through another contraction. The poor young woman was petrified, fear of the unknown written all over her face. Poppy felt the same but she dug deep to hide it. She didn't care what Rick thought of her right now—how capable or not she was. Keeping everyone safe in this strenuous situation was the most important thing.

'Listen, Soph. I'm a nurse, but I've never delivered a baby. We're going to need to learn together, okay?'

Sophie's head rocked in a pained nod as she sucked in quick panting puffs, the relief clear in her eyes despite fear fighting for her attention. Poppy strained to recall the small midwifery unit from university, drawing calming breaths of chilled, late-afternoon air as it crept into the shed. Moving to the farmer's house was no longer an option. Sophie was on all fours, her overwhelming urge to push all-consuming. Early smoko declared, the shearers' mouths slowed with every bite.

Poppy's eyes flew up as Rick approached.

'Are they coming?' It came out as more of a bark—an order—and for a split moment, she raised her guard. He'd always been arrogant, but she'd only ever seen it as confident. But now all she could see was a man who wore possessiveness as a second, more hidden layer, a man she knew she'd wasted two years of her life on, despite Jimmy's subtle warnings she'd stubbornly chosen to ignore. 'I *need* to speak with them if we want this baby to arrive safely.' She lowered her voice, not wanting to escalate Sophie's fear.

'I can't get . . . reception.' His hands fell to his sides, his eyes rolling, like she was purposefully asking him to do the impossible.

And then and there, she realised another true fact about him. It didn't matter what the situation was. If Rick wasn't running the show—in control—then he wasn't happy, regardless of how desperate or important it was to anyone else. But she needed help, and for once, he wasn't the one demanding control over the situation.

'Dave, get those towels laid out on the board behind me, and make enough room for Sophie to lie down. Rick, put the hot water beside me, and try the ambulance again.' Grateful that the farmer's wife had sent along a cake of soap, she snatched it up and washed her hands.

'It won't make any difference.' He stared at her flatly.

'Just. Do. It.'

He let out a long, impatient breath, but tried again.

Relief flooded Poppy at the sound of the dial tone connecting.

'Put it on loudspeaker.' Kneeling beside Sophie, she rubbed her back, begging the connection not to fail. 'Come on, Soph. I need you to lie down. We need to see how close you are.'

Sophie struggled to shift her awkward belly while the increasing pain continued to come more and more frequently. Poppy waited for the next contraction to finish as she grabbed another towel and covered Sophie's lower half, all too aware of the sets of eyes watching on with curious interest.

The phone connected, the woman's voice on the other end of the line filling her with sheer relief. 'We need an ambulance. We have a baby on the way, in a shearing shed.' She didn't miss the quiver in her voice, desperately hoping Rick hadn't picked up on it too. But she wasn't about to risk a look his way to check.

Sophie let out another loud cry.

Poppy gave the address as the operator asked more questions.

'An ambulance is on its way. I'm here with you until they arrive.' The only thing more relieving for Poppy was the thought of them arriving before this baby did.

'Until the bloody call drops out,' Rick said, his sarcasm thick.

'That's enough, Rick!' Poppy's words hissed out before she turned to Sophie, her adrenaline tipping towards panic as she spoke to the operator again.

'I've checked how she's progressing. She's maybe seven centimetres?' It was a guess, but that had to be better than nothing, and Poppy stared at the phone, the wait excruciating. She caught sight of the farmer's wife standing near the wool table, her shaking hand hovering over her mouth as she watched on. Poppy beckoned her over with an urgent nod. If nothing else, the support from another woman would do Sophie the world of good, not to mention herself, while dealing with this baby who was in a rush to arrive.

'Breathe through it, Soph. You can't push yet.' The ten minutes between that check and the operator asking her to reassess Sophie's progress felt like an eternity.

'I think she could be ten centimetres.' *Please tell me that's not possible. She's only been in labour for*—Poppy glanced up at the shed clock ticking ridiculously quickly. How had it been thirty minutes since Sophie's first scream of pain? Weren't first-time babies notoriously slow to arrive?

'Okay, then. You need to tell her that she can push now.'

'But . . . the ambulance isn't here yet.' She needed *them* to take over, to do this. *Not her*. She didn't want to be responsible for anything going wrong. Would she have to leave Tasmania next, too mortified for failing to help this woman in such a crucial time of need?

Not this time. She was staying, and not even Rick was going to ruin what she had going for her.

Sophie let out a determined yell as she gritted her teeth for the next contraction.

'Right, Soph, we can do this together.' Sophie's next scream caused the remaining sheep in the pens to shuffle in panic amongst themselves, and the shearers recoiled their bodies, their toughened faces a picture of distressed unease mixed with genuine wonderment. In the distance, the faint sound of a siren floated on the bleak air.

'How do you know all this?' Rick's tone held scepticism meshed with a heavy dose of distrust as he watched from a safe distance, his gaze daring to hold her to account rather than at the ready should she need help. She'd never told him she had studied nursing. It hadn't seemed important at the time.

She looked up at him, in that moment, realising that nothing had changed. He was still the guy who was blinded by his own good looks and privileged upbringing, the one who didn't know who he truly was, desperate to impress but only able to offer empty loyalty and devotion to his family—anyone—believing his superficial love was worth it.

Tiffany. Where was she now? Left out to dry because the thrill of chasing her instead—two whole states away—gave him all the self-deserving worth and satisfaction he thought he needed to feel like he was actually important.

And she was still the woman who, despite believing she was innocent, had walked away instead of trying to prove herself by dramatic actions and empty words, even if it cost her everything.

'Wait at the front gate, Rick. Wave the ambulance down so they know where to come.' She implored herself to smile, but all it felt was hollow when it came to him.

With a dissatisfied frown and an apathetic nod, he headed outside.

As the sirens grew louder, so did Sophie. Shrill, tired groans were making her hoarse, and she panted between each gripping pain, sweat dripping from her face. The farmer's wife knelt beside her, sympathetically dabbing her forehead with the warm face washer, her earnest smile encouraging her to keep going as she held Sophie's hand.

When Poppy looked back at Sophie, to her surprise, a dark brown head of hair was crowning. 'Okay, Soph. You need to pant. Little puffs, nothing more.' Poppy blew short pants with her as the way-too-young mother fought back against the unrelenting urge to push.

A fresh cause for alarm dawned. Poppy had no idea if the baby was facing the correct way or not, and an alarming wave of worry filled her. 'Puff, Soph. Little puffs. You're doing great.' She blew the stray hair falling around her face aside, only for it to float back in place once more, the anticipation on her face undeniable. This experience was scary and exhilarating, leaving her with a new respect for every mother who had ever gone through this. A little person was about to enter the world, and she could hardly believe she was about to be a part of it.

The sirens ceased, and Poppy felt another rush of adrenaline buzz down her arms and inside her chest. A chilly draft breezed over them, and her body shook in a shiver. Curiosity drew the shearers in a little closer, their mouths agape as she urgently glanced at the doorway.

Come on, or you'll be too late! She looked back. 'Soph, I can see your baby!'

Calm, heavy footsteps paced towards her with purpose, but not fast enough for Poppy. Tiny shoulders were appearing and she held a towel under the baby's head as the paramedics moved either side of her, their reassuring smiles at odds with her nervous energy. Weren't they going to step in, take over from her? Why weren't they doing anything?

'That's it. You're doing great. Keep supporting the baby with each contraction.' Poppy leaned in, cradling the baby's back as it gently slid into the world.

'It's a girl!' Poppy beamed, looking at the farmer's wife, then at Sophie. Claps erupted in the shed, accompanied by loud cheers and whooping.

Rick stared, dumbfounded.

The healthy baby sucked in her first mouthful of frightfully cold air, immediately crumpling her face and letting out a noisy cry. Sheep scattered in the pens.

Ever so carefully and tenderly, Poppy handed the baby to one of the paramedics before shuffling aside, exhausted, resting on her haunches. She soaked in the atmosphere of the shed with disbelieving eyes, and a deep irony of the situation struck her. Here she was, being a nurse, in a shearing shed of all places, when she'd fought so hard not to take on the profession.

This was a moment she would never forget.

Chapter Thirty-Eight

If Tasmania's weather could be summed up in one simple analogy, its steely cold air and determined gales could quite literally fling a rooster over Bass Strait. LJ attempted to blow warmth into his fingers as he pulled up at George's property, his ute loaded with bags of concrete, new pickets, railings, and thick vertical support posts, along with the crisp white paint George had requested. If shearing wasn't an option, then he had to find another way to earn some money, and George's place was in drastic need of a makeover. The old man had been at him for quite some time to do some reno work, so he decided it was high time he started.

Digging post holes, throwing in support posts and pouring concrete to secure them should have been therapeutic, but all it did was give him too much time to ponder how his family farm was ticking along. He stood, swallowing, the work hard enough that he wiped his brow with the back of his hand, but not distracting enough to quell his niggling worry.

Miles . . . How many changes—good or bad—had he made? The nauseous feeling in the pit of his gut each time he thought of the future for the farm never eased. How had things degenerated to this point?

He thrust another post into a fresh hole harder than he'd intended, using a spirit level to check it was straight. It didn't matter what Miles thought of him.

But his father? Before Miles had rejected using his team for crutching, he would've banked on his dad standing up for him, ensuring they gave his team the work, regardless of what he thought about LJ buying the run. But now? It was what hurt him more than anything.

At lunchtime, George tottered out from the house. 'My, that looks a lot better already.'

LJ stepped forward, accepting the plate with a steaming hot pie and sauce that George handed to him.

'It should keep the dogs in.' Rowdy thumped her tail on the verandah, her head lying on her paws as her bright eyes watched on. Sammy was curled up on an old rug next to the front door, his nose tucked under his tail.

'Where's Jazz?' LJ aimed for casual, hoping George didn't pick up on his interest. He took a bite, and the sloppy meat from the pie dribbled down his chin, making him dive forward over his plate as it fell with a splat.

'She's with Poppy. Told her it'd be a good idea to take Jazz to the sheds now she's a bit older, keep her tied up, and the like. You know, get her familiar with the smells and noise.'

'Huh.' LJ did know. His working kelpie he'd trained from a pup, remained at the family farm. His heart pined for the company of the dog he loved. He'd left it at the farm, thinking his father might use it, but in reality, it probably hadn't been let off the chain for a run since he'd left, if he knew his brother.

Another dribble of meat fell, time landing at his feet. In a flash, Rowdy sprang from the verandah and vacuumed up its deliciousness in seconds. She gazed up at him, her delighted tongue licking her lips as she waited for more.

'Sorry, girl, the rest is all mine.' He bent forward to pat her while his thoughts swirled with images of Poppy. Rick was working with her, so he'd heard on the shearer's grapevine, along with the rumour she was his girlfriend. He wished the "sometimes useful" form of communication wasn't as effective as it was right now. He might think the guy was a piece of work, but surely she was smart enough to steer clear of him.

But nothing was going on between them, even if he couldn't get her tender touch out of his mind. So it really wasn't any of his business. He'd done everything to let her down. He needed to face the facts. She was gone, and he'd missed his chance. The ache of loneliness in his chest intensified.

It was late afternoon when the sound of a car approaching had him lifting his head above the railings to see Poppy arriving. His jaw tightened, focusing on the fence, desperate to stop the heat rising on the back of his neck, and the smile coaxing his dark five o'clock shadow into a way-too-pleased smile as he concentrated on her more than the holes he was meant to be pre-drilling.

George was resting on a tatty couch on the verandah, which had seen better days. LJ had positioned it to catch the rays of warmth while ensuring it stayed out of any bad weather—a given around these parts. Sammy was snuggled across the old man's knees like a cosy blanket.

The pup lifted his head and sat up, stretching tall and yawning with a whine as Poppy pulled up. He leapt from George's lap, racing towards the car.

A perky face on the passenger seat popped up like a jack-in-the-box, watching with keen eyes. Before Poppy had fully opened her door, Jazz shot out, racing towards her brother, her mother, LJ, and anyone else willing to embrace her loving licks.

As Poppy stepped from the car, Rowdy nosed her hand. 'Hey, beautiful girl.'

Despite his best efforts, LJ watched on, entranced by Poppy's engaging smile as she lovingly patted Rowdy. But a disappointed frown filled his brow. There was no use wishing for something he couldn't have.

Jazz bounded up the steps, cleaning up the meat pie remnants before one plate smashed to the ground below. Leaping from the verandah, she pounded towards a magpie down the yard who escaped her playful snap by a whisker before Sammy followed suit. The pups wrestled with sassy barks and growls.

LJ paused, hammer in hand, as Poppy approached.

'What are you doing here?' She frowned inquisitively.

'Just filling in my time.' He shrugged, angling away

from her searching gaze. He still found it hard to hide his disappointment at her leaving. He might not deserve an apology, but she should have at least given him, or someone else in the team, an explanation as to why she was going. They were her family too. Couldn't she see that?

'Yeah, I heard. I'm sorry.'

Bloody shearer's telegraph.

'What? Sorry you didn't say goodbye?' He watched her a moment too long, saw the challenge dancing in her eyes. But he couldn't hide the jab his tongue was desperate to say. 'Or sorry you were leaving to join Sweeny?' To his annoyance, she didn't look that taken aback.

'About time you got that fence fixed,' she teased George, a soft smile lingering on her lips, her eyes never leaving him.

Smooth, real smooth. He narrowed his gaze right back at her.

'The rabbits are going to hate you for it, George. How are they going to get their feed of daisies now?' LJ's insides danced with spectacular jolts, immediate surprise apparent on his face before he quickly masked it with an easy smile, the one he was well practised at using, before Sam had passed away. It had been a long time since a woman had tangled with his mind. Her smart eyebrow had almost sent him spinning that first day. And now, with her expression so enchanting, he found himself wanting to bury his face in her neck and breathe in her perfume.

Brow creased, he tipped his head to the side, if for nothing else, to break the locked gaze they'd just shared. With Sam's mischievous smile reminding him every day of his eternal absence, it had been near impossible for LJ to greet the world with his usual optimism. But this woman, with a smile so large it radiated warmth that could cut through a minus-three-degree frost, had him rethinking what love might actually mean to him. His heart raced alongside his thoughts.

'Oh, I almost forgot.' Poppy turned, jogging back to her car before reaching into the passenger side and removing a large pot. As she walked past him, he strained to catch a waft of her fragrance, even if it was out of bounds.

Poppy turned her attention to him from the corner of her eye, her smile ever so subtle, alluring, and totally enthralling him. Was there no end to the torment from this woman?

'Oh, no, you don't,' she chided, angling the pot out of his reach.

'You can have some if you finish the fence. I promise.' She paused, making a show of glancing around before catching his eye once more. 'Then again, you might go hungry.'

A deliciously playful smile caressed her lips. And her earnest dark eyes—the depth within them made him equally nervous and unashamedly determined. He was in deeper than he'd thought was possible, and even more surprisingly, he wasn't searching for a quick escape anymore. How could one woman turn his heart around so quickly and profoundly?

He had to—no, needed to—get her back on his team.

He *wanted* her in his life.

He needed to find out if Rick was telling the truth. Was she still with him?

Walking over the broken stepping stones LJ planned on replacing next, she called over her shoulder. 'Then again, it might be one of George's skinned rabbits with a daisy in its mouth.' She patted the pot as she turned away, her sexy-as-all-heck butt gliding towards the front door, then disappearing inside.

LJ rubbed a hand over his face in an effort to gather some semblance of control over his erratic emotions. Blinking in her direction one last time, he swung the hammer and hit the nail dead on, driving it with acute precision as his heart hammered. Was he turning this whole thing into something more than it could ever be?

The moment Poppy laid eyes on LJ in his rolled-up sleeves, his strong, dusty hands and his work boots scuffed to perfection, her heart had flip-flopped. Then the guilt set in. But some explanations weren't necessary, she reminded herself. He was consistently inconsistent, and she needed more in her life than someone who couldn't make up his mind.

But her senses were on high alert, and it had nothing to do with the delicious fall-off-the-bone chicken swimming in the mouth-watering stock she'd slow-cooked earlier. It had everything to do with her ex-boss standing not twenty feet away, outside. George was a cunning old man. A dinner suggestion with soup on the menu— how convenient. She'd been set up, or rather, they both had. LJ appeared equally rattled, even shocked at her arrival.

And what was she meant to talk about at the dinner table? How working in Sweeny's team was emotionally exhausting?

How working with her ex felt like torture?

His warning to stay away, that day in Ralph's shed, was still crystal clear in her mind. But she could look after herself. And she would.

The tantalising aroma of garlic bread filled the kitchen, and she pulled it out of the oven, draping it in foil. As she dished up the soup, her new phone buzzed on the kitchen bench.

'Hi, Dad.'

'How's work?' He sounded preoccupied, papers rustling in the background.

'Good.' Boots dropped to the verandah outside, the screen door squeaking as someone stepped inside.

'It's been busy, and I delivered a baby, which was a little out of my league.' She impatiently blew a strand of hair away from her face.

Damn these lies. Standing with her back to the doorway, she waited for George to come inside and sit down at the kitchen table.

'It was truly amazing. I brought a baby girl into the world.' Never in her wildest dreams had she considered midwifery while studying nursing.

'Thanks, Dad. Bye.' She ended the call and a cautious smile rose on her lips. He might be a tad overprotective, but that's why she loved him. What she didn't like the sound of was the headaches he'd been suffering from for the past month.

'So, you're a nurse now?' LJ's deep voice was laced with both intrigue and a distinct smidge of suspicion, and she failed to disguise the slight jolt that rifled through her as she swung around to face him, slow heat creeping up her neck.

'I am . . . or, um, I was?' she checked herself, desperately scratching for the right words, her mind rattling between all the mis-truths she was collecting, and had to remember. 'The shedhand in Sweeny's team had her baby in the shed. I had to deliver it.'

See, you didn't lie— this time.

That feeling of exhilaration she'd experienced, seeing Sophie's baby opening her eyes to discover cobwebs and wooden rafters and smells of lanolin and sweat around her for the first time, gave rise to a consoling smile. The overwhelming sensation of holding the bub in her arms, while sheep bleated in pens and awkward shearers stretched their lanky necks to admire the radiant newborn face. In so many ways, it was a shocking entry into the world. And at the same time, so incredibly enchanting.

Memories raced as she shied from his gaze, busying herself with the soup spoons in George's cutlery drawer, while desperately searching for some skerrick of credibility she felt bereft of. But his eyes were searing her through her clothing to the skin on her back.

'That's got to be a first. I see Sweeny can't let go of a good shedhand until the eleventh hour. Is she back at work yet?' His tone was sharp, thick with disgust.

His eyes locked with hers as she spun back, her heart thundering with nervous excitement at how much more handsome he'd become since she'd left his team. And damn it. How could one guy cast such a powerful spell over her, especially when it suited her to be angry with him?

'Not if I have a say.' But with Sophie gone, more than ever, the team needed another shedhand, fast.

'Why didn't you tell me you were leaving?' His words were light but cut deep as his gaze held her with sadness.

'I tried to. But you were all tied up with your girlfriend.' She waved her hand in the air as if that explained her actions away. She wasn't about to let him off the hook, even if he was being Mr—oh so infuriatingly—Nice Guy.

The surprise and realisation that shimmied over his features left her bewildered. Jacinta had certainly made it clear she knew LJ *well*. Besides, she had no claim to his affections. She'd allowed herself to be just as caught up in the moment as he was. His actions since had expressed nothing but a desire to keep his distance.

'I don't like that you're working with Sweeny. He's bad news.' She chose to ignore the concern now filling his gaze, instead planting her hands on her hips.

'So, suddenly you're interested in looking out for me? What did you expect me to do? You knew I needed work and you weren't finding any for me, or the rest of the team.'

Had she gone too far? She had. She shied from the immediate hurt filling his beautiful face, inwardly wincing at her own words. They'd slipped out. What was worse was it wasn't how she'd wanted to tell him she'd wrestled with her decision, agonising at the thought of leaving the team she wished she could still call hers. Or how she'd longed for him to beg her to stay. But she didn't like his accusing tone either, so he could take his concern and shove it, thank you very much. He'd left her with no choice. Couldn't he see that?

A prickly silence fell between them before LJ finally spoke.

'So, how's it going with Sweeny then? His intense gaze bore into her, causing her infuriation to swell. Wasn't he happy without her in his team? He hadn't asked her back. And if he did, she'd tell him no.

'It's fine.' She finished off with a congenial smile, hoping the subject could be dropped. It was dancing way too close to her all-too-real cliff edge, and the rubble was getting slippery.

Dinner was filled with quiet chatter, mainly between LJ and George, with Poppy sneaking cautious glances towards LJ with increasing frequency. Her head was telling her to let him go, but her heart yelled at her to let him back into her life. Why was this man so hard to ignore and forget?

Exasperated, she focused her attention on the three dogs lying hard against the warmth of the AGA oven, their bodies rising and falling in blissful silence.

Keep watching the dogs, Poppy. It was simple enough to do, and a quiet sigh eased from her lips. If only her life was as carefree as theirs was, she'd be home and hosed.

Constantly on the tip of her tongue was the urge to ask LJ about any work coming up, other than Oxley Falls. But with the sentiment of their little tiff earlier still hanging in the air, she couldn't bring herself to do it.

Was she being too hopeful?

Downright stupid?

Were they even talking anymore?

Reality set in. There was no point in hoping to shift back to his team. Sweeny's sheds were giving her all the work she required to ensure she could stay, even if Rick haunted her every move.

For reasons that baffled Poppy, LJ wasn't in any rush to leave George's, and she let out an irritated huff as she plunged the plates and cutlery into the soapy suds, scrubbing them formidably, then placing them into the dish drainer with an effective clunk. She'd wanted to be the last to leave, making sure George knew about the food in the freezer she'd placed there earlier, then check his doors were locked.

George and LJ took their mugs into the lounge room, a poky space with dust streaking the air as George took the single recliner, relishing the company with a broad smile. With only a small, two-seater couch remaining, Poppy frowned, considering where she was supposed to sit, the idea that George had once again set her up a very strong contender. She continued standing, shaking her head in annoyance before finally relenting, taking a seat next to LJ with a disgruntled slump. She could have sworn she'd seen a delighted smirk creep over his lips.

'How's the farm going, LJ?' George lay back on his

recliner with his hands interlaced over his satisfied belly. 'Has Miles forgiven you for dobbing him in all those years ago?' He gave a light chuckle.

'Who's Miles?' She searched LJ's face with renewed interest, hoping it would distract her from the way her heart was suddenly racing thanks to his leg pressing against hers.

'He's my younger brother. And no, George. Don't think I'll have any say over what happens on the farm now. Miles has taken over. Didn't even employ us to do the crutching.'

His brother didn't employ his team? Farming families were a tight-knit bunch, with Rick's no different. Rick's brother was his shearing contractor. If he'd been doing her job and made the mistake she had, regardless of the cost, they would never have sacked him on the spot like they had her. Farming families might not always forgive, but they stuck together.

'Well, that's no good, lad. I hope you're not going to give up that easily. That boy doesn't love the farm. He'll never make it half as successful as you could.'

Poppy's eyes were now trained on LJ. Was he going to let some family rift keep him from the family farm he clearly loved? Could whatever was going on be that bad?

'It doesn't matter. I'm focusing on the run now.' His quick side-eye immediately rankled her. Was he trying to prove a point?

Or was he subtly trying to say he didn't like how things had ended and he'd do anything to get her back?

Or was that simply wishful thinking?

LJ and George discussed the weather, rainfall,

paddocks, and, of all things, rocks. Poppy crossed a leg and kicked her foot in the air as she forced herself not to roll her eyes. What was so damned interesting about rocks? She didn't know where he lived and didn't care. What she wanted was for him to leave.

Finally, albeit with wobbly legs, George managed to find his feet and stand, bidding them goodnight with a contented wave and a cheeky smile as he eyed them both.

She waited . . . staring at the walls, making a mental note to dust the old gas heater, empty the kitchen bin, thinking—stupidly—that if she waited long enough, LJ might take the hint and hop up, then leave. She raised an eyebrow at him, even though he was keenly absorbed in watching his coffee cup.

On the verge of wanting to give him his marching orders, she finally turned in her seat to face him, suddenly wanting to feel the subtle growth of his whiskers beneath her lips because his face held all the sadness of a lost little boy.

He blinked his reverie away as he turned to her. 'That must've been scary, delivering a baby in the shed. Can't say I've ever heard of that one before.' His voice was whisper-thin, genuine, and full of empathy, and Poppy wasn't convinced it was what he'd actually wanted to say.

'It was a bit.' She searched George's threadbare carpet. Couldn't she just tell him she had switched into nurse mode because, well, she was a nurse? Then, at least her untruthfulness with one person could end.

'But we managed. Everyone listened and did what I asked.' She smiled, warmth filling her core as she thought back to the tiny baby, all slippery and warm in her hands, and tenderly delicate. It was an experience she'd treasure for the rest of her life. Her reluctant smile lifted to his, and her heart jolted as he leaned closer, watching her, studying her with eyes full and deep, his delicious smile hovering on his lips.

LJ's heart was a thundering mess, racing like a bullet as he stared into Poppy's dark, engaging eyes, then watched her exquisite lips as they parted softly. Why couldn't he tell her to leave Sweeny and come back to his team—to him?

Because he had no work, that's why.

What she'd done, delivering a baby in a shed? Seriously, that was an action to be applauded. How she'd known what to do was beyond him, but it stirred in him feelings of admiration, attraction and overwhelming awe. This woman could handle anything, and right now, it didn't matter that she hadn't told him she was leaving his team. He wanted to get closer to those irresistible lips.

'I.' He paused, wrangling whether he should verbalise out loud the fact that she still had a boyfriend. If he did, it would answer his question once and for all—the one he desperately hoped wasn't true. But if he didn't? Then he could kiss her like his life depended on it, honestly not knowing he was doing anything wrong.

He drew in a slow breath, summoning what little courage he had left, knowing he wouldn't be able to live with himself unless he knew all the facts first. 'I heard you and Rick were back together.' He searched her face, not shying away, not moving a millimetre closer, simply maintaining their proximity, so close, so tempting. He attempted to subdue his unintended frown he knew full well might write off all his chances of kissing her right there and then.

Poppy recoiled abruptly, filling him with the apprehension he'd been so fearful of. 'Well, you're wrong.' She stood and walked to the door, the air next to him turning icy-cold without her body next to his. She glanced back with what looked like agitation, even anger, before she walked out of the room.

LJ sat shell-shocked. He'd been so sure. When Rick had said he was going to move in with her when he'd rung to tell him he was joining Sweeny's team, what else was he meant to think?

Now, the moment was gone. But it was for the best, he tried to reassure himself. Without work, he couldn't offer anyone financial security. And with Sam's looming inquiry— He just might lose everything.

Something twisted deep in his gut, like shame, maybe, or regret. He'd let fear and assumptions poison what might have been the most important conversation of his life.

Chapter Thirty-Nine

The only thing on LJ's mind as he walked down Grandma Aimee's hallway to the kitchen, was his desperate need for a strong coffee. So, when his phone rang to the tune of Black Betty, he politely ignored it.

Until it rang again.

Reluctantly, he tugged the phone from his pocket, hoping it might be some work for the team.

'Hello.'

'Is this Mr Tanner?'

'Yes.' Weird. No one called him by his surname.

'Ah, good. I'd like to make an appointment with you regarding—'

'Look. I don't want your solar panels, and I like my phone plan. Thanks.' He hung up, the prospect of another week without work gnawing heavily within him. He had to find some way to keep Take Two Shearers afloat. He ran a rough hand through his hair as he flicked on the kettle, allowing a deflated sigh to seep from his lungs.

It had almost killed him that he'd had to stand the team down for the week, but Little Trev was hanging in there, doing mowing and garden jobs to make ends meet. Apart from Dave and now Paul, who had moved across to Sweeny, the other boys were catching up with farm jobs on their own properties. They'd reassured him that they appreciated the "downtime" to prepare for crops, but his hunch told him they were just being polite, exactly what he didn't deserve.

And his two female shedhands, while settling down in the team, had startled him when they'd asked about Poppy returning. But with no work from him, and the reliable shearing grapevine suggesting Sweeny was a shedhand down, he was expecting to hear the brazen thief had poached them for himself too. It was all just a matter of time.

At least he was getting a chance to do more around Grandma Aimee's house. He felt he owed it to her, having lived with her for twelve months after his father had recognised he and Miles weren't getting along, suggesting he move out—just for a while. It had been the final blow and felt like his father's feelings about the purchase of the shearing run were being cemented for good.

When the tune on his phone rang through the air for a second time, he impatiently snatched it up, ready to tell the caller he would block their number. But before he was able to open his mouth, the distinctly perturbed voice on the other end pulled him up short.

'Mr Tanner. I can most adamantly tell you I am not trying to sell you anything, and I suggest you hear me out before you hang up on me again. I will keep calling until you do.'

LJ swallowed hard.

'Good,' the voice said, almost triumphantly. 'It has cost me a great deal of time, and frustration to find you. Have you done this on purpose, perchance?'

Per what? LJ scoffed to himself. 'No.' It pleased him to offer this pompous-sounding man a single-word reply, delivering it with a distinctive 'pffft' tone.

'It will be in your best interest to meet with me immediately. We need to discuss the circumstances surrounding the death of Samuel Whittington.'

The words hit him like physical blows. Jacinta's warnings flooded back like a collection of suffocating bush flies.

WorkSafe, he mouthed.

Oh, crap.

This was it, the moment when everyone would realise it was Lincoln John Tanner who had let his best mate die under his watch.

Sam's image flashed before him—celebrating their National Championship success, dancing on a tabletop at The Night's Helmsmen with his fifth beer raised high.

'LJ, the National Title winner, with Sammy a close second. Woohoo!' Sam tipped his head back, froth sliding down his chin as he raised his empty glass. 'Oh, yeah!'

Another flash: Sam enraged by his father's treatment. 'He left us with nothing but a lifetime of torment.' His fist pounded the table, making LJ jump. 'Mum still can't leave the house some days. The bastard told her she'd be dead if he ever saw us again. I was six!'

LJ stared at the wall as he lowered the phone, long after the call had ended. Being forced to remember might mean he'd never forgive himself. Or live with himself.

And when everyone heard what he had done . . . his life would be over.

Chapter forty

Heavy overnight frost clung desperately across much of Longford and the surrounding districts, reluctant to let the sun melt its grasp. Poppy poked a stick at a puddle, finding ice more than five millimetres thick. Jazz rushed to investigate, her nose nudging under Poppy's finger curiously, tail swishing.

The caravans in the park glistened thanks to the light dusting of snow, making Poppy tug her beanie tighter around her ears. Jazz bounded beside her in a new Driza-Bone jacket—all legs and no real body—and it worried Poppy she didn't have enough baby fat to keep her warm.

Adrian appeared from the side door of his house, waving enthusiastically. She smiled back. Was there no end to his zest for life?

Mrs Potter trudged outside after him, with a fixed,

sullen expression, a steaming bucket of water in hand. Adrian hurried along the road as Jazz excitedly ran to his side for a cuddle.

Poppy was some distance behind, trying not to slip and keeping one eye on Mrs Potter, waiting for the inevitable wrath the moment she noticed Jazz. But her chest swelled as she watched her little dog snuggle Adrian, her paws hugging his neck as she licked him with kisses.

And then it came. 'What do you think you're doin' with that mutt in my caravan park? I warned you—no dogs! Don't go thinkin' that pretty little face of yours will get you outta this,' she warned with a pointed finger. 'That dog is prohibited!' She flung her free arm in rage before swinging to her car, bucket in hand.

'Mrs Potter, don't!' Poppy reached out her hand, horror doing little to sway the woman's filthy mood.

Mrs Potter spun back. 'Don't you tell me *don't*, girly.' Before Poppy could respond, she lifted the bucket, tossing steaming water onto the windscreen of her car. An instantaneous crack filled the air.

'Adrian!' Mrs Potter hollered.

Adrian ran towards the house as Poppy hurried to scoop the pup into her arms, feeling guilty for leaving Adrian to deal with his ranting mother. Saturday mornings meant a trip to George's for a cuppa and a scone from the batch she'd baked this morning. And after that, she was visiting Sophie, excited to have her first cuddle.

Only a faint wisp of smoke rose from the chimney when Poppy pulled up in front of the smart picket fence. She had to admit, LJ had done a great job. A tingle of excitement ran through her, thinking of his deliciously warm lips on hers, despite it happening so long ago. And he'd been incredibly close to doing it again the other night, right up until he'd effectively ruined the moment by mentioning Rick.

She walked towards the house, the ice crystals glistening in the slow-rising sun, reflecting off the white paint and making the entrance to the cottage look like a sparkling fairyland. Jazz trotted behind, her tail swaying frantically, but neither Rowdy nor Sammy came to greet them.

Poppy frowned as she looked about her, everything quiet and in its place. Skipping the steps to the verandah, desperate scratching from behind the door caught her attention. She smiled. They were inside with George.

George's frailty had been worrying her more and more, and she'd purchased a single electric blanket for his bed, hoping it would not only keep him warm but would give her some peace of mind when she wasn't there. Balancing the package under her arm, she knocked on the door, only to be greeted by a loud whine and sharp bark. Rowdy never made a noise unless something was—

Wrong.

Poppy pushed the door open. Rowdy and Sammy

rushed between her legs in a desperate dash for a toilet stop, Jazz hot on their heels, hoping for a game of chasey and a wrestle.

'Damn it.' George hadn't locked his door again, but right now, she wasn't complaining. Dumping the blanket and the scones on the kitchen table, she moved to the AGA, desperate to stoke up the fire despite the sparse coals clinging to life. It had all but gone out, leaving an unfamiliar icy chill. George never let the stove go out.

'George?'

Only the slow rhythmic drip, drip, drip of condensation falling from the ceiling into the bucket made a sound. Biting her lip, her worry grew. Was he just having a sleep-in? The tight hallway was no bigger than a lavatory room, and she hesitated, her eyes wide as she searched for the light switch, for movement, for sound.

Nothing.

'George?'

Opening the door to his bedroom, she stilled. On the bed, curled up in a tight ball with only two thin blankets, lay George, shivering with glazed eyes.

Poppy rushed to his side, followed by Rowdy, who jumped onto the bed, nuzzling the blankets in search of her master's cold hand.

'George, can you hear me?' He was incoherent, but breathing. With her phone to her ear as she waited for "000" to answer, she helped Rowdy shuffle under the thin covering, hoping the dog might transfer some of her warmth to him.

Racing back to the kitchen, she filled the kettle. It would

take time to boil on the AGA stovetop, but the fire was beginning to kick in, and besides, it was all she had. George liked to do things the old-fashioned way, refusing her offer of an electric kettle a couple of years ago.

Setting a teabag in a mug, she ran out to her car and started it up to idle, then called the pups to put them in their puppy pen in the shed. Back inside, she grabbed a hot water bottle from the laundry, shoving it under the hot tap water.

She tugged the electric blanket from its packaging. 'I'm a day too late,' she scolded herself, regret weighing heavily for not dropping by sooner. She snatched the alfoil roll from the drawer.

In George's room, she plugged in the blanket, turning it to the highest setting. Pulling out long lengths of alfoil, she draped it over George's body, then lay the warm blanket on top. Rowdy's nose poked out from the sheet, sniffing, and George wrapped his knobbly hand around his dog. Rowdy exhaled a loud, contented breath, and Poppy hurried back to the kitchen.

With the hot water bottle ready to go and a cup of steaming tea finally in her hands, she headed back to the bedroom. George gave a small cough as she neared, and she set the cuppa down on the bedside table. She squeezed his steadily warming hand, fighting to gain his attention.

'George? George, let's get something warm into you, okay?' Her smile was full of worry and sadness and concern, for George simply getting older and living on his own, and for her not being able to do more for her dear friend. He'd said 'sure, come on over,' when she'd been desperate to escape, his words almost beckoning her to drop everything in Bathurst, and stay. And she had. With just a few clothes she'd thrown together, her phone, and a whole lot of shame and regret, she'd arrived on his doorstep and swamped him in a hug she needed more than he did. But feeling the need to give him back his space and seek her own path, she'd ended up leaving him when he'd needed her most. Her throat clenched tight as her vision blurred. She looked down at him, searching his watery eyes, and they slowly blinked, studying her.

'Tha—. Thank you, m—my dear.' His body shuddered with another shiver, but he was beginning to take on a relieving shade of pink in his cheeks.

'Oh George, how did this happen?' Confident he was now warm enough, she gently eased him up, draping the warm electric blanket around his shoulders and making him comfortable with the pillow behind his back. She placed the hot water bottle on his chest. 'Here, have a sip of tea. It'll warm you up.' She fought to hide the distress in her smile as she held the cup to his lips, watching him sip.

'I—don't remember.' He shook his head in confusion as she rubbed his shoulders with daughterly love. 'But I'm sure glad you turned up.'

'Me too, George. Me too.' Poppy brushed a troubled tear aside.

Finishing his tea, Poppy wrapped George's dressing gown around his shoulders and walked him to her idling car. He slept all the way to hospital, his head resting against the reclined seat, rugs tucked in around his shoulders like he was wrapped in a cocoon. Poppy was sweating with the heater on high, and she glanced at him with concern. He had to make it. She couldn't lose him.

The hospital was ready for their arrival, and a wheelchair was waiting for George as she drove straight to the front entrance of Emergency. Poppy filled in and signed all of his paperwork, only leaving him when he was taken into the ward. With him safe, she had another visit to make. She hoped Sophie had experienced a better night than George had.

'Soph, she's gorgeous.' Poppy rocked the now sleeping baby in her arms, unwilling to put her down in her cot. When she'd first arrived, she had been greeted by dark, shadowed eyes and a wailing baby Rosie. Tiny clothes lay all over the couch beside an empty pizza box. But with the kettle on and scones, jam and cream ready on a plate, Sophie relaxed in the recliner, a tired smile gracing her face as Poppy played auntie.

'I'm not going back.' Sophie's comment broke the tranquillity, and Poppy heard both the gusto and passion with which it was spoken. 'He can't make me. This is my chance to be free of them.'

'You never have to feel forced to do anything,' Poppy reassured her. 'That's never okay.' But Sophie's reality lay in Poppy's arms. She needed to work if she was going to support her newborn daughter.

Sophie gave a sad nod, picking at her fingers buried in

her lap.

'Listen, someone else's opinion is not your responsibility.' If only she could believe that, but right now, giving advice was so much easier than taking it on herself.

'It's your choice and no one else's, no matter what they say.' Poppy leaned forward, tugging Sophie's hand from her lap and squeezing it as she urged a guarded smile from her friend.

'He came and saw me the other day.'

'Who did?' Poppy frowned as she sat back in surprise, resettling the startled Rosie, whose face was scrunched and ready to let rip with a cry.

'Sweeny. Said he wanted me back—that he needed me.' Her lower lip trembled. 'He told me to get rid of Rosie.'

Poppy's mouth gaped as she stared at Sophie with troubled concern. 'You're not considering it . . . are you?' The manipulation was breathtaking—Sweeny preying on a vulnerable teenager's fears to get a worker back.

'I don't know what to do.' Sophie's voice broke. 'I can't afford not to work, but I can't leave her. He said Rosie would be too much trouble and no other contractors would hire someone with a baby.'

Poppy's gaze fell to the rosebud lips and petite eyelashes resting in her arms. This child deserved her mother, and Sophie deserved better. There was no way she would let the young woman struggle or feel forced to work for someone who only thought of himself.

'Soph, promise me you'll keep Rosie. She needs you, and you need her.' Poppy's mind raced. 'Can you get by for the next couple of months without working?'

Sophie twisted her fingers. 'Maybe. I have some savings.'

Hope rose in Poppy's chest. She wasn't sure how yet, but she'd find a way to help Sophie without letting Sweeny exploit her desperation. Some battles were worth fighting, and this was definitely one of them.

'Well, then, I have an idea.'

Chapter Forty-One

With George still recuperating in hospital, LJ continued to work at his place, and Poppy dropped by each evening after work to help. He might have picked up on her response to his suggestion of the two of them working on George's house as a little shocked and a whole lot of cautious, but she'd agreed it would be both a welcome home surprise and that it would give him every chance to look after himself better.

But for LJ, it was the perfect excuse to be with her. Did this mean she'd wanted to spend more time with him, too? He had to hope so.

As the week went on, they found jobs to do which kept them away from one another, and he found himself wishing for an excuse just to bump into her—anything—to take her in his arms and feel those soft lips that had haunted him all week.

He kept himself busy, only going near her when she needed his advice or his muscles to help lift something. Mostly, he spent his time outside, replacing the iron on the roof.

Poppy's striking smile and sparkling eyes came to mind, drawing LJ from his lonely reverie and his hand stilled on the shower rail he'd finished securing in George's bathroom. His lips pressed together in an admiring smile. She possessed an inner beauty that stopped him in his tracks, despite his best intentions. He could smell her perfume lingering in the house well after she'd left. She was working and he wasn't, a fact that, if he were honest with himself, peeved him. What he wouldn't give to have her back in his team, so they could be working at George's house full-time, together, right now. He released a regretful sigh, removed the worn-out old tapware and replaced it with fresh, new ones.

By the following Sunday morning, all that was left to do was rip up the old carpet and replace it, and butterflies sprouted in his stomach as he arrived at George's.

Poppy wasn't due to arrive for another hour, and he needed something to distract him, so attacking the plumbing below the kitchen sink seemed like a good idea. It had a slow leak that had annoyed him all week, and it was something he could do while he waited.

LJ stood, stretching his back after bending under the cupboard for what had felt like hours. Stones on the driveway crunched, and his anticipation had his heart picking up speed. Dropping his tools, he sauntered to the front door, struggling to hide his nervous smile.

'LJ? Can you give me a hand?' Poppy waved her arms

impatiently before reaching deep inside the cabin of her car again, tugging hard.

Leaning against the doorframe, his arms crossed, he watched—almost a little ashamed by his delight—as Poppy tried tugging the heavy carpet out through her car window. With the end of the roll weighing down her shoulders, a frustrated groan coursed from her lips.

'Don't stand there like some stupid jackass, get over here and help me. Please!' Ducking away from the weight, she let the carpet drop onto the window frame and leaned over it, puffing.

Grinning, LJ jogged down the steps and strolled over. It took every inch of his self-control not to wrap his arms around her waist, to support her, of course—not tug her close.

And kiss her.

So instead, he scratched his chin—like that wasn't a dead giveaway he was trying to pretend not to notice her— suppressed his ridiculous grin, then opened the car door, letting the carpet flop away from the window to the ground with a dusty thud. Bundling it in his arms, he shot her a teasing smile, then strolled towards the house, a little too satisfied with his efforts, and earning himself a playful punch to the arm as he passed her. It was totally worth it.

George's humble house was steadily being transformed into an inviting home, with warmth and security to give them all peace of mind. He'd lived for all these years with the odd bits of furniture his brother and sister-in-law had owned before they passed away. It had been years since the wool market had paid satisfactorily to earn him an actual profit. But George had always been happy with his lot, remaining a bachelor, and LJ knew he would never expect all the improvements they were doing for him. But if the old man planned to continue living at home like he was adamant he wanted to, these changes were a priority.

'We did it.' Poppy stood with her hands on her hips as she surveyed the carpet-laying job they had managed to do to what LJ felt was a pretty good standard, all thanks to his crash course from Google.

She smiled his way, reaching out and offering her hand up for a celebratory high-five. LJ caught her small hand in his, his heart pounding as he dared to lace his fingers with hers. He gently squeezed, his grasp tightening as he slowly drew her towards him. She didn't object, accepting his invitation, taking steps closer to him until she stood chest to chest. Their interlaced hands lowered, and the air about them fizzed with electricity as they stared at one another, neither one looking to make the first move. Her eyes danced with, what was it, daring, longing, or was there a touch of mischief, laying out the challenge for him to follow through with the only thing he wanted? Was her face telling him that's what she wanted? Or was that his own hope playing tricks on him? But everything inside screamed at him to take the risk.

A whisper of a smile pinched at Poppy's lips, her gaze steady and captivating as she stared back at him. He studied her face, pulse quickening as his attention drifted from her lips to those mesmerising eyes that held him transfixed. He took in the gentle slope of her nose, the flush of pink across her cheekbones—a testament to her day's work. A loose strand had worked free from her thick braid, and without thinking, he reached up to brush it back, his fingers lingering as he tucked it behind her ear. The tenderness in his expression gave way to something deeper, more intense, as he lowered their entwined hands and drew closer.

He caught her looking at his scabbed cut on his forehead, her curious frown making him fight not to let it steal away this moment. Even Sam would have wanted someone as special as Poppy to come into his world.

With barely a breath of space between them, their noses touched, and the muscles in his cheeks twinged as her warm breath brushed his chin. He searched for a hint she might want to pull away. Closer again, his lips tentatively reached hers, pausing to savour their softness as he brushed them with his own. He kissed her gently, a delightful light-headedness filling him. She made him feel so . . . complete. What spell was she weaving around him?

Poppy drew back slowly, her smile reassuring. His heartbeat stammered as her forehead rested against his, and his breath caught when her fingertips found his jaw, tracing the coarse texture of his beard with featherlight strokes.

'Why did you decide to grow this?' Her voice was velvet-soft, intimate.

The question hit like a stone dropped into still water. His smile faded as he stared down at the worn carpet, wrestling with how much to reveal. Could he trust her with this?

'Hey, I'm sorry. I . . .' Her hands cupped his cheeks with such exquisite tenderness, his chest constricted. 'You don't have to answer.' She tipped her head to catch his eyes.

Yes, he did.

'Because of Sam.' The confession escaped on a shuddering breath. 'Sam always had a beard, like this. When he died, I needed something. Some way to carry him with me.' It felt right.' His shoulders lifted in a helpless shrug, eyes still downcast, until her gentle touch drew his face up again. He didn't need her sympathy. That he knew he didn't deserve. But she was still standing in front of him, even after he'd told her what it might cost him for the rest of his life, just to remember the best mate he'd ever had.

The warring impulses tore at him—the instinct to retreat from such vulnerable intimacy, battling against his desperate hunger for her compassion. Was it selfish to lean into her comfort when his heart still carried such complicated grief?

'It's a beautiful thing to do,' she whispered, rising on her toes to press her soft lips to his lower lip. Her thumb swept across where her lips had been as she settled back, studying him with eyes full of understanding.

'And for what it's worth, I think it's pretty darn sexy too.'

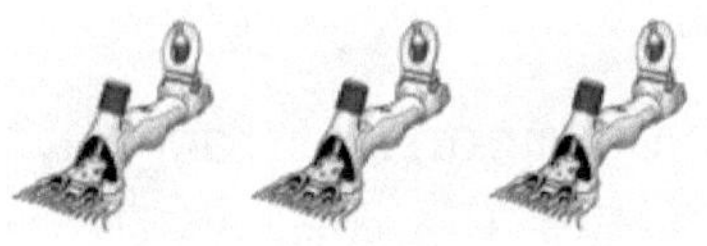

Was he imagining things, or had what he thought had happened at George's—actually happened? LJ sat on his bed as he ran both hands over his face, trying to remember Poppy's entrancing touch. She had kissed him because she'd *wanted* to.

But LJ reminded himself of his reality. It was only one moment, and maybe Poppy wasn't as caught up in it as he was? Had it meant as much to her as it did him? And why had he let his emotions get the better of him anyway? Because this woman was under his skin so deeply, he couldn't imagine her ever being anywhere else but with him.

But Poppy was working with Rick, in Sweeny's team, for as many weeks as she wanted. Word on the wind was Sweeny had all the sheds in the district until Christmas.

And he had one.

How could he not second-guess his chances with Poppy now, regardless of the intimacy they'd shared that continued to steal his every waking moment? She'd chosen to stay where Rick was working. Every guy knew if you stayed near the woman you wanted to be with, your chances of winning her over—or back—doubled. It had been nice while it lasted. If only he could shrug off her effect on him that easily.

With George's house done and dusted, it was back to Grandma Aimee's house to fill in his extended downtime. So, when he received a call from a local farmer asking about the team's availability, a slap from a fly swat could have bowled him over.

'I'd like to start tomorrow. Can you be ready?'

'Um, sure, Clancy. I mean—Yes!' LJ pressed fingers to his lips, his mind racing.

There was a long pause over the line, and LJ pulled his phone from his ear, concern immediately replacing his relief. Had the connection dropped out? Or . . . had he been hung up on again? It was becoming a well-worn habit he'd grown to expect. But Clancy's voice broke through his nervous anticipation.

'Listen, I know I shouldn't talk about your competitors with you, but I've had enough of Sweeny and his bloody light-fingered boys. Had all my combs and cutters go missing after they left last time, and the full oil drum was mysteriously drained dry. I'm telling you, it's no coincidence.'

LJ reeled from Clancy's call as he hung up. As a farmer, he clearly wasn't happy, and LJ felt the immense pressure to perform. But his team wouldn't steal, and he dialled the boys immediately. The best part about this job for him was that Clancy was an owner-classer. He wouldn't need Poppy—despite desperately wishing he had an excuse to bring her back. The family of three brothers were regular country jacks-of-all-trades, so there wasn't even a need for presser, which was perfect. Spider was tied up, having also joined Sweeny's team until LJ could offer him more work.

The only thing he was struggling to organise was a fifth shearer. Dave had stayed on with Sweeny, leaving him short. But there was one last option he could try, and it was worth a shot. It was about time they caught up anyway.

Late afternoon brought rays of setting sunlight poking through the roadside tree branches as LJ drove to the only shearing shop in Launceston. He needed a few supplies before the new shed, and, in a small way, going to the shop to purchase something for the job he loved offered him a glimmer of hope he was beginning to think he could only clutch at.

And from what Clancy had said, others around the district and surrounds shared his sentiment, sick and tired of being robbed, both of farming gear and a job well done. Maybe the flyers he'd spent hours distributing had worked after all?

LJ grabbed a box of new combs and cutters, and a new oil can—he'd left his last one at the shed they'd finished nearly two long months ago. The doorbell tingled behind him, encouraging the brisk air to mingle with the heater's warmth, sending a shiver down his spine.

LJ reached for his wallet, fingers already finding the worn leather in his back pocket, when a voice cut through the shop's quiet like a blade.

'Well, well, if it isn't Little Boy Wonder.'

His hand froze. That voice—cocky, dripping with challenge—belonged to only one person.

'Dunno what he's doing in a shop like this though.' Sweeny's words carried across the space with calculated precision. 'Heard he wasn't getting any work. Heard he wasn't getting any action at all.'

Rough laughter erupted from the cluster of men behind the voice, hands slapping backs in approval. LJ recognised most of them—Sweeny's crew, always ready to feed off their leader's slinging like scavengers.

LJ's jaw tightened as he slowly withdrew his wallet, every movement deliberate. Don't take the bait. Pay and leave. But his pulse had already quickened, adrenaline beginning its familiar burn through his veins.

What the hell is he talking about? LJ's mind raced. There was no way Poppy would consider any of those creeps.

But Rick? His stomach clenched as doubt crept in. He resisted the urge to turn around to see if he was amongst the group.

Heavy footsteps approached, deliberately slow, each one intended to throw him off kilter. LJ kept his back turned, focusing on the bills in his wallet, counting them twice.

'And didn't we have a good time at—' Sweeny's voice grew closer, more intimate, like he was sharing a secret. 'What shed was it again, boys?'

'The Tanner's!' someone called out, and fresh laughter rippled through the group.

LJ's blood turned ice cold. They'd been on his property.

'Are you familiar with that one, LJ?' Sweeny's tone was silk wrapped around a knife. 'Miles reckons the farm is running sweeter than ever now his interfering big brother isn't there to feed his father with harebrained ideas that cost the farm too much.'

He and Sam were regularly brainstorming ideas that could see the farm into the next generation. And Sam wanted to work alongside him to do it.

'And he tells me he has a nice little bit of fun happening on the side, in Launceston.' Sweeny was close enough now that LJ could smell his stale cigarette breath. 'The ladies of the house enjoy his company a real lot. Now there's a man who knows how to let his loins have a party.'

More laughter, louder now, emboldened their leader's confidence. LJ's knuckles went white around his wallet.

'Pity you couldn't learn a thing or two from him, Tanner. It might sweeten you up a bit.'

The final piece clicked into place with sickening clarity. Miles hadn't gone to Sam's funeral because he'd had a more pressing appointment. While LJ had stood at Sam's graveside, watching him being lowered into the earth, Miles had been—

LJ's chest constricted, but years of staying calm in high-pressure situations served him now. He kept his face carefully neutral, despite his breathing turning shallow. The counter edge bit into his palm as he gripped it, anchoring himself.

He could feel all eyes on him, waiting. This was what they'd come for—the show, the breakdown, the moment when grief and rage would finally crack his composure. They wanted him to explode, to give them something to talk about for weeks.

Instead, LJ turned slowly, each degree of movement measured and controlled. His broad frame gradually filled the space between himself and Sweeny's expectant smirk. The man barely reached LJ's collarbone, but his compact build suggested he'd met with fights in the past—thick neck, shoulders that strained his shirt, toughened hands—and had come out the victor.

The shop had gone quiet except for the electric hum of the drinks fridge. Even Sweeny's crew were silent, sensing the shift in atmosphere.

LJ studied Sweeny's face for a long moment, taking in the small, eager eyes, the way his tongue darted out to wet his lips in anticipation. Then he spoke, his voice barely above a whisper.

'My brother is not my concern.'

The lie tasted bitter, but it was strategic. It was better to think about Sam than Miles. Sam would always be his concern, his responsibility, his failure—but he wouldn't give Sweeny that weapon.

LJ took half a step closer, close enough that Sweeny had to crane his neck back to maintain eye contact. He caught the brief flicker of uncertainty that crossed the smaller man's features before the cocky mask slid back into place.

'And if you contemplate laying a hand on my classer,' LJ continued, his tone conversational, almost friendly, 'I will mark you myself with the elastrator, then tie your hands behind your back until your balls turn black and drop off.'

The agricultural reference wasn't lost on anyone in the room. They all knew what happened to rams when you left the rings on too long.

LJ's eyes narrowed, holding Sweeny's gaze with unwavering intensity. The air between them seemed to thicken. LJ didn't move.

'And that,' he said, his voice dropping even lower, 'is a promise.'

Chapter Forty-Two

The fluorescent lights flickered to life in Clancy's shed, interrupting the darkness of the early morning. The smell of mice was subtle, but the presence from their night escapades lay evident across the shearing board. The air lingered with damp lanolin, and LJ breathed it in like it was the lifeblood for his soul.

Strolling towards the shearing stands, he lifted his gear to the small shelf placed above stand two. Wary, large brown eyes stared up at him from behind the pens. Ever so slowly, the ewes stepped backwards, retreating to the far end of the catching pen.

With a considered turn, LJ surveyed the layout of this shed. He had never worked here before, and it was a superfine enterprise. Thoughts of his family farm dangled like a carrot on a stick, and he took in the multitude of pens this large capacity shed held. He might not have Poppy here with him, but at least he had work for his team. That alone was reassuring.

Clancy strolled up, offering a friendly slap on his shoulder. 'G'day, LJ. I'm bloody glad I picked up one of your flyers the other day. Found it floating around down the paddock of all things. Godsend, I say. Didn't know what I was going to do before that.'

'I'm glad you did too. We won't let you down.'

'That's music to my ears, mate.'

But the pressure was on, especially as Clancy would be in the shed the whole time, classing the wool. All they had to do was shear 'em clean and work quick, and they might be offered the job again. That's why the growers paid a little more for his team, right? No bloody way Sweeny could offer a service like that, even with Poppy.

Jase strolled up, dropping his gear to the board. 'Poppy not comin', boss?' The shearer offered a surprised smile as he got his handpiece ready. She was the one thing securing Sweeny's sheds, LJ was sure of it, and he'd lost her, not only for the team, but for himself, too. She'd have to have rocks in her head to consider coming back to his unreliable run.

LJ owned up to himself that he was missing her deeply. Their last kiss, their time together at George's, it had him longing for more, longer than it ought. He swallowed hard, forcing himself to focus on attaching the comb and cutter to his handpiece.

Worse than the longing was the promise he'd made in

anger—telling Sweeny he wouldn't hesitate to mark him like livestock. In that moment, every word had been true. Could he make a different kind of promise now, if Poppy thought him worthy enough?

His gaze swept across the woolly mass filling the shed, but his former classer refused to remove herself from his thoughts. He still couldn't believe Poppy had left his team for Sweeny's. The words burned in his mind. And if by some miraculous chance he secured work, would she return for a couple of weeks over what Sweeny could offer her, months of steady employment? He'd fired and rehired her well beyond any reasonable limit.

The rest of his crew strolled in, setting their gear up and trading news after their forced break. The familiar energy of a new shed buzzed in the brisk air, and B1 and B2 were fluffing their feathers and laughing as if genuinely happy to be back again.

Finally happy with the alignment of his comb and cutter, he tightened it with the shearer's screwdriver as a sense of irony filled his thoughts. The way they'd carried on when Poppy had first come to the shed suggested they were more suited to Sweeny's team than his. The bastard had made them an offer, but they'd turned him down flat, which he couldn't quite believe.

Setting his handpiece down to warm up, LJ's hopes soared. This job was the lucky break he needed—one he had to believe would lead to more work, more farmers willing to give him a shot just as Clancy had suggested. The opportunity felt tangible, within reach. Anticipation coursed through him like electricity.

But what excited LJ was the shearer he'd secured for the fifth stand.

Pa Pat. Not only did he complete the team, but his measured pace of twenty-five sheep per run created a steadying rhythm that ensured quality control and adherence to the Code of Practice.

'Let's get started, boys!' His newfound enthusiasm proved infectious, Jase grinning as he gripped the pen doors, offering a you've-got-this nod before striding in to retrieve his first ewe.

Yep, the team could feel it too—this might be their turning point.

Lunchtime arrived, and everyone enjoyed a hot dinner at the dining table, prepared by Clancy's wife. Roast lamb with an assortment of vegies and gravy was good enough to compare to his mother's, going down an absolute treat. Dessert was berry compote with vanilla ice cream and shortcake.

At half-past twelve, the team wandered back to the shed for their traditional board nap. LJ fell into step with his grandfather, who was patting his satisfied belly with a smug smile.

'Didn't you have a classer? Stan said you were real happy with her. A young woman, wasn't it?'

LJ's chest tightened. 'I did. But when my work dried up, she joined Sweeny's team. Now she's got steady employment and doesn't need me.' The truth of those words cut deep, and he turned away before Pa Pat's shrewd eyes could read much into his expression.

'What's her name?' Pat asked with casual interest.

'Fletcher. She comes from up north on the mainland.' He didn't bother with her first name. Pa Pat never remembered them anyway.

'Long way from home.' Pat's interest piqued, and his mouth turned downwards in thought. 'Knew a shearer once, Spanish bloke, came from up north. Worked here for a good while. We were best mates early on, when we started out.' His distant gaze searched the hills as the trees swayed in the gentle breeze.

LJ thought back to the conversation he'd had with his Pa when he'd mentioned the name Isaac to him. Now he was certain of the connection between their grandfathers. He held back the small smile threatening to engulf his lips as he watched for his grandfather's reaction from the corner of his eye, before looking back to the hills Pa Pat was admiring. 'She said that's one of the reasons she came to Tassie.' Pat's feet slid on the gravel as he stopped, horror washing over his face as he turned to his grandson. 'Not Isaac bloody Fernández, was it?'

'Yeah, I reckon that'd be right.' The image of her shining dark hair invaded his thoughts as he fought back a wistful smile.

'I'd say you're better off without her then.' Pa Pat turned back to face the hills. 'The bugger bloody started double clickin' every time he went into the pens. Couldn't stand that I was faster, so he found a way to cheat me out of my tally.' He growled under his breath, his gaze trained on the gravel. 'And to think I liked the man.' He gave a disbelieving half-laugh.

Despite his animosity, LJ detected the regret threading through Pa Pat's anger. Too many years had passed for one man to nurse a grudge against a mate, and a seemingly good one at that.

Pa Pat's narrowed gaze considered his grandson once more before a wary finger wavered in the air towards him. 'You don't like the girl, now, do you?' His voice carried both accusation and alarm. 'Let her go, son. Find yourself another classer.' He dismissed LJ with an irritated wave as he strode towards the shed, muttering darkly.

Watching his grandfather retreat, LJ heard Sam's familiar laugh echo in his memory. If he'd had more time with his best mate, would they have destroyed their lifelong bond with one another over a stupid offence that might not even be true? No way. Life was too bloody short. Something he understood all too well. Pa Pat had his opinion, but he had his own, and he trusted his own judgement more than ever.

Back in the shed, he heard her before he saw her—the giggle-girl laughter and princess voice which made his already deflated enthusiasm thanks to Pa Pat—plummet dangerously close to the shearing board.

Jacinta pranced in.

How the hell did she find us? He shook his head in disbelief. It was almost enough to have him about face, head for his ute, and the run home.

'Right, everyone, let's go.' LJ ignored her completely, grabbing his first ewe from the pen as she tottered down the board in her work boots, which shone like they'd just come out of the box they'd been purchased in.

He lowered his gaze, focusing on the belly wool he was taking off. As if on command, the sheep bleated an objection.

'Here. Here,' he said to the ewe.

LJ kept Jacinta in his peripheral vision, and when she reached Pa Pat, the old man's eyes lit up like Christmas lights. LJ gritted his teeth. With the handpiece lightly buzzing in his hand and the ewe balanced between his legs, Pa Pat straightened, a cheeky grin filling his face.

'Well, well, this is a nice surprise.' The old devil's eyes twinkled as they slid to LJ, raising his eyebrows in tell-tale approval. LJ shot back a warning glare—with little effect.

Pa Pat finished the ewe and sent her down the chute, his permanently curved spine—from decades of shearing without proper support—more pronounced as he stood. Still grinning, he nodded at LJ as he accepted a welcoming peck on the cheek. 'Where have you been all my life, young lady?'

Jacinta giggled, and LJ squeezed his handpiece tighter. 'Unbelievable,' he muttered.

'You right there, mate? You do know chatting up a sheep is probably a little awkward for her. She'll probably turn you down.' Bent over his own sheep, Jase waited for LJ's retort, grinning.

'Don't you start, smartarse.'

While everyone cleaned up the shed and packed away their gear for the run home, Jacinta followed Bianca like a lost lamb, prattling about the latest town gossip. LJ snorted with amusement. Bianca had zero tolerance for the woman, and the harder she ignored her, the more insistent her pet lamb became.

Pa Pat shuffled out, stooped and tired after a long day's

work, dragging his feet with effort after pushing himself to keep up with the younger "rams" running rings around his tally. LJ followed him to the door.

'Leave your ute here, Pa. It'll be safe. I'll drop you home and pick you up tommorra. Don't try driving tonight.' He kept his tone casual—nobody told Pa Pat what he couldn't do.

Pa stopped without turning around. The only sign of acceptance was the slight nod that barely disturbed his grey hair. LJ gave a relieved smile.

Dusk had claimed the countryside by the time they left, forcing LJ to take the winding roads slowly. Black ice would soon reclaim the cold asphalt for the night. Through sidelong glances, he watched his grandfather's contemplative profile silhouetted against the headlights' glow.

Pa Pat broke the silence in the cabin. 'What's going on with you, son?'

LJ glanced at his grandfather in surprise, missing the concern etched across his face. 'What do you mean?'

'I mean, why is it I'm hearin' things like Miles sayin' it doesn't matter what contractor we use?' He looked across at LJ. 'It was damned disgraceful we didn't use your team for crutching and shearing.' He jerked his head back towards the windscreen.

The emphasis on the name Miles caught in LJ's throat. What *was* going on? He'd like to understand it himself. 'I dunno.' His voice faded into uncertainty.

'Well, you'd better look into it real soon. I get the feelin' your brother has some plans for the farm, and they ain't all good.'

'What makes you say that?' The creases in his forehead deepened as he watched the dividing lines on the road whoosh by. His brother's antagonistic approach towards him was growing thicker every day, and he didn't know what to do about it. Besides, he was certain his father was still salty over the fact he had bought the contracting run against his advice.

'I know I don't know much, and I stay outta things which ain't none of my business, but . . .' Pa Pat's voice trailed into hesitation.

LJ glanced nervously at the passenger seat.

'Somethin's not addin' up. Miles is strutting around the farm like a bull lookin' for a heifer on heat. And I was in the office the other day, trying to find a blasted receipt on that confounded computer for the grain we bought. The funny thing is, I came across the accounts.'

What was wrong with them? He'd tallied them, leaving everything up to date with no issues before he'd left and taken on the run. He recalled Miles's words the day he'd shown him everything.

'Go on, get on with your shiny new shearing run. See if I care.'

LJ thought about his brother's casual dismissal of Sam's funeral and his almost pleased tone when he'd told LJ they'd rejected his team for shearing. It was the final slap in the face he hadn't seen coming, especially when his team felt more like family than his own blood.

In the stillness of the cabin, LJ sensed Pa Pat turn to face him.

'Son, there's a lot of money gone missin'.'

What? Why hadn't his father said something? LJ's temple throbbed as he scanned the grassy edges for kangaroos or stray livestock. Easier to focus on potential hazards than process what he'd just heard. Between searching for work and earning cash from George's renovation projects, he didn't need to call on money from the bank. He couldn't even remember the last time he'd seen a statement.

'So, are you gonna take this? You were in charge of the books.' The tone in Pa Pat's voice was agitated, verging on intolerance.

'Miles won't let me near the books. I can hardly step inside the house without him wanting to throw a king-hit my way. Besides, that's his worry now. There was no problem when I left them to him, so wherever it's gone, it's on him.'

There's no way I could be responsible. And if he was, then he'd have little choice but to sell his run to pay the money back, no matter how much it amounted to. He'd never be able to live with himself if he believed he'd taken something from his own family or the farm he wished he could still be living and working on.

LJ swallowed hard. With the condition his run was in right now, it wouldn't be worth much anyway. His reputation was shot, so he probably wouldn't find a buyer. And if he did, where would that leave him? His team? The answer was pretty clear. Out of work and starting all over again. With nothing.

So where exactly *had* the money gone?

Chapter Forty-Three

Jazz was learning—be it a little too slowly for Poppy—that being tied up was a good lesson. The pup sulked, eyeing Poppy with a guilt stare she'd honed beautifully. She was tethered to a post that held the divider between a couple of the wool bins, and Poppy watched her with a comical grin. Jazz had busied herself, tugging a rogue staple of wool from a nearby bin. She chewed at it, the wool clinging to her tongue. She shook her head as she fought to spit it out, before turning on a sorrowful howl and giving a sharp bark, dropping into a death-roll a crocodile would be impressed with, twisting herself around her chain.

Poppy grinned, gathered the fleece in her arms, and was walking towards the wool bin when Jazz let out a low, drawn-out growl. She turned, ready to remind her pup it wasn't polite, when Rick stopped, watching the dog, before his gaze steadily lifted to Poppy. His body lengthened, his eyes narrowing.

Spider was strolling past, his arms laden with a huge armful of fleeces, and he paused, blinking at, what was it, some kind of unspoken stand-off that was happening between her and Rick? She urged her heart to steady as her gaze shifted back and forth from her dog to Rick, her defences on high alert. Spider didn't move, and she was thankful he was in this team, relieved to have a familiar face working with her.

'Nice pup. Wouldn't like to see her get hurt.'

Was that a threat?

'You never liked kelpies, Rick.'

'They just need to be taught some manners, that's all.'

Spider continued to hover, and Rick glanced at him a moment longer before finally moving away.

'Better get back to work then.' His words were tossed over his shoulder as he walked towards the shearing stands with unnerving ease. Jazz remained silent, but her eyes never left him, her ears on full alert.

With Clancy's shed completed, work had dried up once more. But LJ was hearing that growers were discussing his name, and his reputation was spreading as a contractor true to his word with a good team worth giving a shot.

They just had to start ringing.

A cautious smile crossed his cheeks. Exhaustive hours travelling all those kilometres might have paid off, so why was it so hard for them to call? But if they did, he'd need his classer back. He hadn't heard from her since they'd finished doing up George's place, a fact that had left him bereft and lonely.

Pa Pat's words echoed in his ears. 'Doesn't matter if they don't trust a team, LJ. People always go with someone they know. Sometimes that's better than the unknown.' He still resented his grandfather's words, regardless of whether he was right or not.

So while he waited, he worked on Grandma Aimee's new kitchen, which was coming along nicely. LJ had taken to leaving her a daily note explaining what would change. Some days she growled at him for repeating himself. Other days, she treated the information as though she'd never heard it, excited about the modifications. Her face, with its soft skin and gentle wrinkles, radiated a lifetime of smiles and family love that both warmed and saddened him. But the good days were worth every nail he drove in for her happiness. And if he did get that call Sam was always saying was just around the corner, he'd feel confident he could leave her on her own.

LJ had worked up a sweat, dragging the dining table out of the room and shifting the kitchen dresser into the lounge as he prepared to demolish the kitchen.

Standing, he wiped the sweat from his brow as an amused half-smile toyed on his lips, his thoughts straying to Poppy, coughing and spluttering while waving her hand wildly at the air as she'd pulled up the old carpet in George's lounge room during their week of renos. They'd been tugging a corner of the carpet each, and she'd pulled so hard she'd landed flat on her backside. It felt like a lifetime ago now. He missed their casual lunchtimes together, her sitting on the verandah, her mile-long legs dangling over the edge, him sitting back on George's chair in prime position to admire her long, dark waves running the length of her back as she chased the lettuce spilling out from her sandwich with her mouth. He missed her, and it hurt more than he'd expected. Was it so wrong to honour Sam's dream, have his classer back, and, dare he think it, her love? Was he asking for too much?

'Where are we going to cook dinner tonight, love?'

LJ was down on his knees with his head stuck inside the bottom cupboards amongst fifty years of Tupperware containers and casserole dishes he remembered from when he was a kid. Old mouse droppings littered the crusty newspaper lining the shelves he had started to empty, some with dates going as far back as the mid-forties, when Aimee lived there as a young girl. He ducked his head, backing out of a cupboard, holding a crusty mouse skeleton still intact in a trap.

He sat back on his haunches and studied the mouse in the light, cheekily grinning up at her. 'Well, it definitely won't be this little guy.'

'I should hope not. There's not enough meat on him to share between the two of us.' The twinkle in her eye and her knowing smile, had LJ breathing a little easier. She was having a good day. On a bad day, she might have considered putting the shrivelled up rodent in a pot with some onion, carrots and celery and stewing him up for soup.

'Can I ask, dear, what were you chuckling at before?'

Her curious eyes held his with endless love, and for the briefest of moments, he considered telling her the truth. Would she understand if he confessed he was falling for his wool classer, a girl whose smile reflected family, strength and determination—everything he held dear? A girl with sexy-as sassiness, and the ability to challenge him at every turn, making him a better version of himself? Or should he tell her he was smiling at the memory of a woman who would never accept him because of his inability to keep a promise, and give her the world she deserved?

Unable to face Grandma Aimee's gently probing eyes, he gave the answer he knew she wanted to hear. 'I was thinking of Sammy.' His gaze lowered, and he offered a shallow smile to the dead mouse poised in his hand, reminding him of the loss he now had to face for the rest of his life, and what he could never have because of it.

Two days later, with rain falling on the roof in a soothing rhythm, LJ dragged the last bench cupboard from the kitchen. He'd hoped focusing on the renovation would be a good distraction from everything, but his back was doing enough of that, the painful ache killing him. If he didn't get shearing work soon, it wouldn't only be him who would be unfit for work and in a whole lot of pain when his body moaned at starting up again.

He set aside his pinch bar and dusted his hands in front of him. Coffee was calling.

Cups in hand, he curled around the corner along the hallway to the lounge room, where Grandma Aimee was perched next to the fire, toasting her toes and reading a trashy magazine she insisted kept her mind alert. Who was he to argue?

The room held an eerie loneliness, its dark burgundy walls doing little to reflect the dull light straining to reach inside from the two small windows at the western end of the house. The sun remained behind bleak clouds, and a cool chill ran its fingers over LJ as he entered. He put their drinks down and stooped, reaching for another log to toss onto the coals, the flames instantly waking with eager enthusiasm.

'Ready for a cup of tea, Grandma?' His smile radiated love and patience, something he had to admit wasn't often present these days. Life was beginning to feel a little too hard.

Closing her magazine, she focused on him, and he inclined his head, happy with the silence, but equally, patiently waiting for her to speak.

'You like this girl, don't you?' She gave a soft smile, her discerning eyes holding his. 'You like her a lot.'

LJ almost choked on his mouthful of coffee. He hadn't mentioned Poppy to his grandmother, other than in passing when they ate tea and he told her about his working day. He groaned inwardly. How had his grandmother discovered he liked a woman? And wasn't she supposed to be forgetting things anyway? Except for when he'd gone to throw out the dodgy—decades old—metal ice cube container, and she'd chased him to the recycling bin. 'Not this one, dear. Eddie likes using it for his whisky at night.'

Bewildered, he looked at her before letting his eyes be transfixed on the dancing blaze. 'Who do you mean?' If he played dumb, he'd catch her out. He knew she had no idea.

'That young Poppy. You talk about her more than anyone else. I heard you mention her name while you were asleep on the sofa last night. When are you going to bring the nice girl around here to meet me?' Her warm smile held him captive—by the throat.

He'd let on about his feelings . . . in his sleep? Last night? He blinked his disbelief at the conversation they were having. And how had his grandmother, with her inability to retain his spontaneous remarks, concluded that he was—in love? He coughed against the irritation forming in his throat.

And besides, hadn't she fallen asleep first last night? She'd looked like she was asleep before he'd closed his eyes in front of the telly. He shook his head. The cunning lady had nailed him as securely as he'd nailed the weatherboards to the side of the house. He shot her a side glance, gathering his courage to admit the truth, all while the voice in his ear reminded him that a woman like Poppy would never want him. He was feeling like he was becoming a walking disaster.

'I'd like to introduce you.' But could he? He'd been so sure admitting his feelings to someone else would cause him to recoil, to hide behind the walls he'd built so high around himself after Sam's death.

Instead of the fear and panic he was ready for, a wash of relief claimed him. Could he be ready to offer someone the true Lincoln John Tanner? Even if it came without a shearing run?

Grandma Aimee leaned in, her wrinkled hand patting the skin of his forearm. 'Can you do something for me, dear?' She paused, her kind eyes boring into his. 'Let her know.'

Let her know what? She couldn't be serious. LJ's eyes opened a little wider as she tipped her head towards him, her I-knew-I-was-right smile glowing in the light of the fire as she considered him closely.

'Isn't that worth promising to yourself?'

It was mid-morning, the new kitchen cupboards had arrived, and in keeping with forcing his mind to stay occupied by anything and everything other than Miles, WorkSafe, and his non-existent love life, LJ was keen to get them in. And what was even better was that he had managed to rope Jase into helping install it.

'Hey, Jase. Give me a hand, will ya.' LJ shuffled his feet against the weight of the biggest cabinet when his back pocket buzzed. He shoved the bench into position with his hip, leaving Jase to screw it into place while he stepped outside into the sun's late winter rays as he pressed redial on the number he didn't recognise.

Ten minutes later, with a broad smile plastered to his face, he paused at the kitchen door. Jase stood, wiping the sweat from his face with his forearm. 'Well, come on. Spill.'

'From next week, we're working full-time for August.' His hopeful smile fell away as concern replaced it. 'Only catch is, we need a classer.'

'Hello?' Jen hollered at the screen door, her arms laden with goodies. 'Can you two handsome boys come help me, please? If you want to eat, you're going to have to earn it.'

LJ's chest warmed at his mother's teasing chuckle, and he went to unburden her armful.

'We're already earning it,' Jase said as he followed Jen back out to the car for her second load.

LJ trailed behind, unable to dismiss the smile on his face from the good news, the relief palpable. Maybe things were turning around for him and his team. The only thing better would be hearing from his classer. But he couldn't hold out much hope on that happening. Where else was he going to get a classer with her ability in such a tight timeslot?

Chapter Forty-four

Jazzy snored in puppy bliss as Poppy stroked her while she scanned her phone. She ached to ring LJ and ask about work, the boys, how Cindy's cleaning business was going, and how he was managing with her two favourite shedhands.

But what she really wanted was to hear LJ's warm voice, ask how he was, and hope he'd offer her the classing job back. But despite their growing closeness, uncertainty still warned her he wouldn't commit, not to work, or to being with her. Each time she drew closer to him, he got lost in the moment, then pulled away, his walls carefully lifted like he wasn't prepared to trust.

On the other hand, she needed the work from Sweeny, but she wanted to be free of him and his team's light fingers. Even though she still hadn't witnessed any thefts in the act, given the farmer's growing animosity towards the team in general, she was certain it was happening. Sticking with them only made her look guilty as well.

Even more than that, she wanted to be free from Rick's continual, carefully gauged presence. What she wanted was to sit down with LJ like they had at George's, spilling their salad sandwiches, laughing like they were long lost friends, and chatting about the upcoming weather, jobs around the farm, and the green grass spring would bring.

But what if he'd found another classer . . . making her surplus to his needs? The thought caused a deep ache to swell inside her chest, despite convincing herself it was for the best. The longer she stayed with Sweeny's team, the more she wanted to leave. But unease constricted her throat. Could she guarantee Rick wouldn't up and leave, following her back again? She let out a shaky breath.

Poppy leaned back on her pillow as the wind outside gently rocked her caravan. It was about time she was downright honest with herself. She'd learned to trust herself again, and some of its people—George Adrian, her Tasmanian family—and she pined for a guy who made it his job to keep her at a distance.

Couldn't she have it all? Wasn't it okay to want that?

She rubbed Jazz's soft ears between her fingers as she stared at the phone in her hand, renewed hope sparking inside her. She knew the attraction between her and LJ had been real. She'd seen it in his knowing smile. She'd also seen it vanish in his eyes when she'd held his face in her hands, like he thought he didn't deserve it. What was he hiding? She wanted to understand. Then maybe she could help.

Unable to stop herself, she pressed her speed dial, willing him to answer before she chickened out and hung up. She owed it to him to let him know she'd continued working for Sweeny—make some kind of amends for not telling him earlier.

'Hey, there.' His deep voice resonated, sending warmth and reassurance and hope racing through her. She had to admit, at every turn where she tried to push him away, her heart somehow kept drawing her back to him.

'Hi. How's things? How's the team?' Tell him you want to come back. Tell him you miss him! She shook her head at her own cowardice.

'They're good.' There was a long pause. 'We miss you.'

Poppy's heart suddenly pounded and she sat up, disturbing Jazz who blinked tired eyes at her, then lay her head down on the bed again. Was he saying the team missed her, or did *he* miss her? She waited, wanting to give him a chance to ask her to come back—so she wouldn't have to beg. That had to be what he was going to say next, wasn't it?

But the longer she waited, the more the silence between them grew. Maybe just a little nudge?

'Have you got another classer?' Why did she even say that? She pressed a disbelieving hand to her forehead, her mouth shooting out questions she didn't want to hear the answers to. What was wrong with her? She had to jump in before she heard he wouldn't need her.

'I can tell Sweeny I'm leaving, if you've got work. I can come ba—' There. She'd done it. Told him. Would he pick the desperation in her voice? She swallowed hard, begging him for an answer, and at the same time, not fully ready to hear it.

'So, it's good enough for you to let *him* know you're leaving, but not to tell me?' There was a gentle forthrightness in his tone, but still, that didn't make it any easier to listen to. Except that she totally deserved it. Was he still disappointed in her? Was he worried about her? She wanted to think so, but her Spanish defences spoke up before she had a chance to keep them under control.

'Excuse me?' She might not have told him, but she'd always intended to. What happened to her letting him know she was coming back, like tomorrow? But two could play this game.

'And you can give me work for as long as I like, or is that too hard to ask?'

Touché.

LJ rubbed at his whiskers, struggling to regain his train of thought. Was she actually asking him if she could come back to the team? Why on earth would she do something like that? Was she that silly, willing to throw away a sure career? She was one of the best classers he'd come across; her test results had confirmed it, and bloody Sweeny had her in his team. There was no way she'd give that up, just to make him feel better, and he was pretty sure that's exactly what she was doing.

'I can't make you those promises, Poppy. People don't have enough faith in me yet.'

Bloody promises. Why did everyone expect them from him? It danced on the tip of his tongue to tell her about the upcoming job.

He'd told her he missed her. So why wasn't he prepared to say in what capacity. And if she thought it was for more than the work, was she asking more of him than he was able to give? Hell, he couldn't commit to a decent friendship, let alone a relationship, no matter how he felt about her. She'd only end up disappointed.

'So, you're saying you don't need me then?' Was there an edge of disappointment in her voice?

Miss and *need* were two very different things. He missed her every time he looked around the tearoom, and she wasn't there. He needed her more than he was prepared to admit. But not asking her back . . . it was the only way he wouldn't fail her, or worse. Sam had died on his watch. What if she needed him and he failed her, too?

He closed his eyes, hiding his defeated face behind his hand. What did he tell her? That he hated her being away from the team—from him? Hell, he needed a classer for this coming week!

'Look, you didn't want to listen to us when we tried to warn you about Sweeny's team, and frankly, I don't know why you've stuck with him. But if it floats your boat, then you should stay. You're a great classer. He's giving you all the work you want.'

'So— you don't need me . . . at all?' Her voice trailed away. Was she relieved? Was she giving him the obligatory phone call to finalise her termination of the position?

It wasn't what he'd expected to hear.

It was the last thing he wanted.

'We'll be fine, Poppy. You do what you've gotta do.' Isn't that what she needed to hear, permission to be free of him?

What the heck? Poppy fumed as she stared at her phone in disbelief. Where did he get off telling her she hadn't listened to them? He'd given her no bloody choice. If he'd tried a bit harder and found more work, she'd still be there.

Not with Rick.

With him.

LJ ended the call, kicking the chair leg with his socked toe in frustration, the pain immediate.

'Frustrating, infuriating woman!'

He hopped on one foot, cursing the chair and his pigheadedness as he moved towards the bed. He'd just blown his best chance at getting her back, for what? His opportunity to make some weak kind of rebuff at her that hadn't even worked in his favour? *You're a bloody idiot, Tanner.*

She'd even asked him, outright, to come back. And he'd politely said no thanks? What was wrong with him? He pushed a rough hand through his hair. He'd done it because he couldn't make her any guarantees. She'd said she would come back for Oxley Falls, which was over a month away. What were the chances she'd have more work lined up with Sweeny by then?

Pretty damn high.

The worries of the team looking like they were about to fold, his rejection from his own father and brother . . . the missing money— They were all mounting up, leaving him exhausted, confused, and utterly defeated. He lay back on his bed. He needed to get a look at the farm books, see if he'd made an acceptable mistake, but he knew Miles wouldn't have a bar of it. The last time he went home and ventured into the office, the laptop was absent. When he'd done the books, it had never left the desk.

Unease and frustration squirmed in his gut, and LJ glared at the ceiling. Miles had to be hiding something, or did he simply hate him for reasons he hadn't been able to understand? And why? It had to be a combination of both. A year after Sam and Josie moved in with them, Miles's demeanour had turned sour, his lazy, good-for-nothing attitude bugging LJ.

In their late teens, Sam had drunk a little too much one night and bowled into Miles's room unannounced, catching him watching footage of women he would deem compromising. LJ recalled what Sweeny had said that day at the shearing supply shop.

But treating him like he was no longer a member of the family? What had he done to deserve that? And even worse, why was he turning their father against him?

'Dad said you can go dig your own hole of failure,' Miles had told him.

LJ shook his head. He was trying to make a go of this run, even though it was proving a bigger challenge than he'd first envisaged, especially without Sam's help.

And not shearing at the family farm? That's what gutted him the most. Since when had their family shied away from paying for quality?

Since Miles was running the show.

Chapter Forty-five

George had been laid up in hospital for over three weeks, diagnosed with a serious bout of pneumonia. It didn't help that he had less body fat than a greyhound, but then again, he didn't have the muscle either. But now, he was ready to come home.

Poppy headed to George's house, the early afternoon already allowing the cold air to slink in. She'd been more than happy to help George with the chores around the place while he recovered, but she was all too aware of what the hospital had told her, that George would need to consider moving to a home if he couldn't look after himself. She'd held them off, promising to talk to him about it when he came home; promising to herself she would be there more for him, so she didn't even need to have the conversation.

There was also the matter of avoiding LJ, which was

getting harder and harder. The guy was there every time she turned up, and he was the last person she wanted to see. She'd perfected the knack of scooting straight out the back door the moment LJ entered through the front, and vice versa, even if it was a little—okay, maybe a lot—rude. But when he'd told her he missed her, then dismissed her offer to come back and work with them? Frankly, he deserved what was coming to him. Or was that her vibrant Spanish heritage having the last say? Either way, it felt satisfyingly fitting.

'Finally,' Poppy said out loud as she pulled up and hopped out of her car, relieved LJ's ute wasn't out the front for once.

She went inside and stoked up the AGA fire, then did a runaround, dusting everything and making sure the renovations they'd worked so hard on were set to impress. Her heart warmed as she thought of the fun they'd had. But that was all in the past.

With one more satisfied glance around the lounge, she smiled. The insulation LJ had put inside the walls and ceiling had made a notable difference to the room's ambient temperature, and that relieved her. George would have a better chance of warding off sickness and staying comfortable, giving him every fighting chance to stay longer in his home.

But a sudden sharp stab laced through her. Wasn't it only fair that LJ be here to welcome George home, too? He'd done as much work as she had. Should she tell him? She was torn between the thought of letting him share the moment or staying clear of him.

And that tenderness they'd shared, with his soft gaze,

his—dare she admit it—adoring smile, and the way he'd brushed her stray locks from her face in this very place, were all the things she was now continually tormented by. Why did she have to torture herself by allowing it to repeat over and over in her mind? She needed to keep at the forefront of her mind all the reasons why he shouldn't go with her. And then she remembered the best one yet.

He didn't want her back.

How could she forget?

Without another thought of him, she drove to Launceston.

The hospital corridors felt like a second home to Poppy, thanks to her nursing degree. She might not have wanted to take it up as a career, but everything felt so familiar, from the smell of the disinfectant to the nurses in uniform.

When she turned into George's room, he looked one hundred and eleven percent better than when she'd found him back at his home. His cheeks were reassuringly rosy, and he'd gained a little weight, some showing on his face. His gappy smile welcomed her as he sat perched on the side of the bed.

'I'm sure glad to see you. Took your time getting here, though. You get caught in a river crossing or something?' His cheeky smile was such a relief to see, and she leaned over, putting her hand on his arm as she kissed him on the cheek.

'You silly old bugger, you should know there hasn't been any rain. It was a cattle stampede.'

George chuckled, and Poppy could hear the remnants of the phlegm that persisted in his chest. She'd have to keep a close eye on that.

'Have you got all your anti-ageing tablets?' She gave him a mischievous grin. Antibiotics, puffer, preventer. She'd need to make sure he didn't forget to take them when he got home, or more so, choose to forget all about them, if she knew him.

He patted the side of his duffel bag sitting next to him. 'That I do. The pretty nurse tells me they won't take away the wrinkles, though.' His smile broadened as he looked over her shoulder, and Poppy turned to see a nurse glide in, slowing to stand alongside him. Her courteous smile morphed into disbelief when she registered the woman's face.

'So *you're* the pretty nurse.' Poppy stepped towards the woman, offering a hug before she turned to George. 'Stacey is a friend from . . . um— of mine.' She'd been about to say uni.

'Popps! It's so good to see you.' Stacey stepped back, looking her over, her eyes returning to study her face. 'This outfit doesn't look much like a nursing uniform.' Her head tipped to the side, and her words hung hauntingly in the air, her eyebrow raised in a curious arc. 'Day off?'

Poppy gave a nervous glance towards George, then focused on her friend as her mind raced for answers. Could she tell Stacey the truth? She reminded herself that it didn't matter because Stacey hadn't seen her since their graduation day.

'Um, today? Yes.' She gave a nervous half-chuckle and

looked down at her dusty jeans and flannelette shirt beneath a rugby jumper with serious holes thanks to Jazz taking a liking to it.

'Where are you working? I haven't seen you around here.' Stacey gestured around, her smile holding Poppy's. She ignored Poppy's hesitation, looking to George. 'Poppy finished our nursing degree with honours. Bit of a bright cookie, this one.'

George's brow lifted as he turned to Poppy with interest. And she'd said "nursing" out loud! *Oh no.* How had she managed to get herself into strife yet again? These lies were going to be the death of her, all when things were calming down with her father. She hadn't heard from him in a week.

'No, no, I'm not working *here*,' she interrupted, smoothing it over with a guilty chuckle. But she did work here, didn't she? Launceston was *here*. Would Stacey let it go?

Please shut up. Now!

'Where *are* you working then?'

Poppy froze, and her heart leapt into her throat. She clamped her eyes shut, the words needling her as the deep voice from behind carried perplexed disbelief.

Why? She let her head fall forward. Could this day get any worse? She seriously doubted it.

With her back to the door, Poppy forced her eyes open, sharp blinks helping her to focus as George peered over her shoulder again. 'Ah, g'day. Didn't know you were comin' too.' George gave his trademark smile which shone brighter than Poppy felt good about seeing right now.

He wasn't meant to be. She released a deflated

harrumph.

The room fell quiet, but Stacey broke the silence. 'Hi, I'm Stacey.'

Poppy watched on, aghast, as her friend stepped straight past her. She risked a look, a ridiculous smile on her friend's face as she glanced from his toes, all the way up to his gorgeous smile, reaching her hand out to meet— LJ.

This was all she needed, Stacey being interested in *her* handsome contractor. But Stacey was allowed to be, Poppy sharply reminded herself.

He was available.

She didn't want him.

He hadn't wanted her, a fact he'd made explicitly clear.

Protect your heart at all costs. That was her new motto. But Poppy's finger tapped against her leg as Miss Sunny-side up latched onto LJ by the hand. Poppy fought against the desperate urge not to let her eyes boggle. She gave LJ a less-than-thrilled acknowledgment of his presence as he came to stand beside her, her butterflies refusing to disappear despite her explicit instruction. She cringed as she focused on George, the whole time feeling LJ's gaze on her.

'Well, my dear, I'd like it if you could take me home now. Gotta get the fire stoked in the stove if I want me tea tonight.' He was thrilled to be heading home—she could hear it in his voice. It made knowing all the work they had done so much more satisfying. Had he picked up that she was, in fact, a nurse? Was he trying to save her, not only from Stacey, but from LJ too?

Heat rushed up her neck, prickling against her collar,

and she tugged at it, annoyed. Part of her refused to face LJ, and the other part was desperate to—if nothing other than to see his stunning eyes hopefully still watching her—gauge if there was still a glimmer of something between them, something she could hope might lead to a future. She ached to stare at his way-too-sexy-for-his-own-good beard and watch his crooked smile shine from beneath his lips, the one she'd seen the day he'd stepped back, and she'd looked into his hauntingly despondent eyes.

The day she'd admitted to herself she'd fallen for him when she'd held his face in her hands.

But instead, Poppy stepped forward, grabbing George's bag with determination, offering him her arm to steady himself as he stood. One quick glance at her friend told her that she was moving in for the kill. Her notepad poised and a pen hovering in her now twitchy hands, Stacey swooned towards LJ with devouring eyes. And Poppy didn't blame her. He was gorgeous, in more ways than she hoped Stacey would ever know.

Focusing on the door ahead, she refused to risk meeting his gaze, not even for a millisecond. She was almost home free when his hand reached out with the softest of touches, grazing her arm and her attention. She briefly looked down at it before forgetting every rule she'd put in place, looking up into his eyes that searched her so deeply, tenderly, and desperately.

And she froze.

'I'll see you back at George's. We need to talk.'

Chapter Forty-Six

No. We don't!

The last thing Poppy wanted to do was *talk*. Her finger tapped at the steering wheel as she drove towards George's, arriving in record time.

Nope. Absolutely not!

Never going to happen.

Her mind raced. He'd had his chance and rejected her. Poppy zipped around the house with the speed of her old self, the Sydney girl with too much to do and not enough time to do it. She needed to get George settled in, the dogs fed and snuggled up with him next to the fire, his meds taken—

And then she needed to get out of there.

Fast.

But already, her plans were turning awry. George was

oohing and aahing over all the changes they'd made to the house, taking his time with each detail, at a pace to envy a sloth. She cursed LJ under her breath while George commented for the umpteenth time.

'Look at what you've done.' He marvelled at every alteration they'd made. Couldn't he save this till another time? But it was wonderful that he was appreciating everything they'd done.

They'd done. It had been a joint effort, and she had to admit she would never have been able to do everything if it wasn't for him. She wanted to savour this moment with George, reminisce on how she and LJ had made the modifications and what had happened at each stage. Feelings began to bubble in her tummy. Not so long ago, she hadn't wanted a bar of the infuriating man, and then he went and did things like make her a cup of tea and bring it out to her on the porch, despite her hair looking like a magpie's nest, with dust strewn throughout it that had her looking like she was greying early. She'd been sanding back George's water-stained dining table, preparing it for a fresh protective coat of stain. She'd looked up, into his honest, deep eyes, her mouth parched and her arms feeling like they were about to fall off.

But now? Thanks to Mr oh-so Wonderful, she was in a hurry to get home—or Mt Kosciuszko, right now she wasn't feeling the need to be picky—just far, far away from him, because now he was onto her. She'd kept hidden her nursing to focus on what she wanted; to trust her skills and prove she was better than what Rick had said she was. She'd allowed her lies to grow, and now LJ wouldn't be able to trust her again. She'd all but sealed her chances of returning to his team.

With nerves frazzled, she drove out of George's driveway like a wild dog was chasing her, racing along the road in the opposite direction to where LJ would arrive. The longer drive home would cost her an extra half an hour, but it was worth it not to cross paths with her handsome contractor. But could she call him that anymore? She threw her hands in the air before taking the steering wheel again, glaring at the road as though it too was in her way.

Slowly but steadily, the more distance she put between herself and George's house, the more she breathed, appreciating the final glints of sunlight skirting the dark clouds that had hung low in the sky all day. She squinted, its radiance winking at her. When all else failed, admiring nature's spectacular scenery somehow grounded her in a way nothing else could.

Turning into The Lone Pony, the stones beneath her tyres kicked out as she hit the brakes hard, her eyes straining through the darkness. A tall shadow moved in and out around the back of her caravan.

Heart beating a thousand beats a second, with a shaking hand, she slowly eased her car into reverse, her eyes shifting to the mirror sharply before continuing to watch the shadow as it moved. Slowly. Steadily. She began to reverse, increasing the gap between her and her caravan as steadily as was humanly possible, given the fear fighting to take hold. Reaching the road, she swung onto it before putting the car into drive, desperately fighting against the frantic urge to plant her foot to the floor and raise any unwanted attention.

To the side of her passenger window, she watched a torchlight flash back and forth as someone jogged towards her from the far side of the pony's paddock. The action was reassuringly familiar, and she urged him to hurry with a panicked wave of her upturned hand, leaning towards the passenger door and opening it.

'Quick,' she whispered. 'Get in.'

Adrian panted as he reached the door, fumbling with the door handle as steady movement near the front of her caravan appeared. She eyed Adrian. 'Want to come for a quick drive?' She forced a smile, hoping it might put him at ease. But she could see he was just as shocked and scared. His urgent nod was all she needed.

It almost killed her, but she kept her speed steady despite her shaking leg and hands gripping the steering wheel for dear life. An eerie silence hung between them until she turned left down a corrugated country road not more than five kilometres away, pulling to a stop in front of a large-trunked gumtree, its branches swaying eerily in the lightest of breezes. When she turned her lights off to mask their whereabouts, the full depth of their ominous surroundings loomed in on them.

How dare he! Hadn't she made it clear to LJ that she didn't want to see him, regardless of the lengths he went to? Forget that she was being totally irrational in her reactions. She'd be having words with him—in the daylight—about not only scaring her half to death but also scaring the daylights out of Adrian, too.

'Poppy, there's someone near your caravan.' Adrian's voice was hurried, urgent, and as shaky as her fingers, and

Poppy called on every inch of calm she could scrape up for his sake. 'I think he's looking for you.'

Poppy took a swift breath, shifting her body to face him. It was LJ. It had to be. Right?

'I know. But I don't want to see him.' She stared into the chilling blackness, grateful for Adrian. LJ wouldn't have meant to scare them, but she loved the way Adrian looked out for her.

'You look scared. I was scared too.' Their gazes met and held. 'I don't want to go back yet, Poppy. Do we have to?' His big, round eyes spoke as loudly as his words.

Was she scared? Of facing LJ, yes. But when had he taken to wandering around her caravan in the dark like some creep, instead of sitting in his ute and waiting for her to turn up, approaching her in a civil manner? That wasn't his style. But it did ring true to someone else, and she fought to squash away the disturbing thought.

Poppy reached for Adrian's hand, squeezing it as she begged her concern to settle.

She held her breath for a moment, finally allowing it to ease from her nose in a controlled stream. 'Yes, I was a little scared too.' She forced a smile, nodding in his direction as her mind spun. It had to be LJ, she reassured herself. No one else knew where she lived.

Jimmy came to mind. Where was he when she needed him? She immediately willed him to buy that bloody ticket and get himself over here pronto.

Fifteen minutes passed, and as far as she could tell, no one had driven past on the main road behind them. It should have made her feel a lot better. But it didn't. It was getting cold, and she needed to get Adrian home. All she wanted was a hot shower and a cup of tea. Come to think of it, the shower could wait. There was no way she was trudging over to the shower block in the dark after tonight, or ever again.

'Right, I reckon we should go home now, don't you?' Surely LJ would have lost interest by now and gone home.

'Okay.' She could hear the shake still in his voice and her heart broke just a little more. It was bad enough that she was having to deal with all this. But to drag him into it with her? She hated the realisation she had been so reckless with his beautiful friendship.

Poppy dropped Adrian off at his front door, eying the darkness ahead cautiously. Slowly, she drove forwards, the two hundred metres to her caravan feeling so much longer than it was. Leaning over her steering wheel, she scanned every bush and crevasse with narrowed eyes as her caravan came into view.

She told herself there was no one there.

Her heart hammered.

She tried to convince herself he'd given up.

Her throat clenched.

She pulled up outside her van and locked her car doors.

And waited.

Everything was quiet— Still. Like it always was.

Poppy, seriously, get over yourself, she growled, taking a ratifying breath before determinedly unlocking the car lock, swinging the door open, and leaning out.

She stilled, one leg still inside the cabin, one deathly-tight grip on the steering wheel should she need to get back in, in a hurry. With rapid breaths, she listened, her eyes widening as desperate scratching rattled at her door. 'Jazz,' she whispered, the relief palpable. She'd left her inside her van, unsupervised—not in her crate—for the first time, and had an uncanny hunch at what the outcome she was going to be greeted with. One last glance around her, and she left her car, making for the door, urgently shoving the key into the lock.

Soft foam filling—Poppy guessed from her pillow—spilled down the steps at her feet like frolicking snow the moment the door opened, and Jazz lunged forward, her tail wagging with eagerness as her front paws landed on Poppy's hips with excitement.

She rubbed the pup's ears like they were the tonic she desperately needed to calm her shaking hands. She reached for the light switch, desperate to lock the door behind her.

And then her heart sank. Her meticulous notes she'd taken for the recent shed were shredded. She pointed at her dog. 'I hate to break it to you, pup, but right now, you're not that clever.'

Much to Poppy's surprise, cleaning up was exactly what she needed to distract her from the niggling unease of her unwanted visitor and what he'd "wanted to discuss". She was ninety-nine-point-nine-nine, no, maybe eight percent sure it was LJ, but the remaining point-two percent left her . . . hanging, with an uneasiness she couldn't seem to shrug off. Not even her steaming cup of strong tea was doing the trick tonight.

With her head resting on three bath towels folded as an

impromptu pillow, she shivered against the cold—thanks to Jazz taking on the heater cord in her absence and winning. Or at least she tried to tell herself it was that. She punched at the towels to soften them, her mind still whirring with thoughts that continued to pump adrenaline through her veins.

Jazz jumped up on the bed next to her, and she played with her velvety ears while her mind continued to churn. Could Jazz have scared off whoever had been snooping around? Would she have barked or licked them to death?

Yes, she was mad with LJ.

Yes, she was running away from him. But he'd never scare her intentionally.

But did she know him well enough to believe it?

LJ screwed up the paper with Stacey's phone number and tossed it in the bin. What an annoying time delay that had been. She'd wanted to check George's details, dragging him back to the nurse's station.

It made him think of Poppy.

Her name both danced on his lips and made him want to curse, and he ran a contemplative hand around the back of his neck as he remembered her phone call at the Jenkin's shed, and then at George's the other night. It was all adding up. Was Poppy a nurse? And if so, why the heck would she choose to class wool in dusty, stinky shearing sheds with cocky shedhands and dead-set thieves?

He scratched his jaw as he neared his ute. And when she'd told him she didn't need his help to put the wool away— Her words made him rouse with a smile. 'You're just a shearer.' He recalled the look of shame on her face the moment she'd said it.

A *ding, ding* roused him from his thoughts. He lifted his phone, and his pulse quickened when he saw Poppy's name. Had she been reading his mind?

Hey. Got a favour to ask. Do you need a really good shedhand?

For the briefest of moments, hope flared inside him— was she asking for her job back? That's what he'd wanted to discuss at George's, determined not to be so ridiculously stupid a second time over. He needed her back by next week. He hadn't found anyone to replace her, and the idea of him attempting to do the classing was mildly terrifying, to say the least.

Howdy. Good to see you today.

He wanted to tell her their time had been too brief. He wanted—no, needed—to tell her how he felt. The promise he'd made to Grandma Aimee hung heavy. Part of him clung to the belief his grandmother would forget all about it. He looked towards the sound of the TV humming in the lounge room, then looked back at his phone. He continued his text.

Yeah, that'd be great. Can he/she work next week?

Please say you'll come too . . . A response came back straight away and he looked at it with eagerness.

Depends. Is the farmer's wife a good babysitter?

What? He scratched his head.

Why?

Because she has a baby but needs a job. I promise she's a great worker.

That word— It hit him hard, and he instantly noticed a spot he'd missed when painting the architraves, reaching out to rub it. This had to be the baby she had delivered. His heart immediately swelled. Being a nurse in a shed had its advantages, he mused, catching himself giving a disbelieving chuckle as he tried to subdue his immediate admiration.

'Well, I'll be damned,' he muttered, then caught himself when Grandma Aimee called out.

'Eddie? Is that you?'

'No, Grandma. It's LJ. Sorry.' Grandpa had died when LJ was a little tacker.

Without responding to Poppy, he made a quick call to the farmer.

'Great. Thanks.' He opened her text again.

All good. Yeah, we'd love to have her.

There had been rumours about this girl, stories saying she'd let herself fall pregnant to get her partner to stay. But the way Sweeny had pushed her right up until the birth? Without a doubt, he'd give the woman work, for no other reason than to get her away from the creep.

Great. I promise you won't regret it. Thanks.

Sheesh. That bloody word. It needed to disappear from his vocabulary, for good. He frowned at his phone. And what about today? What about meeting at George's? She'd been and gone when he'd finally broken free from Stacey.

Good night. Smiley face.

He stared at his phone, willing it to ding with a response, and he didn't have to wait long. Another message followed, short and simple, and he bet she had no idea how much it meant.

You too.

Chapter Forty-Seven

Monday morning was frantic, well, at least for LJ. It seemed he was the only one running like a cut cat.

Liam was on stand one. Whippet had moved up to the second stand, and Bear was cruisy on fourth. LJ had managed to find another shearer who'd recently arrived from Queensland, looking for work. He wanted to know who had recommended him, or if the guy had picked up one of his business cards he'd dropped off at countless cafés and hardware stores. He'd even left some at the Tasmanian Wool Centre museum in Ross. That one had been a long shot. What shearer in their right mind would bother dropping by there when they already had sheep on their brains?

His weekend had rushed by in a blur of phone calls all ending with a firm 'no'. The classers he was counting on were adamantly *unavailable*—that had stabbed harder than he'd been expecting—so he was it. He had a fair idea of what he was doing. But achieving the micron difference like Poppy could was a near-impossible task for him. The farmer was counting on him to make him the most money for the clip, and LJ wasn't feeling up to the challenge. He rubbed a weary finger over his eyebrow as he stole a frantic look at the team, *and* their new shedhand, immediate relief filling him. Poppy had been spot on. Sophie was a perfect fit. She was hard-working, obliging, and got on with the job. Finding a babysitter hadn't been a problem. The farmer's daughter was in Year Twelve and on school holidays, and had been delighted to look after little Rosie.

LJ studied Red—his new shearer. He was shearing clean and putting out good numbers. His burly laugh rang out as he roared at yet another of Bear's old sayings and jokes, putting LJ's mind at ease . . . a little.

Shearing ticked along, and the boys sped up, but LJ continued to flail. He was inept at keeping up with the amount of wool being thrown at him, finding an all-new appreciation for Poppy's skills.

If only she were here.

By the end of the day, his brain was fried, and he wasn't sure how much longer he'd be able to keep it up.

The next day began much the same way, with LJ in a woolly frenzy while the boys surged on, dollar signs in their eyes. At smoko, he sank his tired body onto the metal chair at the table in the small tearoom, exhausted, ready for an infusion of coffee. He managed to take a quick sip before a sharp cough at the door caught the team's attention.

As LJ turned in his seat towards the door, his eyes widened, the coffee's bitterness suddenly churning like a concrete mixer in his gut. But there was no mistaking it.

WorkSafe had found him. It was clear as day on the shirt logo.

But how? It wasn't like he was trying to hide from them, he tried to convince himself despite the glimmer of guilt pointing its nosey finger in his chest.

'Ah, Mr Tanner. I had a tip-off I might find you here.'

A tip off? Then it dawned.

Jacinta.

A deflated sigh left his lungs.

The all of four-foot-three man blinked, glancing around the room like he should have been regarded with far more prestige than was being delivered. His steely glare rested on each one of them until—one by one—they stood, greeted with a surreptitious smile as they filed past, LJ noting that for a man of insignificant stature amongst strong, imposing shearers, he had some balls.

And it didn't escape LJ that Bianca and Sophie both received an extra-long, appreciative appraisal as they exited the room, to which Bianca served him with her just-try-and-mess-with-us-and-you'll-be-sorry stare-down.

But not Jase. He remained in his seat, eyeing the man coldly.

LJ was past fighting the inevitable, so he waited for the man to plant his backside on a chair. But it didn't happen. Instead, Mr WorkSafe raised a pointed eyebrow in Jase's direction, who leisurely stretched out in his chair, clearly unfazed. The visitor flicked his finger towards Jase, giving him the "on your way" message.

Jase returned his stony stare. Unmoving.

That's my boy. LJ worked to disguise his inward relief. Staunch friendship counted for a lot in this industry, especially when you were fighting to change the ingrained stigma of a doomed contracting name.

Jase rose, stepping towards their visitor. At six-foot-three, he looked him down the nose, his muscular triceps and forearms crossed firmly over his chest, emphasising his honed shoulders.

'If you want to speak to me, then you can speak to him too.' LJ intercepted, desperate for the coffee in his stomach to settle his apprehension. 'I reckon it'll be okay with you.'

Jase held his ground, and LJ watched one of the man's eyelids flinch— ever so briefly. His mouth began to slip open before he snapped it shut, taking a wide berth to claim Jase's seat next to LJ. Slowly, Jase turned, moving towards him, pausing to loom over his shoulder with the aura of a stealthy, deadly shadow. Mr WorkSafe skittled out of the seat, around the table to the other side, his indignance unashamedly thick.

Taking his seat, he proceeded to shuffle his paperwork, and it didn't escape LJ that Jase was watching him with narrowed eyes and intense focus.

What's bothering him? LJ dismissed the look. If he was going to have a shot at keeping his contracting run, this meeting *had* to go well.

LJ sat forward.

'Mr Tanner.' Pausing for effect, the man sharpened his gaze on LJ. 'Regarding our investigation into the death of Mr Samuel Whittington, whilst we recognise his death was a tragic accident, we do not believe he died without, let us say, a little help.'

Not a hint of sympathy or condolence for his loss was offered, and despite himself, LJ's stare remained glued to this man his future was in the hands of.

'What do you mean by *a little help*?' He sat back hard against his seat, shocked at the unspoken suggestion he could only think was being directed at him, his now sweaty palms flat on the table in front of him. He knew Sam had been drinking—probably more than he should have—but he hadn't been able to keep an eye on him because he'd been distracted by the electrical storm. Power had gone out, and that's when the small fire had started in Cookie's kitchen.

'Humph,' Mr WorkSafe said with satisfaction—clearly in response to LJ's lack of comeback—before he slid his eyes from LJ to peruse his papers with superiority once more.

'Mr Whittington had a deadly cocktail of alcohol and amphetamines in his system the night he died.'

What?

LJ could have sworn the glint in the man's eyes took keen satisfaction in the way his eyes were boggling. He blinked to clear his focus. That— wasn't possible.

With a stranglehold on his paperwork, Mr WorkSafe peered over the top of his thick glasses, studying LJ with intensity. 'You were his next of kin.' He looked down at the paperwork in front of him before returning his unwavering stare. He patted the documents lightly—was that impatience?—the shaft of an eyebrow raising. 'Is that correct, Mr Tanner?'

Was he being accused of killing his best friend—with drugs? Oh God, no.

'Sam never touched drugs!' Not as far as he knew. 'You have to be wrong.'

'Mr Tanner, I am most definitely *not* wrong. The coroner's findings are right here in front of me.'

There it was again, that glimmer of enjoyment—in the man's eyes, in the twitch of his lips—from the power play the job entailed, or his own self-importance, LJ had no clue. All he knew was that he didn't like the accusatory tones being fired his way. He fought with where to look, his mind blown by what he'd just heard. Couldn't the findings have been mixed up? Nothing about this rang true.

'I'm his next of kin. It's what Sam wanted.'

Sam had wanted it so his mother wouldn't have to deal with more fear and grief than she'd already endured with his cowardly letdown of a father. He was the one person who had LJ's back at every turn. And what had he done? Fallen so far short that he couldn't see himself ever deserving or returning to a normal life ever again.

Next to him, LJ sensed Jase's interlaced hands clench as

he placed them on the table overtly, calmly, his body rigid as he leaned forward.

LJ reached for the still pink scar on his forehead, wincing from its tenderness.

He'd tried, desperately, to remember those final moments. To recall the horrific events during that wild storm.

The windmill had lit up, seconds apart, as the rain had pelted him, stinging his face, fuelling his panic. He'd heard a voice, a war cry.

Bianca's screams.

A sheet of iron, hurtling through the air in the blackness.

And then nothing.

Until he woke, searching . . .

And found Sam's limp body lying still—so still—

His heart pounded in his throat. He'd remembered. And now— He wanted nothing more than to forget it, for an eternity.

'And, Mr Tanner, were you aware that the drugs found in his possession by the police the night of his accident were of a *home-grown* variety? You know, a little "raw" or "rough" around the edges? Significantly more potent than something more widely available.'

LJ's Adam's apple worked against his throat, and he realised the action would make him look decidedly more guilty, but he couldn't stop. This was getting worse, not better. If he was getting pinned for something to do with Sam taking drugs, then guilty or not, the final remnants of his reputation would be in tatters. And it wouldn't matter if he tried to get Poppy back to work for him. She wouldn't want anything to do with him ever again.

And if he was pinned for aiding in these "so-called" drugs that were obviously involved— A sudden thought rushed through LJ's mind, to Jase's brother—Mark Twigg. After growing up in Tasmania, Mark moved to the mainland, where he was currently a senior constable in the Western District of Victoria. Could he possibly help? But he dismissed the thought, Tasmania being well out of his jurisdiction.

'After your statement and the police report, Mr Tanner, an entry report was finalised, and you signed the statement of circumstances, did you not?'

What was it with this imbecile and his tosser approach to saying something so simple in such a pompous way?

'Yes.' LJ was baffled as to where this conversation was leading. They couldn't pin something so ridiculously far from the truth on him, could they?

'Right, then.' I need to inform you that, under the legislation of WorkSafe, you have failed in your duty of care as an employer to provide a safe place of work.' He paused, measuring the impact of his next words. 'And as a "friend", to look after the welfare of Samuel Whittington.'

LJ slowly shook his head in bewilderment, wooziness overtaking him. His vision blurred as he stared dumbfounded at the man.

'Mr Tanner. Do you have anything you'd like to add to the statement?'

Was that a note of gleefulness in his voice? *Does he want me to say 'Sure, it's all my fault. In fact, I gave him the stuff.'* His eyes began to dampen, worsening the blur already impeding his sight. This couldn't be happening.

'I have a question for you.' Jase's bold tone broke the tension in the air, taking them both by surprise.

'It's taken me some time to place you, but I reckon I have.' Jase's eyes narrowed. 'You were a cop.'

Mr WorkSafe gave the slightest flinch, enough for both LJ and Jase to see—the slight movement of his jaw; the muscle twitch in his cheek; a guilty swallow. But where was Jase going with this? It had nothing to do with Sam dying.

'We are here to discuss Mr Tanner, thank you. Now, let us stay on—'

'But it's true, isn't it?' Jase leaned forward, his elbows resting on the table, his shoulders flexing in his shearing singlet as his eyes trained on the man whose fingers fiddled nervously with his papers. Jase waited for an answer. When nothing came, he continued.

LJ looked at his mate, perplexed. But the one thing he knew about Jase was his tenacity with the details and his fox terrier nose to sniff out the truth.

'I recognised you from the news. It was a long time ago, but it's you.' Jase's glower clung to him.

'I fail to see how—'

'You were involved with several rape cases. The department did an audit, and admin found you'd neglected to delete several images of abused women taken at crime scenes and from hospitals. *Graphic images*.' Jase raised an accusatory eyebrow.

'Who are *you* anyway?' the small man said, his tone turning irritated, rattled.

'Jason Twigg.'

LJ watched the look of immediate recognition on the man's face from the mention of Jase's surname; he was sure. And he knew Jase was only warming up. He didn't need to fully understand the extent of what it was about. Jase was a stickler for justice, and with a brother in the police force, he'd back Jase's gut instinct every day of the week.

'I . . . ah . . .'

'There were concerns as to why you were retaining them. Your lame excuses wore thin, didn't they, Mr *WorkSafe*?'

The man hit Jase with an incredulous glare. 'That is not my name.'

'Doesn't matter.' Jase dismissed his reaction, his cheek twitching with a triumphant smile.

'Senior management got wind of what you were up to, didn't they? Your explanations for your actions were . . . weak.' Jase casually leaned back in his seat. 'They pressured you to continue your career . . . elsewhere. Wasn't WorkSafe a wonderful option for a small-time bastard like you?' Jase lifted his chin, his eyes unmoving.

LJ stared at his mate, only turning when Bear strode in, having heard everything from the doorway. He stood behind LJ and Jase. 'Mr WorkSafe, I think it's time you left.'

With three Goliath-like men blocking his escape, the man shot each one a nervous look as he began straightening his paperwork with a nervous rat-a-tat tat on the table. He stood, carrying with him his briefcase and what little dignity he had left, and walked out the door of the shed.

LJ leaned forward, his trembling hands covering his face. Jase might have scared his WorkSafe problem away for now, but a weak man like him usually came back with more ammunition for another round.

And what that meant for Take Two Shearers, he hated to think.

Chapter Forty-Eight

It was smoko on Tuesday morning when Poppy picked up her phone and saw the text message, the sausage roll she'd been enjoying suddenly gluing itself inside her tight throat. She fought against the urge to gag.

'Why haven't you taken the job? Ring me.' She glanced at the time on her phone. It was nine-fifty a.m. The message had been sent at eight that morning.

Her stomach coiled with apprehension. 'He's mad, real mad.

And the longer the day went on, the more she convinced herself of one fact. If she pretended the message hadn't come through, he wouldn't be able to blame her for not responding. It was lame, she knew it. But talking to him about this? She'd only be breaking his heart, not to mention his trust. He'd be left feeling let down and disrespected, all of the things she didn't want to do to him.

Argh! Couldn't Dad leave things be? She looked at the screen on her phone as she drove home, relief instantly flooding her. Jimmy's mischievous smile begged her to answer.

Poppy pulled over to the gravel and swiped her finger across the screen. She smiled, opening her mouth to say hello . . . when he spoke first.

'Oh, boy, little sis. You're in trouble now.'

'Thanks for saying hello.' She pouted at the screen.

'Sorry, but shit, Popps, not answering Dad's message? I'm the one copping the fallout. You do know that, don't you? I know you've got reception, and this phone hasn't drowned. What's going on?'

How much did Jimmy know? Play dumb. That's a good idea.

'What's he got his jocks in a knot over this time?'

'Don't give me that bullshit, Pop. The bloody job! Did you get the email?'

Nope, didn't work.

She couldn't believe her father. It was so like him to be thorough, telling Jimmy. It was where she got it from, and right now, she hated him for it. She gave a slow nod, her voice suddenly despondent. 'Yes, I got it.'

'And? Don't tell me. You didn't take it, did you? Did it cross your mind it might be a good idea to at least come home and meet them, turn them down in person because you didn't, I don't know, like the toilet seats in the facility, or something?'

'You know I can't leave! I'm in the middle of a job, and anyway, I thought you were supporting me with this. What's changed?' Her cheeks burned. Had her brother ratted on her?

'Just ring Dad, alright? I don't know. Spin some story. You're good at that.' His tone left her stripped of her sense of pride, ownership of the career she was falling back in love with, and, worse, her relationship with him. His last words left her hanging.

'See ya, Popps.' His voice was deflated, and she knew where this was heading. He'd supported her this whole time.

Now it felt like her favourite sibling was giving up on her too.

'What are you talking about, Dad? The last time I looked at the accounts, I was about to buy the shearing run.' LJ huffed. He heard the same sound from the other end of the line as he stared out at the front garden from Grandma Aimee's loungeroom window.

'Miles tells me it's been missing *since* then.' His father's pause hovered uncomfortably in the air.

LJ rubbed his tired eyes. Was his dad saying he'd pinched the money to buy the business? 'How much are we talking about? Did we buy grain we forgot to log?'

'Son.' The abruptness of the word took LJ by surprise. 'I don't think we would've forgotten a twenty-thousand-dollar bill.'

LJ flinched against the chill in the air. Money like that didn't entirely vanish. He ran a hand through his hair, pausing mid-way. 'Was it taken in one go, or over a long period of time?'

'Shouldn't you know?' The words hit him like a punch in the face.

'All at once.' His father let out a fatigued sigh.

'Does Miles remember anything about it? He's doing the books now. He should know.'

There was a deathly pause on the other end of the phone. 'Dad?'

His father gave a weary groan. 'He reckons you took it.'

'What? Why? I wouldn't—'

Steal money from my parents, or the farm I loved. He always wanted to stay on it, working alongside his Dad. Why would Miles say that? His brother confused him at the best of times. He'd always preferred slouching in a beanbag, shooting bad guys and zombies rather than setting a foot outside.

'Dad. I'd never—' LJ paced the living room. Surely his dad didn't believe this ridiculous accusation.

'You wouldn't listen when I told you not to take on that pitiful shearing run. Had to have it any way you could. Now look where it's got you. LJ, where did you get the money to buy it?'

His father's words were like a snake bite, hard and sharp. But could he rat on his grandfather? If he did, that would be another relationship he would be responsible for destroying.

'I got a loan.' Pa Pat had backed him one hundred

percent, both with the finances and for his ability.

'You're a smart boy,' Pa had said. 'I know you'll make it work. Throw me a bit of work every now and again, and a little super. I don't need the money for anything. By the time I do, you'll be a rich man with a business no one can stay away from.' He'd given his grandson a solid pat on the shoulder. 'You get it back to me when you can.'

And that's exactly what he'd been doing, feeding small amounts into his grandfather's personal account as often as he could. Until lately.

'It all depends on where the loan came from, then, doesn't it?' The terseness of his father's voice indicated their conversation was all but done.

'Dad, are you okay with Miles making all the farm decisions? Since when did you let him start to? He's never—' He started pushing a hand through his hair, stopping mid-way, then flinching from the clunk of the farmhouse phone as he pulled his mobile away from his ear, before quietly finishing his sentence. '. . . wanted anything to do with the farm.' The raw truth of the words settled in deep and hard. *It's always only been me who wanted to live and die there—*

LJ let his hand drop to his side as a flock of New Holland honeyeaters chirped and bathed themselves in the dish of water under the magnolia tree. Miles was pushing him off the farm, of that he was certain. But his gut told him it was more than that. It was from his own family, too—for good.

'Twenty-bloody-thousand-dollars!' It sounded a hell of a lot more when he said it out loud.

Determined to focus on what was more important than

the horrendous amount of missing money, LJ grabbed his keys. Grandma Aimee was in hospital for another round of tests, to determine if she had suffered any more mini-strokes, and he sure needed to be around someone saner than his father right now.

With a posy of pink and white daisies in one hand, and a new trashy magazine in the other, LJ strode into her hospital room. On the shelf sat three cards from long-time friends, and a jar of coconut cookies. A slow smile formed on his face, quietly disappointed he'd missed catching his mother.

He walked in, then stilled, his smile slipping away. Grandma Aimee was sound asleep. He placed the flowers in an empty vase, filled it with water, and approached the bed when her eyes fluttered open. They followed him with a gentle smile.

He placed the vase on her bedside table, smiling warmly as he stepped back.

'It's so good to see you, my dear.' She squeezed his hand in hers.

'You look good, Grandma.' He didn't have the heart to tell her she looked fatigued, a little pale, and, dare he say it, resigned. 'Have they been looking after you?'

Her eyes widened. 'Oh yes, dear. I'm rather spoilt. They bring me my favourite dessert every night.'

He tipped his head to the side a little, studying her closely. Did they feed patients vanilla panna cotta these days? Or was it another figment of her imagination?

'I brought you some riveting reading,' he said, tongue in cheek, giving her a loving wink as he placed the magazine on her lap and took the chair next to the bed. Their conversation covered the usual topics, including her realisation that the kitchen had been done up—for the third time.

'Tell me, darling, have you seen that sweet girl you talk so much about?' Her eyes were expectant as she twisted her head on the pillow to face him.

What could he say? *She doesn't want to talk to me, won't work for me, and is generally making my life miserable.* He wanted to make his grandmother's day, but when it came to women, that just wasn't possible. And how the heck was she remembering all this anyway?

'No.' The floor became his focal point, and he shook his head in slow motion. 'I haven't.'

'Why ever not?'

LJ raised his head, staring at Grandma Aimee in disbelief, her usual serene tone now on the verge of scolding.

'I— I've been busy.' *Lame, LJ. Real lame.*

'Well, if you'd like a piece of advice from an old lady, and I'm only suggesting it,' she said, her tone full of understanding and love while she waited for him to return her gaze. 'You should do it soon. That lovely little thing isn't going to wait around until you decide to get your act into gear, is she?' Her index finger waggled in his direction, her adoring eyes penetrating him. 'You promised me. Remember?' This time, she offered up a cunning smile.

She was right. Poppy hadn't waited around. And what if she never came back? Nursing was calling her loud and clear from what Stacey had said.

'Good afternoon, Aimee. Let's check your stats out, shall we?' The almost too cheerful, pushy tone had a familiar ring, and LJ shook his guilt aside as the nurse brushed past, taking his grandmother's patient chart from the end of the bed.

Oh— Crap.

With the board flipped open, the nurse spoke as she checked the results of Aimee's latest obs. 'We'll take your temp and blood pressure again, and I'll need to take a blood sample . . .' Her voice slowed and her smile rose when she looked up. 'LJ.'

'Is this the lovely girl you were telling me about, sweetheart?' Grandma Aimee looked from him to her. 'So lovely to meet you, my dear.'

LJ's eyes dropped to his hands, and he slowly shook his head. Yet again, he was grateful to Sam for his beard masking the racing heat filling his cheeks.

'Oh, did he just? What a nice surprise.' The nurse studied him, a cursory smile crossing her face. 'I haven't heard from him yet. You might need to have a whisper in his ear about that, Aimee.'

LJ was trapped by Grandma Aimee's misleading suggestion and by Stacey, who sidled up beside him.

'Um, she's not having such a great day today.' His voice turned quiet and concerned as he stood, backing away one cautious step at a time.

'Oh, she's been on my watch all afternoon and been super sharp. Hasn't missed a trick.' With a smug smile, Stacey moved closer, and he recoiled, trapped by the wall, the chair, and a wearisomely pushy nurse.

In the same amount of time it took Stacey to return Grandma Aimee's patient chart to the end of the bed, LJ had kissed his grandmother goodbye and sprinted from the room. He swung a left to the stairwell, his breathing hurried. Since when had he become such a chicken around women?

Since Poppy Fletcher had come on the scene.

Chapter Forty-Nine

LJ examined his wool lines, not happy. They all looked the same, nothing like how Poppy could make them stand out. Was he doing this farmer a major injustice, and inevitably his team? He pressed the back of his hand to his head. This grower would never use them again.

Poppy. He needed her. He'd pay her overtime from his own pocket if she'd come and sort out his mess. Would she come in over the weekend? It wouldn't look good to the grower, but it would pay in the long run. If he was lucky, they'd employ his team again purely for his integrity.

Without warning, his heart bumped inside his chest as Grandma Aimee's words came to mind. His grandmother was right. He wanted—no needed—to come good on a promise. Then he could allow himself to believe he deserved some happiness. He needed to see Poppy and tell her how he felt. He walked out the shed door, shutting it behind him. He'd swing by The Lone Pony, hoping he could catch her.

And after that? He'd cross everything and hope she'd listen.

Poppy's shoulders tensed as she caught another glance her way from stand five.

Bloody Rick. And what annoyed her more was the fact that she found herself constantly looking up with caution to check if he was watching her. She had to stop doing that!

Rick had kept his distance, but only enough to have her thinking he was no longer interested. But his all too regular glances her way as he shore, left her feeling insecure, accountable, and guarded.

Thankfully, the end of the week was here, and she found herself desperate to escape the shed. But as she reached for the door handle of her car, his voice stopped her like a slap. She tipped her head despondently at the dirt around her feet.

'Hey, Poppy, what are you doing this weekend?' Rick strolled up casually, but she wasn't fooled. He carried the ambience of a cunning wolf in a sheep's woolly coat.

'Nothing much.' She shrugged, hoping he'd get the message as she lowered herself into her car and reached for the ignition. What she did was none of his business.

'Wanna grab a pizza, catch a movie, you know, like old times? I'd love—'

'Sorry. I've already got a date.' Her heart swelled with love, appreciation, and sheer relief at the thought of Adrian. She cherished their Friday night takeaway dinners.

Poppy took keen delight in his shocked face, but almost immediately, tightly wound coils gripped her stomach, his displeased expression revealing the truth about his real thoughts.

'Right. No worries. Enjoy.' His nod might have been meant to say he wasn't bothered by what she'd just told him, but the shift in his gaze, coupled with his narrowed eyes, told her he felt put out.

She feigned interest in her phone as she waited for him to drive away, before waving to the farmer as he drenched the last mob in the yards. The afternoon sun hung low in the early spring sky, the nights continuing to throw decent frosts, but the days were warm enough to encourage small blades of grass to shoot. Poppy inhaled the freshness in the air and flexed her shoulders, forcing them to loosen. She didn't have to see Rick for two whole days, and puppy training was high on her schedule thanks to Grandpa Isaac's training book arriving. She was also going to visit George.

She cranked the heater up and headed towards town. With the music pumping, her fingers tapped to the beat. She sang at the top of her voice, relieved to feel her tight muscles finally beginning to relax.

Inhaling the sensational smell of pizza as she entered the

shop, she headed towards the counter. Twenty minutes later, one steaming *capricciosa* sat next to her on the passenger seat and she was salivating before rounding the first corner.

When she turned into the driveway, the pony nickered and she pulled over. The mare had developed a routine of waiting for her arrival, where she'd present her with an apple she'd saved from her lunch. She scratched the horse on the forelock as it chewed contentedly, and Adrian came jogging down the drive, his smile bigger than the full moon due that night.

'It smells yummy, Poppy,' he said, stopping at the open car door.

They sat at Poppy's small dining table with the box open and their mouths shut, savouring every mouthful. Adrian broke the silence, a long piece of mozzarella dangling from his lip.

'Did you have a good day, Poppy?'

A piece of mozzarella dangled from his lip, and Poppy stifled a smile. 'It was okay, but it's great now.'

'There's people coming to stay tonight.' Adrian smiled. 'We're going to be busy.' He took another enthusiastic bite.

Poppy held back a sigh. She understood they needed guests, but she loved the stillness of the surrounding bush without the disruption of people coming and going. It was selfish to think that way, but how was she going to keep sneaking Jazz in if customers were wandering around everywhere?

'What do you say we go get an ice cream for dessert? I'm in the mood for something vanilla.'

'Yes, yes!' Adrian's smile almost outdid his jigging on

the spot as he stood, gulping down his last bit of pizza.

The wind was picking up, rocking the car, and she held the steering wheel a little tighter. The supermarket car park was almost deserted when Poppy pulled up out front, waving to Bianca as she drove away.

Poppy sat still, her heart heavy. If they'd arrived a little sooner, she could've asked Bianca how the team were; how LJ was. But in that split second, she realised she didn't need to know because she hadn't heard from him. He was obviously getting along just fine without her.

Adrian was out of the car in a flash and through the door to the ice cream cabinet before she'd locked the car.

She paid for their dessert, and Adrian ripped open his Drumstick, searching for a rubbish bin at the front of the store. The sliding doors slid open and a strong gust blew his footy beanie from his head. Poppy snatched it up from the floor, pushing it back around his ears. 'There you go.' She smiled warmly, turning back towards the door when her appetite fell away.

'Rick.' Her ice cream began to drip.

'Nice date.' He looked from Adrian to her, stepping forward to reach for her hand. 'Poppy. Let's talk.' He did a quick, dismissive glance in Adrian's direction.

'No, Rick.' She pulled her hand away and turned to Adrian. 'Let's go.' She hoped desperately that he wouldn't pick up on the nervous edge her voice had suddenly developed.

Rick stuck his hand out, taking her by the arm, gently but firmly enough that it sent a flare of wariness rushing through her. She shucked her arm from his grip.

'Rick, this is not the place,' and she flicked a glance at Adrian, 'or the time. I'm. Not. Interested.'

Adrian looked at Poppy wide-eyed, then stepped forward, his protective glare fixed on Rick. She drew alongside Adrian, but he took another half-step forward, like a guardian.

'Poppy doesn't want to talk.' Adrian crossed his arms, his ice cream angled precariously.

She put a protective arm around his shoulder, hoping she'd disguised the shake as she set her eyes on Rick. 'Have a good weekend, Rick. Let's go, Adrian.'

Making it to the car, she glanced over her shoulder. Rick had turned to watch her, his eyes narrowed, determined, and definitely disgruntled. Everything deep down she had feared. He held her gaze a moment longer before he strode to his car, reassurance flooding her.

'Hey, Poppy. Can I get a packet of chips? We can watch a movie on your telly.'

Poppy's eyes shot to Adrian's. If they went into the shop again, it would be a good test to see if Rick would leave; the likelihood of him following them back inside doubtful. His persistence was beginning to wear her down. She snuck a peek over Adrian's shoulder to see Rick sitting in his car, immersed in his phone.

'Okay. Good idea.'

The lights in the store glared at her, making it impossible to see through the darkness now surrounding them. Her body gave a shiver. They walked along the chip aisle, directly in line with Rick's ute lights, Poppy unable to peel her wary eyes from them. Adrian leaned in close to her shoulder.

'I don't like him.'

Poppy couldn't help but smile. 'Me either.'

Turning away from the front window, she scanned their choices. 'What flavour do you feel like?' Thanks to Rick, the pizza now sat like a crowbar in her stomach, and the ice cream had coated her hand in a sticky mess.

Unconsciously moving to the next aisle, Poppy's shoulders slumped as the headlights of the ute stayed on, unmoving. Why wasn't he leaving?

Without any particular thought, she marched to the large array of chocolate bars. 'We need chocolate. Lots of it.' She started grabbing every different flavour and variety she could hold in her arms.

'Adrian, we need washing detergent. And a toothbrush. And new socks.' She threw a broom into Adrian's arms for good measure, because Jazz was sure to destroy another pillow, or heaven forbid, her doona, one of these days. The checkout chick watched them suspiciously, and she knew they couldn't lurk much longer, even if they could manage to hold just one more item. She rounded the next corner and to her relief, finally, the ute lights had gone.

Relief flooded her, and she dumped what she termed her "ridiculous shopping" items onto the conveyor belt, the pimply-faced teenager giving her the impression she was working well past her bedtime. She flashed her a "I seriously need all these things" smile, scanned her card, then snatched up their purchases, sharing them between both hers and Adrian's arms. She'd be finding a new supermarket to shop from now on, regardless of whether it was kilometres away.

The roads were quiet as she drove back to the caravan park, but she couldn't stop the way her eyes gave nervous glances to her rear vision mirror all too regularly, the uneasiness that they might be being followed all too unshakable. She lightly thrummed the steering wheel as a distraction. Why had she allowed Rick to wind her up this much all over again? And why did his presence make her nerve endings crawl? She'd watched him take out his frustration on his family, telling them how useless they were. But it was only now she recalled the way he would follow this up by looking around the shed to see who had watched on.

And then smiled.

Then he did it to her.

And she didn't hang around.

Poppy turned into the entrance, scanning the park for unexpected cars or utes. All she could see was the glow of the moon highlighting the pony standing at the far end of the paddock. It looked up with slight curiosity, then dropped her head again to resume her snooze.

The sound of a baby crying in the distance broke the still night air as they hopped out of the car. She was dying to get inside and put the kettle on, and she could almost taste the chocolate and salty chips. With bags in hand, she was about to head towards the caravan door when she stilled, squinting into the darkness, forcing her eyes to focus. Was there . . . movement in the shadows?

Dismissing her hyperactive imagination, she started towards her caravan when a rustle stopped her in her tracks. Was it Adrian? But he was already inside the caravan, the TV humming. From behind a thick-trunked tree, Rick stepped forward, his palms in the air in what appeared to be some kind of "I'm not here to scare you" apology, but she was far from believing he meant it.

A slight shade of panic fought its way to the surface, her heart pounding inside her chest.

The other night—

'Poppy, I just need you to hear me out.' His voice was controlled, set. 'What we had was great, and it still can be.' He stepped closer, his appealing smile the one of old—the one she'd all too easily fallen for.

'What do you really want, Rick? Was he putting on the charm because that's the way he always got what he wanted? Had she been the first one to say this behaviour wasn't okay?

She couldn't move, only stare at him in utter disbelief. The wind whipped her hair around her face, the disturbance of car engines approaching from behind.

'All you've got to do is give us a go again, Poppy.' He took a step closer, his arms out in front of him. Had he stooped to a new low, begging her?

'Come back to the farm, class for us.' For a split second, Poppy genuinely thought she was seeing an honest version of Rick, his face almost pleading, even desperate, before it hardened. Then she remembered.

'And what? Believe you won't throw me under the bus again? You let me take the fall for someone else's mistake.' That's all it could be, she sincerely believed it. In the glow of the caravan light, anger was building behind his eyes.

Car doors opened and shut, then footsteps paced

towards them. If it was guests staying nearby, she'd be grateful to know she could call on some help if she needed it. But it wouldn't come to that.

Poppy took as casual a step back as she could, not wanting to give Rick any indication he had her flustered, nervous, and her heart wanting to explode inside her chest. He took another step towards her, his hands now lowered, his eyes turning steely. Why was he doing this? He had everything he wanted. A farm, a family to run it with, and his *other* woman.

'Rick, you don't get to come around here and expect I'll— What is it you want me to do? Fall at your feet? I might've fallen for your smooth charm once, but there's no way I'm doing that again.' She'd been the one who was the fool, thinking she needed him.

This time, it was her who took a step closer. 'And don't follow me anymore.' She pointed at him. 'Not now. Not ever!'

'If I didn't know better, I'd say you're scared, Poppy.' A delighted smile crept over his face, his eyes penetrating hers.

'You'd better leave, Rick. I don't think Poppy wants you here,' a deep voice from behind spoke.

What? *Dad*? But how? Poppy's eyes widened, but she didn't dare turn and look.

Yet another voice spoke up.

'Rick. Let it go. Poppy has told you she doesn't want you here.' This voice was composed, warm and oh so familiar. Poppy's throat clenched with shock.

'Stay out of it, Jimmy. This is none of your concern.' Rick's anger flared as he pointed past Poppy's shoulder, and she desperately wanted to look behind her. But that would only leave her vulnerable, and Rick was seriously starting to frighten her.

'Why don't you tell Poppy the truth, Rick? Tell her how it was you who set her up.'

He— What?

Rick stepped to within a foot of her, reaching out and grabbing her upper arms, looking deeply into her eyes with desperation. 'I don't know what he's talking about.' His grip tightened.

'What did you do, Rick?'

'Nothing I didn't have to. You just needed to be put in your place. That's all. My family were talking you up like you were the best classer they'd ever had, but they told me you'd never hang around. And they were right.' Spittle sprayed from his mouth as he looked at her in disgust. I was meant to do the classing, but because of you, they wouldn't give me a shot.'

'How on earth were you supposed to class the clip, Rick? You never finished getting your classer's ticket.'

'With your stencil.' His voice rose. 'But no. Miss High and Mighty wasn't about to let me use it.' His jaw clenched as he leaned closer, and Poppy squirmed against his grip. 'Face it, Poppy. You weren't *that* good.'

She stared at him, dumbfounded. Never mind the fact it was downright irresponsible to lend out your stencil—risking your whole reputation on the skills, or lack thereof from someone else. 'So, you threw me under the bus instead?' Now it was all beginning to make sense. '*You* put the black wool in the bales. Your best line. But why?'

'He repressed the whole eight bales. It was enough for

his family to think you'd stuffed up their entire clip, and never want you back,' Jimmy said.

'How would you know?' Rick's nostrils flared as he released a hand, jabbing a pointed finger at Jimmy.

'Tiffany.' He shrugged, giving the appearance that it was casual. 'I'm good mates with her brother. She got sick of you, too, didn't she.'

'Shut the—'

'So why do you want me back, Rick?' Poppy wasn't fooled. Rick only ever wanted something if it was going to serve his own purposes.

'He didn't want you back. He wanted your stencil,' Jimmy said.

'So that's why you followed me? To steal it?' Never more than now was she grateful to her inner hunch to keep it with her at all times.

'And you frickin never let it out of your bloody sight.'

With stealth, Adrian snuck up behind Rick, and Rick stooped forward, his face aghast as a fragrant shower of washing powder doused him from behind. The wind blew it wildly into the air, and Rick coughed and spluttered, then yelped before falling on his knees. Poppy gasped for breath, taking the opportunity to pull herself free, unknowingly stepping straight back into Jimmy's arms.

Poppy spun around, brushing the powdery scent from her face as she looked up at him. 'You *finally* bought your ticket!'

Chapter Fifty

LJ skidded to a stop behind the car that had stopped in front of Poppy and Rick, watching the scene unfold. Rick was being held down on the ground by Adrian and an older man. But who was the guy Poppy was hugging so tightly? His body stiffened. He'd been so busy not seeing a future for himself, had he just lost what could have been his, here and now?

Moving from his ute, he walked towards Adrian, whose bright eyes and big smile were beaming as he stood. LJ put a brotherly arm around his shoulder.

'So, how'd you do it, buddy?' Jimmy strolled over to them, grin large, his focus set on Adrian.

'We bought a broom. I threw the washing powder over his head, then hit him behind his knees. He was hurting Poppy.' Adrian gave a fierce nod, and LJ protectively squeezed his shoulder.

'Well, Adrian, I'm Jimmy, and I like your handiwork.' Jimmy's infectious smile glowed as he reached out to shake Adrian's hand.

'Thanks.' Adrian gave a shy grin. 'Are . . . you Poppy's brother?'

LJ's brow rose.

'Sure am.' Both men grinned from ear to ear, and LJ swung his relieved gaze towards Poppy. *Her brother?* He offered her a flash of his smile, catching her eye as she turned. But her gaze was cautious, unsure, and he softened his own, hoping it was enough to convey what he was thinking and all that he wanted. Right now, he didn't care if anyone else was watching or what they thought. There was something he had to say.

In one final gesture to convince her, he tipped his head to the side, begging her to come over with a soft smile. Her small frown asked if he was sure, and he gave a gentle nod. As she approached, he began to chuckle, his head rocking in disbelief. 'You look like you've been in a snowstorm.'

'Feels like I've been through the washing machine.' Her laugh made his heart leap, and he reached for her hand, gently tugging her to him and holding her tight. His nose began to buzz. With a hand cradling the back of her head as she rested against his chest, his cheek nestled into her hair, and he suddenly let out a sneeze.

She giggled.

Jimmy came over to them, and LJ straightened. He lifted his right arm over Poppy and offered it to him. 'G'day.

I'm LJ.'

'Ah. You're the contractor.' Jimmy shook his hand, offering a knowing smirk at Poppy.

'Yeah?' LJ glanced warily at Poppy, unsure what exactly was going on.

'You're the one who couldn't get a homing pigeon to base camp if he tried.' Jimmy's good-natured wink brought a flush to LJ's cheeks. She'd told him that?

'Yeah, that'd be me.' He nodded, giving a steady chuckle, and Poppy a teasing tickle in the ribs. Her smile was priceless, her eyes shining up at him.

Jimmy eyed her suspiciously. 'You know, Popps, you're looking a little aged. That early Spanish greying trait sure has hit you earlier than me.' He brushed his dark hair with a smooth hand, flicking his head with pretend finesse. 'Don't think it ever will either.' But his cheeky smile slipped away the moment he copped a sisterly backhand to his stomach.

'Whaat? It's true,' he teased.

'Poppy?'

She turned back to LJ, her expression unreadable as he brushed the powder from the side of her face with gentle fingers. He opened his mouth to speak, then stopped. His rueful smile hid what his racing mind was thinking. He had to tell her, now. 'I was the idiot . . .'

'No, you weren't. It was me.' She shook her head as LJ put a tender finger to her lips, silencing her.

He searched her eyes as he fought for the courage to speak, and brushed the loose hair framing her face, tenderly behind both ears.

'It was Sam's death.' *There, I said it.* But could he admit the truth?

'I made promises I didn't keep.' He looked away, ashamed. 'And I'm not sure I can keep them anymore.' He fingered the hair at the side of her neck before finally gathering the courage to look at her again. 'I should've tried harder to get the team more work. I should've fought harder to get you back because, well, I need you.'

'Do you need me for the shearing run, or do you need *me*?' Her eyes were earnest, begging for his heartfelt honesty. And that's what he gave her.

He looked deep into her rich brown eyes, his heart shuddering. 'I need both. You're under my skin, Pop, and I want you to stay there. Forever.'

Poppy reluctantly let go of LJ's arms, squeezing his hands after one last kiss before reaching for his face, cupping his cheeks and offering a reassuring smile. It felt so good to hold him, finally. But she needed to take care of something else before she allowed herself to become swept away in the moment—the first of many she hoped.

Poppy cautiously walked towards her father, who was now leaning against the hire car, thanks to Jimmy keeping a firm hold of Rick as sirens in the distance sounded. His arms were folded over his well-rounded belly, a thoughtful, serious look on his face as he watched her approach. When she reached him, she hung back, expecting to get a lecture for being careless, scaring him half to death, and . . . for lying.

'Dad, I'm, um—' She shied from his gaze. 'I'm sorry I lied.' There. She'd said it. She blinked at her powder-coated sneakers, shame and embarrassment descending on her at a rapid pace. 'It's—' She shrugged. 'I had to prove to myself I hadn't lost my nerve.' Risking a cautious glance his way, she begged him to understand. 'I don't want to do nursing. I never have.'

Her father offered a steady nod, considering her before he spoke. 'I'm sorry you thought you had to lie. And, I admit, I didn't make it easy.' He looked away as he shook his head. 'After your mother died, all I could think was, what if that happened to me? And these headaches I've been suffering—' He pushed himself off the car, taking a step towards her. 'They scared me, Poppy. We fought hard to keep nurses available for your mother. But, if something like that were to happen to me too . . . well, I thought if you did nursing, you'd be there if I needed you.' He hung his head in shame.

'I'll always be there for you, Dad, especially if you need me because you're unwell.' She searched his reluctant eyes.

'I don't want to lose you, Poppy.'

She grabbed him around the waist, nuzzling into his chest.

'You never will, Dad. Ever.'

Chapter Fifty-One

Everything in LJ screamed at him to stay well away from the farm. But so much more called for him to front up and face the firing squad. He just hoped he'd picked the right time to do it.

As he drove along the narrow driveway, his mother's fruit trees in the side paddock popped with spring bursts of soft pinks and pale whites. LJ held the memories of a happy childhood, playing goodies and baddies with slingshots and wooden sticks for guns with Brad, Sam and Miles. He chuckled lightly. They'd never let Bianca join in. Deep down, he knew she would have slain them if they'd given her half a chance.

His father stood on the verandah, his arms crossed and feet wide apart as LJ pulled to a stop. Behind him stood Miles, his smugness unmistakable. LJ stepped from his ute, the apprehension making him want to throw up.

'Ha, you have some nerve turning up here. Good thing we're around to keep an eye on you, light fingers 'n all.' Miles's menacing tone had LJ clenching his fingers at his side.

As he walked towards the steps to greet his mother, his father stopped him with a flat hand in the air. 'Not a good idea, son.' Stan gave him a warning look, and he stepped back, blinking in disbelief. His perplexed gaze drifted to the kitchen window, where his mother's devastated expression gouged deep inside his chest.

As if to justify his actions, his father continued. 'I don't think we, *I*, can trust you anymore.'

'I didn't steal any money, Dad.'

Miles scoffed.

'Here. Check my accounts.' He'd come prepared, and when he handed the paperwork to his father, Miles stepped in, snatching them out of his hands.

'What did you do, have a little talk to the bank manager? Come up with a clever plan? She is rather pretty, isn't she?' Miles's sneer was laced with suggestion, and it dawned on LJ that the brothel wasn't the only place his brother may have frequented.

'You'd know better than me.' His eyes narrowed on his brother, the implication in his tone distinct, determined. He turned to his father. 'Take a look at the papers, Dad. I haven't touched a thing.'

'I don't think that's necessary,' Miles said, crushing the papers in his fist.

LJ's gaze shifted from Miles to his father's. 'Out of interest, Dad, have you actually looked at the accounts yourself?' LJ watched his father carefully for a change in his father's expression. When he was still living at the farm, he'd taken over the books because his father hated that part of the farm work. He hadn't liked it either, but at that stage, no one else was volunteering.

'It's all there to see in black and white, LJ.' His gruff tone became impatient, and he waved a dismissive hand in the air.

'But have you? It's only fair to let me take a look, prove my innocence.'

'And let you alter what you like to cover your butt? What do you think we are? *Stupid?* You always did think you knew everything.' Miles crossed his arms, looking away from LJ in disgust.

Their father looked at his boots.

It was obvious to LJ that, for now, he wasn't going to get far. This had been his best shot at clearing his name, and he'd half-expected it to fail. But there were other ways to get to the truth.

With a respectful nod to his father, LJ strode back to his ute, catching sight of the smirk spreading across Miles's face as he watched him wring his paperwork into a twisted knot. They had been good mates when they were young, right up until Sam and Josie had come to live with them.

It had never been the same since.

Taking one last, regretful glance at the kitchen window, his mother's pained face searched his before she too turned away.

LJ drove in a non-hurried manner down the driveway.

He needed to set some wheels in motion, but it would take some time.

Something he wasn't sure he had.

'Did you find it?' LJ stared at Pa Pat expectantly before he took a seat beside his grandfather at the computer. They had LJ's bank transactions on the screen.

'I found a withdrawal for the twenty thousand dollars. But son, it's got your name next to it.' Pa watched him with a deep frown, his glasses perched low on his nose. 'He's made you look batshit guilty.'

'No. There must be something to prove I didn't. If we don't find it, I'm going to lose the shearing run.' He ran a damp hand down his thigh, despising the admission. 'I'll never be able to repay you.'

'Don't go thinkin' like that now, lad. You didn't do it, so we'll prove it.'

LJ nodded, though doubt gnawed at him. 'Can I see the printout?' Pa passed it to him, and he studied it as he stood to put the kettle on.

The answer *had* to be in front of him. Somewhere. He took his original statement, grateful he'd only given his father—or rather Miles—a photocopy. He compared his name—the branch—everything matched.

Taking a seat at the kitchen table, his grandfather leaned

over his shoulder, placing a steaming coffee in front of him, then paused. His callused finger hovered before sliding to the small account number beside the withdrawal amount.

'Bingo.' Pa Pat tapped the paper with his finger, then pushed his glasses back up. LJ could see it too—the crucial slip-up. Sure, it might be his name on the account saying he'd taken the money, but it wasn't his account number. LJ traced his finger down the figures.

And there it was. A match.

Pa Pat clapped him on the back. 'Now let's go save that shearing run of yours!'

LJ took off in the ute with Pa Pat clutching the sides of the seat. 'Slow down, son. We've gotta get there in one piece first!'

But urgency drove LJ harder. Part of him wanted to call the police immediately, but something held him back—he wanted the chance to confront Miles first, to understand why. His brother had already stolen that opportunity once.

As they approached the house, LJ's foot hit the brake. A police car was sitting in the driveway.

A uniformed officer emerged and turned towards their approaching vehicle. LJ's hands grew clammy on the steering wheel. Miles stood at the verandah steps, arms crossed, wearing an expression of pure satisfaction. LJ's stomach dropped as he parked and stepped from his ute, his breathing shallow and fast.

Miles broke the silence.

'Perfect timing, boys. There he is.' Miles pointed an accusing finger at LJ. 'Arrest him and get him off my premises.' His laugh was cold and triumphant.

The second officer joined his colleague as they approached LJ with grim determination. 'Are you Miles Tanner? We need to ask you a few questions.' The first officer stood two metres away from him, while his partner watched on, his hand resting near his holster

LJ's brow creased. Weren't they here for him?

'No, I'm not.' He glanced at Miles, who was still basking in anticipated vindication, oblivious to what the officer had actually said. 'That's him up there.' LJ pointed towards the verandah.

The officers turned towards Miles, whose triumphant expression suddenly crumbled. 'What are you doing? Arrest him!' He jabbed his finger at LJ as the second officer climbed the steps.

'Mr Tanner, we have a search warrant for materials related to the death of Samuel Whittington. You need to come with us for questioning.'

LJ's mind reeled. What did any of this have to do with Sam?

'You bastard, Lincoln!' Miles struggled against the officer's grip as handcuffs clicked into place. They escorted him to the patrol car.

LJ stood frozen, watching his brother's arrest when he'd expected to face his own. Why Miles, not him?

'Sam had to pay, Lincoln. And it was so easy.' Miles's bitter laugh echoed across the yard. 'All he wanted was to forget his old man.'

Confusion clouded LJ's features. What did Sam need to pay for? The officer slammed the car door, cutting off Miles's words.

Stan burst through the screen door, hurrying toward the officer who displayed his badge. 'What's happening?' His worried gaze darted between the officer, LJ, and Miles, now sitting in the backseat.

'Seems Miles has got himself into some serious trouble,' Pa Pat said quietly, shaking his head at his grandson with profound disappointment.

A second patrol car arrived. Three more officers entered the house, emerging with several evidence bags. Bianca's car came hurtling down the driveway, gravel spraying as she skidded to a stop and ran to LJ as the police drove away with Miles.

Hours later, they gathered in the kitchen to hear the news. Stan hung up the phone and turned to face them, his complexion wan.

'Miles pleaded guilty to drug trafficking and dealing.' He stopped short, and LJ slumped onto the nearest chair at the kitchen table before his legs collapsed beneath him. He fought against the urge to vomit.

'Apparently, he detested Sam moving in with us all those years ago.' Stan turned to LJ. 'He blamed Sam for taking you away from him, and he knew it was only a matter of time before Sam would drink himself silly again.'

'No, Sam!' LJ said, burying his face in his hands as his chest heaved.

Chapter Fifty-Two

Shearing at the new shed was delayed by a week while LJ cleared his name over the missing money with the police. He also needed to let Poppy finish her last job with Sweeny's team. The biggest shock news came when Poppy rang to let LJ know on Wednesday that the police had turned up at her work, taking Sweeny away for questioning.

By Friday, the police informed LJ and the family of their findings. Ryan Sweeny had been working with Miles to traffic and sell homegrown drugs amongst the brothel women.

Miles had convinced Sam to buy some of their drugs because they would make him forget what his dad had done, and, combined with the amount of alcohol in his system the night of his death, he'd hallucinated and jumped.

LJ stood beside the kitchen bench at his parents' place,

the smell of his mother's freshly cooked tea cake the last thing he could stomach right now. He knew they all needed to talk, but LJ couldn't seem to find his voice.

'I'm sorry, son.' Stan's eyes were tired and drawn. 'I knew it didn't sound like you, but—' He shook his head in shame. 'Miles had me fully convinced.'

LJ watched a lone tear roll from his father's eye, the first he'd ever seen him shed. He swallowed hard against the tightness in his throat as a soft knock sounded at the door. Everyone looked up.

'May I come in?'

'Oh, God, please— No.' LJ backed away, his face draining of colour as his limbs went weak. There was no way he could face her, and he moved towards the door.

'LJ?' Josie's fragile voice begged for his attention, and he froze, clenching his eyes. He couldn't do this. He fought to steady his breathing.

'I— I want you to know you did keep your promise.' Josie sniffled.

LJ's eyes flew open, and he shook his head at the floor. 'No, I didn't.'

'Yes, you did. I know it because of this.' She held out a small, tattered note, creased from folding. LJ forced himself to turn and face Sam's mother, his eyes red-rimmed as he avoided her gaze. She nodded encouragingly, coaxing him to take it.

LJ traced his thumb over it as a memory surfaced, bringing a faint smile to his lips. He drew in a shaky breath before opening the note.

'LJ never took his eyes off me, Mum. I took my eyes off

him.'

What? LJ read the words again. How had Sam known about the promise he'd made to Josie? His chest tightened, and he struggled for breath; the pain and guilt of promises unkept finally beginning to lift.

'Oh, man.' His hand rushed to brush away the tears, and he stepped towards Josie, holding her like only a son could do. He kissed the top of her head, and she shuddered in his arms, her body shaking with grief over the loss of one son, but rejoicing with the love of Sam's best friend—the one she loved like her own.

Chapter Fifty-Three

LJ had worked all weekend to finish painting Grandma Aimee's laundry and complete the cabinetry. He'd navigated around the plumber who had fitted a new toilet, a vast improvement on the original one with its side-mounted pull flush.

The renovations were complete, including a covered-in back verandah which faced the north. He'd bought a new recliner with a footrest, and a white coffee table for the space, and had a split system air conditioner installed. Below it hung an enlarged photo of her late husband, Eddie.

Dawn was breaking, and excitement bubbled in his belly. His mother was bringing Grandma Aimee home from hospital, and with the renovations complete, he was eager to see her reaction.

With time to spare, he went back to the kitchen and checked—for the third time—the cheese and dip he'd bought. He made sure the bottle of Tempranillo red was at the front door so he wouldn't forget it, along with two tall wine glasses. Pacing the hallway, he checked his phone again. Poppy hadn't replied to his earlier voicemail.

'Woo-hoo,' his mother called as they came through the front door, and LJ couldn't hide his excitement as he watched his grandmother move through the house, her face bright with pleasure.

'It's all so lovely.' She turned to LJ, beaming. 'When did you get the time to do all this? Did you sneak in while I wasn't at home?'

Oh Grandma. LJ hid the bittersweet smile creeping over his face. If this was going to be his grandmother from now on, he'd do everything possible to make her happy. She'd made him realise love was worth the risk. Gratitude was only the beginning of what he was feeling.

His mother called from the kitchen, and when he reached the door, Jen stood still, gazing up at him. 'Hey, LJ.'

He moved towards her. 'Something smells good.'

'Sweetheart. This all looks amazing.' Jen spun to admire the kitchen. 'A lot better than what it was when I was growing up.' His mother's smile meant more than he could say. 'It's all so beautiful, LJ.' She rubbed his arm before they stepped into the warmth of the back room, where the morning sun streamed through the windows. Grandma Aimee was nestled in her new recliner, gazing in delight at the opposite wall. LJ followed her line of sight and paused, looking back to her with concern.

'There's my Eddie.' Her smile lit up her face. 'I won't lose you now.' She pointed a spindly finger at the picture.

LJ's throat tightened. The fact that she could now talk to Eddie anytime she wanted meant more to him than the entire renovation; his only regret was not thinking to print a photo sooner.

Comfortable that she was settled, he returned to the kitchen where Jen was filling the kettle. 'Staying for a cuppa?' Her face searched his, almost pleading for him to stay.

'Thanks, Mum, but no. I have a few things I need to do today.' He gathered his items from the fridge and put them into an old basket he'd found in the shed. He'd also added a cutting board, cheese knife, and a box of crackers, then glanced up to catch his mother's knowing smile.

'Going somewhere special?'

LJ slowed as he turned into The Lone Pony. Adrian was giving the white mare a carrot when he pulled up beside him, opening the passenger window. 'How's our superhero going?'

'I'm good.'

LJ gave a chuckle, Adrian's beaming smile as infectious as ever. 'Good to hear. See you, buddy.'

Adrian waved as LJ drove past Mrs Potter, who nearly

dropped her basket of washing to wave at him. He shook his head and smiled, offering a courteous wave in return.

As he pulled up at the caravan, an excited bark erupted from behind the door. It opened, and Jazz bounded down the steps, racing to the door where LJ was climbing out, her tail a frenzy of energy. She clambered up his leg, begging for a cuddle. He reached and stroked her soft head and ears. 'You smell like you've had a bath.'

'She needed one! I'd had enough of the smell of sheep poo inside the caravan.'

LJ looked up at the sound of her voice, his delighted smile morphing into pleasant disbelief as two long legs in a knee-length floral dress descended the steps, moving towards him. His heart somersaulted as his hand stilled on the pup. Over her dress, Poppy wore a pale denim jacket and casual dress sneakers, her long hair draping her shoulders and back.

Jazz licked at his hand for more attention, but right now, the pup was the last thing on his mind. The only female he wanted in his arms was the wool classer sauntering his way.

LJ drew her in by the waist, the silken material of her dress highlighting her soft curves beneath his hands. If ever he'd wanted someone in his life, it was in this moment, with this woman. He'd finally found the love of his life and was not going to let her slip through his fingers ever again.

'You look stunning.' His eyes trailed over hers, then slipped to her lips. Unable to stop himself, he moved closer, pressing his lips to hers. His slow kiss morphed into a smile before he stepped back. 'How about we get going?'

Poppy nodded with a smile, taking his hand.

LJ clipped Jazz on the back of the ute to save Poppy's caravan from a second ransacking. He drove past the washing line and Mrs Potter waved with enthusiasm, that was, until she set eyes on Poppy.

'I see she still doesn't like you.' LJ gave her a sideways wink.

'I see she's still drooling over you.' She held his gaze with equal amusement.

As they drove, the sun shone over the rolling hills covered in a fuzz of new spring growth, and the sheep picked contentedly at the green grass. It took every inch of his self-control to watch where he was driving instead of staring at the gorgeous woman he had sitting beside him. He reached for her hand. 'I want to take you somewhere that means a lot to me.'

'Aren't we near the Jenkins shed?' She frowned, looking around.

He slowed not a hundred metres on, then turned into a gateway. Driving through it, he slipped the ute into four-wheel drive and headed towards a large willow tree. Pulling up, his eyebrows danced in her direction and he jumped out, grabbing the basket. Rounding the bonnet of the ute, she shut her door, then entwined her hand in his.

'Follow me,' he smiled.

When they reached the tree, LJ reluctantly let go of Poppy's hand and lowered the basket. He tossed out the picnic rug like a freshly shorn fleece, and it floated to the ground, settling in the dappled shade. He set up the cutting board with crackers, cheeses, grapes and strawberries. Jazz gave an I'm-being-neglected yap from the back of the ute. They ignored her.

'Did you ask Ralph if we could come onto his place?' She narrowed her gaze his way, her look of disbelief clear.

'Didn't have to. It's my family farm.' The relief as he said the words felt deep, tangible, reaching his heart and making it race. While he was sorry that Miles was in prison, he no longer needed to worry about what was happening on the farm. His father had assured him they would only use his contracting team for all the sheep work, and that meant his run had a good chance of success, so long as the farmers continued to ring him.

He watched Poppy as she gazed across the paddocks. 'Now I understand your apparent interest in rocks,' she teased, elbowing him in the side.

'What do you mean?' He feigned innocence. 'George and I love rocks.' But he'd kept his best reveal until last, passing her the two glasses, before pulling out the bottle of wine.

She gasped. 'This is my absolute favourite!' She looked at him, amazed. 'How did you know?'

A surge of love rushed through him as he looked across the land, watching their pregnant superfine ewes graze, close to lambing.

LJ shifted to face her, her stunning eyes searching his face as her hair moved in the gentle breeze. 'I read that some Spanish wines are hard to pass up.'

He opened the bottle and poured a glass for each of them. He wanted to pinch himself, so in awe of her radiant pink cheeks and olive complexion, thankful she was back in his life, forever. 'Cheers.' Their glasses clinked, and he watched as

Poppy sipped her wine, her eyes closing in bliss.

379

Chapter fifty-four

One week on, the shearing plants whirred at the new superfine shed LJ had secured.

Poppy smiled to herself as she tugged on the staple of wool in her fingers, and looked across to the shearing board where Jase, LJ, Bear, and Whippet worked on the four-stand shed. B1 and B2 were there, along with Bianca, Little Trev, and Spider. Not only was the team back together again, but she was with people she considered like family as she travelled with them from job to job. And unlike her last team, these guys had proven through their loyalty, they had the tenacity to look out for one another when the going got tough.

Oxley Falls was booked in for the following week, and she couldn't wait. Her heart skipped a beat as LJ looked up, having sent his last sheep down the chute for the run, dazzling her with his generous smile and sending delicious shivers all over her body.

He sat down next to her in the smoko room as she wrestled with a huge piece of orange and poppyseed cake that Cookie had made especially to welcome her back. She giggled, leaning forward as she took a bite, the crumbs falling to the floor. LJ grinned, brushing away the last of the crumbs from the side of her mouth, and she leaned into his hand, relishing its roughness before he kissed her on the nose.

'Had a phone call during the run. We've got a job at a property called Twin Lanes, straight after we finish Oxley Falls.' LJ sat back and took a big bite of his own slice of cake.

Poppy frowned. 'I've heard that name before. Just can't think where.'

That evening, LJ watched on with a satisfied smile as all the people important to Poppy sat with them at The Night's Helmsmen. Her father and Jimmy had decided to stay on for the week and see what Tasmania had to offer.

Adrian sat next to George, and laughter erupted. Jimmy was in fine form, telling them of Poppy's many antics on their grandparents' farm.

'Well, you weren't going to help me, were you!' Poppy glared at Jimmy as he laughed uncontrollably.

'No way, Tinker Belle. You wanted to shovel manure to

earn the money, not me.'

'I wanted to go halves with you! Grandpa Isaac was going to pay us to remove it, and we'd make money when we sold it. It was a great deal.'

'Yeah, but instead of getting paid, all you got was peed on from above!' Jimmy snorted, laughing again as he hopped up to get another jug of beer and Coke for the table.

'Well, no one bothered to tell me the rams were in the pens above me, did they?' she yelled out over the noise of the pub.

LJ loved the way she laughed and pretended to sulk. Jimmy had the upper hand when it came to picking on her. He needed to hear a few more stories in private for valuable ammunition.

'My Pa Pat knew a shearer named Isaac many years ago.' He said it by the way, but everyone stopped, staring at him. He lifted his focus from his glass of Coke to their puzzled faces.

'What was his surname?' Poppy's eyes were glued to him as she twisted in her seat.

'Um, can't remember. Might have been something beginning with F. Fern . . . án . . . dez?' His eyes held a glint of mischief as he watched her eyes widen.

Jimmy rocked his head in disbelief as he chased another piece of lamb around the plate, unable to stop grinning. 'Oh, man. What have you got yourself into this time, Popps?'

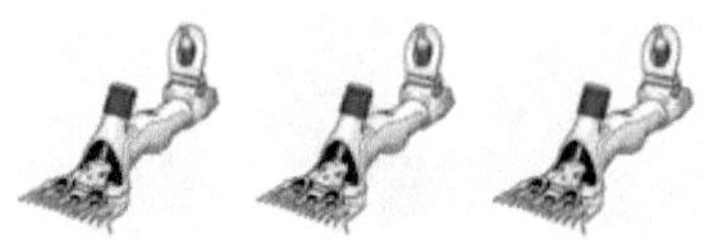

Poppy was speechless as she swung her head towards her father when he began to speak to LJ.

'Did your Pa Pat have a barney with this Isaac because he accused your Pa of double clicking?' Her father looked intrigued and waited for an answer, his piece of chicken schnitzel hanging mid-air on his fork, but it was Poppy who almost fell off her chair. Did her father actually know that story?

'They were best mates, until that day. Haven't spoken since, as far as I know.'

'I don't believe it. They *know* each other?' Poppy said.

Her sceptical grin filled her face as she spun around to LJ once more. 'Your grandfather *and* my grandfather are those two men?'

'Yeah, isn't that incredible?' he said, his smile so wide, Poppy didn't know whether to wring his neck or hug him.

'You knew all this time and you didn't tell me?' She dropped her fork to her plate and gave him a teasing thump on the arm, shaking her head as everyone else laughed.

LJ leaned in and nudged her with his shoulder, squeezing her knee under the table. 'Well, they're going to have to see each other again now, aren't they?' He stole a quick kiss, leaving her lips wanting for more.

The following Thursday night LJ arrived home from work to find a letter sitting on the kitchen bench. He stared at the title in the left-hand corner of the envelope.

"WorkSafe".

His lips parted as he looked about him, wishing for more painting to do, a cupboard to reassemble, anything to prolong the agony of what the letter contained. He dropped it back on the table and started to walk away, then slowed, about facing. He took it in his hands, staring at it before reluctantly taking a seat. He needed to know what it said. He couldn't keep accepting work from farmers if WorkSafe were going to take it all away from him. His fingers shook as he tore at the envelope and unfolded the letter.

Dear Mr Tanner.

I am writing to inform you that WorkSafe finds you not liable for negligence in the matter of the death of Mr Samuel Whittington.

Thank you for your cooperation regarding the matter.

Yours sincerely,

J.S. Shriver.

LJ's shoulders sagged and his breath let go in a rush. He pressed fingers to his eyes before Grandma Aimee walked in on him.

'Are you alright, Eddie?' Her hand rested on his shoulder as she peered down at him, her smile tender.

He took her hand in his, squeezing it as he smiled up at her. 'Yes, Aimee. I'm fine.'

'Does your coffee taste alright?' Bear frowned, looking into his mug and scrunching his nose in disgust. Whippet and Jase took sips of their teas, and Whippet spat his out in a splatter over the floor in front of him, earning himself a punch in the arm from Bianca.

LJ cringed against the mouthful he forced down, then walked over to the urn. Removing the lid, he peered inside.

'Oh, bloody hell.' He looked up and everyone turned to him.

'Spider!'

Spider loped in from his cigarette break outside, unfazed by the exasperated holler of his name. He strolled up to the urn, looking inside with a satisfied nod, and grinning back at LJ as he took a plate and a pair of tongs. Reaching into the hot water, he retrieved five steaming hot dogs. The team then stared as he sat at the table and proceeded to eat his lunch without a care in the world, but not before giving Bear a goofy smile as he chewed, raising the hot dog in salute before taking another bite.

Poppy giggled as she cuddled baby Rosie. Sophie was enjoying her reprieve and the farmer's wife was cooking a cake for afternoon smoko, which meant she was on babysitting duty.

She stared down at the beautiful face as Rosie slept peacefully, marvelling at how this baby girl was already growing up with all things sheep in her world.

Looking up from Rosie, she smiled when the owner of Twin Lanes stopped in front of her.

'I wanted to tell you you're doing a ripper job, Poppy. I can't thank Adrian enough for recommending the team to me.'

Poppy's eyes widened, and she soothed the startled Rosie back to sleep before she looked up at him again. 'You mean— Adrian Potter?'

'Yes. He told me all about you.' The farmer gave her a chuffed smile, leaving her to solemnly swear to herself that she would never brush aside a comment from Adrian again. The little guy really had come through.

LJ rested his back against the big willow tree—now their favourite place—and Poppy eased herself up against his chest, the two of them sitting in comfortable silence, watching the sheep graze and the lambs run and bounce on top of the boulders, leaping to chase one another around the paddock.

He broke the silence. 'Pop. I need to make you a promise.' She lifted her head from where it was resting against his shoulder, twisting towards him.

'What do you mean?'

'I want you to know— No, I need you to know, I'll

never sack you again.'

'Technically, I sacked you too.' They both burst out laughing as LJ leaned in to catch her lips with his before she pulled back, searching him with teasing determination.

'And I promise, if you try to, I'll get Adrian to use my broom on you.'

A Shearer's Run

Orange Poppyseed Cake
(Poppy's favourite)

This delicious recipe is one I came across many years ago,
stashing it in my folder of favourites. It's by a wonderful
CWA lady by the name of Elsie. While I didn't personally
know this amazing woman (deceased 15th December 2019,
aged 100years, 8 months), her photo next to the recipe
reminds me of the many farming women who have lived and
breathed dirt, floods, rain, fire, manure and shearing sheds,
amongst other farming smells, for most of their lives. These
women are, to me, the strong pillars of their families, cooking
for hungry shearers (more often in the past than these days)
and keeping their loved ones united in home-cooked meals
made with love. That's who Cookie is to me.

Thank you, Elsie. Your CWA award-winning recipe is

one I call on often, taking it out to share at properties I work on, to be enjoyed by farmers, some of whom once had a loving wife like you to bake for them. And thank you to your family for giving me permission to share it. I sincerely hope you love this recipe as much as I do.

Enjoy xx

♥ Laurelle

A Shearer's Run

Ingredients:

1 ½ cups Self-raising Flour, sifted

¾ cup Caster Sugar

2 Eggs — at room temperature

1 Egg yolk

½ cup Milk

185g Butter, softened

3 teaspoons finely grated Orange rind, OR you can use Lemon rind instead if you like.

40g Poppyseeds

Pinch of Salt

Icing:

1 cup Pure Icing sugar, sifted

1 teaspoon Butter, softened

½ teaspoon Milk

Method:

1. Preheat oven to 180° C; 160° C Fan force. Grease and line a 20cm (base) round cake tin.
2. Combine flour, sugar, eggs, egg yolk, milk, butter, orange rind, poppyseeds and a pinch of salt in a bowl. Using an electric mixer, beat on medium speed for 6 minutes, or until thick.
3. Pour batter into the cake pan and smooth the surface. Bake for 50-60 minutes, or until a skewer inserted into the centre comes out clean. Stand the cake in the pan for 5 minutes. Turn onto a wire rack to cool.
4. **Make icing:** Combine icing sugar, butter and

enough milk to make a thick icing.

5. Spread icing over the top of the cooled cake. Allow to set before serving.

6. **Winner's tip:** 'You lose points in the CWA cookery contest if the judges find wire rack marks on the bottom of your cake. To avoid this, I actually turn it out directly onto a clean tea towel on the benchtop. And before you ask, no, this doesn't make the underside soggy!'

Thanks, Elsie. You are a true Aussie legend.

A Shearer's Run

Acknowledgements

This "rooly and truly" is the best part, because remembering the ones who walked with me in this traditionally solitary job, allows me to honour everyone who kept me on track, fed with musk Life Savers (you know who you are), made me laugh when I wanted to cry, and made me laugh when I wanted to laugh! It really is the best kind of medicine.

Lois, what a trooper you are! You have been there through the highs, the hopes, and the rejections, and you came to my rescue only weeks ago after my SOS call explaining I couldn't see how I was going to pull this story into shape with structural edits testing me. But just talking it through with you, we came up with a plan of attack. And it worked! That's true, unequivocal support and belief in a friend, and I am so, so lucky to have you on my team! I might write alone but I definitely don't do it alone. Thank you for your extreme patience to read and re-read several versions—sometimes in tight turnaround times—with fresh eyes and endless enthusiasm, until the very end. I couldn't do it without you! xox

Annie Seaton, you had me scampering on this one and I am so glad you did! I might say that I put my characters through the wringer, but it was you who put me through one in the end! Now, because of that, this story is so much stronger than it was. So, thank you.

Mike. No words except I love you.

Kelli, here's to keeping the laughs, adventures and general all 'round life mishaps alive. I couldn't do without my bestie in my life! xox

Dave Melhuish, thank you for sharing your knowledge of WorkSafe firsthand, and helping inspire "Mr WorkSafe" and his background story to life.

Tan Ryan and Amy Doak, I am so grateful for our brekky catch ups, debriefs and accountability check-ins! Not only are you wonderful friends, Tan, you keep me on the straight and narrow socials pathway, and Amy, you remind me "I can" when I'm adamant "I can't". Thank you for always being there. xo

To all my incredible book reviewers, the world's biggest thank you! I am so grateful to your support, honesty and feedback. You make me want to write even better stories!

Ida Brady, you might live in Ireland but that doesn't stop us chatting! You keep me pumped up when my air is running dangerously low, and celebrate the smallest of successes. Hugs, hugs, and more hugs.

Tracey Hoffmann, thank you for your nursing advice about the different roles within a hospital.

A special thank you to Elsie Storm for your wonderful orange and poppyseed cake recipe that has given many—especially me—such pleasure at morning and afternoon smokos. Thank you to Ann Storm, Elsie's daughter who gave me permission to share this delicious recipe and honour a true CWA woman.

My family. You're the best and I couldn't be more proud or more grateful to you all for believing in me, supporting me and celebrating with me in publishing my books. I wouldn't be "me" without "you". Anna, your favourite quirky little line: 'It's a definite maybe', was perfect!

Jeanette (and Jeff), the more I know you, the more I love our friendship. You are truly special people. xo

Ceeny, I'm always feeling your love and support, even though we live so far apart. xo

I wrote this story several years ago, and it has seen many drafts, probably in search of the true GMC (Goal, Motivation and Conflict) source. It was a story I one hundred percent knew the setting for. I knew it was always going to be about a shearing contractor and a wool classer, but finding the true premise for both of them proved a little more difficult. I've spent a lot of time in the shearing shed and the industry itself, being inspired and dealing with many different—not always easy—characters. While none of the characters are based on any real person, inspiration comes from so many places, so LJ and Poppy's story is just the start for the Shearer's Arms series which I am excited about.

To my wonderful readers, now and in the future. I give my all when I write a character into being, and I fall in love with them like a best friend. I sincerely hope they are as unforgettable to you as they are to me. I so appreciate your incredible support as I continue to bring many more memorable characters to life, all who share with us in our wide and awe-inspiring Aussie landscape.

 Laurelle xox